# catching pretty

LOVELY BROKEN DOLL
*book two*

USA TODAY BESTSELLING AUTHOR
## SIENNA BLAKE

# CATCHING PRETTY

LOVELY BROKEN DOLL
BOOK TWO

SIENNA BLAKE

Catching Pretty: a novel / by Sienna Blake. – 1st Ed.
First Edition: Feb 2025
Published by SB Publishing
Copyright 2025 Sienna Blake
Cover art copyright 2024 Pretty Little Cover design © The Pretty Little Design Co. www.theprettylittledesignco.co.uk.
All Rights Reserved Sienna Blake.
Editing services by Kimberly Dawn: editingbykimberlydawn@gmail.com

The characters and events portrayed in this book are fictional. Any similarity to real persons, living or dead, is coincidental and not intended by the author.

*For my dark romance girlies,
I don't know what kind of messed-up shit you've been through,
but, girl, we fucking survived it!*

*Welcome home.*

*Now sit the fuck down.
The Warden is waiting.*

## AUTHOR'S NOTE

Claiming Pretty is darker than Book 1.
It romanticizes obsessive behaviors, kidnapping and *very* dubious consent.
It deals with SA and violence (not between the two main characters).

It also contains:
Drug usage, non consent, sex while being drugged/unconscious, kidnapping, captivity & Stockholm syndrome, murder, implied human experimentation, forced abortion, suicide ideation, torture, SA and abuse of a minor (flashbacks), primal/chasing play, edging, breath play, bondage, taboo foster brother relationship and an incredibly inappropriate use of a garden tool…

The dark scenarios in this book are *pure* fantasy. I do not condone any of the behavior in real life.

*Please consider your mental health before deciding to read this novel.*

# THE WARDEN

As I waited for the automatic wrought-iron gates to open, I stared at Ava still sleeping in my passenger seat, her face soft and peaceful in the pale moonlight filtering through the window.

She had no idea what was waiting for her.

For a moment, I let myself look at her, *really* look—the way her lashes brushed her cheeks, the way her lips parted slightly as she breathed in slow, steady rhythms.

The tension she always carried, the fire, the sharpness, had melted away. She looked... delicate. Almost fragile.

My chest tightened, a familiar ache rising inside me, no matter how hard I tried to keep my emotions under control.

She was so damn beautiful, more so in sleep, when her walls were down and all I could see was the girl I had loved for years. The girl who had haunted my every thought, my every breath, my every fucking move.

I wanted to reach out, to touch the softness of her cheek, to brush a lock of hair away from her face, but I clenched the wheel tighter, knuckles white as I fought against the pull of it.

I did lean over to her, though.

"*Is leatsa thú*," I whispered to her in Irish.

*You are mine.*

Ava didn't respond. She didn't wake. The drug I'd injected her with still held her under.

But not for long.

I caught a whiff of her familiar scent, which unlocked a part of me I'd long since repressed.

Jasmine.

I gave in, the need overtaking me, and my hands slipped from the wheel. I buried my nose in her hair and inhaled deeply.

Her scent threatened to undo me and my breath caught in my throat.

The moment was finally here.

She was *here*. With *me*. With no way of escaping.

After all those years when I'd survived only by imagining this moment—the moment when she was *mine*.

The gates clanged into their final resting place, signaling for me to enter the grounds.

I took a moment to brush the hair from her cheek, my fingers lingering on her pale slender neck as the spot where her steady pulse beat, before I composed myself and straightened.

*We're here, my hummingbird.*

The gravel crunched beneath the tires as I drove down the long, winding driveway toward Halla an Draighean, *Blackthorn Hall* in Irish.

The looming silhouette of the gothic mansion rose up

ahead, dark and imposing against the gray sky, its jagged spires and towering chimneys cutting through the horizon like sharp teeth.

The ivy that clung to the stone walls was thick, as if trying to swallow up the cursed place from the world, and the tall blackthorn trees lined the driveway, their gnarled branches clawing toward the sky.

The medieval arched windows stared down at me like dark, empty eyes, and the sprawling structure seemed both beautiful and haunting at the same time.

I repressed a shiver. To be back here...

I should've felt relieved. This was home, after all. But that sense of home came with too many jagged edges. Too much pain woven into the walls.

The windows were dark, like hollow eyes that followed me, watching, always watching.

Blackthorn Hall wasn't just a building—it was a force, alive with the echoes of laughter and the weight of sorrow.

The darkness of it wrapped around my chest, squeezing tighter the closer I got and I feared that she wouldn't let me leave this time.

Even the air inside seemed heavier as I drove the car into the garage, a sense of dread mixed with familiarity as the door rattled down, shutting behind me, trapping me in.

Trapping *us* inside.

At least, this time, I wasn't alone.

In the dim light I could see the purple circles under her eyes, the smears of mud and blood over her cheeks, the tattered remains of her torn clothes.

I gritted my teeth against the anger that surged inside me. For a few moments, I let myself imagine the bloody painful vengeance I'd unleashed upon the people who'd hurt her. But only a few moments.

That was all the indulgence I would allow myself.

Because what we were here to do was more important than revenge.

"Welcome home, hummingbird," I whispered against her jasmine hair.

I carefully gathered Ava into my arms. She felt no different held against my chest than she had all those years ago. As I carried her inside, it was tempting to believe that no time had passed at all.

I carried her to her dark wood paneled bedroom and laid her down on the pale-pink silk duvet before lighting a fire in the stone fireplace.

Even though it was late spring, the nights in the remote west of Ireland were still cool, and this cavernous old place was full of ghosts and drafts.

The flames danced on her icy skin as I stood there, watching her sleep.

The room felt impossibly still.

For years, I'd dreamed of her every night, planned every step, every detail of this exact moment. But nothing, not even the wildest reaches of my imagination, could have prepared me for the reality of seeing her here.

Real. *Alive.*

Right in front of me, the girl who had haunted my dreams. And now… here she was, within reach, her chest rising and falling with each peaceful breath.

It took everything in me not to crumble under the weight of it—the overwhelming awe, the disbelief, the longing that had clawed at me for years.

It made my chest ache.

I wanted to touch her, to make sure she was real and not just another ghost my mind had conjured. But I didn't.

I turned away from her hypnotic allure to enter the en suite bathroom.

I ran a bath and gathered along the edge of the giant antique claw-foot tub all the soaps and liquids I would require.

I turned on her *bath time* playlist, a mix of classical piano music and Einaudi.

The white noise of the stream of water helped to focus my mind. What was to come next would be difficult, the first true test of what I was capable of. Or not.

I tested the temperature of the bath and lingered just a little too long on whether it was a little too hot, a little too cold.

The truth was I feared myself, feared how easily I might give in.

With controlled steps, I returned to the bedroom.

The warmth from the fire had already brought some color back to Ava's cheeks, though her skin was still too cold.

My heart rate accelerated as I reached for her hem and tugged off her top.

Her small pink nipples peaked from the lingering chill of the rain and they shifted on the pale-white swell of her breasts like cherries atop fresh cream.

I longed to taste them despite the muddy streaks marring her beautiful chest, but I chastised myself.

Not the time. Not now.

I slipped off her heels and let them fall with a thud to the carpet beneath the bed. I rolled her torn stockings down the long length of her shapely legs, careful not to scratch her perfect skin.

I couldn't figure out how to undo her pleated skirt, so I ripped it off her.

Ava lay before me, naked except for simple white cotton panties with the girlish trim of dainty lace.

I dug my fingernails into my palms because the need to claim her right then and there was threatening to overwhelm me.

I ran my fingers down her neck and over her breasts, the blood droplets now dried so they flaked off.

She was extraordinarily beautiful, even with leaves in her hair and a monster's blood splattered on her skin.

*Stay strong.*

My fingers trembled as I ran my palm over her stomach and along the edge of her panties.

I pulled them down over the soft curve of her hips, pushing her knees to her chest so I could get it over the supple globes of her ass.

My dick surged with blood.

It would be so easy, so fucking easy to take her, claim her right now.

*Control yourself!*

I forced myself to step back, to lower her legs back to the mattress.

But the rebellious part of me, the part that screamed to lose control, drew her panties up to my nose.

Fuck. Musky and sweet.

My cock surged with blood and my cells screamed for me to just fucking take her.

For so many years I'd deadened myself, burning off all my emotions and nerves so I didn't have to feel, but I was coming alive again.

Because of her.

I clamped my teeth around her panties like it was a leather bit as I steadied my breath.

*In. Out.*

I drew the familiar lines against my thigh, a grounding technique that Eamon taught me. I drew them over and over until the fire in my blood retracted, until my breath steadied and I was back in control.

I tucked her panties into my pocket. For later.

They would be my reward for remaining in control.

*Later.*

I lifted her into my arms and held her to my chest, her bare heat searing into my body.

The proximity of her naked body was a true test of my control.

If I wanted, I could touch her. Taste her. *Take* her. Unleash every single fantasy I'd had of her over the long years.

The thought made my knees weak as I carried her into the bathroom and climbed with her into the tub, my shoes and clothes still on.

*Patience.*

I reclined against the side of the tub and positioned Ava between my legs, her back against my chest. Making sure her mouth and nose stayed above the surface of the warm water, I began to bathe her.

I lifted one arm and then the other to wipe them clean

with a sudsy sponge, the water droplets tinkling against the bathwater sounding playful.

Cold, murderous anger swelled in my chest as I discovered the bruises beneath the dirt. As I cleaned the raw skin around her wrists.

I painstakingly cleaned each inch of her skin and wished I'd had more time to make that bastard pay for hurting her. I imagined all the different ways I could have tortured him, drawn out his suffering, made him beg for death.

For a while, these thoughts served to keep me distracted. But there was only so much of Ava's body to clean before I had nothing left but the most tempting parts.

When I shifted the sponge over her breast and then the other, there was no thinking of Cormac, of blood and pain and vengeance.

My cock swelled beneath the surface, straining between Ava's ass cheeks. I wondered why I even ran a bath in the first place. I could have licked every inch of her, lapped at her flesh till she glistened with me.

Arousal struck me so hard that I had to pause with the sponge against Ava's belly before dipping it further to clean between her legs.

Closing my eyes was no good because all I could see was me dragging her from the tub and fucking her against the flooded bathroom tiles, her perfect breasts bouncing with streaks of bubbles still on them.

I forced my eyes to stay open and punished myself with the sight of Ava's beautiful body beneath the water in front of me.

I *had* to remain in control.

This was my test.

My test of worth.

With slow, cautious movements, I allowed myself to stroke the sponge along Ava's pussy.

Everything inside of me yearned to feel her velvety lips with my own fingers, but I kept the sponge between her and me.

I didn't dare trust myself otherwise, not even with a brush of my pinky against the soft, dark hair over her pretty little pussy.

My cock screamed in protest, but I pulled the sponge away from between her legs and did nothing more than look down at her, drinking in the sight of her naked and wet.

I stayed in control, even if my chest was shuddering against Ava's back as I admired her naked body in my arms, even if I could hardly breathe knowing she was now all mine.

One day soon, she'd let me do this to her when she was awake.

But all in good time.

Bathwater sloshed over the side of the tub as I leaned over to retrieve the special bottle of shampoo.

"I have all your favorites," I whispered, leaning my lips in close to her ear.

I poured the shampoo into my palm and massaged it into Ava's raven hair. The scent of jasmine filled the steamy bathroom, intoxicating me with memories.

Cupping water in my hand, I started to rinse the shampoo from Ava's scalp, my head clearing with every pass, the realities of what I was going to do to her flooding back in.

"If you'll only trust me," I said to her as her clean hair swirled around her breasts, "I think you'll come to like it here. With me."

I admired my work even as I thought of all that was left to do.

"One day you'll even come to love it," I said, pulling her naked body in tighter against my chest. "To love... *me*."

# AVA

I woke to darkness. My head pounded, my thoughts slow and sluggish, like they were wading through mud.

For a second, I didn't know where I was, didn't know *why* I couldn't see. Panic flooded my chest, tightening around my lungs, as I tried to blink away the blackness—until I realized something was tied around my head, my eyelids pressing against cool silk.

A blindfold.

*Oh God.*

I jerked my arms, only to feel the sharp bite of rope cutting into my wrists. I was tied down—my hands, my ankles—everything was bound.

The chair beneath me creaked with my frantic movements as I struggled against the restraints, the rough fibers digging into my skin still raw.

My heart thundered in my chest, the echoes of my pulse deafening in my ears. Every breath felt too loud, too sharp in the oppressive silence surrounding me as my last memories slammed back into me.

Cormac had kidnapped me and tied me up in a basement. He was handing me over to... *them*. To the High Lord of a dangerous secret society.

Oh God.

The High Lord had killed Cormac, slit his throat right in front of me.

I thought it was Scáth wearing the skeleton mask. I had been so sure it was Scáth who came for me in that cellar.

But it hadn't been.

Scáth would have me in his arms by now, his heat radiating against my ice-cold skin.

He wouldn't have been able to hold himself back from me. He didn't have the kind of self-restraint to leave me like this to wake up alone, struggling against the thick fog in my mind.

He would have forced me awake, claimed me roughly and passionately, marked me as his. With teeth. With tongue. With his cock.

Whoever had been standing over me, hidden in the shadows of that black hood, hadn't been Scáth. I didn't know much, but I knew I wasn't saved.

My torment wasn't over.

If anything, it was just beginning.

Oh God. The High Lord had been stalking me as well.

And now, he had me. God knows where.

I strained my ears, trying to make out any sounds around me. A voice, a footstep, distant traffic—anything that would tell me where I was.

And if I was alone. Or if *he* was in here with me.

But all I could hear was my own ragged breathing, loud and erratic, drowning out everything else. I was shaking, my chest rising and falling too fast, and the blindfold pressed tighter against my face with every panicked breath.

*Calm down, Ava.*

My throat tightened with fear, but I forced myself to focus, to take slow, measured breaths. In and out. In and out.

My breathing steadied, just enough for me to try again. I listened, this time with more control, forcing myself to stay quiet.

But I didn't hear anything. No voices, no footsteps. Nothing but the oppressive silence and the darkness pressing in on me.

Not the distant sound of cars passing. No birds. Where the hell was I that I could hear *nothing*?

I had to get loose.

The rope cut into my wrists as I flexed my fingers, testing the knots again, but they didn't budge.

I tried to pull at my legs but I was bound tightly to two wooden chair legs, forcing my thighs apart. I couldn't even press my knees together.

Cool air on my inner thighs made my skin goose pimple. And I realized based on the weight and feeling on my skin that I wasn't wearing the same clothes as before.

The High Lord had redressed me.

I was wearing something lightweight. Silk? And it felt loose around my breasts but tight around my waist. Gods, it was short, barely covering my thighs.

He had stripped me and redressed me in some sort of silk robe.

Panic surged against the lingering effects of the drugs when I tried to place my hands over myself—an instinctive response—but they too were tied tightly.

A muffled sound came from my right and I snapped my head to face it—whatever *it* was.

The strong scent of jasmine wafted from my hair. My *freshly* washed hair.

I realized that I no longer felt dried cracking mud or a gritty film on my skin.

Fuck, did that asshole *bathe* me as well? And using my jasmine shampoo?

Did he steal it from my bathroom or… had he bought it specially for me because he *knew* it was my favorite?

I shivered, a cold sweat breaking out over my whole body, because I wasn't sure what was worse.

I imagined my masked stalker touching my naked body, his breath heavy under his skeleton mask, taking fucking liberties with my body.

I repressed a shudder and tried to ignore the strange awareness that had flooded to my core. I was way too exposed. Too vulnerable like this.

More unsettling than the fact that my kidnapper was playing with me like a fucking doll was the uncertainty of *why* he had kept me alive.

What did he want with me?

I couldn't stick around to find out. I had to get out of here *now*, before he came back.

Panic gnawed at the edges of my mind, but I shoved it down, focusing on the rope digging into my wrists.

I fumbled with my right hand, twisting my wrist painfully against the rough fibers, trying to find any slack, any way to loosen it. My fingers strained, shaking with effort, but I had to keep going. I couldn't just sit here.

The air felt too still, too heavy, pressing down on me like a weight, thick and suffocating. My heart pounded in my chest, each thud echoing in the quiet.

And then, out of nowhere, there was a soft creak.

The door opening.

My breath hitched, my blood running cold as the sound sliced through the silence.

Then I heard the footsteps.

They weren't rushed. Slow, deliberate—each step landing heavily on what sounded like old wooden floorboards before being muffled, probably by a rug.

The measured pace felt torturous against the racing of my heart. Each step seemed to stretch time, the steady rhythm mocking the frantic chaos inside me.

My breath caught in my throat as every step felt like a countdown, each one heavier than the last.

Closer. And closer.

*He* was coming.

Each footfall sent another wave of panic crashing through me, but I couldn't scream. Couldn't move. The blindfold pressed harder against my eyes as I sat frozen, helpless, waiting for the inevitable.

Until I could practically feel the vibrations in the floor beneath my chair.

I became hyper-aware of how exposed I was. From behind my blindfold it felt like I was splayed open for him, the delicate edge of the robe ending way up my thigh, and there was nothing I could do to draw my knees closer together.

My heartbeat slammed even louder in my ears when I realized I wasn't wearing any panties.

Bastard.

He could *see* me. All of me.

I imagined the hungry way he was looking at me over his skeleton mask, thinking through all the ways he could violate me while I remained entirely unable to stop him.

The footsteps ceased right in front of me and silence flooded back in.

I smelled his masculine scent—his dark and earthy scent of musk and sandalwood—through flared nostrils, my breath coming shallow and fast.

The same scent from the cellar, from Cormac's killer, from *my* kidnapper.

I knew it was the High Lord, the same man who had approached me beneath his mask with disinterest, who had injected me with a needle without sympathy.

I trembled as I waited for something to happen, for him to grab me, slap me, hit me till I recorded a ransom message for Ebony, lip busted and nipples bruised.

But all he did was stand in front of me. Gawking at me, I bet.

I could just make out his controlled breathing if I held my breath for long enough.

He must have been the one to bathe and redress me. Had he touched me while I'd been under? Raped me? Would I know if I had been?

I shifted in my chair. My pussy didn't feel sore.

But surely there was a reason he'd dressed me and tied me to that chair.

*Maybe he wanted me awake for whatever he had planned.*

I wanted him to just come out with it already. Just fucking do it already, whatever sick, twisted thing he was going to do to me.

I bit back a scream as the silence threatened to drive me mad, his eyes devouring whatever he pleased. I would *not* give him the satisfaction of seeing me break.

"W-who are you?" I said, my voice shaking with false bravado. I had no power. No leverage. Nothing.

I was completely at his mercy. Under his control.

"What do you want?" I tried again.

He pressed something cold against my lips.

I whimpered in fear and turned my face away out of instinct.

He grabbed my chin with strong, calloused fingers, forcing it back, harder this time.

Plastic cracked against my teeth and ice water dripped down my chin, soaking through the gauzy material of my robe. The chill made my nipples hard and I was certain I was giving him a wet t-shirt show.

But I didn't want to give him the satisfaction of drinking the water. God knows what kind of drug it was laced with. I spit it out, hoping some of it hit his face.

*Take that, bastard.*

More water dribbled over my lips.

An iron hand clamped onto my jaw and this thumb applied pressure to a muscle at the side of my cheek which opened my mouth against my will.

I choked on the water he poured down my throat, the terror of drowning seizing my chest like a fist.

When I started to cough violently, bucking in the chair, he threw my face away roughly with a *tsk*.

My chin sagged to my chest, water still dripping from it. My breasts and lap were soaked.

"W-what do you want with me?" I said, biting back tears.

He grabbed my chin again and raised my face back up, jamming his fingers into the sides of my cheeks so I couldn't close my mouth.

I heard a sick *squelch* and he forced a finger into my mouth.

It was sweet. A banana mashed into a wet paste.

It disgusted me, him feeding me like that.

It was vulgar, the way his finger smeared the food across my tongue, the way he kept my mouth open with his other hand and pushed so easily past my lips.

It was a violation.

At last, his finger left my mouth. And he loosened the fingers of his other hand so I could chew.

I thought about spitting the banana out at him, too.

But my stomach growled. I was starving. Depending on how long I'd been unconscious, it could have been days since I'd last eaten.

And I didn't want to make a mess across my clothes. Water would dry. But if I spilled food, I didn't want to find out if he would change me again.

I swallowed the banana.

To my horror, he stroked my hair as if to say, *good girl.*

His hand returned to my jaw and his finger returned to my mouth, coated in more banana.

This time, I didn't exactly let him. But I didn't fight him either.

Like the first time, after I swallowed, he stroked my hair.

A strange sensation settled into my lower belly.

The next time, I may have licked him a little as he withdrew his finger. An involuntary flick of my tongue.

I was just trying to get it all. At least, that's what I told myself.

He fed me several more times and each time I licked him a little more hungrily, sucking just a little harder.

Each time his finger stayed in my mouth just a little longer, his *good girl* head stroke lingering more and more.

My mouth opened wider for him and I enveloped his finger with my tongue, drawing along its full length to get every last taste.

Then I heard him: a small deep masculine groan escaping his lips. A crack in his control.

He grabbed my neck and I gasped with surprise. He plunged two fingers into my mouth; there was no food this time and neither was there controlled patience.

I gagged as he began to finger my mouth.

My wrists strained against my bindings, but there was absolutely no give. I just had to take it as he thrust his fingers in and out.

If I tried to bite down, he tightened his grip on my jaw, forcing my mouth open once more.

My stomach muscles contracted and I thought I was going to throw up. He did not relent.

If anything, he brutalized my mouth harder, fucking it with his fingers like it was my pussy.

Over my muffled groans, I strained to hear him again, whether it was a grunt of twisted arousal or just a quickened breath.

But he was as silent as the grave.

My mind tried to tell me that it was wrong, nasty.

But heat began to grow between my legs, my nipples straining against the delicate silk fabric.

A moan bubbled up around his thrusting fingers as I imagined my masked stalker fucking me with those fingers, holding me in place with his strong hands.

It was too easy to imagine behind my blindfold that this was just a twisted little game we were playing.

I found myself sucking at his fingers, flicking my tongue along the grooves of his fingerprints.

What the fuck was wrong with me? I hardly understood it myself, getting turned on by my kidnapper's abuse of my mouth.

Heat pooled deeper in my stomach as my eyelashes fluttered against my silk blindfold.

The room that I was being held in had become stiflingly hot, the air thick and unmoving. It condensed on my skin like I'd been fucking for hours.

He kicked back the chair and I whimpered, my body flailing against my binds as I fell back. But he caught the chair, held it on two legs, holding me by my throat as he loomed over me and slid his fingers in and out of my mouth.

I was totally in his hands. Under his control. Under his spell.

He held me partly suspended over the floor like he was some sort of god. Or, at least in this moment, he was my god.

I began to leak from my pussy onto the wooden chair, thighs sliding with nothing between me and it. The smell of my musk filled my nostrils as I breathed through my nose.

He pulled me back suddenly, his fingers sliding from my lips, his hand leaving my throat.

I landed back down hard and rocked before stilling, sending shocks up my legs and into my core.

I swallowed big gulps of air, but the relief of being able to breathe was minor compared to the frustration of my empty mouth, my naked tongue, my aching clit.

I flinched when a damp rag pressed against the corner of my lips.

He wiped my mouth clean gently, almost tenderly.

For some reason, this was a million times more horrible after he'd choked and fingered me. I'd revealed my pleasure too easily.

He now had my moans of arousal and my humiliation and I still had nothing from him.

Not his name.

Nor his face.

Or why he kidnapped me.

Heat flooded my cheeks and I ached to be able to close my legs.

Could he smell my arousal? Could he see the shimmering moisture between my legs?

I could feel the heaviness of his gaze searing my skin as he drew the rag across my chin, down the length of my throat, and over the dampness between my breasts.

I felt the sudden urge to cry, I was so embarrassed. Had that been some kind of test? A sick twisted Stockholm Syndrome game?

He tended to me like a child. His touch feeling innocent and harmless.

And here I was, his prisoner, exposed for him. Wet for him. Like some kind of whore.

Before any tears could fall from my covered eyes, an invading fog began to fill my mind.

I shook my head from side to side, trying to clear it, but it only grew.

Soon, I could no longer keep my head up.

The food. He'd drugged it. He'd drugged me. *Again*.

"You fucking coward. Fuck you, asshole." I thrashed and yanked against the ropes holding my wrists and ankles. "When I get free, I'm going to scratch out your eyes and feed them to the crows."

But my limbs were too heavy. I sank deeper into the chair and knew it was no use. I was going to be unconscious once more. At his mercy. Pliable to his whims. I groaned with the last of my strength.

A hand sweetly cupped my cheek.

A vile hatred for him surged inside of me and for a moment, I thought I'd garnered enough energy to bite him before passing out. Teeth sinking in. Drawing blood.

Even then, I didn't elicit a single fucking sound from him—of pain, of pleasure, I didn't care. It was his silence I could no longer stand.

Before I was lost to the darkness, I had a single terrifying thought.

I'd been taken by a cold, emotionless psychopath.

# THE WARDEN

It gave me more pleasure than I expected to see Ava struggle.

Her slender wrists already red raw, tugging against my expert knots, wet silk clinging to her bouncing breasts as she jerked to escape the chair, the curses spitting from her, before everything slowed and her chin fell to her chest.

She was never going to win. I knew that from the exact amount I'd laced her food.

But she'd given me what I wanted from her: *fight*.

"Good girl," I whispered as I tucked her silky hair behind one ear and then the next. "You're already doing so well for me."

She was out, asleep, but just under the surface. Yet there was a part of her that could sense what was happening. Part of her body that was still aware.

That was what I was counting on.

I lifted her face and ran my thumbs over her blindfolded

eyes. I longed for her to see me, to *know* me. But it was a temptation that I had to resist for the time being.

"You'll know me soon enough," I told her.

We had all the time in the world.

No one knew where she was and no one would come looking for her here.

Her lips were slightly parted in her drug-induced sleep. My cock twitched, imagining what it would be like to push past those lips. To have her tongue flick over my sensitive head the way she did to my fingers.

Fuck. I remembered the moment when she'd started sucking at my finger. And that little moan I'd elicited from fucking her mouth that way.

I'd almost given in. Almost taken out my cock and pushed it past her lips.

It took everything in my power to hold back.

Just like it would take everything in my power to do what needed to be done.

"I've imagined this—*you*—for years, Ava, and now that I have you," I said, tracing her plump mouth. "I'm *never* letting you go."

I kept brushing my fingers down her chest, pushing aside the damp silk to reveal those perfect mounds, her nipple hardening against my thumb.

One day, soon, I'd spend hours teasing those nipples with my teeth and my tongue.

But today, I had other plans.

I tugged at the ties around her waist and groaned as her robe fell apart and I feasted my eyes on the glistening folds of her pussy, her legs tied apart just for me.

She was perfection. A work of art.

I slid my fingers along her folds.

Fuck, she was already wet.

Her breath hitched and her brows furrowed together in her sleep.

I brushed my thumb in circles on her clit and this time I was rewarded with a whimper.

She might not know who I was—yet—but she wanted what I could give her.

I remembered the way she stared at me when I let her see me as I watched her through the window. I felt the electricity that arced between us.

I slipped two fingers into her warmth, the same two fingers I'd had in her mouth, still damp with her own saliva.

Fuck. She was so tight around my fingers.

My teeth sank into my lip, expecting how she'd have to stretch for the size of my cock. How pain would etch her pretty features. How sweetly she'd groan in my ear when she adjusted and I began to rock against her.

I kept rubbing her clit, kept pushing in, stretching her.

Her pussy kept drawing me in, clenching me, her nipples hardening in response.

Such a good girl.

Then, when my fingers were in at the hilt, I slowly slid them back out, drawing more moisture from her.

The musky scent that greeted me made my cock harden even further.

Even though she was under, her hips rocked forward, asking for more.

My girl wanted more.

And I would give that to her.

A murmur of pleasure came from Ava's parted lips as I

pushed my fingers deep inside of her and curled them around to massage her G-spot.

A thrill shot down my spine as it made her breath quicken and brought a blushing pink to her pale cheeks.

"I'm going to wash you clean of him," I said as I pulled my fingers out and gently slid them back in. "Every inch of your skin, every cell of your body. I'm going to cleanse you."

She moaned in rhythm with my fingers. Her eyes moved against her eyelids and her wrists tugged slightly at the bindings, but I knew the drug well enough to know she would not come out of it.

She was trapped in this blissful dream. For now.

"I'm not going to stop till all you feel is *me*," I told her, my own voice strained as I fought against my arousal.

I'd indulge Ava when she deserved it. But there was no give for me. Never.

"Till I'm all over you." I exhaled. "Till you're full of me. Only *me*."

Ava was close to coming. I knew by the pitch of her moans, by how the muscles along her inner thighs were twitching, and most of all by how dripping wet she was as she clenched on my thrusting fingers.

It would have been so easy to take her over the edge.

She'd already been so aroused when I fucked her mouth. She'd wanted to come then. She wanted to come now.

I gritted my teeth because I wanted so fucking badly to see that. To see how her body trembled, how her head fell back, how she sagged, boneless in the end. I wanted to see her spent and empty because of me.

But as Ava whimpered at a fever pitch, I withdrew my fingers, wet with her arousal. My hand shook beyond my control as I raised my fingers to my lips and sucked, drinking down her honey, finally letting out the unrestrained groan.

My cock needed friction, release. It needed her sweet, hungry lips wrapped around it, sucking it, swallowing all I had to give.

I groaned loudly as I released my rock-hard cock from my pants.

My fingers wrapped around its base and I felt my pulse throbbing, my hot blood pounding.

I stroked my length a few times as I devoured Ava with my hungry gaze.

I should have been more worried about my reaction. About how close I was to losing control. But I was too consumed with the way Ava's hips bucked, straining forward, searching for me.

I reveled in the way she whimpered, so fucking needy for my touch.

I wanted to give it to her. Everything she wanted. And more.

And I would.

But she had to *beg* for it.

I grabbed her chin and lifted her mouth, holding it open the way I had when I fed her.

Then I stood with my legs on either side of hers and eased the tip of my cock past her lips.

The feeling of her soft wet tongue on my head as I thrust in and out of her mouth made my legs tremble, made my vision go white.

Fuck, I wasn't going to last long.

I was losing control. And I'd barely started with her.

I loved her, but in this moment, I wanted to destroy her.

I imagined her eyes open, pupils blown wide as she gazed up at me from her knees, eager to choke on my dick.

I wanted to kiss my cum off her mouth, taste myself on her innocent little lips. Goosebumps erupted down my spine at the thought and I had to grip myself tight to keep from coming.

My panting filled the room. My groans became more and more animalistic as I thrust my rapidly leaking cock down her throat.

I wasn't in control, no matter what I might have said to convince myself otherwise.

She'd reduced me to nothing more than a beast.

I wanted to tear into her, consume her.

I wanted her to be mine, only mine. Only ever mine.

All I'd told myself about keeping control, of following the plan was for nothing. I never stood a chance against her.

I pulled out as I came hard, my cum filling her mouth and dribbling down her chin and over her breasts.

To my surprise she let out a moan and her throat bobbed as she swallowed down my cum.

Such a good girl.

I grabbed on to the back of her chair to stop myself from falling over as the wave of pleasure subsided.

Fuck, look at the mess I made.

Anger at myself flared up in my hollowed chest. How could I have been so weak? How could I have risked everything I'd planned?

I stuffed my still half-hard cock back into my pants. I'd have to bathe her again. Clean her up.

But my cock was already hardening at the thought of

washing her beautiful body, of soaping her skin as she lay with her back to my chest.

Fuck. I'd been so prepared. I'd built up my self-control for years. It had been impenetrable, a fortress. And yet it had crumbled like a child's sandcastle at the nearness of her.

She was more dangerous than I ever thought possible. And I had no defenses against her.

My exhale came out shaky and uneven as I ran yet another bath for her, my desire for her already creeping back in as my cock began to harden once more.

I didn't know what to do, how to hold myself back. I was helpless.

I'd put locks on the doors to keep Ava in.

But it seemed I needed them to keep *me* out.

# AVA

"This will hurt," a younger Ty said, standing between my thighs as I sat on the bed at the school nurse's office.

The door had closed behind the nurse only a few moments ago, but the silence in the small office was deafening.

It was as if we had always been alone together, him and I.

He dabbed the antiseptic onto a cotton pad, but as he applied it to my scratched knee, I barely felt it at all.

I only felt his hand resting flat and firmly against my inner thigh.

His breathing quickened.

Mine did, too.

I looked at his face as he followed his hand's movement up my thigh with his eyes.

His lips were slightly parted, bright and wet. His dark eyebrows were knitted together; he was focused, but there was something more.

He was upset. But not quite upset.

It was an emotion I couldn't put a name to nor explain, except that I felt something similar stirring in my lower belly. A strange heat.

When he lifted his gaze, I was shocked by his eyes.

The blue of his irises was gone, consumed by pupils as dark and shimmering as an oil pit.

Outside, birds chirped and the last shouts of children before being called back into class could be heard. But they seemed so far away from where I was, from where *we* were.

"I'm going to wash you clean of him," he said, his voice so husky it was almost unrecognizable. "Every inch of your skin, every cell of your body. I'm going to cleanse you."

His thumb made small, reassuring circles and when he grazed the scalloped lace edge of my panties, a hot ache went through me.

My breath hitched as something tightened in my belly.

I... I shouldn't be feeling things like this for him. It was wrong.

Then, somehow, I wasn't wearing any panties.

What? How did that happen?

I dug my teeth into my lower lip as he brushed his finger between my legs.

The sensation made me break out in goosebumps all over my body. I'd never experienced anything like it before.

And I wanted more.

I bucked my hips slightly, afraid to put into words this urgent need I hadn't even known existed inside of me.

The crepe paper on the examination table crinkled as I gripped the edge.

When he slipped just the tip of two fingers *into me*, it took everything I had not to cry out.

My first instinct was pain.

But as he held his fingers there, I realized it wasn't pain.

It was intensity.

*A need.*

*There was a wetness between my thighs, and I worried I was leaking onto the crepe paper.*

*But when he pushed his fingers in, I felt how easily they slid deeper into me, all the way in, filling a part of me I never knew needed filling.*

*I forgot about the examination table. The nurse. The school.*

*All that existed was the pleasure that his fingers pushing in and out of me was giving me.*

*At first, he moved slowly, almost tenderly, but then it went faster. And then faster still.*

*I could feel his breath on my forehead. "I'm not going to stop till all you feel is* me."

*I wanted to tell him that I didn't want him to stop. But I couldn't speak. I could only whimper and moan as he worked my body.*

*I wanted to grab ahold of him, to hold him, to kiss him, to pull his hand closer, urging his fingers deeper.*

*But I couldn't move apart from rocking my hips toward him.*

*It was as if my hands were tied down by my sides. I could almost feel ropes around them, even though I couldn't see them.*

*The need for some kind of release soon became all that I could think about. A heated pressure had built in my stomach and I knew it couldn't just keep growing. Could it?*

*There was something on the other side of this. I longed with every cell in my body to get there, wherever* there *was.*

*This wave began to crest, about to crash over me, and I wanted to scream at the pressure of it. But only a moan left my lips.*

*"Till I'm all over you," he promised. "Till you're full of me. Only me."*

My eyes shot open as I gasped for air, my heart pounding, disoriented and groggy from whatever drug was still coursing through my veins.

For a second, I just lay there, staring up at the delicate fabric of the pale-pink canopy above my head, struggling to piece together where I was.

The sheets felt like silk against my skin, cool and smooth, while the pillows cradled my head in a cloudlike softness. It was the kind of bed that should have offered comfort and safety.

But it didn't.

The luxury, the comfort—it all felt wrong. Like a cage disguised in velvet.

My wrists throbbed, the skin raw and stinging from where the ropes had dug in. There was a bruise on the back of my neck and on my knees, too.

My throat was sore and dry from whatever he'd given me and something musky coated my tongue.

Between my legs I was soaked. I could feel my wetness dripping down the crook of my leg, running across my ass, pooling on the mattress.

A needy ache burned in my lower belly like a furnace and I squirmed in the bed.

I had been dreaming. And the sensation during my dream had been so real. The pressure of his fingers, the urgency as it thrust into me with increasing violence, the almost painful strain of every muscle in my body as I tried to come.

The agony of being denied it at the very last moment.

I glanced down. I was in a silk nightgown in a deep-crimson color. No robe. The bastard had changed me again.

Had my captor *touched* me while I was passed out? Was

that why my memory of Ty had morphed into a dream of him fingering me?

I tried to feel for any lingering proof of *him* between my legs. But I couldn't be sure, dream mixing with reality to muddy my drugged memory.

I just knew that I couldn't give him a second chance to claim me against my will.

And I couldn't give myself the temptation of liking it.

I sat up slowly, and a wave of dizziness hit me, making me press my hand to my forehead. The drug's effects were still wearing off, leaving me foggy and weak.

When the room stopped spinning, I took in my surroundings.

I was in a four-poster bed, the dark wood spindles towering above me, intricately carved with designs that seemed almost too detailed to focus on.

I was in a cavernous bedroom, elegant in a way that felt far removed from reality. Gleaming wood floors stretched out before me, polished to a high shine that reflected the dim light filtering down from above.

Heavy dark wood furniture filled the room—ornate dressers and armoires, each piece meticulously carved with the same intricate detail as the bed.

There were touches of pale pink scattered throughout the room, softening the otherwise imposing atmosphere.

Something flickered in the back of my mind—a strange sense of familiarity.

I *knew* this place.

But figuring out where I knew this room from wasn't my first concern. My first concern was getting the hell out of here.

I pushed the covers off me, wincing as my shoulder joints ached, and pushed myself out of the bed.

My legs were weak from disuse and from the drugs. Just getting my feet back underneath me took my breath away. Swaying dizzily, I stumbled forward and caught myself with my hands flat against the door.

I knew instantly that this hadn't been the original door. It was lined with a flat piece of bolted steel, a strange industrial oddity in this dark gothic room.

Perhaps if I'd stopped to think, I'd have realized that a psychopath who took the time to line the fucking door with metal, wasn't going to leave it unlocked.

I yanked at the door handle nonetheless, dots flashing in my vision as blood rushed to my head.

Locked.

Fucking locked.

"Let me out, asshole," I screamed, banging my fists against the iron sheet.

Each slam sent sharp jolts of pain through my hand, but I didn't stop. Not at first. Panic and adrenaline overrode the sting, fueled my desperate need to escape.

But as I kept going, it hit me—*how pointless this was.*

I'd seen people do the same thing in movies, banging and yelling like that's all it would take for their captor to have a change of heart, unlock the door, and say, *"Well, because you asked so nicely..."*

The absurdity of it hit me like a slap. I was trapped, and this—this pathetic display—wasn't going to change a damn thing.

I stopped, gasping for breath, my lungs wheezing as I

leaned forward and rested my forehead against the cool, smooth surface.

My breath came out in ragged bursts, and I squeezed my eyes shut, a dull throb in my right hand.

I would not escape by the door.

But I would not give up.

The windows.

I ran to the pink drapes, certain a window would be behind it, perhaps even a door to a balcony, and my freedom.

If it was locked like the door, I'd use one of the dark wood armchairs to shatter the glass.

If I was lucky, I was on the ground floor and I could climb out.

If the bedroom where I was being held captive was on a high floor, I'd climb down a gutter, a vine of ivy, a few jutting stones on the facade of the house because risking my life would be better than staying prisoner.

My heart raced and sweat pricked at the back of my neck as I threw back the curtains, their soft rustle and scrape sounding like the scuttle of cockroaches.

My skin crawled as I stumbled back from the windows. A heavy pit sank deeper in my stomach. There was no way I was going to break through the glass in the window, because there was no glass at all in the window.

There was only red exposed brick, messy globs of concrete between them as if he'd done it himself.

He'd fucking bricked me in.

No light from the outside world. No chance I could catch the attention of a passing car or use a mirror to signal to a nearby house. I couldn't even see where the fuck I was being kept.

*Oh God.* I was trapped. A prisoner.

Fuck him. I'd been stupid enough to think escape would be that simple.

He'd planned for this. Planned for me. He'd already thought of every way that I might escape and he'd *foiled it in advance*. He was one step ahead of me.

I could feel the walls closing in around me, the room tightening, suffocating. Panic swelled in my chest, threatening to take over.

*Calm down, Ava. Think.*

I forced myself to stop, to breathe.

I turned back to face the room, wringing my hands together to try and stop them shaking. I had to figure out my next move.

There had to be a way out, something I wasn't seeing yet.

The first thing that caught my attention was the full-length mirror that took up the whole wall. It didn't seem to fit the gothic bedroom. Too modern. Like it had been installed recently.

I walked toward it—toward my own reflection, the short crimson slip shifting across my body as I walked, an uneasy feeling growing in me.

I remembered Lisa grabbing my wrist before I started to change in one of those double-sized change rooms at Brown Thomas and telling me to always place my fingernail against the reflective surface.

If there was no gap between your fingernail and the reflected image, it was a one-way mirror.

I lifted my finger to the glass and pressed the tip of my finger to it.

Shit. There was no gap.

*He* was watching me from the other side.

A shiver went up my spine as I imagined my hulking masked stalker standing directly in front of me, watching me, his breath fogging up the glass.

I did what any self-respecting girl would do in my position. I stuck both my middle fingers up at him.

"Fuck you, asshole."

Later I'd figure out a way to cover up at least some of this mirror.

If I hadn't escaped, that was. Escape was still plan number one.

Through a second door I spotted an en suite. A quick inspection showed me a dark marble bathroom, a large claw-foot tub in the center, its white porcelain contrasting starkly with the shadowy tones of the room, the bronze clawed feet adding a touch of vintage opulence. The polished marble floor gleamed under the soft, warm light of a hanging chandelier.

The air was thick with the smell of jasmine and I knew he'd bathed me in here.

In here was yet another full-length mirror taking up most of one wall.

I used the toilet, scowling at the mirror because I knew he was still watching.

I walked back into the bedroom and studied the room and found more details in the low lighting from an iron chandelier.

The dark wood paneled ceilings were high and molded. I

bedside table. Without thinking, I snatched it up, gripping the cool metal tightly in my shaking hands.

The footsteps stopped right outside the door.

My breath hitched, my pulse roaring in my ears as several locks clicked from the other side, the sound muffled by the metal.

The door creaked open, and I raised the lamp, ready to strike.

But the second I saw him—now without his skeleton mask on—the weapon slipped from my hands, falling to the floor with a dull thud.

He stood there, his dark figure framed by the dim light of the hallway. Confusion crashed into me, so intense it left me breathless.

*Scáth.*

My stalker, my protector—*he* had kidnapped me.

# AVA

Scáth stood in front of me, his arms crossed over his chest, the black button-up shirt he wore clinging to his muscled frame like a second skin.

His eyes, icy and piercing, locked on mine with an intensity that sent a shiver down my spine.

I stared at his face, the face of the man I loved, unable to believe my eyes.

The face so familiar I could draw it with my eyes closed, trace every stern line and curve.

The face I loved.

But there was something unsettling about the way they watched me, like a predator assessing his prey, his gaze devoid of warmth, his lips set in a hard, emotionless line.

No, this couldn't be Scáth. It couldn't.

I was hallucinating. Dreaming. Trapped in a nightmare.

"Ty?" My voice shook as it came out as barely a whisper.

He smirked, but it was cold and cruel. "Hello, Ava, darling. Did you miss me?"

It *was* Scáth.

The feeling of betrayal hit my chest with such force that for a moment I couldn't breathe. I gasped at the sight of him as if he had his hand back around my throat.

Scáth had drugged me.

He'd kidnapped me. Kept me blindfolded and in the dark for days.

*Scáth* had made me his captive.

But... why?

A thought so cruel struck me like a steel knife to the heart.

He had been playing a twisted little game with me. Everything before was just a lie. He hated me so much that he wanted to make me love him before he destroyed me.

What did I do to make him hate me so much? Why couldn't I remember it?

A shiver went down my spine. Did I even want to remember?

Even as I fell apart, Scáth—*Ty*—stood so coolly, so unaffectedly, watching with only a slight arch of his dark brow.

Scáth looked meaner, crueler than I'd ever seen him before. His cheekbones seemed sharper, his jawline even sterner, and the darkness in his glare made his blue eyes seem almost black.

Even when he stalked me through the campus of Darkmoor, even when he appeared at my bedroom door as silent as the grave, even when he chased me through the library and pinned my arms above my head against the stacks, he never looked like this.

Never looked at *me* like this.

This wasn't the face of the boy I grew up with, the protector who had always been there in the shadows, watching over me. No, this was someone colder, sharper, like all the warmth had been carved out of him and replaced with something darker.

And his eyes—the way he looked at me. Where once there had been fire and intensity, now there was only ice. Cold and cruel, his gaze sent a shiver down my spine, as if he was calculating, weighing me against whatever twisted plans he had.

And beneath it all, something far more terrifying lurked, something I had never seen in him before. A glint of madness flickered in his eyes, just enough to make my breath hitch.

It was like I didn't even recognize him anymore.

This was a stranger wearing the face of the man I loved.

"What's going on?" My voice came out shaky, barely more than a whisper. "Why am I here? Why are you keeping me prisoner?"

He took a step toward me, slow and deliberate, his eyes dark with intent.

I instinctively backed up, my feet moving on their own, my mind scrambling for any sign of a weapon. *Anything* I could use to defend myself.

"I have plans for you, Ava," he said, his voice low and menacing. "And I'm afraid you're not going to like them."

His words sent a chill down my spine, and I felt the floor tilt beneath me. "W-what?"

No weapons. And there wasn't much room left to retreat.

Panic surged. I needed a plan, something else—I couldn't just stand here and let him close the distance.

"Stop right there," I stammered, calculating my next move. "Stay back."

If I could just get around him, make a run for the door—

In a burst of desperation, I darted to the side, trying to duck past him.

But Ty moved quicker, stepping directly into my path, cutting off my escape.

He *tsked* as if I'd disappointed him. "So many fucking years… perfecting my plans."

I gasped and stumbled farther back, my pulse racing even faster.

"Why would you kidnap me?" My voice cracked as panic clawed at me. "Bring me here? If you'd just asked me to come with you, I would've gone willingly."

My feet shuffled blindly, and within seconds, my back collided with the hard wall behind me. My heart leaped into my throat.

I was trapped.

Ty's eyes gleamed with something cold, something unrecognizable. "Would you? I don't know about that. It almost seemed like you'd *forgotten* all about me."

Before I could respond, he closed the distance between us in one swift, terrifying move, his chest pressed against mine, pinning me between him and the wall.

His body pressed into me, firm, unyielding. I could feel his breath against my skin, feel the dark heat radiating off him.

There was nowhere to go, no more room to escape.

For the first time, genuine fear gripped me, sinking its icy claws deep into my chest.

Up until now, no matter how twisted or dangerous things had gotten, I'd always known, *deep down*, that Scáth —*my* Scáth—would never hurt me. There had been something in him, a thread of restraint, a silent promise that no matter how dark things became, I'd be safe in his presence.

But now... this wasn't him. Not the man I'd known.

This version of Scáth—this *Ty*—was different. Cold. Detached. There was no flicker of recognition, no hint of the boy I had once trusted. The look in his eyes told me everything I needed to know.

He was planning to hurt me; he said so himself. It wasn't a matter of *if* anymore. It was *when*.

And the real, sickening question that twisted in my gut was *how much*? How far was he willing to go?

"W-what happened to you?" I asked, my voice barely more than a whisper, my hands pressing against the wall as if I could somehow melt into it. "You're... you're acting crazy."

Ty scoffed, his breath hot against my cheek as he leaned in closer.

"Me? Acting *crazy*?"

His hands slammed against the wall on either side of my head, the sound echoing through the room like a gunshot.

I flinched, my whole body jolting in fear as the force of his movement made the plaster vibrate behind me.

"I suppose five fucking years in a maximum-security prison will make a man a little... *crazy*," he said, the wicked glint in his eyes sending a fresh wave of terror through me.

A realization hit me so hard I could barely breathe.

*Crazy.*

*No.* It couldn't be.

Something had happened to him in that prison. Something dark. Something that had split him in two.

*Two distinct sides of him,* I realized with a sickening jolt.

But then again, he'd always been that way, hadn't he. There had been signs. I'd seen it before, even when we were younger.

My protector and my bully.

The Ty who loved me and the Ty who hated me then.

The Ty I loved now, my *Scáth*—and this... monster standing in front of me.

Ty had a split personality.

And the one standing before me *wasn't* the man I had fallen for.

*Split personality.*

I'd read about it when researching for an article—Dissociative Identity Disorder.

Different personalities could be triggered by trauma, emotional stress, or specific memories. Those triggers could force one personality to the surface while pushing the other back into the shadows.

The personalities might not even know what the other had done while in control, like living two separate lives in one body.

My Scáth had a dark side. A *dominant* side.

*Ty.*

"What happened to you, Ty?" I reached out to brush his dark hair back from his face.

He flinched—*flinched*—from my touch before his hand

lashed out and grabbed me by the wrist, holding me back from him.

"I suppose I have changed since you last saw me." He leaned in, brushing his lips against my cheek, sending shivers and heat down my spine. "I became who I needed to be… *for you.*"

My heart pounded as I pieced it together, the memories lining up too perfectly to ignore.

*Ty* must've been triggered when I was kidnapped by Cormac, when the danger had become too real. When *Scáth* wasn't enough anymore.

I swallowed hard, feeling the weight of that truth settle into my bones.

My voice was barely a whisper, swallowed by the dread tightening around my throat. "W-what are you going to do to me?"

Ty's lips brushed against my ear, his voice like a caress, soft, intimate—horrifying.

"I'm going to break you," he murmured, as though he were whispering sweet nothings. "So that I can rebuild you."

My heart stuttered, my mind spinning. I couldn't breathe. Couldn't think.

His words were venomous, yet the way he spoke them, the tenderness in his voice—it was as if he was confessing his love, not telling me something dark and twisted.

"You're going to… torture me?" I managed, though it felt like the word might strangle me.

His lips ghosted over my cheekbone, his breath warm against my skin.

This might not be *my* Scáth. But my body was reacting like it was, the familiar need coursing through my veins. His nearness, and the fact that I'd been left so unsatisfied from my dream earlier, had me wet between my legs.

"Torture is such a vile word," he whispered, pushing a strand of hair behind my ear with a gentleness that made my stomach churn. "I prefer... *therapy.*"

# AVA

"*Therapy?*" I echoed, my voice barely more than a whisper.

My head spun with the weight of the word, the implications swirling in dark, dizzying circles. Every possible meaning twisted into something vile, something horrifying.

My pulse thundered in my ears, and I could feel the sickening contrast between the gentle way he touched me—his fingers brushing lightly along my skin—and the cold menace in his words.

I loved Scáth—*my* Scáth—but this man, this version of Ty... he was terrifying, and yet the nearness of him still stirred something in me, made me ache, made me want to give in to him.

I didn't know how to handle the confusion, the horror of it.

"W-what kind of therapy?" I forced out, my body trembling beneath his proximity.

Ty chuckled softly, but the sound was dark, humorless. "Not the kind that Dr. Vale wasted your time with."

He reached into his pocket and pulled out a small vial, the glass catching the dim light of the room as it glinted in his hand.

Terror surged through me, crawling up from the depths of my chest like a dark wave, my body locking up as memories clawed at the edges of my mind—fragments of something I'd buried deep, something too painful to look at.

But I felt it now, felt it stir as if Ty had opened the latch on Pandora's box.

*No. Not that.*

Ty popped the cork and waved the vial under my nose.

The scent hit me like a punch to the gut, the air thickening with the unmistakable, sickly-sweet aroma of the liquid that had haunted my nightmares.

The same one his father—*the professor*—had used on me all those years ago.

My chest tightened painfully, and I couldn't stop the images that flickered in my mind—those dark, vile memories.

*No, please.*

"You will take this paralytic," he whispered, brushing his lips against my temple as if he were offering comfort, not horror, "and you will start to remember."

"No."

"But don't worry, I'll be there to help you through it. To cleanse you of *him,* until there is only *me. My* touch. *My* love."

I wanted to scream, to run, but my legs felt like lead, my

mind like quicksand, dragging me down into a place where I couldn't escape.

His fingers, so tender as they traced the line of my jaw, contrasted violently with the nightmare I knew was coming.

I needed to figure out how to bring *him* back. Scáth. And I needed to do it now.

My mind raced, scrambling through every piece of information I could remember about split personalities, anything I'd read or researched.

I knew triggers could switch them—stress, memories, emotional connections. If I could just find the right words, the right thing to say, maybe I could reach the part of him that was still *my* Scáth.

He was in there somewhere, buried beneath this cruel version of Ty.

*The name.* Names had power, didn't they? I'd read that before.

Scáth wasn't just his name—it was a symbol of who he was to me. He was my shadow, my protector. If I could remind him of that, pull him back with it, maybe… maybe I could bring him to the surface.

I swallowed hard, feeling the tremor in my voice. "Please… Scáth—"

"*Don't* call me that," he snarled, his voice low and dangerous, like the growl of an animal ready to strike.

I flinched, recoiling from him like he'd actually struck me.

His eyes were dark, furious, a complete stranger's. There was nothing of the man I loved, the man I knew, in his expression.

Yet he was in there. Somewhere. But did Ty know about him?

"So, you know about Scáth?" I dared to ask. I needed to understand how far this went, how much he knew.

Ty threw his head back and laughed, the sound cold and harsh, sending a shiver down my spine. His eyes glittered with something dark and twisted.

"Of course, I know all about your precious *Scáth*," he sneered. "Your Scáth has coddled you, babied you. He'd cover you in bubble wrap if he could, keep you safe in your little cage."

My stomach turned at the way he said *your Scáth*, like he was mocking everything I'd thought I knew about the man who had protected me.

"Your Scáth is too much of a coward to do what needs to be done." His voice dropped lower, a dangerous edge creeping into his tone. "But *I* am not."

My breath caught in my throat. *What does that mean? What does he plan to do?*

"Does Scáth know about you?" I dared to ask, my voice trembling, barely able to get the words out. "Does he know what you've got planned?"

Ty's lips curled into a sinister smile, something cruel flashing in his eyes.

"No," he said, a quiet chuckle rumbling through him. "He's clueless. Just how I planned it."

A cold pit of dread settled in my stomach. Ty was in control, and Scáth had no idea. The man who had protected me, the one who would have *never* hurt me—he was in the dark. Helpless.

My chest tightened, panic swelling inside me. I had to

bring Scáth back—I *had to*. If I lost him to this darker side of himself, I might never get him back.

But as I stared at him, standing before me like a towering storm, I realized how delicate this was.

One wrong word, one wrong move, and I might push him further into this... *monster*.

My heart pounded as I clung to the one thing I knew might break through his cold, terrifying exterior—the bond we'd shared.

Scáth's feelings for me.

His love.

*My* Scáth, the one who watched over me, who protected me, who would never hurt me. If I could just tap into that, bring him back to the surface, maybe—just maybe—I could get him to remember who he really was.

Then Scáth would let me go.

"I know you care about me," I said, my voice trembling but firm. I had to believe that the man I loved was still in there, buried under all this darkness.

His eyes flickered, the mask of cold indifference slipping for just a heartbeat before hardening again.

"Of course I care," he growled, leaning closer until I could feel his breath on my skin, his lips brushing the edge of my jaw, the gentle touch so wrong against the cruel tension in his words. "I love you more, Ava. I always have."

For a second, the words hung between us, and my heart squeezed painfully in my chest.

*He loves me.*

"Then if you love me, you wouldn't hurt me," I whispered, my voice desperate now, pleading. "The real you wouldn't do this. I need you to remember that."

He paused, and for a moment his eyes softened.

*Yes, please, Scáth. Come back to me.*

But then his eyes hardened.

"You don't get it, do you, Ava?" His voice was low, menacing, as though I'd missed some crucial piece of this twisted puzzle.

I swallowed hard, fear tightening around my throat like a noose. "Get what?"

His hand wrapped around my throat to pin my head to the wall, not hard enough to cut off my oxygen. But firm enough to make a point, to infuse his next words with deadly promise.

"I'm doing this *because* I love you."

I had one last card to play—one desperate attempt to reach him, to reach *Scáth*.

Sometimes touch could be grounding, pulling someone back to the surface. Maybe if I could create that physical connection, it would spark something deep inside of him, something that could remind him of who he really was.

My heart pounded in my chest as I grabbed the back of his neck and pulled him to me.

To my surprise, he didn't fight me.

His lips crashed into mine.

*God, please let this work.*

With his free hand, he grabbed the wrist of the hand I had around his neck and he wrenched it off him, as if he couldn't stand my touch. He pinned my hand above my head and kept his other hand around my throat, trapping me, as he took control of my mouth, my lips, my tongue.

Owning me.

Possessing me.

*Taking* my submission.

He didn't make a sound. No soft groan of pleasure, no sigh against my lips the way Scáth would.

The silence felt suffocating, eerie, like he was holding back more than just his voice. As if even in this moment of supposed intimacy, he needed to maintain control, to remind me that he was in charge.

Yet my body responded instinctively, as though it *was* the man I loved, every nerve alight with conflicting sensations. Need surged through me, tightening my nipples to painful points, making my pussy ache and stealing groans from my throat.

My heart, however, slammed against my ribs in terror, a visceral reminder that this wasn't the same man. That his kiss was different from Scáth's—colder, more controlled, lacking the wildfire that I'd come to know.

*God, I missed Scáth. I loved him. Please... come back to me.*

I poured every ounce of that love into the kiss, as if somehow, by sheer force of will, I could reach inside him—deep down where Scáth was hiding—and pull him back. To save us both.

Ty tore his lips away from mine, the sudden loss of his touch so sharp it was like a slap.

I fought the urge to whimper, to show any weakness.

His eyes were dark and unreadable, not a single trace of warmth in them.

"I'll take that as a yes," he said, his voice so casual, so detached, it made my stomach turn.

"No," I forced out, my voice shaking but defiant. "I won't do it."

I braced myself for his anger, for the explosion of rage that would follow my disobedience.

But instead, he just stared at me, cold and emotionless, like he was studying me, trying to figure out how best to break me.

"Oh, you'll agree." His voice was unnervingly calm, almost as though he were stating a fact. A promise.

"Never," I spat, my chest tightening with each breath, but I refused to show him any fear. He couldn't win. I wouldn't let him.

Ty backed up slowly, his gaze never leaving mine. He moved with that predatory grace, all the way to the door, pausing just before he stepped out. A smirk tugged at the corner of his mouth, one that sent a cold shiver down my spine.

"Fight me," he said softly, almost teasingly. "I like it when you fight."

And with that, he turned and slammed the door shut, the locks clicking into place with an eerie finality. The sound echoed in the room, but his words lingered even louder in the silence. His terrifying promise ringing in my ears.

"I won't stop until you bend to my will."

# AVA

I was going to escape. Or die trying.

My attempts to bring Scáth out of Ty had failed and I would not—could not—stick around to find out exactly how he planned to break my will.

I just had to hope I would succeed.

But I knew I couldn't be too obvious.

I had to assume he was watching me from behind the mirror. So I had to bide my time and wait patiently in my gilded prison until he returned.

I lay in the familiar softness of my childhood bed, staring up at the pale-pink canopy that draped above me like a delicate veil, straining my ears for the sound of his footsteps approaching, the creak of the door, anything to signal his return.

But the room was still and quiet, so quiet that every faint sound seemed amplified—the soft ticking of the antique clock on the mantle and the distant creak of the house settling around me.

The sheets beneath me were luxurious, cool against my skin, smelling fresh with a hint of jasmine, but no amount of comfort could ease the tight knot in my chest.

My body was tense, every muscle coiled tight, ready to spring into action when the moment came.

My wrists still ached, the dull soreness a constant reminder of the ropes that had bound me. I could still feel the phantom sensation of being tied, of being trapped, and the lingering panic that I was once again a prisoner.

Every shadow in the room seemed to creep closer, closing in around me as I waited for him—*Ty*—to return. My heart thudded in my chest, not from fear, but from the anticipation of what I had to do.

I had one chance.

He would not be fooled again.

At last, I heard his footsteps approaching from down the hall. I had to move swiftly.

I slipped out of the bed and stuffed my pillows beneath the comforter, creating a mound like I was still lying there. It wouldn't stand up to scrutiny, but I didn't need it to.

I tiptoed behind the door, just in time to hear the first dead bolt shift open.

I didn't have any time to consider whether this was, in fact, a horrible idea.

He was here.

The reverberations of the second and third dead bolts were indistinguishable from the painful thudding of my heart.

I had just the tiniest moment to gasp one last final deep breath as the door swung open, concealing me behind it.

I heard his confident steps into the room before his back came into view.

He slowed as he reached the bed. "Ava? Wake up."

He was holding a tray in his arms, my dinner, I guessed.

Although whether it'd be drugged again or not, I wasn't waiting around to find out.

This was my one shot. It had to be perfect.

I didn't bother with stealth. I just moved as fast as I could.

I sprinted out from around the door and ran out.

"Ava?" His stern voice chastised me as if I were a child.

I grabbed the handle from the outside and yanked it shut behind me.

I was shaking like a leaf as I tugged a heavy, utility grade dead bolt into place. What he shifted back and forth like a switch, I had to grunt and heave at, muscles quivering.

But I managed it in the end.

For a brief moment, I stared at the bar crossing the door, a trembling hand over my mouth.

I'd done it.

I'd trapped *him*.

I didn't bother with the other two locks. I ignored the door handle turning as he attempted to get out and turned.

I found myself in a long hallway with closed doors and glowing wall sconces lining each side. There was a single window at the very end, the soft dove-gray light filtering in illuminating thick motes of dust. Trepidation lifted the hairs at the nape of my neck.

None of these identical doors looked like an exit. And I saw no stairway.

The hallway looked strange. It looked... *staged*.

And what chilled me more was the fact that Ty wasn't even banging on the door behind me like I expected him to.

But I didn't stop to consider it any further.

I ran to the first door, but I found it locked. Yanking on the next one's brass knob, I discovered it was no different.

Zigzagging down the hallway, I grew more and more desperate; they were all locked.

I was trapped.

Had he known I'd try and escape?

Panic gripped my chest, making it difficult to breathe, as I found door after door... locked.

As I came to the end of the hallway, I could see it branched off left and right in a T. But all I could focus on was the window.

Closer, I could now see that the window was barred and all I could see at the moment was a sheet of uninterrupted white sky. What more was out there?

I moved to the window, hardly feeling my footsteps on the well-worn oriental runner as if I were in a dream.

Despite their ice-cold bite, I wrapped my fingers around the icy bars and I pressed my nose between them. I needed something to steady me as I gazed out.

There was nothing around for miles.

Nothing but thick woods and empty green hills. No road, no path—nowhere to flag down a helpful passerby.

Oh God. We were completely isolated.

The elation of freedom was gone, leaving me feeling empty.

Peering down, a sprawling, meticulously manicured garden stretched out below.

Dark hedges carved into winding patterns framed flower beds bursting with crimson roses and other dark-petaled blooms.

Gravel paths wove between the beds, the garden's symmetry precise, almost unnervingly so, each shrub and blossom too perfect, as if tended with an obsessive hand.

My gaze traced the length of the garden until it came to a dark corner where stood an all-too familiar greenhouse.

Memories slammed into me.

"Ready or not..."

*I could hear Ty's footsteps pounding behind me, the crunch of black pebbles under his boots as he chased me through the manicured gardens.*

*The air was thick with the scent of roses and lilies, mingling with the faint smell of wet moss that always seemed to hover around the estate.*

*I glanced back, heart racing, catching a glimpse of his pale-blue eyes through the towering bushes. He was close—too close—but I wasn't about to let him catch me. Not yet.*

*I darted down one of the narrow paths, my skirt flaring out as I weaved between the flower beds, dodging the roses with their bright petals and thorny stems.*

*Even though it was still daytime, the sun never seemed to break through the thick trees, casting dark shadows across the paths.*

*His footsteps seemed to fade behind me, swallowed by the sounds of the garden.*

*For a moment, I thought I'd lost him.*

*But ahead he stepped out from behind a thick bush, smirking like he'd known all along where I'd go. Like this was all just a game.*

*"...here I come."*

*I yelped and skidded to a stop, barely managing to spin away before he could catch me, his fingers grazing the hem of my skirt.*

*Without thinking, I veered off the path, sprinting toward the old greenhouse at the edge of the garden. I slammed against the glass door, the entire lower level of the greenhouse covered as always with a dark curtain, and I grabbed for the handle.*

*Behind me, Ty's voice shifted, panic creeping into his usually steady tone.*

*"No, Ava! Don't go in there!" he shouted, his words chased by the sound of his footsteps getting closer again.*

*I pushed open the creaky ivy-covered door and took a small step inside.*

*The air inside was warmer, thicker, with a strange, sweet smell that hung in the air, mixing with the scent of damp earth and leaves.*

*"Ava, get out. He'll get so mad if he finds you!"*

*I glanced over my shoulder.*

*Ty wasn't laughing anymore—his face was serious, almost scared.*

*My pulse quickened, but not from fear. Why did it matter if I went inside? What was so terrible about this place?*

*"Ava, stop!"*

*But I didn't stop. His words only fueled the curiosity that had been bubbling inside me for months.*

*So I stepped farther in, my eyes adjusting to the dim light, taking in the strange shapes around me as the door shut behind me.*

I gasped, my fingers gripping the cold bars of the window so tightly that my knuckles blanched, trembling with the force of my desperation.

I willed myself to remember more—*please, remember.*

But with each flicker of memory, with each flash of twisting vines and strange looming shapes in that forbidden place, came an equal wave of dread, tightening in my chest.

The terror of *what* I might recall was almost as suffocating as the blank spaces themselves.

What had been in the greenhouse? What had I found?

And the professor... *Had he caught me?*

My pulse quickened, a cold sweat breaking across my skin as fragments of fear whispered through my mind. If he had caught me—how had he punished me?

A dark, sinking feeling twisted in my stomach. The answers hovered just out of reach, but with them loomed something far worse than anything I could prepare myself for.

"You are really testing me, Ava."

Ty's deep voice from behind me made me jolt, the aching familiarity chilling my bones.

I spun around, my heart lodging itself in my throat as fear clawed its way up my spine.

Down at the end of the hallway, Ty stepped out from the locked room, his dangerous eyes locking on mine.

*No.* My breath hitched. *How did he get out of that bedroom?*

I'd dead bolted it—I was sure of it. The click of the lock had echoed in my mind, a promise that he couldn't follow me.

But there he was, standing tall, unhurried, as if the lock had never mattered.

He must have had some kind of failsafe way of getting out. A key to unlock it from the inside.

A horrible thought entered my mind.

*He'd prepared for everything, including my escape.*

Panic gripped me tighter. My only hope now was to find a way out before he caught me.

My mind raced, scrambling for memories of this place—somewhere deep down I knew there had to be an escape. I just had to remember. *Remember.*

But the harder I tried, the more the memories slipped through my fingers like smoke.

Instinct took over, and I bolted down another hallway, my feet pounding against the floor. But dread already coiled in my gut, a sinking realization that I'd made the wrong choice.

At the end of the hall was a single door. Just one door. My only hope for freedom.

Behind me, I could hear Ty's steady footsteps.

He wasn't even running, each slow, deliberate step sending a chill down my spine. He didn't need to rush. He knew there was no way out for me.

I slammed against the door, my whole body shaking with the force, the wood rattling in its frame. My hands fumbled for the handle—*please, please be unlocked.*

To my surprise, it turned.

The door swung open, and I stumbled inside, breathless and frantic.

The room was enormous, a master bedroom bigger than I remembered, with a grand four-poster bed, heavy curtains framing the windows, and bookshelves lining the walls like a library. There was even a small sitting area, plush chairs and a fireplace that flickered with low flames.

But my eyes were drawn to one thing—the red velvet couch.

I froze, my breath hitching as recognition slammed into me like a tidal wave.

*The couch from my nightmares.*

The very one I'd tried so hard to forget. The place where I'd experienced things I never should have, *felt* things I'd buried deep. And now, standing here again, the memories threatened to break free, clawing at the edges of my mind.

Behind me, I could hear Ty's footsteps growing closer, his presence like a shadow creeping over me.

My pulse raced, my body screaming for me to run, but my feet were rooted to the spot, my gaze locked on that cursed couch.

I wasn't just running from him anymore. I was running from the past. From what I couldn't afford to remember.

Ty caught me before I could even think to scream. His hands clamped down on my arms, and no matter how hard I struggled, his strength easily overpowered me. He threw me over his shoulder like I weighed nothing.

"No, no!" I shouted, my voice breaking as I beat my fists against his back, but it was like pounding on solid rock.

He barely flinched.

"Let me go!" I screamed, twisting against him as he carried me through the house, back to my prison.

His heat seared through me, so much like Scáth's warmth, his nearness making my body betray me in the worst way.

My heart raced, not just from fear, but from a deep, twisted ache that I hated myself for feeling.

I kicked and pushed, hammering my fists into him with every ounce of strength I had, but it was useless.

He was too strong, his body rigid, unmoved by my resistance.

There was almost a hint of regret in his voice, a softness beneath the steel as he said, "I'm sorry, Ava. But this is how it has to be."

His words made me falter for a heartbeat, but the fury and panic surged back in an instant.

*How it has to be?* I would never accept that.

I tried grabbing for the doorframe as he walked back into my prison, but he was too strong, his step unfaltering and my fingers lost their grip.

He threw me onto the bed and I scrambled back until my back hit the headboard.

He nodded toward the tray sitting by my bedside. "Eat."

His command was firm, and I could see the finality in his gaze as if my choice didn't matter.

*Fuck him. FUCK HIM.*

Without thinking, I snatched up the closest thing on the tray to me—a soft bread roll still warm and smelling like heaven—and hurled it at him with every bit of force I could muster.

"You bastard!" I screamed, my chest heaving with anger.

The roll bounced off him, uselessly falling to the floor as if my anger had no effect on him at all.

Ty didn't react.

He simply turned, his shoulders tense as he walked out, the door slamming shut behind him with a brutal finality.

I heard the locks closing, trapping me again.

"No!" I screamed, my voice breaking.

I pounded my fists into the mattress as helplessness

threatened to consume me. Tears stung my eyes, but I didn't let them fall, the fury fueling me as I kept beating at the bed, as if that would somehow shatter the walls closing in around me.

A crackling sound cut through the room, and I realized it was coming from speakers in the ceiling.

"Eat," his voice echoed, the command distant yet inescapable.

"Make me," I yelled back to the ceiling, my stomach growling with disgust and anger.

And hunger.

A part of me—shamefully, pathetically—half hoped my defiance would bring him storming through the door again, just so I wouldn't be left alone.

The silence gnawed at me, twisting the fear into something darker, more suffocating.

Because as much as I *hated* him, as much as I wanted to escape, the loneliness was worse.

I crossed my arms, sitting on the bed defiantly. I wouldn't give him the satisfaction. I wouldn't eat.

He'd have to tie me down and force-feed me.

The memory of him fucking my mouth with his fingers sent a wave of heat through my body, and my previous unsated need rose up like a tide.

My clit throbbed and my pussy ached. From the memory of being tied in the chair at Ty's command, at the forceful way he invaded my mouth with his fingers, at the nearness of him, at his frustratingly stubborn dominance over me.

At *everything*.

And I knew I was so fucked.

Because despite how much I hated my captor, hated this version of Scáth—hated *Ty*—I wanted him. Wanted him with an ache that burned like poison.

I refused to give in. Refused to want it. Want *him*.

But I wasn't sure how long I could hold out.

# THE WARDEN

The one-way mirror stretched the whole height of the wall. I'd designed it that way because I hadn't wanted to miss a single inch of her.

Especially now as she sulked in her bed, her arms crossed over her chest.

That wasn't the only thing she was feeling, though.

Her cheeks were flushed and her nipples were hard points through her thin dress. And she kept pressing her thighs together, her knees up.

I saw. I knew.

Because I studied everything about her. Noticed every minute change in her breathing, in her skin color. I could read her moods, just like I could when we were younger.

She bit her lip as she covertly rubbed a forearm against her breast.

And I thanked my decision to forgo buying her any bras. From what little I knew of them, they were torture instruments. And the most finicky things to fit for a woman. So I didn't bother.

*Thank you, past me.*

She rubbed her thighs together, her eyes moving back and forth across the full-length mirror, breath hitching as she parted her knees just slightly.

I pressed my finger against the glass right where I could see her wet cotton-covered mound was.

*I can help you with that, little hummingbird.*

She slipped her hand into her panties, moving it against herself.

"Are you watching, asshole?" she spat out, her voice coming clearly out of the speaker thanks to the microphones I'd hidden around the room.

There was nowhere for her to hide. And it seemed my little bird was hungry. Too hungry to care that I was watching her.

Perfect. Just where I wanted her.

Her breath grew heavy, her head falling back against the headboard and her eyelashes fluttered. I didn't even care that it wasn't *me* that she was thinking about. At least not yet.

My cock swelled in anticipation of what I was about to do. What I had to do. All part of the plan.

She began to moan, the sounds coming out clearly into my observation room, her voice sounding like it was in my ear, sending wildfire down my spine.

My cock ached and I grasped at the glass as if I could close my fingers around her, an involuntary motion.

Soon.

There was nothing I wanted more than to watch her fall over the edge. To be the reason for it.

*Sorry, hummingbird. Not yet.*

I pulled a small remote from my pocket and pressed one of the buttons.

Instantly, a white gas began to pour in from some of the vents above her head and a hissing noise filled the speakers.

She jolted on the bed, but she was half-gone, half-uncaring, her hand moving faster as she chased the orgasm. "No, you bastard."

The orgasm that I wouldn't let her have.

She covered her mouth and nose, trying to hold her breath. But it only staved off the inevitable by moments.

But it was inevitable.

Just like she and I were inevitable, had been from the start.

Her needy gasp caught in her throat as her eyes fluttered closed and her hand stilled.

I waited another sixty torturous seconds, just in case she was faking, before I pressed another button on the remote and turned off the gas. It swirled in wisps as it sank to the ground, creating a soft cloud around the bed.

I pressed another button on my remote which turned on the exhaust, sucking all the lovely gas away.

My control panel beeped when it registered that the air in the room had been filtered and the exhaust switched off automatically.

A thrill went through me.

*Oh, Ava. Ready or not... here I come.*

I entered Ava's bedroom, my nerves already jangling in my bones.

Ava was sitting slumped against the headboard, her long slender legs askew.

The sheets rustled as I pulled her legs down the mattress

so she was lying flat on the luxurious bed, then I rearranged the pillows under her head.

There. Much more comfortable for my pretty little bird.

I took a moment to just look at her, her chest slowly rising and falling with each steady breath, her features soft and peaceful.

God, she was so stunning it *ached*.

Her beauty was almost unbearable, from the full, plushness of her lips to the delicate flutter of her long dark lashes against her flawless cheeks.

Even the gentle rise and fall of her chest, causing her supple breasts to bounce with each breath, was enough to send shivers down my spine.

Her dress had already ridden up around her waist, showing off the curve of her hip and her soft mound, her panties soaked.

I grabbed the edges of them and drew them down her body and off her feet. I pocketed them for later before crawling on the bed and kneeling between her legs.

I pushed her creamy thighs apart so she was spread out for me.

Her pussy glistened with moisture, her pretty folds begging to be touched.

Fucking glorious. She was a temple that I wanted to spend the rest of my fucking life worshipping.

I lowered my face to her folds and inhaled her musky scent, my cock aching to be released.

Fuck me. Her worn panties didn't do this scent justice.

The first lick of her, my first sweet taste of her, exploded on my tongue. I let out a groan as I sank further against her folds.

Her brows furrowed and her hips twitched toward me.

My darling girl was so needy. I wondered what she was dreaming about. Me? What I was doing to her?

Even though she was out, her breathy moans and gasps filled the room, mixed with my own low growls as I devoured her, tracing my tongue in circles on her clit, teasing her with light flicks and licks, before sucking the sensitive bud into my mouth.

I couldn't get enough of her taste and my lapping became hungrier as a deep primal need took over. I gripped her hips, holding her in place as her body writhed with need even in her sleep, as I devoured her, sucking and licking her pussy like I was starving.

I pushed two fingers into her and fucked her with my tongue and my fingers as I ground against the bed. She rewarded me by soaking her thighs and my face with her arousal.

I had only planned to finger her. Just tease her just before the peak of pleasure. And walk away.

But she—this, the scent of her—the way her hips rocked against my mouth and fingers with every thrust. It was making me crazy.

I let out a growl as I sat up and released my cock from my zipper.

I shouldn't be doing this. But I was past reasoning with myself. This was Ava's fault for making me fucking crazy.

I lined up my dick with her slick entrance and pushed in.

*Frrrrrk.*

She was so tight. The feeling of her gripping me was overwhelming.

I pushed in deeper, spreading her, splitting her open,

even though I knew she was going to feel me for days afterward.

Good. Soon I would be *all* that she felt.

I held myself over her with my arms, and once again I was struck by how stunning she was, her mouth parting on a gasp.

I thrust once again and this time, I slid in to the hilt. I slid home.

The pleasure hit me like a tidal wave, crashing over me with such force that it stole the breath from my lungs.

My heart pounded in my chest, the world around me blurring at the edges.

My body felt too small to contain the storm of emotions swirling within me—pleasure, rage for every minute of her that I missed out on, pain for having been torn from her, and something far more dangerous, something I couldn't name.

I'd gone so long without letting myself *feel* that having all of it rush in all at once was overwhelming.

For a moment, I thought I might pass out, my vision darkening as the all-consuming feelings threatened to pull me under.

I fucked her, my hips slamming into her, my breath hard around her cheeks as I pressed my forehead on hers.

But I couldn't stop. I'd lost control. All the years of building up my willpower, brick by brick, were gone.

I sucked on her tongue, drinking down her moans as her body trembled underneath me, as her cunt grew hotter and wetter.

When her pussy started clenching around me, I knew she wasn't far off. Neither was I.

At least I had the sense to pull out just before she came.

I jerked myself off as she whimpered, her hips rocking forward, her thighs clenching on air, chasing my cock, my fingers, anything to get her over the line.

But there would be no satisfaction for her. No nectar for my hummingbird.

My orgasm slammed into me and I pushed the tip of my cock into her entrance, flooding her with my hot cum.

I sagged, barely holding myself up with one shaking arm on the mattress, my breath heaving.

I wasn't even recovered before I began to chastise myself.

*Fucking weak. Look at you crumbling before you've even really started.*

Even after all these years, my critical self-talk sounded like *him*.

I should have known that when it came to Ava, I was helpless.

I'd always been helpless. No amount of time, no hardened resolve, could change that.

She was the one thing in this world that could unravel me, could strip away all the layers of control I'd meticulously built over the years.

And now, here I was, losing control again. Because of her.

My cum dribbled out of her pretty folds, a flower bursting with nectar.

I pushed it back into her with two fingers, a sick thrill going through me at the sight and at the feeling of her tight pussy filled with my seed.

When she was last under, I surgically put an implant rod in the back of her neck so there would be no accidents.

One day, I thought as I brushed her flat stomach, your belly will grow with my child. But not yet. You have a long dark journey ahead of you.

I kissed the furrows on her forehead, lightly damp with sweat.

*But don't worry, my hummingbird, I'll be with you every step of the way.*

You are *mine*. And I am *yours*.

Even if you try to run, you will *never* escape me.

# AVA

I jolted awake, gasping for air like I'd been drowning. My body felt heavy, sluggish, but my mind quickly caught up, the familiar bedroom around me spinning into focus as I lay on the bed.

My *prison*.

The last thing I remembered was... touching myself and then... the gas—thick, suffocating. My throat felt raw, my lungs still burning from the inside out.

*He stopped me from coming.*

I looked down.

Fuck, I was in the same dress as before but he'd taken my fucking panties.

Between my legs, my inner thighs were soaked and I was leaking onto the covers.

There was an ache in my pussy. Like... like he'd done something to me while I was under. I felt stretched, used, like he'd filled me.

A heated shiver slid down my spine and more moisture leaked onto my thighs.

*He'd stopped me from coming, put me under, and then he used my pussy?*

Did he use his fingers? Or his cock?

What did it say about me that a part of me *liked* not knowing? That a twisted thrill ran down my spine at all the potential ways he might have debased me.

But one thing I knew for certain was he hadn't let me come.

I was so turned on. So desperately unsatisfied. So hungry it felt like my body was turning on itself, the need clawing under my skin, mingling with the rage simmering just beneath the surface.

I could barely think past the hollow ache in my core. The need was primal, scratching at my insides like a beast, my body demanding to be fucked.

*Bastard. He did that on purpose.*

I leaped out of bed, my legs unsteady but driven by fury, and stormed toward the mirror.

He had to be watching. He always was.

"What's your fucking game, huh?" I spat, glaring into the mirror, reflecting back my crazed wide eyes and hair wild around my face. "You sick fuck, tell me!"

The silence in the room was deafening, pressing down on me as I waited for a response, half daring him to show himself.

Speakers in the ceiling crackled to life, the sound making my stomach flip.

His voice followed, deep, smooth, and all too familiar. It slithered through the room like a serpent, making my skin crawl and yet at the same time, making me press my thighs together.

"You only get to come," Ty's voice echoed, cold and detached, "during therapy."

His words were casual, like he was talking about something as simple as the weather. But the weight of them sank into me, like a heavy stone dropping into the pit of my stomach.

*Therapy.* The word twisted into something vile, something dark.

My fists clenched, trembling with a mix of rage and desperation, as I paced in front of the mirror, my dress swishing around my slick thighs, my nipples brushing painfully against the silky material.

"Therapy?" I shouted. "You think starving me of an orgasm will make me agree to *that*?"

He chuckled—the asshole *chuckled*. "I guess we'll find out, huh?"

"You *cruel* bastard, you're fucking insane if you think I'll ever bend to you!"

Tears welled up in my eyes, blurring the edges of my vision as the full weight of my fear, anger, and desperation crashed over me, too powerful to hold back any longer.

I was breaking apart from the inside, every emotion I had bottled up bursting through me like a dam that had finally given way. I banged my fists against the glass, sobbing uncontrollably, my voice trembling with the rawness of my plea.

The man behind that glass wasn't the boy I knew, the one who protected me. But *he* was in there, I could feel it, buried under this darkness, trapped beneath everything Ty had become.

"Please, let me go," I whispered, pressing both palms to

the glass, feeling the divide between us like a wound. "The boy I knew is still in there. *You.* The one who would never hurt me. The one who kept me safe, who cared for me when no one else did."

Silence echoed through the room, the tension so thick I could barely breathe.

His breathing came through the speakers, uneven, like he was struggling with something, like a part of him was trying to break through.

"Do you remember?" I continued, my voice cracking as I tried to push through to him—to Scáth, *my* Scáth. "The nights you stayed with me, watched over me, made sure I was never alone. You promised me we'd run away together one day, far from all of this. Where's that promise? What happened to it?"

My fingers curled against the glass. I could almost feel him—so close, yet so far away.

The static in the speakers shifted, his breath heavy, but I couldn't stop. I had to reach him.

"You're not this... monster," I said, pleading, my voice low and desperate. "I know you think you've changed, that you're different, but... you're still the same deep down. I *know* you are. You're still the boy I knew... the man I love..."

I closed my eyes, pressing harder against the glass as if I could reach him through sheer force of will.

A low, bitter laugh rippled through the speakers, sending a chill down my spine.

"The boy you knew?" His voice dripped with cold disdain. "He's dead, Ava. That part of me? It's gone. I'm all that's left."

"No," I whispered, shaking my head as my chest tightened. "You want me to believe that, but I don't. I *won't*."

I closed my eyes again, feeling the heat of my tears sliding down my cheeks as the weight of it all pressed down on me.

What if Scáth was truly lost? What if Ty was right, and somehow, he had "killed" Scáth—his good side—buried him so deep that there was no coming back? What if this man, this monster standing behind the glass, was all I had left?

The thought gripped me with a terror so intense I almost broke down right there.

No. I couldn't believe that. I wouldn't.

I forced myself to take a breath, swallowing back the sob rising in my throat. I had to keep the faith, had to cling to the hope that Scáth was still in there somewhere.

I wasn't going to give up on him, no matter how much Ty tried to convince me otherwise. I couldn't let Ty win.

I would find a way to bring Scáth back to me, and once I did, we would figure this out together. We'd find a way to keep Ty at bay, to lock him away where he couldn't hurt either of us again.

My chest ached with fear, but I wasn't giving up on Scáth. Not now. Not ever.

"Please..." I begged, my voice barely audible as it cracked with desperation. "Let me go. We can find another way. We can—"

"There is *no other way*," Ty's voice boomed through the speaker.

The finality of his words crushed me, hollowing out the last fragile thread of hope. Silence settled between us like a suffocating weight, pressing down on my chest.

I leaned my forehead against the glass, the cool surface offering no comfort as my breath fogged up the glass, blurring my reflection. I wasn't sure I could take any more.

Ty sighed through the speaker, a soft exhale that rippled through the room. It was the closest thing to regret I'd ever heard from him.

"Perhaps I have been… too hard on you," he said, his voice softened, just enough to make me pause. "Perhaps you need a carrot, not just the stick."

A flicker of hope ignited inside me, fragile and fleeting, but it was enough to make my heart skip.

I pressed my palms harder against the glass, straining toward him. Maybe this was it—the small crack in his armor, the chance to reach the man I once knew.

"Yes?" The word tumbled out of me, hope making my throat tight.

"With every therapy session, more and more of the house will be open to you."

My pulse quickened. Freedom. It sounded like freedom, even if it was wrapped in chains.

I pushed harder against the glass, as if I could somehow force myself through it, force myself closer to him.

"And when I'm done with therapy?" I dared to ask, my voice no louder than a breath.

There was another pause, the kind that gnawed at the edges of my sanity.

Then his voice came through the speaker, colder this time, sharper. "When you're done… then, and only then, will we leave this place."

The air seemed to rush from my lungs as my chest tightened, and the tiny flame of hope I'd nurtured withered.

I felt the floor beneath me fall away, as if I were sinking into the darkness of this house all over again.

Leave this place... The words tasted like poison. Because I had to go through hell first. The therapy. The memories. The red couch.

Panic crawled up my throat. Already I could feel the cursed velvet beneath my fingertips, could already smell the drug seeping into my skin, my mind, making me lose control.

My stomach twisted as the thought of those buried memories surfacing made my blood run cold.

How could I face that room again? How could I face the things I wasn't ready to remember?

But I had no choice. Ty was making sure of that, bending me until I would break.

I forced myself to breathe, to pull air into my lungs even though everything inside me screamed to run, to fight, to get away.

Maybe, just maybe, if I agreed to this, if I went through the therapy, Scáth would come back to the surface. Maybe it would awaken him, bring him back to me. I had to believe that.

I bit down on the wave of nausea and nodded, barely managing to choke out the words.

"Okay." It was a whisper of defeat. "I'll go back to therapy."

# AVA

I lingered too long in the shower, my forehead pressed against the cool, marble wall as the hot water cascaded over my shoulders. I tried to let the heat soothe me, but it barely touched the ache in my chest, the gnawing feeling of dread that was tearing me from the inside out.

What had I done, agreeing to his twisted therapy?

The very idea of it was a nightmare, a cruel invention that no sane person would even consider—let alone devise, let alone enforce.

Who kidnaps someone, holds her captive, and forces her into reliving her worst memories as a form of healing?

A shiver crept through me at the sheer madness behind it.

Ty—Scáth—*had* gone mad.

I could only hope that he'd break before me. That the pain it caused me to relive my abuse would change his mind, would bring Scáth back to the surface.

After what felt like hours, I forced myself out, the loss of heat from the shower sending a chill over my skin.

Wrapping myself in a soft fluffy robe, I stepped into the bedroom, my stomach giving a hollow growl.

My eyes locked on the emerald gown shimmering as it hung on the closet door.

It hadn't been there when I went for my shower.

*He* must have left it while I was in there.

A shiver traced its way down my spine, and I glanced back toward the bathroom door. I'd left it open. Had he seen me naked, showering? Had he been watching?

My gaze flickered to the one-way mirror, that silent, sinister presence.

He was *always* watching.

A shiver traced my spine, caught somewhere between unease and… something darker, something I couldn't name but felt deep in my bones.

Pinned to the hanger was a note, neatly folded and concise in his familiar hand.

*Get ready.*

I noticed the ornate antique jewelry box sitting on the dresser, its dark mahogany wood polished to a warm sheen and intricate mother-of-pearl inlays that caught the light in glimmers.

That had just appeared, too.

The tiny drawers beneath opened with a soft creak, lined with faded crimson velvet that still held a faint scent of peony perfume, whispering of secrets and memories locked away.

My fingers grazed over the brand-new Chanel makeup—all suited to my coloring.

I knew it was silly, stupid even, to get made up for my kidnapper, but I did it anyway.

I brushed a hint of shimmer on my cheeks, a coat of mascara on my lashes, and a swipe of gloss on my lips.

The gown felt weightless as I lifted it, the delicate, silky material slipping through my fingers, cool against my skin as I held it against myself.

I didn't even care that wearing this dress was yet another command; it was too gorgeous.

I couldn't help the small thrill that ran down my spine as I slipped it on, letting the fabric cascade over me, smoothing it over my hips.

I stared at myself in the mirror and gasped, a blush coming to my face.

Was that really me?

The gown was exquisite, a deep, shimmering emerald that caught the light in a way that made it seem almost alive. It hugged my torso snugly, tailored to fit every curve with flawless precision, flowing down to the floor in a cascade of silk.

The bodice was cut just across the top of my breasts, exposing my collarbones and the slight rise of my shoulders, tiny emerald gemstones scattered across the bodice, adding a subtle, sparkling texture that mirrored stars as I moved.

At the back, the gown dipped into a deep V that swept down my spine, revealing just enough skin to feel scandalous yet somehow restrained, ending just above the base of my back.

The silk felt cool and smooth against my skin, as if the fabric itself was some kind of second skin—luxurious, delicate, and eerily intimate.

It felt almost too grand, too regal.

The gown felt weighty, not from its actual fabric, but from the significance it seemed to carry. As if by slipping into it, I'd agreed to something wordless and binding.

As I smoothed the gown over my hips, a disquieting realization crept into my mind: this wasn't an off-the-rack dress.

It was couture, tailored to fit my body like a second skin. Every inch, every seam, every contour was perfectly aligned to me.

Ty must have given the dressmaker my exact measurements.

My head spun as I wondered just how he could have gotten them.

Had he measured my body himself, while I was asleep, his hands tracing over every line and curve? The thought sent a shiver down my spine, equal parts unsettling and... something else.

Or had he simply studied me for so long, observing each detail, that he'd known exactly how to craft a dress that would fit me so flawlessly—by sight alone?

I didn't know whether to feel exposed, violated, or... seen.

And I couldn't shake the feeling that this dress was as much an invitation as it was a trap.

Then I heard it—the unmistakable sound of the three locks sliding open.

I hated the way my heart tripped over itself as I instinctively moved toward the door, then paused, chastising myself for being eager to see my kidnapper and tormentor.

The door swung inward, and Ty appeared in the doorway, silhouetted against the dim hall light, making my breath catch.

He was dressed in all black, from his tailored suit to the slim tie that lay flat against his firm chest, his dark hair slicked back, revealing the strong lines of his face.

He looked… devastating.

His gaze came to rest on me standing in the middle of the room, clasping my hands in front of me because I didn't know what to do with them.

His eyes widened, his lips parting in something that almost looked like shock.

"Wow, A-Ava…" He cleared his throat, his voice catching slightly.

If I didn't know any better, I'd say my kidnapper was nervous.

If I didn't know any better, I'd think this was a date.

But I knew better. Right?

Ty stepped toward me, each step deliberate, his eyes tracing over me like he was memorizing every detail. "Perfect fit."

When he circled behind me, his presence sent a shiver down my spine, the heat of him somehow burning through the space between us.

His breath brushed against my ear. "Hold still."

He lifted a length of smooth fabric over my eyes.

"What are you doing?" I protested, jerking my head back, but his grip was gentle yet unyielding as he tied the blindfold.

"It's a surprise," he murmured, his voice low and warm. "Do you trust me?"

"No." A scoff escaped my lips.

He sighed as if he expected that answer. "No blindfold, no surprise."

I clenched my jaw, silently cursing my relentless curiosity. Maybe that's why journalism had always called to me—an insatiable drive to uncover what lay hidden, even when I wished I didn't care.

"*Fine.*" The word slipped out before I could stop myself.

"Good girl," he murmured, his words striking a chord deep within me.

He finished tying the fabric, snug but not uncomfortable, blocking out the dim light of the room.

A shiver traveled through me as his fingers brushed the length of my hair off my shoulders.

With his hand burning into the small of my back, he guided me forward.

With my sight taken from me, every other sense sharpened, stretching thin with anticipation and an edge of fear.

Every sound seemed magnified: the creak of floorboards, the soft brush of the skirt against my legs, his steady breathing close to my ear. Slivers of light from the wall sconces threaded past the slip under my blindfold as he led me through the hallway.

Ty's grip was firm and unyielding, his hand warm around my elbow, steady, as if he knew every step by heart.

Underfoot, I could feel the cool, polished floor shifting

as we turned left, and a faint draft told me we'd passed into a different wing, the air carrying an almost forgotten hint of roses and old wood.

Somewhere in the depths of the mansion, a clock ticked faintly, an almost hypnotic beat against the eerie silence around us.

My pulse quickened, nerves crackling, a thousand questions crowding my mind. Was this truly a surprise or something else? Part of me wanted to tug away, to break the blindfold and run, but curiosity held me just as firmly as his hand.

If this was a trick, why bother with the gown? Why soften the experience with elegance only to bring fear? Why dress me up if this was just another game?

But then, this was a twisted stranger in the body of the man I knew as Ty, and everything with him was tangled, leaving me unable to separate threat from thrill.

My heart thudded heavily in my chest, the unknown stretching out before me, both terrifying and tantalizing. Each step took me closer, but to what?

"Careful of the stairs," he warned, his hand moving to my elbow and slowing me down.

I stepped cautiously, but the fabric of my gown caught underfoot, and I stumbled forward.

Ty's arms caught me, pulling me firmly against his chest. His heart beat strong beneath the soft material of his suit, and for a moment, his hands lingered at my waist, holding me steady. My cheeks warmed, though I couldn't see his face.

He picked me up in his arms and I let out a yelp, my arms instinctively going around his neck.

"I can walk," I muttered, squirming slightly, feeling my pulse race.

"Obviously not without tripping," he replied, the hint of amusement in his voice.

"Who blindfolded me in the first place?" I shot back.

But I couldn't help but soften in his arms, the feeling too familiar... too safe.

My blindfold had shifted just enough for a narrow view of the dark curling staircase, the main stairs I remembered. And there, at the bottom of the sweeping staircase, was the front door.

The door to freedom.

When we reached the base of the stairs, he set me down gently, my bare feet landing on the cool marble floor.

His hand slid into mine, firm and steady, and I couldn't quite bring myself to pull away. The warmth of his grasp seeped through me, traveling up my arm in an unsettling current.

My mind buzzed as I counted each step, each twist and corner, my silent rebellion, until he stopped and released my hand.

His fingers brushed over my cheek as he pulled the blindfold away.

Blinking against the sudden candlelight, I gasped, the familiarity of this place hitting me in the solar plexus.

Before me was the Blackthorn dining hall, rich red and black drapery cascading down the walls, accented by deep shadows that only intensified the glow of hundreds of candles scattered across the grand dining table and lining the walls.

The tall arched windows—newly barred, I noted—shimmered with moonlight, casting silver glints across the dark wood floors, while the candlelight danced in a warm, inviting glow that contrasted the dark, brooding colors.

A luxurious table for two sat draped in black velvet. Gleaming silverware and platters awaited; the teasing smells of roasted meat and garlic made my stomach grumble.

The heavy black candelabras on either end of the table seemed to belong to another time, their wax dripping in elegant rivulets, adding to the decadent, almost forbidden allure of the room.

I turned to Ty, my breath catching. "You did all this?"

He pulled out a chair for me with a modest shrug, but a gleam of pride flickered in his eyes, almost boyish beneath the intensity of his gaze.

Ty served me before serving himself, carefully adding each dish to my plate, a freshly baked bread roll, some roasted vegetables, slices of roast chicken, and a portion of rich, creamy mash.

But it was the gleaming silver knife that caught my attention, tucked just beside my plate.

A *real* weapon.

I knew I shouldn't stare, but my eyes kept flicking back to it, waiting for the right moment when he was distracted enough.

He finished piling food on his own plate and took his seat, his eyes flickering to me.

"So," he began, voice smooth, attempting a pleasant tone, "tell me how college is going?"

I raised an eyebrow, my tone dripping with sarcasm. "Oh, just great. If you don't count the part where I couldn't do exams because I was kidnapped by some psycho."

Ty's lips twitched, clearly amused. "No exams? Some might say I'm doing you a favor."

I snorted. "Some might prefer freedom over an excuse for missing exams."

He tore a piece off his steaming bread roll and popped it into his mouth. "There's freedom in submission, hummingbird."

I hated the way he lowered his voice like he was speaking to a lover not his captive.

"Why do you call me that?"

He didn't answer, he merely continued with his meal, his gaze firmly on me.

If I wanted a chance to steal the knife, I'd have to create a distraction.

I spotted the decanter of red wine on the sideboard, glinting temptingly in the candlelight.

Perfect.

"Could I have a glass?" I asked, keeping my voice even, casual.

Ty's eyes narrowed with that familiar, calculating look.

After a beat, he stood, his chair scraping softly against the floor as he walked over to the sideboard. He glanced over his shoulder once, making me tense, before he picked up the decanter and poured two glasses.

The second he turned his back, I seized the knife and slipped it into my lap, pressing it beneath the folds of my gown.

My heart pounded, fingers tingling with adrenaline.

When he turned around, glasses in hand, I froze, my body tense.

But he didn't react; he just returned to the table and handed me a glass, his fingers brushing mine as I accepted it.

My hand tightened on the wineglass, and I took a sip—only to make a face. "That's not wine."

"No," he said, casually eating a forkful of vegetables. "It's grape juice."

I huffed, annoyed. "I'm old enough to drink, you know."

He just smirked as he pointed his fork at me. "You should thank me for not letting you SUI."

"SUI?"

"Yes." He let out a quiet chuckle, clearly amused with himself. "Stabbing under the influence."

My blood ran cold. Did he know I'd stolen the knife?

I forced myself to stay composed, hoping the guilt wasn't written all over my face.

I watched him as he cut up his food, eating as if I were no threat, as if I couldn't possibly have it in me to attack him.

The knife weighed heavily in my lap, my fingers itching to show him just how much of a threat I could be.

*I'll show you.*

I seized the knife from my lap and lunged, aiming for his arm.

But he was faster.

His hand shot out, catching my wrist mid-swing. He twisted my wrist just enough to disarm me and I yelped at the flash of pain. The knife slipped from my fingers and clattered to the table.

With his grip loosening, I wrenched myself free and bolted, running for the door, hoping to retrace the twists and turns of the mansion.

*Front door, front door,* I repeated in my head, feeling the thrill of escape tightening in my chest.

I didn't even make it out of the dining room.

A powerful hand clamped on my shoulder, spinning me around and shoving me against the wall.

Ty's body pressed close, pinning me there with his hand wrapped around my throat like an iron clamp.

"*Really*, Ava?" he murmured, his voice low and deadly, his hand firm on my neck, locking me in place, as his eyes—dark and challenging—scanned my face. "We were having such a nice time."

# THE WARDEN

Ava tried to stab me.

A dark thrill sparked through me.

My girl had guts. She had fire. Fuck, I loved that about her.

But a sharper edge of irritation simmered beneath it, the frustration that even now, after everything, she was still fighting me. She might have agreed to my plans, but her defiance still flickered just below the surface.

"You could have at least waited until dessert," I complained. "I made opera cake. Your favorite. The cake knife would have at least been a decent knife to come at me with."

"You bastard," she hissed as she struggled. "Let me go."

But I knew she didn't really want me to; her nipples were hard, pressing into my chest.

I shoved a knee between her thighs, bunching her emerald gown as I pressed my thigh against her clit.

Her pupils dilated, her cheeks flushing, and she made an

adorable gurgle in the back of her throat as she tried not to moan.

"Let me go." Her voice was barely above a whisper, and her tongue darted out to lick her lips.

"Now why would I do that when I can do this instead?"

I ground my thigh against her, making her gasp and shove against my chest. But her traitorous fingers gripped into me, as if wanting to pull me closer.

I tried to push my hand up her dress, gathering the endless skirt before frustration got the better of me. I ripped it off, the lovely Valentino gown tearing at the nipped-in waist.

She looked up at me, her lips parting in a breathless gasp. "You ruined it."

"I'll buy ten more," I promised.

I kicked her legs apart and pushed aside her panties, groaning when I found her soaked.

"Soaked," I *tsked*. "Oh, Ava. You naughty girl, what would your precious Scáth say if he knew you were gushing for your cruel, mean kidnapper."

I ran a finger through her folds, circling her clit, and she gasped, trying to move against me. But my other hand kept her still, pressed up against the wall by her throat, as my fingers dipped into her.

Heat and shame flushed her cheeks. "You bastard. Stop."

Fuck, she felt so tight, so hot and wet. My cock ached to replace my fingers.

"No," I said. "I don't think I will. Don't think you really want me to either."

I kissed her, stealing the gasp she made when I pushed three fingers into her, thrusting them fast and hard.

She beat at my chest as I claimed her lips, kissing her as I fingerfucked her. But her hits soon weakened, her fingers curling into my suit lapels and drawing me in closer.

"Such a good little captive," I crooned. "Maybe I'll even let you come. Beg for me and make it pretty."

Her eyes glittered with unshed tears as I abused her pussy with my fingers roughly, my anger getting the better of me.

She bit her lip, a refusal to beg.

"Fuck. You." She glared at me, but her breath caught, her body jerking and shuddering against me.

"Excellent idea, hummingbird. I'll be doing that."

I could feel her walls clenching me as she neared orgasm.

I squeezed two pressure points in her neck, cutting off the blood to her brain.

"What are you—?" She gasped, sucking in air as her eyes rolled into her head.

I caught her in my arms as she passed out.

I picked up an unconscious Ava and laid her on the heavy dark wood table, shoving dishes out of the way so they smashed against the floor.

*You've ruined dinner. But I will enjoy punishing you.*

I sat at the chair between her legs and pulled her toward me so that her ass was at the table's edge and her legs were resting on the arms of my chair.

I tore off her panties, and the heady smell of her arousal filled the room.

I looked down at her, lying unconscious on the table, a feast for my eyes in the way the emerald bodice set off her creamy skin and the way her thighs parted, her pink pussy glistening like dew.

She was beautiful, like a fallen angel.

Or a devil.

I dove my mouth to her pussy, ravaging her folds with my mouth and tongue.

Her hips rocked, the movement coming from deep inside her, her eyes fluttering even as she remained under.

She tasted so fucking sweet. So wet and tight.

I tongued along her folds and sucked her clit into my mouth, feeling it swell as I brought her to the edge. Even though she was unconscious, her hips rocked toward my mouth, her breath growing shallow and rapid.

My fingers dug into her creamy thighs as I slowly lost my mind.

The smell of her. The taste of her.

The *feel* of her.

I needed all of her.

Now.

Fuck the rules. She tried to stab me. She needed to be punished.

I pulled away, licking my lips of her sweet taste, and unbuckled my pants, letting my cock spring free.

It was already hard and throbbing, the tip leaking pre-cum.

I lined myself up at her entrance and pushed inside, inch by glorious inch, until I was fully inside of her.

Fuck, she felt like heaven.

Abusing her like this would send me to hell. But it was a place that I would gladly burn in for all of eternity.

I thrust in and out, slowly, taking my time, not wanting to go too quickly, despite the urgency screaming inside me.

I could feel her pulse around me, her walls fluttering, the orgasm coming, her body ready.

A groan slipped past her lips and more wetness soaked my cock and her thighs. Even though she was unconscious, she wanted more, needed more.

And I gave her more.

I gripped her hips and thrust into her again and again, feeling her walls grip me like a vise.

Just before the orgasm rocked through her, I pulled out.

Her brows furrowed, her nipples hard as I climbed over her. On the table, I turned to face her feet, planted my knees on either side of her head, and pushed my cock past her plump lips.

My hand slid around her throat, my fingers pushing the pressure points, making sure she didn't wake as I abused her mouth.

Her throat was loose and relaxed so I could push all the way down past her voice box.

Fuck, so deep. So tight.

I fucked her face, her eyes leaking tears, smearing her mascara, making her look like a beautiful, ruined doll.

She was so beautiful like this. Her hair messy, her makeup smeared, her dress ripped and torn, her lips swollen from my abuse.

And I was so close.

But there was one final punishment that she deserved.

I pulled my cock from her lips, groaning as it sprung free and slapped her lips.

I climbed off the table and rolled her to her front, positioning her hips at the edge.

Her back hole seemed to wink at me, the only hole I hadn't punished yet.

I plunged my fingers into her pussy and scooped up moisture from her, working it up to her back hole.

As I touched her, her back arched toward me as if begging for more.

With her asshole wet, I worked two fingers inside her first, stretching her.

*You'll feel me for days, hummingbird. A reminder for you to be a good girl.*

I worked her hole, stretching her, taking my time. She loosened easily for me, so relaxed in her unconscious state.

When she was ready, I slipped the tip of my cock in and hissed at the feel of her like a tight wet fist.

Her hips rocked, trying to take more of me.

My cock throbbed and twitched, wanting more.

"Good girl, Ava," I said as I stroked her back. "I can't wait until you're awake. I want to hear you beg."

I inched my way into her asshole, feeling her walls stretch, her body taking me so well.

"That's it, Ava, take all of it."

Passed out, her walls were relaxed, taking me easier than if she were awake. Once I was fully in, I began to thrust, slowly at first, then harder.

I pounded her, gripping her ass cheeks and squeezing them, the flesh so supple and firm, a work of art.

"So fucking good."

Her tight little ass pulled at me as I pumped into her, her

hips twitching, her mouth parted and gasping and fogging against the polished wooden table.

I groaned, thrusting, my cock pulsing as I came.

I pulled out, stroking myself, cum splattering all over her ass and lower back, covering her in my seed.

"Yes," I hissed, my heart racing like it was trying to bang out of my chest.

I held myself up with trembling arms on the table as whimpers came from her, as she rocked her hips, begging for more.

*Sorry, hummingbird,* I thought as I cleaned her up with a napkin. *You only get to come in therapy.*

# AVA

I woke up to a hollow, gnawing ache in my stomach and my pussy.

Frustration simmered as I remembered last night—the disastrous dinner, the knife I'd tried to swipe, and Ty's smug, unbothered gaze as if he knew all along before he knocked me out.

And now this.

I was starving and desperately needy. And I knew Ty had left me like this on purpose.

This was his silent punishment, his way of reminding me who held all the cards.

I rolled over, groaning, my body twisting with *hunger*.

I could *feel* how he'd punished me, my throat, my pussy, and my asshole deliciously sore.

And still, despite how much I hated him, how much it killed me to know that he'd taken advantage of me when I was passed out, I burned for him.

Burned for more.

Ached to be sated, filled… punished some more.

Without windows, the passage of time felt like a distant memory, swallowed by the same four walls.

I had no idea how much time had passed since the dinner.

Two days, maybe? I based it on the number of meals Ty had shoved into my room, a vast difference to the elaborate dinner he'd planned.

More punishment.

My heart betrayed me every time I heard the door creak open, anticipation rising like a tidal wave.

Every time, I hoped it would be Scáth, his eyes soft with apology, his lips finding mine with that same fire I'd grown to crave.

But it was never the persona I longed for.

It was always Ty.

His rigid posture, his cold, expressionless face. It seemed he was totally in control.

He'd step inside with a tray, perfectly balanced, the scent of rich food filling the air, and place it in front of me like I was a prisoner being fed by a warden.

Roast pork with vegetables and thick gravy, rib-eye steak seared to perfection, chicken and leek pie with buttery peas. Meals that belonged to another life, one I barely remembered.

Then he'd sit in an armchair and watch me eat, refusing to let me leave a single crumb on my plate.

"Eat. You need your strength." His voice was flat, devoid of warmth, as if the very idea of kindness had been drained from him.

I bit my tongue, fighting back the urge to snap, to

remind him it was *his* fault I was this weak in the first place. But what would be the point?

I had to play Ty's game, at least for now.

Until I found a way to bring Scáth back.

Or to escape.

But for now, I had to suffer through *therapy*.

And I had no idea what was about to happen—what I would remember—but the fear that had been gnawing at me all day surged, threatening to swallow me whole.

I was close to backing out. So close.

The sound of the locks on my bedroom door sliding open before my first "session" sent a jolt of dread through my entire body.

My heart started hammering in my chest.

It got worse as the door creaked open, and Ty, dressed in his usual button-up black shirt and black slacks, stepped into my room with that same unreadable expression on his face, the one I'd grown to dread.

He didn't bother shutting the door behind him. It's not like there was anywhere for me to run even if I tried to.

He walked toward me, slow and deliberate, his black boots heavy on the wooden floor. He was wearing all black so that the folded white material that he was carrying in his hands looked stark.

Ty stopped just before me, too close.

My heart pounded harder, and my breath hitched as his nearness sent a conflicting wave of heat through me.

It was the kind of closeness that made my body react instinctively, pulling me toward him even as my mind screamed at me to keep my distance.

The soft fabric in his hands brushed against my arm, making my skin prickle with nervous energy.

My pulse quickened, and a knot twisted tighter in my stomach, the apprehension mixing with something I didn't want to admit—something dangerous, something that made me *want* to get closer, even though I knew I should be pulling away.

His intense gaze locked on mine, reading me too easily, like he always did.

"Are you ready?" he asked, the question soft, almost coaxing, but laced with something darker underneath.

I swallowed hard, my throat tight, the weight of his presence suffocating me. I nodded, even though my body was trembling, my legs weak beneath me.

He stayed quiet, watching me, waiting.

I cleared my throat, trying to sound braver than I felt.

"What… what is that?" I gestured at the fabric in his hands, my voice barely above a whisper.

His lips curved slightly, but there was no warmth in it, only a shadow of satisfaction.

"It's for you," he said softly, his eyes flicking down to the material and back up to meet mine. "Part of your therapy."

He moved with eerie precision, laying the soft and delicate fabric out on the bed.

A nightgown.

He fussed over it, smoothing it out, making sure it was laid out just right.

I watched, frozen, my breath caught in my throat as a terrible sense of recognition washed over me.

*No.*

My blood ran cold as the memory hit me like a slap.

*That* nightgown...

The lacy nightgown the professor used to make me wear when I was younger. The one that had clung to my skin like a prison, trapping me in his sick games.

And now here it was, in an adult-sized version. The same delicate lace, the same soft white material.

A sickening wave of nausea rolled through me as I realized what this meant.

Ty had brought this for me to wear. This was part of his so-called "therapy."

What had I agreed to? What the hell had I signed myself up for?

My fingers curled into fists, my nails biting into my palms as I stared at the nightgown, willing myself not to break down.

But inside, I was crumbling, the walls I had tried so hard to keep up collapsing all around me.

I couldn't do this. Not again.

I felt numb as Ty reached for me, his fingers grazing the hem of my dress.

The tension thickened in the air, wrapping around us as he pulled the dress over my head, leaving me exposed, standing in only a pair of white lace panties. Cool air rushed over my skin, tightening my nipples to points.

My skin prickled, a shiver running down my spine, but I was too numb to react. Too distant from the part of me that should have resisted.

The world around me dulled, fading into the background. His nearness, the steady rhythm of his breath, and the quiet authority in his eyes took up all the space in my mind.

I didn't protest. I couldn't.

Ty dropped my dress to the floor and for a moment he just stood there, inches away, just staring at me, at my half-naked body.

I should have felt more embarrassed, should have moved to cover myself up, but I couldn't move. Like my brain wasn't attached to my body.

For a fleeting moment, his cold mask slipped, and a flicker of awe crossed his face, so brief I almost questioned if I'd imagined it. But just as quickly, it vanished, swallowed up by the cold mask he now wore.

A familiar heat coiled low in my stomach, my pulse quickening in response to his nearness, his scent of musk and sandalwood, the way he loomed over me.

It was *wrong*—so wrong. This wasn't Scáth. This wasn't the man I loved.

But my body didn't seem to care.

I tried to force the reaction down, to shove the feeling away. I told myself it was only because Ty and Scáth were the same person.

My body couldn't tell the difference—but *I* could.

I just had to ignore these unwanted feelings. I had to push it away.

But as his breath ghosted over my skin, sending shivers down my spine, it was harder to silence that pull than I thought. And I hated myself for it.

I *loved* Scáth. How could I react this way to the version of him who was keeping me here, forcing me into a twisted form of therapy?

*This is wrong. This is a betrayal.*

But my body wasn't listening.

"Arms up," he commanded.

My body reacted instinctively, lifting my arms.

The tension thickened in the air, wrapping around us as he pulled the nightgown over my head, the familiar fabric brushing against my skin—soft, lacy, and *wrong*.

He reached up, his fingers grazing my collarbone as he pulled my hair out from the neckline and laid it along my back.

His touch was careful, almost reverent, as if this was all part of some twisted ritual he had perfected in his mind.

As he tied the ribbons closing the front, the faint, warm brush of his fingers against my skin sent a ripple of goosebumps over my arms, and I hated that I felt it. Hated the way my body responded to my captor.

I was lost in the thick fog of his control, moving through the motions, letting him dress me like I was a doll. Because I didn't know what else to do.

Because soon there'd been nothing left but to start *therapy*.

My breathing grew unsteady, each inhale shallow and ragged as the fear crept in, threatening to take over. I felt like I was sinking, spiraling into a place where I wouldn't be able to claw my way out.

Ty's fingers were firm as they gripped my chin, forcing my gaze to lock on his.

"You won't be alone," he said, his voice low, steady. "I'll be right here, the whole way through."

There was something about his touch, something grounding in the way his fingers held me in place, as if his very presence was the anchor I so desperately needed.

His words seeped into me, calming the frantic pulse of fear as it beat against my chest.

I wouldn't be alone.

Ty pulled back slightly, studying me, his eyes searching my face with a strange softness, concern clouding the coldness.

For the first time in years, I saw *him*. Not the monster he'd become—but the boy who used to be my best friend, buried beneath the layers of pain and scars.

And for some reason, despite everything, I trusted *him*. Maybe it was foolish, maybe it was reckless, but in that moment, I believed *him*. I believed the boy who used to be my best friend. Who took care of my wounds. Who used to hold me at night through all my nightmares.

He really was still there deep inside.

I nodded, my breath still shaky. "I'm okay."

My voice wavered, but I wasn't lying. At least not entirely.

Ty took a moment to study me, his gaze flickering across my face, as if he was looking for any trace that I wasn't okay.

Then the tiniest smile curved his lips, barely noticeable, but it was there. "Good girl."

The praise sparked something inside me, something warm and unsettling. I hated how much it affected me, how that small acknowledgment bolstered my determination.

I straightened my shoulders, trying to push my nerves down.

He held out a glass vial, the clear liquid inside swirling slightly as it caught the dim light.

"Drink it," he said, his voice soft, but the command unmistakable.

I took the vial, my hands trembling slightly as I popped the cork.

The smell hit me instantly—a familiar medicinal and slightly sweet scent that sent a jolt of recognition through me. My heart lurched.

"This is the same drug," I whispered, staring at the vial. "The one Liath was drugged with."

The words tumbled out before I could stop them, confusion swirling in my head. How could two girls—Liath and me—on opposite sides of the country, separated by years, have been drugged with the exact same substance? It didn't make sense.

Ty's gaze darkened, his expression turning grim. "My father wasn't just a botanist; he was a chemist. He *created* this drug."

His words sent a chill through me.

The pieces started to fall into place, but it wasn't a puzzle I wanted to solve. Something bigger, darker, was at play here.

Something that connected my foster father, Liath, Dr. Vale... and *me*.

I felt the world closing in around me as the realization took hold.

The professor created the drug and the recipe *didn't* die with him. It had spread, poisoned lives, mine and Liath's among them.

Ty continued, his voice growing tight. "I used his recipe, but I adapted it. I took out the scopolamine, the memory suppressor, so..."

So this time, I'd remember *everything*.

I held the vial tighter, the weight of what I was about to do sinking in.

Before I could rethink it, I knocked back the entire vial in a single shot.

The liquid slid down easily, almost tasteless, with just the faintest hint of something medicinal.

*God, it could have been laced in anything,* I realized. *No one would ever know they were being drugged.*

The thought barely had time to settle before I felt it—the drug moving through me, rushing through my veins and creeping into my muscles.

My body began to betray me, limbs growing heavier by the second. Panic surged in my chest.

Oh God, what had I done?

# AVA

I'd drunk the cursed vial and I couldn't do anything about it. Couldn't run to the bathroom to throw it up. I couldn't move.

My knees buckled as the paralysis took hold, but before I could hit the ground, Ty caught me.

His arms slid under me with practiced ease, and he pulled me up effortlessly, cradling me against his chest.

For a moment, a flash of something crossed his face—concern, regret, maybe—but it was gone too quickly for me to be sure.

As he carried me out of the bedroom, my limbs limp, the memory hit me like a soft, distant echo: the day he'd carried me to the nurse's office when we were younger. Just like this.

Despite the fear knotting inside me, for a fleeting second, I gave in to the sensation of weightlessness, of being held.

His chest was firm against my cheek, the steady thrum

of his heartbeat a strange comfort. For just a moment, I let myself feel it, enjoy it, even if I knew I shouldn't.

The hallway passed in a blur as Ty carried me through the mansion, his steps steady and purposeful.

My heart hammered in my chest as confusion clouded my thoughts. Where was he taking me?

Then it hit me.

*The professor's bedroom.*

A wave of terror surged through me. I tried to scream, tried to thrash in his arms, to do anything to stop him.

But I couldn't move. My body was locked in place, helpless.

And the look on Ty's face—cold, determined—told me he wasn't going to stop.

No matter what I wanted.

Ty kicked open the door and it let out a loud creak like a wail.

He carried me inside the professor's master bedroom, the heavy, oppressive air settling around me like a cage.

Ty carried me to the red velvet couch and gently laid me down, my head lolling on the cushion, not even the sight of the beautiful bookshelves and rows of books bringing me peace.

As soon as my fingers brushed the velvet, memories began to claw at the edges of my vision, pushing their way through the haze of my mind.

The texture of the fabric, smooth and suffocating, threatened to unleash the darkness inside me, pulling at pieces of my past I had worked so hard to bury. It was cracking something open inside me, something I wasn't sure I could ever close again.

No. I didn't want to do this. I wasn't ready.

But it was too late.

I felt the memories rattling their cage, like a monster I couldn't escape.

I wanted to scream, to run, to *stop* this.

But all I could do was lie there, trapped in the paralysis, waiting for the nightmare to hit.

Ty sat at my side, the cushion beneath me sinking slightly with the weight of his presence.

Every movement felt magnified in the thick silence, the tension between us so palpable it was as if the air itself was pressing in around me.

He took his time, brushing strands of hair away from my face, his fingers lingering as he arranged the strands over my shoulders, his touch gentle, almost reverent.

It was like he was delaying the inevitable. His movements slow, almost hesitant, as if he knew what was coming would break me.

For a moment, I wanted to lean into it, to find solace in his tenderness. But I couldn't.

My muscles were locked in place. But even though my body was paralyzed, my mind wasn't—and it raced with growing panic.

As if a switch flipped, his mood shifted. I watched the darkness flicker across his face, his eyes hardening, his jaw tightening.

He whispered softly, so low I almost didn't hear it. "I'm sorry."

Those two words clawed at my throat, igniting the panic that had been simmering just beneath the surface.

My breath hitched, my chest constricting with fear as his

fingers reached out, tugging at the delicate tie at my throat. Each pull, each soft brush of his skin against mine, felt like the world unraveling around me.

"Sweet, sweet girl." *His sour breath swirled around my cheeks as he tugged the ribbon loose from the top of my nightgown.*

Ty's fingers were shaking as he undid the first button. Then the second.

Each pop echoed in the room like a gunshot, my body rigid as the nightgown peeled open, exposing me, my skin prickling with cold air and dread.

But the real cold was inside me—an icy grip that wrapped tighter and tighter around my heart.

Button by button, he undid my defenses, each small release peeling back layers I had buried deep.

*His thick fingers undid my buttons. I could smell his sweat, hear his labored panting.*

*He waited until they were all undone before he peeled me open, like I was a present, the sick hunger lighting up his dark dead eyes at the sight of me.*

I wanted to beg him to stop, to claw at Ty's hands, to make him stop—but my body remained limp, unresponsive.

I couldn't fight it. I couldn't stop it. And worst of all, I couldn't stop *him*.

Ty kept going. He grabbed the hem of my gown and pulled it up over my head.

*His rough hands pulled my nightgown over my head. Through a tangle of raven hair, I saw his face looming over me as he began to peel my soul open.*

*I wanted to scream, but I couldn't, the lingering sweetness of hot chocolate on my paralyzed tongue, making my stomach turn.*

"Ava. It's me. I'm right here."

*His* rough touch became Ty's gentle hands. *His* face, twisted with cruel delight moments before, morphed into Ty's handsome features, twisted with concern and mirrored pain.

Black soulless eyes melted away, replaced by the pale-blue eyes of the man I loved.

No, this was *Ty*. I didn't love Ty. I loved *Scáth*.

"It's me, Ava," Ty said as he massaged my nipple to hardness even as pain lingered on his face.

"It's only ever *me*," he repeated as he kissed down my body, his warm lips feeling so much like Scáth's that I couldn't help but react, my body surging with heat. With need. Despite how twisted this was.

"*I* am touching you. These are *my* fingers," Ty said as he trailed his hands down my stomach to spread my folds.

His touch sent electric shocks through me, igniting every nerve ending.

I wanted to arch into him, to writhe and moan, but my body remained motionless, a prisoner of the drug coursing through my veins.

"These are *my* lips."

The scent of sandalwood and leather filled my nostrils as Ty pressed hot kisses across the crease of my inner thigh.

So close. But not where I wanted him. Where I needed him.

No, I shouldn't want this. This was wrong.

Shame and desire warred within me as I saw Scáth's hungry gaze as he looked up at me from between my legs. His eyes were icy pools, promising both pleasure and pain.

But it wasn't Scáth, was it? Not really.

And that's where the guilt settled, like a heavy weight in

my chest. Scáth was buried deep inside this shell of a person.

Or at least, that's what I told myself. I clung to the hope that somewhere, underneath Ty's cruel mask, the man I loved still existed.

My attraction to *this* version of him? It was twisted.

The room felt too warm, too close. Shadows danced on the walls, cast by flickering candles. Their unsteady light made the scene feel dreamlike, unreal.

But the sensations were all too vivid—Ty's hot breath on my most intimate places, the soft velvet beneath my immobile body, the pounding of my heart echoing in my ears.

"This is *my* tongue."

He licked my aching center, long and slow, and a silent scream reverberated through my mind. The pleasure was exquisite torture—I couldn't move, couldn't vocalize. I could only lie there and *feel* as wave after wave of sensation crashed over me.

His skilled mouth worked me relentlessly, bringing me to the precipice again and again, only to back off at the last moment.

"It's only me," he kept repeating over and over like a mantra until his voice echoed in my mind.

I was drowning in sensation, losing myself. Nothing existed but Ty's mouth on me, his hands gripping my thighs.

He slipped a finger inside of me, drawing it out with a careful, steady pace, always keeping a reassuring hand on my thigh. His eyes never let mine go as he muttered against my clit.

"It's *me*. Only ever *me*."

He worked me without hurry, two, then three fingers

filling me, the steadiness of his movements building the pleasure so torturously slow.

I wanted to grab his hair and rock my hips up, to urge him faster, to demand *more*.

But I could do nothing except submit.

He had total control over my body.

That was, I guessed, how I justified this to myself. Justified taking pleasure from Ty when it was Scáth that I loved, Scáth that I had promised myself to.

This was just *therapy*.

But deep down, I knew it was a lie.

As my body hummed with pleasure, my mind wrestled with the morality of it, turning over the question again and again. Would Scáth be angry with me if—*when*—he resurfaced?

Would he understand that I had no choice? Or would he see it as a betrayal, proof that I was weak, that I'd let myself be manipulated by the dark side of him—Ty—who had locked me in this twisted version of therapy?

Would he forgive me? Could I even forgive myself?

The thought made my stomach twist with guilt.

Scáth had always been my protector, my rock.

But now, in this dark place, it felt like Ty had taken his place.

And even though I told myself it was because they were the same—two sides of the same coin—the doubt gnawed at me.

I wasn't supposed to like this. I wasn't supposed to *need* this.

But I did, and that thread of guilt wove its way through

me, tightening with each passing moment, even as pleasure threatened to tear me apart.

My orgasm built to breaking, and the walls of my pussy began to constrict around his fingers.

Ty made a hum of approval against my clit, vibrating through my pussy. That was all it took.

I exploded, the feeling blasting through my body from my core out to my toes, to my fingers. Electricity skittered across my skin and over my scalp as fire burned inside me.

My vision went completely white as the darkness was vanquished.

Over and over the pleasure smashed around inside my motionless body like waves, shaking me to my soul, sucking out all the fight I had left.

But I knew even as I experienced heaven, I had damned myself to hell.

And I wasn't sure I'd survive it.

# AVA

Ty lifted me from the couch and carried me back to my bedroom—to my prison.

Then he pulled me onto his lap on the bed and rocked me, his fingers brushing tenderly over my hair.

My breath hitched as Ty wiped away hot tears that poured down my cheeks, his hands steady against my trembling body.

My fingers twitched as control over my body slowly returned, and I curled into myself, into the fetal position, as if I could protect what little pieces of me were left.

Ty didn't try to pull me out of it. He didn't force me to move or unravel.

Instead, he cradled me in the hollow of his body. My cold feet pressed against his thighs, my knees wedged into his ribs, but he didn't complain. He just held me.

I wanted to disappear. To let myself be swallowed by the darkness, to fall asleep and never wake up again.

"No." My voice was a rasp, a sound barely recognizable as my own. It felt foreign, as if I'd forgotten how to use it.

"That never happened to me. They were... hallucinations. *False memories.*"

Ty's face seemed to crack open, as if his carefully constructed mask was fracturing under the weight of my words.

My throat constricted painfully around the words. "*You gave me fake memories.*"

Hatred burned hot in my belly, and I clung to it like a lifeline. Better to hold on to anger, let it consume me with its fire, than to sink under the crushing icy weight of grief.

I *hated* Ty. He did this to me. He forced me to rip open wounds I'd rather have kept hidden.

Scáth would never have done this. Scáth would have let me run away, to keep these painful memories buried until I followed them into the ground.

He would have protected me. Kept me safe from my own past.

He would have run away with me. Run far away and kept running so my past would never catch up with me.

I missed Scáth. Missed his protection. Missed the way he stood between me and the darkness—even when that darkness was inside me.

If only I had listened to him sooner.

Ty stroked my hair gently, his breath shuddering, holding me to him even as I beat at his chest.

"I'm sorry," he whispered, the words slipping from his mouth like a confession, like a plea.

The dam inside me broke.

At first, just a tear or two slipped down my cheeks, but the flood quickly followed.

My back heaved with sobs, my breath catching painfully

in my throat as I choked on the waves of grief and horror that threatened to pull me under.

"No," I cried, my voice raw, broken. *"That never happened to me."*

Ty lowered his head, resting his cheek against the crown of mine, and the warmth of that simple gesture made me cry even harder.

I shuddered violently in his arms, and he responded by tightening his grip around me, holding me together as my world crumbled apart.

Slowly, my sobs subsided, the tears drying up, leaving me empty and hollow. It was as if the pain had carved me out, leaving nothing but a brittle shell in its wake.

My chest ached, but not from crying—from the sheer exhaustion of feeling too much all at once. I didn't know if I had anything left to give.

"So... we're done, right?" My voice was flat, almost numb, as if the words were coming from someone else. "I remember now."

But even as I said it, I knew it wasn't entirely true. I remembered pieces of it. Fractured memories, like shards of glass slicing through my mind. Pieces that were enough to cut.

I didn't need to remember more. I couldn't.

Ty's breath hitched, rough and ragged, like he was also suffocating under the weight of all this. He lowered his head, his eyes shadowed, and I could see the guilt behind them.

"Ava," he whispered, his voice heavy with regret, "we're only just beginning."

No. I couldn't handle remembering more. The thought

of reliving the past clawed at my insides, panic rising like bile in my throat.

I shoved myself off Ty's lap, my limbs sluggish and uncooperative from the drug. Every movement felt wrong, too slow, too heavy, but I forced myself to crawl clumsily across the bed.

My heart raced, each beat hammering in my chest like frantic drums as I stumbled toward the open door. Freedom. Escape. Just a few more steps.

But before I could slip through, Ty's arm wrapped tightly around my waist, his grip unyielding.

In one swift motion, he reached past me and slammed the door shut, the sharp crack of wood and metal echoing in my ears.

I barely had time to gasp before my body was pinned between the solid door and his. My naked chest pressed hard against the cold surface, my breath caught as his weight caged me in.

Trapped.

"P-please... why are you doing this to me?" My voice cracked, the words barely escaping between my sobs.

I felt so small, so powerless, trapped in a nightmare that I couldn't wake up from.

"Because Ava..." His voice faltered, sorrow leaking through every word, catching me off guard. "You are sick. *He* is buried inside you like a disease. And I am the only one who loves you enough to force you to get *real* treatment."

"*Scáth* loves me," I cried out, my fingers sliding down the cold metal door, the words slipping from my lips like a prayer.

"No!" His raw voice exploded in my ear, his palm slamming against the door, sending vibrations through the metal, rattling it against my head. "*I love you.*"

I flinched, the force of his words cutting through me, making my chest constrict.

*Sick. Diseased.* The words hit me like a punch to the gut. It felt like a poison creeping under my skin, spreading through me until it reached the darkest parts of my mind.

But they were more than just words. They were keys, unlocking something deep inside me.

My breath hitched, and a memory slammed into me with the force of a speeding train. It knocked the air from my lungs, leaving me gasping, as the floodgates of my mind opened wide and the past came roaring back.

*I shoved open the campus doors and the glare of the sun was so intense I had to blink several times before I spotted him.*

*My bully had his hands stuffed deep into his pockets, his shoulders rounded forward. His uniform tie was loose around his untidy collar and the breeze which blew my hair into my face sent it fluttering wildly behind him.*

*"It was you," I accused him as I stormed up to him, my fists by my sides. "You spread those nasty rumors about me."*

*The sun backlit his head as I searched his face, masked in the silhouette, for any sort of remorse.*

*"Why?" I asked and hoped he didn't hear how my voice cracked.*

*All at once, his casual facade dropped, and the cruelty beneath it surfaced, like Mr. Hyde clawing his way to the surface. His eyes darkened, his voice sharp as a blade.*

*"Because you're diseased, Ava," he hissed, his words venomous. "You're sick."*

*"No... it's not true," I whispered, my voice shaking.*

"It is. I was the only one who saw it, but now they all know."

He leaned closer, the space between us shrinking as his presence overwhelmed me.

My body screamed for action—run, fight, do something—but all I could do was stand there, frozen, staring up at him with wide, helpless eyes.

His thumb ran over my wet cheek, and I flinched. Not because it hurt, but because it was too soft, too gentle, and that somehow made it worse.

"Why else would you let him touch you?" His voice was hard, laced with bitterness. The accusation hung in the air, heavy and confusing.

I didn't even know what he meant.

All I knew was that his thumb drifted lower, brushing across my lips.

My breath hitched, my lips parting on an unsteady inhale. The sensation was overwhelming, like being submerged in ice water and fire at the same time, and I couldn't think past it.

The conflict inside me raged—fear, disgust, and something else, something terrifyingly close to desire.

Before I could stop myself, I was rising onto my tiptoes, instinctively chasing the feeling, desperate for more.

He shoved me away so swiftly and so violently that I barely realized I was falling until I felt the pain flare across my knees and hands.

I bit my lower lip to fight back the prickle of tears in my eyes as pebbles burrowed into my torn skin, hot with fresh blood, stinging terribly.

A tiny sob escaped as I tried to push myself up, thin arms shaking, only to collapse back down.

A pair of strong hands caught me.

"Leave her alone," Ty said into my hair.

*My bully just laughed at me, a cruel bitter sound, and slipped his hands back into his pockets just as casually as before.*

*Just before Ty pulled me into his arms, I glanced up at my bully.*

*My heart jammed in my throat to be met with those same pale-blue eyes.*

The full memory of that day hit me like a freight train, slamming into my body. It was like someone had flipped a switch in my mind, lighting up the dark corners where I'd hidden the truth from myself.

Scáth *didn't* have split personality.

No—*they were twins.*

# THE SHADOW

I sped down the dirt road, the Darkmoor forest blurring around me, branches whipping at the car as if trying to slow me down. The tires kicked up clouds of dust, the engine roaring louder than my thoughts, but I couldn't bring myself to care about the noise.

I couldn't think about strategy, couldn't think about anything except *her*.

Ava.

My heart pounded in my chest like it was going to burst, each beat a painful reminder of how fragile time was. If I was too late—

*Don't think it.*

I slammed on the brakes, the car skidding to a halt in front of the crumbling, abandoned building.

I couldn't afford to waste a second. I threw the door open and sprinted through the pouring rain toward the entrance, my breath ragged, prayers slipping through clenched teeth.

*Please let her be alive.*

I shoved through the broken wooden door, the hinges creaking as it swung back with a hollow thud. The place reeked of decay and dark secrets, and my gut twisted at the thought of her trapped in there.

The place was *too* quiet, the kind of silence that gnawed at you, that made every shadow feel like a threat.

My pulse pounded in my ears, and my breath came in short, panicked bursts as I stared around the old stone building, barely standing.

What had once been several floors had caved in, leaving jagged beams and broken stone scattered across the space.

Part of the ceiling was gone entirely, exposing a patch of gray sky through the remains of the flooring. Dust floated in the pale light filtering in, making the whole place feel like a crumbling tomb.

No one was here.

I scanned the ruins, my heart thudding in my chest, hoping for any sign of her—*anything*—but the silence pressed down harder. Then my eyes landed on the stairs leading *down* into the darkness below.

I sprinted down the stairs, barely feeling the impact as I took them two at a time.

"Ava!" I screamed, my voice raw, cracking with desperation. The echo bounced back at me, mocking me with the silence that followed.

*Please. Please let her answer.*

As I descended, I swept my flashlight through the darkness. I stopped breathing when I saw the pair of legs, bent at an odd angle on the floor below.

*No.*

A body lay sprawled on the ground, half in shadow, unmoving.

I stumbled to the bottom of the stairs, my throat closed up, a sharp pain stabbing through my chest.

*No, please, God, no.*

I rushed to the body, dropping to my knees so hard I barely felt the impact. My hands shook as I reached out, my heart pounding so violently I thought I might collapse under the weight of it.

The beam of my flashlight illuminated the face—*Cormac*.

Relief hit me like a punch to the gut, so sharp and overwhelming that for a second, I couldn't breathe. I collapsed forward, my hands pressed to my knees, and I let out a shuddering breath.

Thank God.

But relief had never been so torturous. Because if she wasn't here, then *where was she?*

Fear prickled at my spine as I leaned over him to get a better look at the body and saw the source of all the blood. The huge open gash across his neck from ear to ear, done with a sharp blade.

Whoever had killed Cormac knew what they were doing. That kind of precision murder took strength, but above all, it took self-control. It was the work of a steady hand and an even steadier mind.

He'd been a loose end, tied up in a bloody knot. The Sochai didn't need him anymore. So they disposed of him as carelessly as a used rag.

But then why was Cormac's eye socket a red, pulpy mess? And why was the poor bastard's horrified eye staring at me from the back of his mouth?

I could handle a hit man. A professional in every sense of the word. But there was something personal about this that caused whoever it was to lose that requisite restraint.

It didn't matter why.

*They* had Ava.

I would track them down. I would dismember each and every one of them limb by limb before bringing her back where she rightfully belonged—with *me*.

Outside, I threw open the trunk and Dr. Vale blinked against the downpour.

I hauled him out and threw him to the mud. I shook the rain from my hair and unsheathed a blade—Dundee.

He screamed and began trying to crawl away with bound hands and wrists.

I lifted him by his hair, deriving small pleasures at the pops of hair tugging out, and placed my knife to his throat.

"Where is she?" I demanded, my voice cutting through the downpour like a blade.

"W-what?" Dr. Vale stuttered, blinking furiously as rain splattered against his face.

"She's *gone*," I growled. My grip tightened on him, my knuckles white. "Where did they take her?"

"You won't find her now." Dr. Vale whimpered, blinking against the relentless rain. "The *Tiarna Ard* has her." The *High Lord*.

"Unacceptable."

I dropped him to the ground in disgust and grabbed his ear, slicing it right off.

He screamed, his cries echoing through the trees, causing birds to take off in fear.

I threw the offending ear aside, my insides cold.

"*Who* is the High Lord?" I demanded, my knife's glinting edge perilously close to his jugular vein.

No, I couldn't lose control. If I killed him, I'd learn nothing.

I shifted the knife so that there was no chance my hand would slip in my rage.

He shook his head, his lips going pale as he clutched his bleeding head with bound hands. "I d-don't know, I swear."

"Then give me a fucking name—*any* name."

I'd carve my way through the fucking Society to get to Ava.

Dr. Vale shook his head. "They'll kill me."

Snarling and drawing his face close to mine, I hissed, "*I'll kill you.*"

Dr. Vale blinked at me from behind his eyeglasses, askew and covered with droplets of water. "Maybe. But it'll be infinitely *less* painful than if *they* do it."

I laughed, wrenching his head back and pressing the knife against his Adam's apple so he could feel the blade when he swallowed.

"Are you so sure, Doc?" I asked, ready to prove my point.

He answered before I even had a chance.

"Yes."

His response was chilling. There was no lie in it. No trick.

The *Sochai* had the man not just terrified, but more terrified than he was of *me*.

And I was a monster.

With a growl of frustration, I shoved Dr. Vale back down to the mud.

He landed on his face, his glasses shattering. He rolled over with a groan and blood mixed with the rainwater.

I loomed over him with the knife at my side in a white-knuckled grip.

When I found Ava—and I *would* find her—I wanted to be *more* for her.

She hadn't wanted me to become like the Society when she told me not to torture Dr. Vale for answers. I'd promised her I wouldn't.

But even with all the promises I made, all bets were off now that her life was at stake.

"W-wait, wait…" Dr. Vale held out his bound hands. "I'll tell you the truth about your father if you let me go."

Squatting down beside him in the mud, I blinked the raindrops from my eyelashes. "What do you know about my father?"

Dr. Vale nodded. "I can tell you everything."

I tilted my head to the side and gave him a pitiful look. "Oh, Dr. Vale, you went to shrink school and everything."

Blinded without his glasses, he frowned in confusion, squinting to see my face better. "What?"

"Took you years to earn that degree, I'm sure."

His smile faltered.

I patted his cheek. "All that to end up dying because you couldn't properly read someone's psychology."

I slit his throat, ear to ear, before he could put it together.

Before I could change my mind.

He wasn't going to tell me anything more. I tried to justify it, pushing down the small voice in my head that chastised me for being reckless, for not thinking things through—again.

For acting on impulse, just like I always did.

The rain fell heavier, but I barely noticed as I watched the blood pour from his neck, steaming as it mixed with the cold. It gushed hot and fast, staining the ground beneath him.

The light in his eyes flickered, then dimmed entirely, leaving them blank, staring lifelessly at the circle of trees and the tower piercing the low gray clouds above.

I took a deep breath, the gravity of what I'd done barely registering. I only had one thought left in my mind.

I would get Ava back.

No matter what.

No matter how much of a monster I had to become to make it happen.

Even if it meant she couldn't stand to look at me, even if I destroyed everything good between us. As long as she was safe, as long as I could save her from this nightmare... I'd pay *any* price.

I pushed myself to my feet and cleaned my blade against my pants. I dragged Dr. Vale down to the basement and tossed him next to Cormac.

"You see, Dr. Vale," I said to his corpse. "I already know the truth about my father."

Unlike Ava, I couldn't forget my father, couldn't unsee his sins.

And I already knew more than I wanted to.

I knew that he never learned Gaelic, too busy with his precious plants and their Latin roots.

I'd only ever heard him say three words in Gaelic: *An Tiarna Ard*.

*The High Lord.*

My father had been part of this Society. The doc didn't have to tell me. I already knew.

And it was the reason Ava had been targeted.

# AVA

~~~~~

It was every orphan's dream to be adopted.

But as I stepped into Blackthorn Hall, the weight of the place seemed to settle on my shoulders.

Shadows clung to the walls, and the grand staircase twisted up before me, intimidating in its dark wood and wrought-iron railings. I drank in the intricate carvings and the monstrous iron tiered chandelier hanging above as I took in the mansion's dark grandeur.

The professor, my new foster father, had said, "Go on inside, I'll be right with you."

So for the moment I stood there alone.

I glanced over my shoulder but I could not see him.

"Hello?"

I moved farther in, unsure of where to go, and a sound caught my attention from the curling dark wood grand staircase.

I looked up to see two figures racing down, elbowing and nudging each other, shoving and jostling as they competed to reach the bottom first.

*They skidded to a stop in front of me, barely managing to look composed.*

*Both of them were tall, dark-haired, and unmistakably gorgeous.*

*One of them was dressed in a cornflower-blue sweater, highlighting his broad shoulders and layered over a white-collared shirt, with the sleeves carefully rolled up just past his elbows. His hair was neatly brushed back, every strand in place.*

*He exuded an intensity that seemed almost... contained, like he was holding something back just beneath the surface. His eyes flicked over me with curiosity and a softness that was somehow at odds with the imposing hall around us.*

*Beside him was his mirror image and yet his exact opposite.*

*He wore a leather jacket, worn and scuffed in places, with a black t-shirt beneath it that clung to his frame, a silver chain glinting at his throat, stark against his skin.*

*His hair was a bit longer and hung casually over his forehead, tousled like he'd just come in from a windstorm—or a fight.*

*There was a ruggedness to him, a rawness, with a glint in his eye that hinted at trouble.*

*The preppy one, slightly breathless, flashed a grin and nudged the rebel aside, reaching out his hand.*

*"I'm Ty," he said, his voice warm, his eyes intent on me.*

*"You're... twins!" I said, surprise in my voice.*

*I'd never met a real set of twins before.*

*"And you're lovely." He blinked, catching himself, a blush creeping to his cheeks. "I mean... who are you?"*

*"I'm Ava," I said.*

*The other boy rolled his eyes, stepping forward with a sly grin. "Ignore him, Ava. I'm Ciaran. And I'm obviously the better brother."*

*He gave Ty a shove, claiming my hand for himself.*

*"Please," Ty scoffed, nudging Ciaran back. "My grades are better than yours."*

*"Yeah?" Ciaran winked at me, the hint of a dare in his smile. "Well, I'm the* fun *brother."*

*I glanced between them, taken aback by their striking similarity and the playful, competitive energy crackling between them.*

*Both so handsome, yet so different.*

*But as I stood between them, I couldn't shake the feeling that this wouldn't be the last time I'd find myself caught between them.*

I lay wrapped in my pale-pink comforter, the truth sinking deep into my bones, wrapping around me like heavy chains.

They were *twins*.

Not two sides of the same broken man, but two different people.

How could I have forgotten? How could I have blocked it out so completely, the fact that the professor had *two sons*?

The Donahue twins—my foster brothers—shared the same face, but their hearts couldn't be more different.

My Scáth—*Ty*—had been the kind one, the one who had protected me, who held me when I had nightmares, had been my childhood best friend.

And then... the other one.

Ciaran.

His name rose up from the depths of my memories like a dark shadow, filling me with a cold, hollow dread.

*Scáth* wasn't some split personality of Ty's. No—Scáth was Ty, the boy I trusted, the boy who had shielded me from the worst of it.

And this... this bullying bastard who now held me captive was *Ciaran*.

He had been the cruel one.

The one who bullied me relentlessly, who spread rumors about me at school, who made my life hell.

And now he had me trapped in this house, playing his sick games.

I refused therapy after that. I told him I wouldn't go through with it again, not after everything. And now, here I was, locked in this room, left alone to rot until I "came to my senses."

For days, he hadn't even shown his face.

He slipped trays of food through a small hatch at the bottom of the door, the only sign he was still out there.

I hated the silence, the cold emptiness that surrounded me. But what I hated more was the aching pull inside me, the part of me that missed him.

Not just Scáth—I missed *him* too.

The guilt, sharp and bitter, gnawed at my insides. I should have known. I should have fought harder, resisted more.

But I let Ciaran touch me. I let him put me through his twisted therapy, let him bring me to orgasm, thinking somehow it was okay because deep down this was Scáth.

It wasn't. I'd betrayed Scáth, my protector. The one who would have saved me from all this if I'd let him.

Ciaran had hated me then, with a bitterness I couldn't understand, and now that hatred burned even brighter.

*He hated me even more now.*

And how I *hated* him.

The lower panel on the door slid open, and like Pavlov's

dog, I reacted instinctively. My heart gave a pathetic flutter as I sat up, eyes glued to the slim opening.

Every part of me ached for a glimpse of him—his hand, his fingers—anything that wasn't the endless monotony of this room.

Ciaran's pale hand appeared, pushing a tray through, those familiar strong fingers I shouldn't want to see, shouldn't care about. But there they were, and the sight sent a shiver of something I didn't want to name skittering through my body.

His hand disappeared and the panel slammed shut, a wave of disappointment going through me.

Dinnertime? Lunch? I didn't know anymore. The days bled into each other, marked only by these small moments.

I pushed myself out of bed and staggered toward the tray. It wasn't hunger driving me, not really. My appetite had vanished, along with any real sense of time. But I needed something to do, something to break up the crushing emptiness that surrounded me.

I lifted the tray with cold fingers, the metal chilling my skin as I carried it to the small table by the bricked-up windows.

The cloche gleamed under the dim light, and for a second, a flicker of hope stirred in me—maybe there'd be food, maybe just a small slice of normalcy.

But when I pulled it off, all that sat there was a single vial, glinting under the light.

Mocking me.

A wave of fury tore through me. I snatched the vial and hurled it against the wall with all my strength. The sharp sound of glass shattering echoed through the room, the pieces scattering across the floor like sanity.

Frustration boiled over, searing through my veins and I couldn't fucking stand it anymore. The helplessness, the constant feeling of being trapped, the suffocating control—it all snapped inside me like a brittle thread.

I wasn't going to just sit here and be his prisoner, his toy. Not anymore.

I grabbed the nearest chair, adrenaline surging through me like a tidal wave. With every ounce of strength I had, I hurled it at the glass, my heart pounding in my chest. I ducked instinctively, bracing for the sound of shattering glass.

The chair cracked on impact, one of its legs snapping clean off as it clattered to the floor in pieces.

But the glass didn't break.

It barely wobbled. There wasn't a single fracture or splinter in the smooth surface. It must have been made out of some sort of shatterproof glass.

The sight of the untouched glass felt like a punch to the gut, my hope of escape slipping further away as the reality of my captivity closed in around me again.

*I was never getting out of here.*

No, I *would* leave this place, one way or another.

I yanked the silk sheets off the bed in a fury, my hands trembling as I twisted them together, forming a crude knot. My heart pounded as I looped the fabric into a noose, every motion fueled by pure, reckless rage.

"Show your face!" I screamed at the glass, my voice hoarse and raw. "Show your fucking face, or I swear to God, I'll hang myself right here!"

I couldn't even tell if I meant it. But the desperation was real, the unbearable weight of being watched without end, of being toyed with, like my life was nothing but a sick game.

The crackling of the speakers made me pause, my grip on the makeshift noose tightening.

Then his voice came through, colder than I'd ever heard it.

"Ava," Ciaran warned, a sharp edge slicing through his usually composed tone. "Stop acting crazy."

Me? *Me* acting crazy?!

I pulled the noose tighter, my breath coming in sharp, erratic bursts.

"You think I won't?" I hissed, my eyes locked on the glass, daring him to stop me. "You think I'll let you keep doing this to me?"

A curse cut through the speaker, low and vicious, then the crackling abruptly stopped.

Silence fell over the room, heavy and suffocating.

He was watching. I *knew* he was watching, but for the first time, I had him rattled.

His footsteps stormed through the hallway outside, each one tightening the knot of fear in my stomach.

I held the twisted sheet in my hands, my heart still racing, the power of the moment washing over me like a bitter, twisted victory. I had forced his hand. Even if just for a moment, I had taken control.

He was coming.

I spotted the broken chair leg lying on the floor—*a weapon*. My pulse quickened as I dropped the sheets and snatched up the leg, my hands trembling as I gripped the jagged wood like a bat.

The locks clicked open, and the door creaked as it swung inward.

Ciaran stepped into the room, his tall frame filling the doorway.

For a split second, the sight of him, familiar and imposing, made me hesitate. There was something in the way he moved, in the way he seemed so unshakably in control, that made me second-guess everything.

But my survival instinct kicked in, stronger than anything else. I lunged at him before I could stop myself, the chair leg raised high as I swung with everything I had.

But Ciaran's reflexes were quick, his hand shooting up to catch the chair leg in mid-swing.

For a moment, the two of us were locked in a silent battle, the piece of wood hanging between us as we strained against each other.

My muscles screamed in protest, my teeth grinding together as I pushed harder, determined to overpower him.

But it was useless. His strength was so calm, so effortless, like I was nothing more than a mild distraction.

And that realization—more than anything—made me want to scream.

He made a strange sound—low, almost guttural.

It took me too long to realize what it was. *He was laughing.*

Ciaran's lips curled into a dark smile, his eyes flashing with something wicked as he easily snatched the chair leg out of my hands.

"Is this your grand plan, Ava?" he asked, his voice thick with amusement. "Fighting me with a chair leg?"

His laughter sent a chill down my spine, the ease with which he overpowered me only fueling the burning frustration that twisted inside me.

The next thing I knew I was on the cold wooden floor, gasping for the air which had been knocked out of my lungs, his knee digging painfully into my chest.

Through teary eyes I watched him toss the leg harmlessly aside.

"Try again," Ciaran said, staring down at me with cold detachment.

"Fuck you," I growled.

He had no reaction to this at all. Instead, he just stared at me with no emotion as he waited.

His calm arrogance ignited something in me, setting my skin on fire and making my thoughts unravel.

I kicked a foot toward his knee, hoping to pop it out of its socket, but Ciaran sidestepped me easily and my heel thudded painfully back on the floor.

"That's not trying," he said.

The asshole was toying with me. I knew I'd be giving him exactly what he wanted by attacking him again.

But more than wanting to deny him, I wanted to fucking hurt him.

I pushed myself up from the floor and launched myself at him, swinging at his face with a clenched fist.

He moved with the speed of a viper, catching my wrist and spinning me around to pin me to his chest.

I whipped back my head, hoping to break his nose or

knock out a tooth, but he predicted this too and moved aside to send me toppling back over.

From the floor, I glared up at him as he stood calmly with arms casually crossed over his black button-up shirt.

My dark hair hung over my red cheeks as my breasts heaved beneath the thin silk dress.

I could still feel his touch on my skin. I didn't want to admit even to myself that the hard strength of his chest was something I wanted to lean against, that I imagined with his speed and agility how he might be able to manipulate my body in bed.

Fuck him. I hated that he looked so much like the man I loved. Like the man I wanted. It seemed my body couldn't tell the difference.

I was wet. Achy in places I shouldn't be. That I was embarrassed to be.

I dragged myself up to try again, roaring as I ran at him.

He didn't even bother moving out of the way. He just stood there, seemingly unaffected, while I wore myself out, pounding my fists against his chest, my breasts heaving.

His eyes flashed black before his hand shot out to my throat.

I gasped as he walked me backward all the way across the room.

My shoulders at last collided with the opposite wall and when he pressed himself against me, I was horrified to find his cock hard along my thigh. Even as my clit throbbed.

"You're further behind than I thought," he growled, his mouth dangerously close to mine.

I snapped at his lips with my teeth, narrowly missing him.

He assessed me with cool eyes. I bucked my hips against his and he hissed in pain as part of my leg I connected with his throbbing erection.

His fingers tightened around my throat, but the asshole smirked.

"Better."

He jerked his own hips against me so violently that I cried out.

His strength was terrifying and I hated that I got wet imagining his cock splitting me in two, those brutal thrusts breaking me apart.

My body was rebelling against me.

I stilled, frozen like a frightened animal, when Ciaran's chest rubbed against mine and his dick twitched between us.

I saw in his eyes that he'd felt how hard my nipples were for him.

"You have to hate me if you're going to succeed in killing me," Ciaran said softly, tucking a strand of hair behind my ear, his gaze burning down my body.

"I do hate you," I snarled.

Ciaran slipped his free hand beneath the hem of my dress and I screamed till he squeezed hard enough to choke off my voice.

His searing hot touch traveled up my quivering inner thigh.

I had to stop him. I had to do something.

But I was frozen. Even if I could move, he had me pinned tight against the wall.

He pushed his knee between my legs, forcing my legs to

spread wider, giving him even more access as his calloused fingers moved closer and closer.

I let out a whimper. I knew what Ciaran was going to find when his fingers slipped inside my panties. I hated that I couldn't seem to control my body around him.

I hated *him*.

At this point there was no stopping it. I shivered like I was in the grip of a deadly fever and my heart pounded out of my chest.

Even over the blood rushing in my ears I heard him groan as his fingers slid across my slit. I was fucking soaking wet.

"*This* is hate?" he asked, dragging his dripping fingers along my slick folds.

Goosebumps covered my flesh as he smeared my wetness over my engorged clit and I bit back a groan.

"Go on, tell me how much you hate me," Ciaran whispered in my ear.

"I hate you," I stuttered as he teased the entrance of my pussy.

"Tell me how you're going to kill me," he said, licking a hot trail along my jaw.

Shallowly, he fucked me with his finger. Already my cunt was clenching for him, begging to take all of him inside its pulsing heat.

In my mind, I burned with fury for him. He was humiliating me, turning my body against me.

My eyes fixed on his as I promised, "I *am* going to kill you."

He plunged two fingers into me and my eyes rolled back against my will. The beautifully ornate ceiling was hazy as his hand closed firmly around my throat, choking me.

Stars danced before my eyes, and my legs trembled as he fucked me with his fingers, bringing me dangerously close to the edge.

"This pussy is weeping for me," Ciaran said as he rutted his cock against my hip. He squeezed my throat and growled, "Do you have so little control?"

My cheeks flared even hotter at the embarrassment.

His disdain as my body continued to be a slut for him was excruciating.

"Tell me to stop," he commanded.

I wanted to. My mind was screaming at my lips to form the words.

But Ciaran was right; I wasn't in control.

My body responded to his touch so intensely that I was helpless. A dripping wet puppet. A boneless doll.

His heat burned inside of me, destroying all my self-will.

"Tell me to stop, Ava," Ciaran snarled.

But I couldn't.

Especially when he curled his finger around to abuse that sensitive spot inside me.

His nearness, his hand around my throat, deciding how much oxygen I was allowed, his cruel dominance over my body, it was too much.

That added with my frustration over the last few days, the unfulfilled desire overlapping in layers, the fucking pressure built up so much that I thought I'd explode.

There was the edge. I was so close to coming that I could barely breathe.

He pulled his fingers from my pussy and shoved himself

away from me. I fell to my knees without him there to catch me.

"You only get to come," he said, his voice a single cruel note, "during therapy."

There were tears in my eyes as I watched him walk away. I'd needed to come so badly that my whole body was in agony.

"Fuck you!" I screamed after him, arms wrapped protectively around my stomach, not sure if I was going to throw up or pass out.

God, I wanted to shove my hands between my legs and finish myself off. But I knew that if I tried, he'd just knock me out again. Knock me out and do God knows what to me.

Leaving me unsatisfied and even more hungry.

And I knew that this wasn't even the worst torture to come. Agreeing to his fucked-up *therapy* would give me relief, but the darkness he would unleash from the depths of me would destroy me.

I wasn't sure I could survive it.

"Tynan will find me," I shouted desperately. "Ty will rescue me."

"Oh, Ava." Ciaran's laughter was just as cruel as he glanced back at me from the doorway. "*I* am Tynan."

# AVA

"I am Tynan."

I wasn't sure which was worse: his malicious smile or the amusement in his unflinching eyes.

My breath stuttered in my chest and I laughed to stave off the fear. But it didn't come out the way I wanted it to. Even to my own ears I sounded like a little kid trying not to be afraid of the dark.

"You're lying!" I screamed at the imposter.

He arched a long, elegant eyebrow at me, gazing across the bedroom at me like I was a creature in a cage, pity in his cruel eyes.

It stirred anger in my belly. The heat of rage was better than the ice-cold fear and I clung to it even as my knees trembled.

"*You* are Ciaran," I said, snarling at him. "My bully bastard foster brother. You're trying to trick me. You're being cruel. You've *always* been cruel."

The corners of his seductive lips curled up just the slightest bit. Just enough for me to see.

They looked just like the lips I loved: Scáth's lips, the lips that I loved on my mouth, my aching nipples, my swollen clit.

But they were different: hardened, cruel, with a scar running through the top that I just noticed.

How did I ever mistake him for *my* Scáth? And how could my body betray me, betray Scáth, by wanting this monster?

The betrayal of my desire turned my stomach. I hated myself.

I hated *him*.

"Ty went to prison for me!" I said, trying to convince myself. "He knows what it's like to be held against his will and he would *never* do the same to me... like you have. You're either insane or unbelievably cruel!"

With a mix of horror and sick intrigue, I watched as he tugged his shirt out of his black pants. He began to unbutton his shirt all the way open, his icy eyes glittering with madness.

It should have reminded me of the terrible things that happened to helpless girls in twisted fairy tales, but instead it thrilled me with anticipation, a heat building between my thighs.

He shrugged his shirt from his broad shoulders, the soft rustle of fabric falling to the floor echoing in the silence, sending chills all the way up my arms.

The sweltering heat of the room seemed to vanish in an instant, leaving me cold and unsettled.

I wrapped my arms around myself, trying to stay warm, but it wasn't just the temperature that made me shiver—it was *him*.

My eyes drifted to his bare torso, and I couldn't tear them away.

I sucked in a breath at the rugged beauty of his muscled body. It was ruined, but it was perfect.

Tattoos stretched across his firm chest and rippling abs, dark ink marking him in ways I couldn't begin to understand. Each one seemed to hold a story, a memory of a place I couldn't imagine—a place that had hardened him, that had stolen whatever softness might have once been there.

But it wasn't just the tattoos. Scars crisscrossed his skin, rough and pale against his flesh. Some were thin and long, like they'd been carved by blades, others jagged, like the remnants of violent fights.

My eyes caught on one in particular—a deep scar on his side, circular and ugly. Was that... a bullet wound? It looked old, faded, but the sight of it made my stomach twist.

*This* was the body of a man who had been to hell and back.

I thought of Scáth, of how perfect his skin was when I'd touched him under his clothes, unmarred by anything more than a stray scratch.

Scáth's body was like armor, but my captor's... his was a battlefield.

I swallowed hard, my mind spinning.

Standing before me wasn't just the man I once knew. This was someone forged by years of pain, of survival, and it was written in every scar, every tattoo, every wound.

The twin who'd gone to prison. The proof was written all over his body.

"Insane or unbelievably cruel..." Holding out his

tattooed arms, my captor gave a dark, charming smile. "Why not both, hummingbird?"

"You are Ty," I whispered, shuddering as soon as the admission left my lips.

My head spun with the implications. I shook it as if it might force the pieces of the puzzle to fall into place.

*This* was Ty.

He stood there so patiently, so assured, while my entire world collapsed around me.

I felt like I was crumbling, but he remained solid, watching as the ground beneath me gave way.

Shakily, I managed to whisper, "But Scáth told me that *he* was—"

The end of my sentence fell away as the truth slammed into me like a wrecking ball. I was wrong.

Scáth had never called himself that cursed name—*Ty*.

*I* had called him that.

I could hear his reply to my accusation in the mansion as clearly as if he was whispering it into my ear: *Don't call me that... I like Scáth.*

And then it hit me with brutal clarity. Outrage swelled inside me, thick and suffocating, threatening to choke the air from my lungs.

*Scáth*—no, *Ciaran*—had lied to me.

He had deceived me, twisted the truth until I couldn't tell the difference anymore.

I had fallen in love with a sick, twisted bully who had manipulated my heart.

And worse—*I had almost run away with him.*

I was ready to throw my entire life away for a cruel

bully, for the boy who had never deserved my trust, my love, or the pieces of myself I'd given to him.

The weight of my own blindness, my own mistakes, crushed me. I had trusted him. I had believed him. And he had made a fool of me.

"Ciaran always was a cunning boy," Ty said. "But I have become... more cunning."

I was hyperventilating, my heart erratically skipping beats, and Ty picked up his shirt from the floor of my bedroom and laid it casually over his arm.

I hated him for being so nonchalant with his wickedness. For not caring at all that I was teetering on the verge of a complete mental breakdown.

For being right.

My warden was Ty. My childhood best friend. The twin who went to prison for me.

My shadow was Ciaran. My childhood bully. The twin whose eyes always burned with hatred at me from among the black baccara roses. The twin who had *lied* to me.

But another truth—fragile, desperate—wrapped its fingers around me, clinging to a thread of hope.

Yes, Ciaran had lied to me, he had deceived me, twisted me into knots. But I *knew* he loved me. I could feel it in every fiber of my being, as broken as it was.

And despite everything, I loved him, too.

He would find me.

"Ciaran," I whispered, his name tasting foreign and heavy on my tongue. "He'll find me. He'll come for me. He *loves* me."

Ty's expression didn't change. His face was unreadable, lips pressed into a firm, unyielding line. His eyes were cold, focused, detached—like he was already miles away from me. His posture was rigid, shoulders squared like a judge about to deliver a final, irreversible sentence.

And like an executioner, he wasn't finished destroying me yet.

"No," Ty said, his voice low, final. "He won't even consider that I have you. He won't come back to this cursed house, not ever again."

My heart stuttered in my chest, cold terror crawling through my veins as Ty's next words fell like a hammer.

"Because he thinks I'm *dead*."

I flashed back to that moment in my kitchen, remembering what Scáth had said when I'd called him Ty.

*"Don't call me Ty... Ty is dead."*

At the time, I had thought he was speaking figuratively, metaphorically—like a part of him had died inside. But now I realized he had meant it *literally*.

He believed his brother, Ty, was dead.

Which meant Ty was right. Scáth would never think to look for me here.

Scáth wasn't coming.

Ty moved so quickly, I barely had time to react. My mind and body were frozen in place, paralyzed by the weight of his revelation.

He dropped his shirt, scooped me up off the floor as if I weighed nothing, and dumped me onto the bed with a swift, careless motion.

I shook my head, trying to force the shattered pieces of the truth to fit together, but they just rattled around inside me like a broken doll tossed in a box. "You... how? Why?"

His voice was low, calm—too calm for what he was

admitting. "I faked my death in order to escape prison. So I could return to *you*."

I saw it in his deadened, fixated eyes that he had a plan for me and neither heaven nor hell could keep him from it.

I crumpled against the sheets of the bed in a fit of frightened, despairing tears because there was no escaping this nightmare.

I sobbed till I couldn't breathe, thinking about what lay ahead for me, inescapable and horrifying.

His iron grip on my chin made me cry out in surprised pain.

"There's only ever been *you*, Ava."

He claimed my mouth with his. His tongue was fire against mine and the warmth spread straight down between my thighs.

My hands were on his solid chest to push him away, but I never found the strength. Instead, my lips melted against his and I groaned with sickening arousal, my fingers searching out every knotted scar, every bump and line of his beautiful ruined body.

Gripping my neck, he forced me onto my back on the bed.

I should have felt trapped with his big body atop mine, but the friction of his marble chest against my hard nipples was delicious, and when Ty rutted his cock against me, my hips rocked back.

My breathing became ragged when Ty licked my throat.

"I'll wash every single trace of him from you," he said. The wet heat of his tongue was everywhere all at once: the line of my jaw, the hollow between my collarbones, the swell of my breast. "I won't stop until you're cleansed. Until you're all *mine*."

My body was buzzing with white-hot pleasure, but his words made me shiver.

Ty tore my dress apart down the middle with his hands.

"I'll suck out every memory of him," he promised as he licked my nipple, the pleasure making me moan despite my rising panic. "From every dark corner."

Nausea swept over me when past Ty's shoulder I saw the shadowed corners of my bedroom reaching out for me. Bile rose in my throat as the soft bed underneath me turned into the cursed velvet couch damp with my own sweat beneath me.

This house was where I was abused.

Ty had brought me here on purpose. He wanted to torture me with my past. He wasn't loving me. This was all just another part of his sick little game.

"No," I cried out as I struggled against Ty as his tongue circled my nipple.

Ty just pressed my hips deeper against the bed with his hands.

"I'm sorry, but this is the way it must be," he said before he plunged his face into my folds.

I fought against him as he licked my swollen clit, but he was way too strong.

I made a noise that was half moan, half whimper as he ravaged my pussy with his mouth because it felt so fucking good and I didn't want it to.

I hated the way my body responded against my will.

"You'll never be free of him until you face the darkness," Ty said between laps of my pussy, his cruel burning eyes never leaving mine. "You need to be broken before you can be put back together again, Ava. And no one loves you enough to do it but *me*."

His two fingers thrusting inside me choked off my scream. I bucked and thrashed beneath him, but I was trapped.

"You're a sadist!" I screamed as he sucked my clit between his teeth, his fingers working my pussy, my wet desperate sounds making me burn with self-loathing.

I shook my head, refusing to let the despair take hold, my survival instincts scrambling desperately for another thread of hope to cling to.

"Ebony," I cried. "She'll send the fucking cavalry after me. The whole of Ireland's police force will be looking for me. She won't stop until she's found me."

Ty chuckled, sending a lash of fear down my spine. "I'm sorry to be the bearer of bad news, but *no one* is looking for you."

"You don't know Lisa. Or Ebony. They'll—"

"They all think you're in Greece, sailing around with a friend with hardly any Wi-Fi all summer. That's what you told them in your messages."

"W-what?"

Ty smiled at me from between my legs, and the sight of it chilled me to my bones. "It's not hard to fake messages, fake post updates on your socials from Greece. Hashtag wish you were here."

I could feel the color draining from my face. A cold chill crept over my skin. My vision narrowed down to Ty's dark, victorious eyes.

"I spent every single waking moment in my tiny cell

planning for this—for *you*. Don't think for a second I haven't put in place every single possible measure to make sure that we are left undisturbed and that you will *never* escape."

No one was going to find me. Because no one was looking.

"No." The word slipped out, barely a whisper, as hopelessness seeped into every inch of me, numbing me from the inside out.

"Yes," he hissed before he lowered his face into my pussy again.

"No, no," I begged. I fought against his tongue, against his fingers, even as my body screamed *yes, yes*!

My thighs trembled around his ears as my orgasm crested but he slowed his thrusts.

Fuck him. He knew exactly how to keep me on the edge.

He wouldn't stop until I submitted once and for all to his evil torture—his *therapy*.

No. I couldn't say yes. I couldn't face what had happened to me again. It would shatter me, break me into pieces I'd never be able to put back together.

But what choice did I have? He'd stripped it all away—my hope, my options—until I was left with nothing. Nothing but this.

Nothing but *him*.

"Okay, I'll do it," I cried as tears spilled out over my eyes and I sealed my own fate.

# THE SHADOW

I slammed my palm on my desk as the satellite image took its sweet fucking time to load, my breath coming too fast, too shallow. *Come on, come on.*

Ava wasn't in the basement. Dr. Vale had said she'd be there, that she hadn't been moved yet. But he lied. *Or he didn't know.*

The High Lord had her now. The bastard who'd, at best, kill her—at worse…

And if I didn't find her soon…

No. I couldn't think like that. Couldn't let the panic swallow me whole. But it was clawing at the edges of my mind, trying to tear through my control.

I had to stay focused. Had to get ahead of them before it was too late.

Finally, the aerial map of the Darkmoor campus flashed up on one of my many screens.

I located the clearing in the woods with the stone tower where Dr. Vale had led me. From there, I spotted the service road, which was the one I'd taken.

My car's tires tracks, melting away in the rain, had been the only tracks on the road I'd used.

But I'd discovered two more sets of tracks.

One leading to Cormac's car, hidden around the other side of the building.

And a second, leading through a small dirt track, the overgrown bushes partly hiding it.

On my aerial map, I zoomed in on this second path, smaller and overgrown, where the Society's tire tracks had disappeared down.

I traced it along, sometimes losing it as it was nothing more than a faint impression among the treetops, until it exited onto a small side road.

My hands trembled as I hacked into the city's traffic cameras, tapping into the grid of Dublin's network.

It wasn't the first time I'd done this, but never with stakes this high. Every second that passed was one second closer to losing her.

Normally, it would take me less than a minute to get in. This time it took just over five.

I was rushing. Too emotional, near panic. I wanted Ava back too badly. It made me sloppy.

Finally…

I found a traffic camera on a light at the nearest intersection to the side road. I could just see the mostly hidden exit from Darkmoor forest.

My already thumping heart began to race even faster as I rewound the footage to the time just after Ava left me at Dr. Vale's office.

But even with speeding up the tape, the process was agonizingly slow.

My foot bounced uncontrollably against the leg of the chair and my skin felt like it was on fire. I scratched constantly at the back of my neck, rubbed at my burning eyes till they were raw, and drummed my fingers on the desk till the sound drove me mad.

My skin prickled as a black sedan pulled into the rain-soaked intersection on the video feed.

I sat up, my heart thudding in my chest as I squinted at the two figures in the car. Was that Ava in the passenger seat?

I paused it and zoomed in. I couldn't see the passenger's face, but they appeared to be sleeping.

Ava was in that sedan. I *knew* it.

*I've got you, rabbit. Hang on. I'm coming.*

I couldn't see the face of the man driving. He was nothing more than a shadow behind a rain-speckled windshield, wearing a baseball cap pulled down low under a black hood, concealing his face from any cameras, most likely on purpose.

I couldn't shake the cold dread from the base of my neck.

They were a pro. They knew someone—*me*—might be coming for them.

But *who*? Who was this High Lord?

I was used to wild swings of emotion. Passion and lust, anger and fury. But those were the kind of emotions that burned the blood. This inescapable cold was new to me: *fear*.

This Society was bigger than me. And what was most frightening was that they seemed to want Ava just as much as I did.

I was going to go after her. I was never going to stop. I was going to sacrifice everything to find her. I'd burn down the world to get her back.

But I couldn't shake off that sickly chill as I continued to stare at the hidden figure on my screen.

*It might not be enough.*

I looked up the license plate in the police database, hoping, praying that this High Lord was arrogant and used their own car. That my search would give me a name and an address.

Shit. The vehicle had recently been reported stolen.

Guess they were smart enough to cover their tracks. I could only hope I was smarter. Or at least more desperate.

The world was full of too much pain and evil to stop it all. No one could be expected to take that on their shoulders. Women would always disappear.

But they'd made one fatal mistake.

They'd taken *mine*.

Using the traffic cameras, I followed the black sedan, tracing its path through the streets as it made its way out of the city.

My stomach dropped as the black sedan merged onto the main highway that connected Dublin to the rest of Ireland.

There were dozens of exits and offramps. Hundreds of possible destinations. The chances of tracing the sedan using traffic cameras became next to impossible. It was like looking for a needle in a hundred different haystacks.

This left me with only one last option: hacking into the black sedan's GPS.

Most people didn't realize their cars had GPS trackers

built into their navigation systems. Manufacturers said it was for safety. I planned on turning that against them.

I started by running the car's make and model against the database of known GPS systems. Then using the plate number, I hacked into the network.

Every second I spent at that keyboard, I pictured what might be happening to Ava. My hands were shaking, my breath coming out in uneven bursts.

*Focus. Stay on task.*

But self-control had never been my strong suit. Sweat slicked my skin, dripping down my forehead as my fingers flew over the keys. I clenched my jaw, fighting the urge to smash the keyboard into the wall and watch it shatter.

When I finally cracked into the black sedan's GPS, my body was running on fumes.

I hadn't slept, hadn't eaten—hell, I didn't even know when I'd last showered. The stench of my own sweat clung to me, but I didn't care. None of it mattered. Not compared to this.

The locator blinked on the screen, a single pin on the outskirts of Dublin. An abandoned mansion.

I leaned closer, my pulse thudding in my ears. *I found you.* And now I had an address.

*Hang on, Ava. I'm coming.*

On the open highway, I willed the engine faster as I pictured arriving too late, finding Ava's battered body submerged in some murky pond, the rain splattering her cold, blue lips.

The engine screamed against my ears and the countryside whipped past without me seeing it as I neared the locator pin.

I nearly sent the car flipping side over side when I took the turn between some overgrown weeds. The tires lifted and crashed heavily back down onto an unpaved road lined with trees whose shadows were like mangled limbs in my hurtling headlights.

It was madness to push the car even faster on that uneven, pothole-riddled road, risking a broken axle, but I didn't care. I'd carry Ava back to Dublin in my arms if I had to.

The rusted gates that came into view were open and I accelerated through them without hesitation. Ava was somewhere at the end of this drive.

I could see little else than the throbbing blue locator pin on my phone and the second of clear windshield after the wipers cleared it before the droplets flooded back in.

I braked with such violence at the end of the drive that my seat belt choked off my breath and tore viciously at my throat. Gravel flew up from the tires and the car slid all the way to the base of the wide stone steps.

I lurched painfully back against the seat and gasped for air as the windshield wipers lashed against the downpour.

I was at a sprawling mansion whose farthest wings disappeared into the early dusk among low-hanging clouds. A large set of double doors were illuminated in the headlights before me.

I checked the screen of my phone as the rain hissed and popped on the overheated hood. I had arrived at the location of the pin.

I stepped out into the rain with my hand on the knife at my hip I'd named Dantès.

My eyes scanned the weed-infested drive. Another flash

of lightning illuminated a set of tire tracks flooded with water. Beneath a dead oak, I spotted the black sedan.

Ava was here.

This was the place.

If I had time to think things through, I may have chosen stealth as my entry strategy. But I was mad with desperation. I was being careless. I just had to hope I—or Ava—wouldn't pay for it.

The door of the mansion fell from its rusted hinges as I kicked it in. A billow of choking dust rose in the darkness. The beam of my flashlight cast my shadow long across a marble floor littered with dried leaves which scuttled like rats in the sudden rain-slashed gust of wind.

My heavy boots echoed in the vacuous space. I looked up in the center of the foyer and drops of rain fell from a hole in the ornate stained-glass ceiling, splashing onto my cheeks and eyelids. The cold seeped down into my entire body.

Where was Ava?

Just a few steps up the wooden grand staircase the boards creaked and moaned, threatening to give way if I pressed farther.

I retreated. It would have been impossible for someone to carry a limp body up those stairs without crashing through.

I investigated each room down the hallway on the first floor, kicking open every door with a cloud of dust.

A strike of lightning revealed chandeliers shattered on the floor and molding furniture covered in torn shrouds of plastic.

But I found no sign that anyone had been inside for years.

No High Lord.

No Ava.

My breath caught painfully in my chest and I lowered my gun.

No. But this is where the GPS had led me…

Fear crept into my mind. The silence of the empty mansion pressed against my ears. Had I underestimated my opponent? Was he clever enough to change vehicles? To use this as a decoy location?

My faceless enemy grew larger among the shadows.

I raced back through every room, just in case I'd missed something. I couldn't afford to panic, but I felt its cold grip closing in around my racing heart.

But the truth was inescapable; Ava was gone.

∼

By the time I got back to Dublin and pulled up on Dr. Vale's street, the fire trucks were already there, the street blocked off by yellow tape.

Firefighters swarmed the house like ants, and smoke billowed from the roof in thick, black clouds, staining the gray sky above.

*Bastards.* The Society was covering their tracks, scrubbing any trace of evidence I might've uncovered.

Everything that could've tied them to Liath's disappearance, to Ava, was gone.

*I'm too late.*

The flames were licking away every secret, every lie within Dr. Vale's house.

But they'd miscalculated. They thought they'd burned it all, but they hadn't.

Because I had one thing. One lead.

I had the foresight to grab Liath's video—the one marked *Insurance*—and it was more than enough to turn the tide.

I knew who Dr. Vale had been protecting.

I knew who had hurt Liath. And he was going to learn what real fear felt like.

He thought he could bury his secrets. But monsters like him had no idea what real monsters looked like.

I wasn't going to stop until I had every answer. Until I had him.

And this time, I wasn't playing by anyone's rules but my own.

I just had to hope it wasn't too late.

## AVA

Only when Ty had left me alone again could I fully process everything I'd learned.

Betrayal simmered in my veins, bitter and heavy. I felt betrayed by the fragments of my memories, by everything I thought I'd known.

*Scáth* was my childhood bully.

*Scáth*—the man who saved me, who put his life on the line, who haunted the shadows to keep me safe... that was Ciaran.

The boy I had hated.

The boy who hated me, despised me, who wanted nothing but to see me suffer.

He had been my protector all along.

And Ty—the gentle, protective boy who held my hand when I cried, who held me when I had nightmares, who swore to keep me safe—*that* Ty had become... this.

My captor.

My tormentor.

How could the caring boy I knew become this cold, controlling stranger?

My mind struggled to reconcile the memories of his boyish laughter, his kindness, and his sweet affection, with the man who now held me captive.

It didn't make sense. I couldn't fit the pieces together. Even though they were true.

Which meant Scáth—*Ciaran*—had lied to me.

He'd led me to believe that he was Ty.

The revelation crashed over me, leaving me dizzy, disoriented.

Had it been just another game to Ciaran? A sick game to manipulate me, to watch me fall in love with a ghost from my past? And to what end?

If Ty hadn't kidnapped me, would I have run away with Ciaran to have him... what? Leave me stranded on a remote island?

Was he just trying to get rid of me?

I'd given him my secrets, my fears, even pieces of my heart that I'd thought were unreachable.

How could I trust him now, knowing he'd worn a mask, knowing he'd hidden parts of himself just to keep me close?

That trust, once a steady heartbeat between us, was breaking, crumbling with every thought of his deception.

I could feel it—an ache that pulsed deep, a wound I didn't know how to heal.

Now I understood why I'd forgotten everything.

My time at Blackthorn—with Ty, Ciaran, and the professor—it was all too tightly knotted together, every memory twisted up with another, impossible to pull one out without dragging the rest along with it.

So, I'd buried it all, locked it away somewhere deep and dark, a place where none of it could reach me, my mind doing everything it could to protect me.

But being back here... this mansion was like a key, unlocking the parts of my mind I'd bolted shut.

Here in Blackthorn, my ghosts weren't just in my head. They were waiting in every room, shadows of the past slipping out from every corner, urging me to remember things I'd sworn I'd left behind.

The longer I stayed, the more memories dislodged, like old ghosts coming out of hiding, determined to remind me of the past I'd tried so hard to erase.

God. Too many memories assaulted me in this place.

After that first day when both brothers had crawled all over each other to befriend me, something had changed soon after.

I remembered the day Ciaran's behavior had switched, as if a totally different boy had taken over him.

*The rough wooden boards of the treehouse scratched at the thin fabric of my summer dress beneath my stomach, but I didn't care.*

*I should've.*

*It had only been a month since I arrived at Blackthorn Hall, but I already knew I'd get into trouble if the professor saw me dirty—always stay clean and presentable. That was the rule.*

*But hiding up here in the treehouse felt too good to care about that.*

*I lost myself in the pages of my pink leather journal, another present from Ty, the scratching of my pencil a quiet rhythm against the stillness of the afternoon. So when someone climbed up through the hatch next to me, I didn't notice right away.*

*The clearing of a throat—sharp and annoyed—cut through the peaceful silence, jolting me back to reality.*

*My heart skipped a beat, and I turned my head, a smile already forming.*

*But Ciaran glared at me with a hatred that I'd never seen on his face before.*

*"Get out of my treehouse." He spat out the words.*

*I blinked, struggling to process his words, trying to understand where this venom was coming from.*

*His treehouse? He and Ty had always shared it with me. The three of us had spent afternoons together up here, escaping the world below. Why was he suddenly acting like this?*

*"Ciaran... what did I do?" I asked, my voice small, unsure.*

*He folded his arms, scowling down at me with an expression that twisted my stomach. "You think you can just waltz in here and make everyone love you, don't you? You think you're so... special."*

*He said the last word like it was something foul, something he wanted to spit out.*

*"Ciaran, I..." I faltered, searching for the right thing to say.*

*Why was he so angry? A knot of worry settled in my chest as I reached out a hand, instinctively wanting to soothe him, to make things right.*

*But he jerked back, flinching as if my touch burned.*

*"Don't touch me, you orphaned freak."*

*I felt my cheeks flush with shame, instinctively curling my hand over the pink leather cover.*

*"Why are you being so mean?" The words slipped out, my voice barely above a whisper, the confusion thick in my throat.*

*For a split second, something flickered in his eyes—something almost like regret. But just as quickly, his gaze hardened, and he sneered down at me.*

*"Get out."*

*I stammered, but nothing I thought to say felt right. His face and mine were too close as we stared at one another.*

*I shivered, but there had been no breeze at all. The air hung heavy and still, like just before a terrible storm.*

*"Ty said I could be here," I answered, finally finding my voice. "He said—"*

*"I don't give a shit what Ty said," came his low, trembling voice. "You* don't *belong here."*

*His hands shook on the sides of the ladder, his jaw tightened so intensely that I thought it might break.*

*"I have every right to be here," I said, defiance rising in me. "I'm the professor's daughter."*

*He laughed wickedly. "You're not his real daughter, are you? You're no one's daughter."*

*"You're my brother," I continued. "And brothers share."*

*With horrifying speed, he wrapped his fingers around my wrist with a bone-cracking grip. A cry of pain slipped from my lips.*

*This only seemed to enrage him more. He looked at me with fury in his icy eyes.*

*"Brother?" he hissed, "Never call me that disgusting word ever again."*

Something had changed in Ciaran that day.

At the time I hadn't understood what. Why.

But now I did.

He must have seen his father *with* me. How, I had no idea. But he'd gotten the wrong idea.

His behavior toward me just got worse after that. It

ended up driving a wedge not just between him and me, but also him and Ty.

His cruelness grew worse and even more twisted—I remember finding the pages of my journal, the secrets of my young tender heart, wallpapered across the school lockers.

I'd walked into the hallway to find Ciaran, surrounded by students, reading them out to everyone in a high-pitched voice and twirling his pretend hair, mocking me. *"Ciaran is so cute but why does he have to be so mean? ...Ty accidentally touched my boob last night and my nipple ached but not in a bad way."*

I remembered how he'd taunted me about how ghosts roamed the Blackthorn Halls, that they hated little girls, especially stupid ones named Ava. I hadn't been able to sleep after that, at least not until Ty started creeping into my bed.

I remembered how Ciaran would steal my shoes and drag them through the mud, leaving them around the mansion for the professor to find and punish *me* for it.

Ciaran had *hated* me. So how had he become my protector? How much of him—of Scáth—was really *him*.

And why would he let me think he was his brother?

But deep down, I knew.

Ty had been my safe place, my sanctuary from the twisted world we grew up in.

And Ciaran... he still carried the weight of guilt from how he'd treated me, how he'd been so cruel to me, punishing me for a crime I never committed, when he thought I was complicit with his father.

He knew how deeply Ty and I had connected, and he'd used that bond to pull me close to him.

Maybe it was his way of rewriting the past, of giving us both a second chance at something real. A way to be the person he hadn't been then—only now, under the shadow of his brother's name.

Despite my anger at Ciaran, I knew, somewhere deep within me, that he'd come to love me.

I couldn't pinpoint when or how it had shifted, but somehow, the boy who'd once tormented me had become the man who cared.

I had to trust in that.

I had to believe he loved me, missed me, and was out there searching for me—otherwise, I wouldn't survive here.

I wouldn't have any reason to fight, to plan, to cling to that faint hope of finding my way back to Dublin. Back to Scáth—back to Ciaran.

A surge of hope welled in my chest.

Scáth and I loved each other; we could start over, build something real from the ashes. If we could make it to the other side of all this, maybe we could finally be together, without secrets or shadows.

But first, I had to escape. And so far, every attempt had failed me.

I realized with a sinking feeling that there was no one left to save me.

I had no choice but to do Ty's twisted therapy. And hope I could save myself.

# THE WARDEN

◈

I held out another vial to Ava, knowing what it meant. Knowing that she'd hate me for it.

And she did, standing there in the cursed nightgown I forced her to wear, her eyes burning into me, like the hatred she carried for me was an actual, physical heat.

I'd prepared myself for this, steeled myself against her hatred, against feeling anything at all.

But it was harder than I ever imagined to be the target of her disgust—her loathing. It dug under my skin in ways I wasn't equipped for.

Her fingers brushed against mine when she took the vial, sending a shiver through me, one I couldn't suppress fast enough. My body betrayed me every time she was near.

For a second, she gripped the vial in her hand, her forearm trembling, her knuckles white. I thought she was going to throw it, just like she had before. Smash it against the wall and unleash that fury I'd seen flickering behind her eyes since I'd brought her here.

But she didn't. She pulled out the stopper and drank

down the vial in one long gulp, her throat working against the liquid.

I watched her, my chest tight, desperate to say something, anything, to bridge the impossible distance between us.

She frowned, her nose scrunching.

"I added strawberry flavor," I said, the words tumbling out too eagerly, my voice awkward in the silence. "It won't affect the active ingredients, but... I just thought..."

I trailed off, watching her reaction, searching for anything in her expression that might show she remembered liking the sweet red fruit. Or maybe she didn't anymore.

It had been five years. Five long years. Too long.

She'd grown into a woman, and the only way I'd known her was through the fractured lens of stalking her after I'd escaped from prison, watching from afar like a mere ghost tethered to her life.

And then I'd kidnapped her. The weight of that settled in my chest like a stone.

For a moment, jealousy ripped through me. Ciaran had been the one by her side, watching her every day. He got to be her shadow.

Hell, she even called him that now. Her *Scáth*.

It was a name I could never claim, not now, not after everything.

There was flicker of something in Ava's eyes, maybe confusion, maybe... gratitude?

I couldn't tell. Emotions had become a foreign language to me after so many years of deadening them, callousing myself over, like burying them under thick layers of ice.

At least, I thought they were dead.

But Ava…

Everything about Ava made my nerves raw and jangled. Like all the emotions I'd repressed over the last five years were all resurfacing at once, battering underneath a sheet of ice that was getting thinner with every second in her presence.

I wasn't sure how to handle it. Any of it.

But I had to. I had to be her rock while she fell apart.

I had to be her safety as I broke her, so I could put her back together again.

My eyes never left her, watching every subtle shift in her body.

I noticed the tremble in her knees first, the way her breath caught as the drug started to take hold. Every little thing about her, I noticed.

And I was ready when she fell, catching her in my arms before she hit the ground.

Holding her close, my heart screamed with apologies that I'd never let pass my lips.

*I'm sorry, Ava. I love you too much to stop now.*

I carried her through the mansion, the eerie silence broken only by the sound of my footsteps echoing off the wooden floors. Every creak of the ancient wood, every shift of the shadows felt like it carried the weight of a hundred unseen eyes watching me.

This place, once grand, now felt like a tomb—filled with memories that should have stayed buried.

But it wasn't just the house. It was the past clawing at my heels, threatening to pull me under with every step I took.

Especially as I passed the familiar polished wood of my brother's now empty room.

*I kicked open the door into Ciaran's bedroom, the walls covered in posters of metal bands—Slipknot, Metallica, Iron Maiden—the kind of noise that made my head hurt.*

*The heavy smell of cigarette smoke hit me before I even spotted him, lounging by the open window like he didn't have a care in the world.*

*His back was half turned to me, one leg hanging over the side of the window, the other propped up casually on the sill.*

*For a moment, I wished I could be him—untouchable, careless, cool, like the world couldn't affect his fun no matter what it threw his way.*

*But I couldn't be like him. I was too different. Too sensitive. I cared too much about everything.*

*"You stole my biology textbook," I snapped, not bothering with a greeting.*

*I slammed the door behind me with enough force to rattle the posters on the walls and stormed across the room.*

*Ciaran glanced at me, flicking ash from his cigarette out the window, completely unfazed by my outburst.*

*"Nice to see you, too, brother," he muttered, barely lifting his eyes.*

*I grabbed him by the collar, yanking him back from the window so he had no choice but to look at me.*

*"Where is it?" I demanded, my voice tight, my frustration boiling over.*

*Ciaran didn't even flinch. He just flicked his cigarette out the window, watching it fall onto the gravel below before turning his lazy gaze back to me. "Chill, nerd. It's just a textbook."*

*"It's* mine.*"*

*Ciaran smirked, shrugging my hands off him like none of this mattered. And to him, it didn't. Not anymore. Not since Ma died.*

*I'd thrown myself into studying after she passed. I needed something to focus on, something to drown out the emptiness she left behind. Debate team, science club, the fencing team, endless hours buried in textbooks. I thought maybe if I kept my head down, if I stayed busy enough, the grief wouldn't catch up to me.*

*Ciaran... he went the opposite way.*

*He lit cigarettes instead of candles, downed whiskey instead of tears. Stole our father's Rolls Royce to impress college girls or drove his damned motorbike recklessly through the county like he was invincible.*

*We used to be inseparable, almost impossible to tell us apart—we'd play the most outrageous pranks on our servants, tricking them as we pretended to be the same boy.*

*Our ma's death several years ago was like a lightning strike, swift and cruel, cleaving us into two different people.*

*But he was still my brother.*

*And I missed him.*

*Even though he pissed me off more than anyone ever could, I still missed him.*

*Before I could yell at him some more, the sound of our father's car crunching over the gravel below cut through the tension like a knife.*

*Ciaran's smug look faltered for a second, a flash of something close to fear crossing his face.*

*I slammed his window shut before our father could notice us.*

*We both froze, staring out through the glass as the old doors of the Rolls Royce groaned open.*

*Our father, ever the stoic figure, stepped out in his usual crisp, tailored suit.*

*But it wasn't just him.*

*The other passenger door opened and out stepped a girl.*

*She had dark hair, long and slightly tousled, catching the afternoon light as it brushed across her face like a soft whisper.*

*I sucked in a breath, my heart beating faster in my chest.*

*The way she nervously tucked her hair behind her ear, her delicate face framed by that cascade of dark waves—she was... ethereal.*

*She was the most beautiful girl I'd ever seen.*

*"She's hot," Ciaran said, his voice cutting through my awe like a blunt knife.*

*"She makes the stars pale by comparison," I muttered under my breath, feeling a pull inside me I couldn't quite explain.*

*Ciaran let out a sharp snort, giving me a sideways look. "That's what I fucking said."*

*With my nose pressed against the glass, I couldn't tear my eyes away from her as she stood there, staring up at the towering gothic structure that was Blackthorn Hall.*

*There was fear in her eyes, uncertainty, and all I wanted to do was protect her. To promise her that nothing in this godforsaken house would ever touch her.*

*"Dibs," Ciaran declared, his own nose pressed against the glass now, mirroring mine.*

*I turned and shoved his shoulder hard. "She's a person, Ciaran. You can't just call dibs on her."*

*"I can and I fucking did, nerd." He shoved me back, his tone light, but his eyes gleamed with something darker, something more possessive.*

Ciaran and I had been fighting for Ava ever since. For a while, I'd been winning.

But it appeared I had now lost.

I'd waited too long. Stayed away too long. Taken too much time in making sure everything was perfect. But perfection was a lie I'd told myself. A lie to mask my cowardice.

While I was planning, Ciaran was acting.

He broke his promise—the promise he made because of what I did *for him*. The sacrifice I made *for him*.

And now? Now he'd stolen her from me. He got to her first, wormed his way into her heart, into her soul. He had tainted her, twisted everything that was meant to be mine. Corrupted her in ways I couldn't undo.

And the worst part? She loved him for it.

It was in the way she said his name, as if it carried a weight mine never could. It cut me, sharper than any blade.

Her eyes—when she thought I was him—burned with a kind of longing I'd never seen directed at me. She looked at him like he was her salvation.

What did that make me?

I wasn't her protector. I wasn't her savior. I was the one who let her slip through my fingers. And no matter how many ghosts haunted this place, none haunted me more than the thought of her loving him.

I'd lost her to him, and I wasn't sure I could ever get her back.

The bitter truth gnawed at me, hollowing out the pit of my stomach, as I carried her to the place that haunted her.

The pain I would force upon her—even for her own good—would drive a wedge even further between us.

I could already see it happening, feel the distance between us growing. Every time she looked at me, she saw her captor, her tormentor. Her warden.

Not the boy who loved her, not the one who was trying to save her. No.

She saw the monster in me.

It didn't matter, though. Saving Ava was the most important thing. More important than my pride, more important than my heart, more important than the future I had dreamed of with her.

Because that's what it might come down to in the end. To save her, I'd have to destroy parts of her, rip out the darkness buried deep inside, expose the wounds that had festered for years.

I'd break her to rebuild her, and she might never forgive me for it.

But I had no other choice.

Even if it meant losing her forever.

I lowered Ava to the couch, taking my time as I arranged her limbs and hair. Even though she couldn't move, tears shone in her eyes and her breath was jagged and shallow. She was terrified.

I reached for the buttons of her nightgown, but my fingers felt thick and clumsy.

As I undressed her, my heart pounded like I was a scared teenage boy again. I couldn't help but stare at her nakedness.

At her creamy skin, marred only by fading rope burns on her wrists.

Her wide, frantic eyes glazed over, like she was staring into the jagged maw of whatever horrors lay buried in her past.

Her fear hit me square in the chest, knocking the breath

out of me. The fear in her eyes, the way her body trembled even in its paralysis—it was unbearable.

I wanted to turn away, to pretend I wasn't the one doing this to her.

But I couldn't look away. I had put her here, forced her into this. So I had to *be here* with her.

Her pain wasn't just hers—it was mine, a sharp, twisting knife that dug into my gut every time her breath hitched or her eyes glazed over with terror.

It made me want to pull her into my arms, tell her it was all over, that she didn't have to do this anymore.

For a moment, fury surged within me—directed entirely at myself. *What the hell are you doing to her? How could you put her through this agony?*

Bastard. Evil. Monster.

The self-loathing clawed at me, but I pushed it down. I had to. This was the only way. The only way to save her.

She had to fall into the depths of hell before she could climb her way back out reborn—but I would do it with her. I would not leave her side. Even when she begged me to. Even when she hated me for it.

"It's *me*, Ava," I whispered, my voice breaking as I pressed kisses down her naked body, licking away the ghost of his hands, of his filth. "It's *my* mouth. *My* tongue."

She was already soaked when I reached her pussy lips, her inner thighs coated with her arousal.

The glistening proof that this was actually working—the therapy, the unraveling of her past—was the only thing that kept me going.

It was the single thread I clung to, the faint signal beneath her fear that told me I wasn't just torturing her for nothing. This wasn't cruelty for cruelty's sake. It was a means to an end. A way to cleanse her, to rewrite her history.

Every tremble, every flicker of pain in her eyes, wasn't just reliving the worst moments of her life—it was erasing them, piece by piece.

I was recording over her memories with my hands and my tongue, wiping them clean. Flushing out the darkness that had burrowed so deep inside her. If I could just suck that poison out of her mind, no matter how much it hurt in the process, then maybe—*maybe*—I could save her.

Her juices running down her thighs and soaking the couch was proof that this pain had a purpose. Proof that I wasn't just breaking her but fixing her.

Her musky scent drew me in, inspiring a primal need in me that took over as I buried my face into her folds and thrust my tongue into her entrance.

"My tongue, Ava," I muttered against her clit. "I won't stop until there's only *me*."

Like a conductor, I slowly, achingly brought her body up to the edge, using all the minute signs of her body to guide me—the way her pupils dilated and her breath quickened. The hardening of her nipples and the goosebumps that scattered across her skin.

Deep down, beneath the need to save her, I had a selfish reason.

A hope—no, more than that, a desperate craving—that this therapy would do more than just cleanse her of the past.

That it would strip away any trace of my brother from her. Erase the imprint he'd left on her mind, on her body. I wanted her to forget the way her heart had learned to beat for him, the loyalty she'd mistakenly attached to him.

She wasn't meant for him. She was meant for *me*.

Before Ava tipped over the edge, I pulled away and quickly stripped so that I was as naked and vulnerable as she was.

I pulled myself up her body, my cock naturally falling between her legs. The need to thrust into her surged in me at the feel of her soaked entrance, but I pushed it down.

Ava came first. Whatever my needs were, they came second.

She looked through me, seeing the ghost of the man who hurt her, fear and pain clouding her eyes, spilling over as tears.

I gripped her chin. "Eyes on me, Ava."

Her gaze darted wildly around, then locked on mine. Her pupils focused, and the darkness cleared.

The corner of my mouth tipped up. "There you are, my hummingbird."

I licked the salt from her cheeks and I held her, kept her eyes on mine, willing her to stay with me as I pushed into her.

# AVA

The matted curls of the professor's sweaty chest hovered over my face as he stole from me.

Inside my frozen body I screamed and threw myself against the bars of my physical prison, my own body turned into a cage.

The weight of him and the sourness of his sweat making bile rise up my throat.

"Eyes on me, Ava."

Ty's voice sliced through the suffocating fog, shattering the professor into a blur of tears.

*Ty? Where are you? Save me!*

I searched the mist for him, my thoughts swirling in panic, but then his face broke through like a lighthouse piercing the night. The sharp, chiseled lines of his features came into focus, and a wave of relief crashed over me.

My body stilled as I became painfully aware of the heat radiating from him, his hard, muscled body pressed flush against mine, and his thick cock resting at my pussy entrance, leaving me feeling empty and needing to be filled.

The corner of Ty's perfect lips pulled up into a faint unexpected smile. *Wow, the cold warden smiles.*

"There you are, my hummingbird." he said, his voice warm like he was welcoming me home.

He cleaned up my tears from my cheeks with his warm tongue and the tip of his cock slipped into my entrance.

For a moment, panic surged through me, clawing at my chest.

*No, don't.*

I wasn't his.

I was Ciaran's.

Every nerve screamed that *this* would be a betrayal—that somehow the *therapy* that had come before might be excused as... cleansing.

But for Ty to *know* me—to mesh with my body while he stared into my eyes—was unforgiveable.

But I couldn't stop him. I couldn't pull away. I couldn't even plead with him, *no*.

My body wouldn't respond to my mind, and I was trapped in this moment where the lines between the two brothers blurred.

Ty slid his cock into me, the hollowness filling, my wet, soft body welcoming him even as it betrayed me.

As guilt weaved inside me, a louder voice whispered through the cracks—insistent, unrelenting. Let go. Give in. Accept.

This was out of my control.

Wasn't it?

My limbs were paralyzed, my body no longer mine to command. If I couldn't stop him, if I couldn't fight back, did that make me complicit? Was it even my fault?

Could I really be blamed for surrendering to the inevitable? For letting Ty—no, forcing Ty—to make these decisions for me?

Guilt weaved through me, but with it came a strange, twisted sense of relief.

I didn't have to fight. I couldn't. And that thought made the burden just a little easier to bear.

Pleasure slammed through me as he began to thrust, slowly at first, then faster. This time, inside my frozen body, I twisted around in its fiery delight, letting it burn away my demons.

Even when the darkness edged at my vision, all I *felt* was Ty. He might be my warden, but he was also my guard. My protector.

Ty gripped my face, trapping me in his stare, and pulled my thigh up around his hip so he could fuck me deeper. His cock slammed against that sensitive spot inside me.

"You're *mine*," he whispered, he promised. "Only ever *mine*."

My body exploded and a blinding light burned through everything. Every nerve was on fire, every cell exploding with energy.

In my mind I was screaming, but the sound was swallowed by the overwhelming sensation of my world shattering into a million pieces.

I became aware of Ty pulling me into his arms, holding me as my body stitched itself back together again. This time I straddled him, my thighs around his waist, my head on his shoulder as the life returned to my limbs.

I wanted to tell him that I hated him, but I swallowed it down.

I feared I'd start crying if I spoke. I was tired of crying. And I feared he would call me out, point out how easily my pussy welcomed him, proof of my lie. That I didn't really hate him at all. Or at least, my pussy didn't.

He was still hard inside me. He... he hadn't let himself come.

Why not?

"It's going to be okay," he promised against my hair.

I buried my face deeper into his neck, letting the scent of sandalwood and musk envelop me—a scent that, against all logic, had begun to feel like safety. How had it come to this?

My tormentor was becoming my solace.

Even though I knew he would hurt me again, that more pain was inevitable, there was something undeniable about the way he held me. As twisted as it was, he was also my salvation. The balm to my wounds. My safe harbor in the storm.

Over Ty's shoulder, I stared at part of the wall as a distant memory shimmered.

The shadow of a younger Ciaran appeared, watching from the narrow crack... of a secret panel I'd forgotten existed.

He was breathtaking, with that angelic face and the predator's gleam in his icy eyes. Like a panther lurking in the dark, beautiful and lethal, fury radiating off him in waves.

*"How could you let him touch you?"*

His words, once spat at me, now wrapped around my throat, tightening, stealing my breath.

Guilt clawed at my insides. Ciaran had to understand, didn't he? This wasn't intimacy—it was survival. It was Ty's twisted form of therapy. I wasn't responsible. I wasn't to blame for the way my body responded. I couldn't be.

Could I?

The pleasure that flickered through me wasn't my fault. It couldn't be. But that whisper of guilt gnawed at me. *How could you let him touch you?*

I blinked, and the memory of Ciaran vanished, the secret panel closing. But the consequences remained, lingering in the space between my skin and Ty's touch.

And I feared that even when Ty set me free, when I returned to Ciaran, it could never be the same. I wouldn't be the same girl he knew; I could never be *her* again.

And that might destroy us.

∼

I woke slowly, the heaviness of sleep lingering in my limbs.

For a moment, confusion swirled in my head—no nightmares. I'd expected them, as if I deserved to be tormented in my sleep after everything that I'd remembered.

But there was only silence.

Then I realized why.

I felt a presence behind me before I heard the softest masculine sigh, the sound drifting over my skin like a cold breeze, sending a shiver down the back of my neck.

*Ty.*

Slowly, I turned to face him, my heart leaping as my eyes locked on his face.

It was softened from sleep, his features less guarded, more... vulnerable than I had seen in days.

His presence, so close and warm, bled into me, and I

hated that it felt… comforting. I should have been afraid. I should have moved away, but instead, something in me softened.

*I blinked drowsily, brushing the dried tears from my eyes as my mattress dipped and a familiar warmth settled in beside me. I knew, even half-asleep, that it was Ty.*

*Somehow, despite the professor locking me in my bedroom, unfair punishment for muddy shoes that hadn't been mine, he'd found a way in. Again.*

*"How did you get in?" I whispered, rolling over to face him, the edges of his face barely visible in the dim moonlight.*

*Ty gave a quiet scoff, wrapping an arm around my waist. "You really think a locked door is going to keep me from you?"*

*A small shiver ran down my spine as his breath fanned softly against my hair. The scent of him—sandalwood, something dark and comforting—wrapped around me.*

*"If he finds you here, you'll get in trouble," I murmured, my voice barely audible, but even I knew it didn't sound like much of a protest.*

*He buried his face in my hair and breathed in deeply, as if memorizing the smell of me, sending another shiver through me. "Worth it."*

We'd just slept next to each other. Nothing had happened. I hadn't done anything wrong, so why did guilt twist in my gut like this?

Flashes from last night crept in. I remembered Ty carrying me to my bed after that horrific therapy had drained every ounce of energy from my body. I remember him tucking me in and climbing in after me, spooning me, wrapping me in his warmth.

And I took it, greedy for his solace.

I thought I even remembered begging him to please stay.

He did. He hadn't left. He'd stayed beside me all night.

It was exactly what he used to do when we were younger whenever I had nightmares or was too afraid of the darkness around Blackthorn Hall.

That memory made something inside me soften, made something warm and familiar coil in my belly.

No. This wasn't the same boy who'd been my best friend, my protector. This wasn't *him* anymore. This man was a stranger. A monster.

Ty's lids fluttered, his brows furrowing.

"No," he muttered, his limbs thrashing against the sheets. "*Stop.*"

The fear in his voice bled into my chest, tightening around my heart, making it seize.

He was having a nightmare.

I knew about those. Too well.

Without thinking, I lunged forward, risking the wild swing of his strong arms, and wrapped myself around him. As if I could anchor him to the present, pull him away from the nightmare.

"Ty, wake up," I begged. "It's just a nightmare."

I squeezed him, willing him to come back to me, to now.

His eyes snapped open with a gasp, but they didn't see me at first. They looked *through* me, past me, as if I wasn't even there.

For a moment, I saw a glimmer of raw fear in those pale-blue eyes—something I shouldn't recognize in him, but I did.

His fear mirrored my own.

Then his gaze focused on mine. He blinked, his gaze

darting around my room and the coldness bled over his tormented features, slowly erasing the vulnerability I had caught a glimpse of.

I shouldn't have cared. This man—my captor, my tormentor—shouldn't have been a mystery I needed to solve. But his pain mirrored mine too much. It snuck under my skin, becoming a part of me.

And I needed to know.

"What were you dreaming about?" I dared to ask, my voice barely above a whisper.

Ty shook his head as if to banish the last of the shadows clinging to him. His jaw tightened, and the mask slid back into place, rigid and unyielding.

Disappointment wove through me, bitter and unexpected.

Ty cleared his throat. The mattress shifted as he climbed out of bed and walked around to my side.

"Go wash your face," he said in that infuriatingly calm voice. "Then we'll start."

His shadow loomed over me, and a jolt of fear crawled up my spine.

But I kept my voice steady. "Are you making me do therapy today?"

He tilted his head, expression unreadable. "In a way."

My head spun at the possibilities, dread settling like lead in my stomach. *What does that mean?*

Fear gripped me, tightening around my throat as the memories from yesterday surged back—memories I'd been trying to shove deep down where they couldn't hurt me. I recoiled from the images that flashed across my mind, bile rising in my throat.

"This exercise will make you feel better," he added softly.

Better? What twisted form of "better" could he possibly mean?

He held out his hand toward me, an offering—or a demand. His face was calm, but there was something in his eyes, a flicker of hesitation.

I stared at his outstretched hand, my pulse quickening.

"You used to trust me," he said quietly, the tiniest crack of vulnerability breaking through his cold facade.

I swallowed hard. "You've never held me hostage before."

A flash of something crossed his face—regret, maybe, or frustration—before he schooled his features back into that cold mask. His hand remained outstretched, unmoving.

I sighed, knowing full well I didn't have a choice.

Ty liked to make it seem like I did, but in the end, it was all an illusion. I could fight him every step of the way and just wear myself out, or I could surrender now and get whatever new torture he had in store out of the way.

My hand trembled as I reached for his. "Let's get this over with."

# AVA

After I came out of the bathroom, Ty was gone. The room felt colder without him in it, an unsettling emptiness lingering in the air.

I crossed to the door, testing the handle, but of course it was still locked.

"Hello?" I called, frustration spilling out. "Ty?"

No answer. Just silence. Not even the crackle of speakers.

A cool draft tousled my hair, causing me to spin on my heel, eyes darting around. That's when I noticed something off about one of the ornate wall panels.

I stepped closer, and another waft of cold air brushed my skin, prickling goosebumps up my arm.

The panel was slightly ajar. It was a secret door.

My heart raced at the discovery.

*So that's how Ty always managed to slip into my room at night.* Even when the professor locked me in as punishment, Ty always found a way in.

I grabbed the edge of the panel and swung it open like a door.

Behind it, a narrow, dim passageway stretched ahead, the air thick with the smell of damp and musty old wood.

My breath hitched as I peered inside. Thin streams of light filtered through ornate vents high above, just enough to reveal a few meters ahead.

*Secret passageways.* I'd heard that old mansions like this had them, narrow tunnels between the walls so the staff could move unseen. Some of them might even lead to a secret way out.

Goosebumps rippled over my skin as I stepped inside, feeling the icy draft wrap around me.

With my fingertips, I traced the rough walls as I moved forward. Each step took me closer to whatever twisted game Ty had planned for me.

My heart thundered in my chest, my breath loud and harsh in the confined space. Claustrophobia tightened around me like a vise, the walls pressing closer as the air became even colder.

Then, up ahead, I saw it. Light.

I stumbled forward, pushing open the panel, and to my surprise, it opened into the grand ballroom of Blackthorn Hall that took my breath away.

Gleaming ornate gold designs curved along the dark walls and the arched ceilings. Crystal chandeliers hung overhead, dripping with gold and casting fractured light across the room.

The dark wood floors stretched on forever, polished to the point that I could almost see my reflection—faint, ghostlike. The reflection of me from long ago as a memory fragment hit me.

*Ty led me around the ballroom, his hand warm around mine, guiding me as if he belonged to this grand, golden room.*

*I caught my breath as I took it all in, the massive chandelier casting a warm glow over the dark polished floors and the shimmering walls.*

*It was the most beautiful room I'd ever seen, like something out of a fairy tale.*

*I felt out of place in my plain dress and bare feet.*

*Ty turned, his gaze finding mine as he smiled, that soft, steady smile that always managed to calm me.*

*"Dance with me," he murmured, his voice deep and warm, a teasing glint in his eyes.*

*"But... I don't know how," I managed, a bit lost for words, barely noticing as his hands slid to my waist, pulling me closer.*

*"Just let me..."*

*My heart raced, and I looked up at him, not sure what to say or feel.*

*He was so gentle, his touch respectful as he moved us around the room, as though he were handling something precious.*

*Images of Ciaran flashed through my thoughts—his intense, sharp-eyed gaze, the way his presence filled a room, reckless and challenging.*

*The thought startled me, guilt prickling at my skin as I tried to push it away.*

*I wished it was Ciaran here holding me instead.*

I blinked and I was back in the present, back in the Blackthorn ballroom.

The vast space had been altered—turned into a makeshift gym, weights and mats lined up on one side.

There were a few machines I vaguely recognized from the sporadic health kicks Lisa and I hopped on (and off)—a treadmill, a punching bag, medicine balls, yoga mats, and God knows what other torture devices.

The grandeur of it clashed violently with the raw, utilitarian setup.

"Do you remember what I told you?" Ty's voice startled me.

I whipped around and saw him leaning casually against the ropes of a boxing ring I hadn't noticed before.

He was watching me, his gaze heavy with the same intensity that always made my stomach twist in a mix of fear and... something else.

"You said a lot of things," I replied, forcing nonchalance as I stepped slowly toward him, my eyes scanning the once lavish ballroom.

I remembered this place. I remembered hiding behind the velvet curtains, watching the professor's guests in their fine clothes as they danced and laughed.

My eyes flicked to the towering glass door stretching from floor to ceiling that led out to a wraparound stone balcony.

They were all barred. And locked, I bet.

No way out. Still no escape.

Ty had swapped his usual black button-up shirt for a tight black tank. It revealed his tattoos, their vivid black color made his untouched skin look like marble. With black tape around his wrists, black pants, and a black mat in the ring, his blue eyes flashed like sapphires.

"You're strong, Ava," he said, the same words he'd whispered to me last night as I fell asleep taking root in the corners of my heart. "You just need someone to *show* you."

I paused halfway to the ring and crossed my arms over my chest, fighting back a shiver.

"Come here," he said.

I ran my tongue along my teeth, hesitating. Strong? I felt anything but. My legs shook beneath me, my pulse refusing to settle.

"Don't make me come get you," Ty said in the same calm voice, but it was clear it was a threat.

I had a feeling that *this* Ty didn't bluff.

Setting my jaw, I stepped forward and stopped at the edge of the raised ring.

He leaned over the ropes and his hands encircled my waist, lifting me from the floor like I weighed nothing. He placed me on the edge of the platform with nothing but the ropes between us.

For a moment, we stood toe to toe, his fingers gripping my waist, the warmth of his breath brushing my forehead.

The icy exterior of his mask seemed to dissolve, his gaze flickering with an intensity that seared through me.

It was too much—too close.

My pulse quickened, my mind screaming for distance, yet my body betrayed me, drawn in by the heat between us.

I wasn't supposed to be looking at him like this, as though I wanted his lips on mine.

I tore my eyes away from his, my gaze catching on the ink across his firm upper chest, a raven with wings outstretched across his collarbone as though ready to take flight. Its mechanical heart was exposed, gears and cogs spilling out as if being torn apart.

My fingers twitched with the urge to touch the ink, to trace the lines, but I held back.

Ty lifted the rope, his eyes cold and fixed on mine, waiting.

I ducked beneath, the weight of his gaze as heavy as chains.

"Your clothes are in the corner," he said.

I found a pile with a sports bra, gym shorts, socks, and shoes, all in black. All in my size.

"Where do I change?" I asked.

Ty stood in the corner opposite me, adjusting the straps on his wrists. He lifted his eyes to me.

"This is no time to become modest, Ava." His eyes flashed with something hungry. "It's not like I haven't seen it all before."

I repressed the urge to sarcastically remind him that he'd only seen me naked because he drugged me and stripped me.

I gritted my teeth, grabbed the hem of my night slip, and pulled it off over my head.

Naked again before Ty except for a simple pair of black panties, I shivered under his dark gaze.

Heat flooded my cheeks, and I hated it. Hated how aware I was of his attention, how my skin burned under his gaze. Hated how I rushed to pull on the workout clothes, hated the flush of heat that rose in his presence.

When I'd fully dressed, I took my time braiding my hair back off my face. Delaying the inevitable.

When I finally turned around, Ty stepped toward me, another set of straps in hand. He unrolled them with slow precision, his eyes never leaving mine, a silent promise hanging between us.

Without a word, he wrapped my wrists, every brush of his fingers against my skin sending shivers across my body. A wetness trickled into my panties and my hardened nipples poked against my sports bra.

There was no hope in thinking he didn't notice. Nothing escaped him.

I stared at the mat and tried to get my breathing back under control as Ty finished and stepped away.

"Attack me," he said as he faced me from the center of the ring.

I laughed weakly.

"You've attacked me before," he said.

"I ended up on the floor," I reminded him.

"You're going to learn *not* to end up on the floor. Now attack me."

I walked up to him and made a lame effort of pushing my fist into his chest.

Ty shoved me back. I slammed back onto the mat so hard it stole the air from my lungs.

"What was that for?" I asked angrily when I could finally breathe.

"That was for not taking this seriously," he said.

I propped myself up on my elbows, chest heaving. "And what exactly is 'this'?"

Ty's face darkened at the sarcastic tone of my voice. He glared at me as an ominous silence descended over the ballroom.

"Get up."

When he growled in that low voice, everything in me wanted to obey.

The second I was on my feet, Ty advanced on me. Even before, in the bedroom, he hadn't been fast like this.

He spun me around and crushed me to his chest. He grabbed a handful of my hair before I even had time to think of escaping.

# AVA

I'd made the mistake of underestimating Ty's viciousness.

He held me in his brutal grasp and I was left breathless and shaking like a leaf against the iron of his body.

I closed my eyes and bit my trembling lower lip as Ty ran his free palm across my breast, down along my stomach, and over my hip to my pinned wrist.

His fingers forced mine into a fist.

I yelped with fear when he twisted my body, forcing my hips open.

His leg wrapped around mine and pushed it backward. He pulled my hair till my chin was lifted, oblivious to my whimpers of pain.

His breath was hot and pressing against my ear. "*This* is how you stand."

With his fingers wrapped around my hand, he guided my fist forward.

"Power comes from here," he said, urging his groin against my buttocks and upper thigh.

Our bodies twisted together as he repeated the movement with my fist, his hips and body guiding mine.

"You must be balanced yet light," he growled into my ear. "Nimble. In control."

Ty's heat had melted into me. His closeness had made my limbs pliant to his command.

When I'd felt the hardness of his against my back, unwanted need surged through me.

"Like *you* were in control when you *punished* me in the dining room?" I hissed.

Ty shoved me roughly away from him.

I caught myself against the ropes, gripping them till my knuckles shone white.

"Attack me," he said.

This time I didn't laugh. I didn't hesitate. I wanted to hurt him.

I lashed out, my punch connecting with Ty's jaw with enough force to make me cry out and clutch my hand to my chest.

"Good rotation through the hips," Ty said, rolling his jaw. "But you need to keep your weight more centered. Try again."

I stared at him, on the verge of tears.

"Push *through* the pain," he said.

"Fuck you."

"There's no other way to the other side."

Snarling at him, I said, "*Ciaran* had a way."

Ty advanced on me and I slipped out of his reach, circling along the ropes to keep distance between us.

Ty grinned darkly. "Good."

He swung at me, but I could tell he was doing it deliberately slow.

I ducked before glancing a blow off his arm.

"Better."

My heart rate accelerated as he forced me toward a corner. He had me trapped.

I reacted out of instinct and I punched at his ribs to create an opening to escape.

It wasn't until I was gasping for breath that I noticed—I'd used the hand I thought I'd injured.

I stretched out my fingers, the ache sharp but not unbearable. My knuckles throbbed, but nothing was broken. I flexed them again, slower this time, testing their strength.

When I looked up, Ty was watching me, his lips curved into the hint of a wicked grin. His eyes gleamed with something dark, something knowing.

"Pain isn't to be feared," he said. "*Use* it."

I curled my fingers into a fist. The ache was still there, but it was different. It was physical, something I could grasp, something I could control. It cut through the chaos inside, grounding me, giving me a way to cope.

This pain was tangible. Manageable. And it drowned out the pain on the inside.

I circled Ty again and my heart raced, an unfamiliar sense of power creeping into my veins, a smile creeping over my face.

I could fight. I could fight him.

Maybe I could fight the demons inside me, too.

Ty kneeled beside the claw-foot tub in my bathroom, testing the water with his hand until it was perfect, steam curling up into the air, lit candles casting flickering shadows along the walls. Black rose petals drifted among the bath oils, their velvety scent mixing with the faint perfume of jasmine.

I stood near him wearing my sweat-drenched workout clothes.

Ty wore just his gray sweatpants.

I felt almost shy as my eyes trailed over Ty's back—the rippling muscles, several long scars almost silver against the vivid black ink.

Across his upper back, a Grim Reaper lay asleep, shrouded in tattered robes, resembling a cursed prince from a twisted fairy tale. A dark-haired girl stood above him, with trees growing out of her eye sockets, leaning in as though about to kiss him awake.

Like a twisted Sleeping Beauty.

I ached to trace my fingers across the black lines, the puckered scars, but I didn't dare.

His manliness, his raw masculinity, made me feel... young, almost virginal. Even though I was far from one.

I pressed one foot over the other and shivered as I waited, my body temperature having dropped too quickly after the rigorous hours of training Ty had led me through and the drafty passageway had chilled my dampened skin.

Seemingly satisfied, Ty stood and faced me. His towering height and wide shoulders made me feel even smaller than I was. I repressed a shiver.

He turned me around and undid my braid, working his fingers through my hair carefully so as not to tug. Every time his fingers brushed against my scalp, shivers spread down my arms.

When Ty helped peel my sports bra off me, I tried to ignore the weight of his nearness, trying to convince myself that this was like a nurse tending to a patient. Professional. Meaningless.

But it wasn't.

The brush of his fingers against my skin sent a shiver down my spine, and I bit down hard on the inside of my cheek to keep from reacting.

When he grabbed the waistband of my pants, I tried to push his hands way, but he was unmovable. He seemed determined to do it all for me, like I was a breakable little doll.

"I'm not useless, you know," I muttered, crossing my arms over my bare chest as he tugged my leggings down and kneeled at my feet.

The only sign that he'd heard me was the slight press of his eyebrows. "I'm not doing this because you *need* my help. I'm doing it because I *want* to."

As he lifted my legs one by one, tugging my leggings off my feet, his hands slid so tenderly across my calf that it sent shivers up my leg.

He stood and before I could say a word, he pushed down his sweatpants, his thick cock springing free.

Shit. This was the first time I was seeing him naked.

I tried not to look, I really did. But I couldn't help myself, drinking in his beauty, thick cords of muscle painted in ink, the scars only adding to his brutal beauty.

Then my gaze landed on his cock, thick and long and, fuck, it was swelling under my stare.

I gasped and tore my gaze away, landing on his face where he was already staring at me.

The tension was thick, palpable in the small bathroom, making the air feel heavier than it should.

I thought he might try something. Especially when he stepped into me, his cock grazing my thigh.

But he just picked me up by my waist and lowered me into the bath, getting in behind me. The hot water was pure bliss as Ty lowered us down into it, soothing my aching muscles after the brutal workout Ty had just put me through.

He arranged me in front of him, his back against the tub, my back against his chest, my thighs within his.

I could feel his heartbeat against my back, steady and calm, like this was the most natural thing in the world. But it wasn't natural. None of this was.

He took his time washing my hair with my favorite jasmine shampoo, his fingers combing through my strands with deliberate care. His touch sent tingles across my scalp, down my neck, and I found myself relaxing against him, despite everything.

When he was done, he draped my hair over one shoulder and started massaging the tension out of my neck and shoulders, his strong hands working out knots I didn't even realize were there.

It felt too good. Too intimate.

A groan slipped past my lips before I could stop it, my body betraying me as I melted further into him.

Guilt twisted in my chest. This felt wrong. More wrong than the 'therapy' sessions. More wrong than sex.

This felt deeper, like we were crossing a line we hadn't even acknowledged yet.

I let out an awkward laugh, trying to shake off the confusion. "Who are you and what have you done with Ty?"

His fingers found a particularly thick knot in the base of my neck. "What do you mean?"

"Well, you know," I said as I repressed another moan. His fingers really were magic. "You're usually cold and mean. Why are you being so… nice?"

He stilled behind me, his hands halting their soothing rhythm. I felt the tension ripple through him, a tightness I couldn't decipher.

The warmth of the bath, the softness of the moment disappeared as I waited for an answer, but he didn't give one.

The silence stretched out, thick and heavy, like the weight of something unsaid pressing between us.

The thick tension was still there like weighted air when he wrapped me in a soft white robe, his fingers lingering just a moment too long as he brushed the damp strands of hair from my face.

And when he made me sit in front of him so he could massage cream into my raw knuckles, unused to hitting a bag for so long.

Then he placed a massive steak in front of me, cooked to perfection, the smell alone enough to make my stomach rumble in anticipation.

I stared at the steak surrounded by buttery mash and

perfectly steamed broccoli, then at him, and lifted a single brow.

He frowned, glancing from the plate to my face. "Did I not cook it the way you like?"

"I'm waiting for you to cut it up and feed me," I snarked. "You've done everything else for me."

He snorted and rolled his eyes. "Eat your damn steak."

But I glimpsed it. A tiny smile.

The victory sent a surge of satisfaction through me, a dangerous pleasure in chipping away at his icy exterior, revealing something—*someone*—beneath it.

I grabbed my knife and fork, hiding the smirk pulling at my own lips as I cut into the steak.

But as I took the first bite, something unsettling hit me so hard I almost dropped my cutlery.

There it was, lingering like a guilty secret.

Oh God, I *liked* my warden.

## AVA

Ty had promised me access to more of the mansion.

Now, walking down the long, dimly lit hallway, the weight of the place pressed in around me, heavy with uncovered secrets.

My fingers trailed over the locked doors, one by one, and excitement mingled with tension in my veins.

Behind each door held the possibility of more memories. More mysteries.

More pain.

Behind me, I could feel Ty's presence. Silent, watchful, his eyes boring into my back.

I resisted the urge to turn around and meet his gaze, choosing instead to savor the anticipation as I moved farther down the hall.

I paused when I reached a certain door, my fingertips lingering on the wood, tracing its grain as though it were the contours of a face I longed to see again.

This was Ciaran's room.

Even the thought of his name sent a pang of longing through me, sharp and sudden.

I pressed my hand against the door as if I could feel him there, just beyond it.

"This one," I murmured, barely daring to hope as I looked back at Ty.

His expression changed in an instant. His jaw set, eyes darkening with something hard, almost possessive, as he took in the way my hand rested on the door.

"No." His voice was curt, final. "Pick any other room."

I turned fully toward him, feeling my own frustration flare up. "Why not? You promised me more freedom, Ty. That was the deal."

He stared back, unyielding. "*Not* that room."

A protest rose in my throat. "But—"

"Pick another. Or pick *none*."

The bluntness of his words clawed at me, each syllable a reminder of his control.

My fists clenched at my sides, fighting against the helplessness pressing in.

He twisted the rules to suit himself, always a step ahead, always reminding me of my place.

My pride wanted to stand its ground, to refuse him outright, but the threat lingered heavy in the air—one wrong move, and I'd be back in that cold, windowless bedroom.

A thought struck me, a memory from years ago, a door kept locked for the entire time I'd lived here, the only room in the mansion I'd never been in.

*The forbidden room.*

A dark curiosity flared up inside me. If he wouldn't give me Ciaran's room, then I'd take the secrets behind that one.

Without a word, I strode down the hallway, Ty's footsteps following close behind, a current running down my spine.

I stopped in front of the door of the forbidden bedroom and slapped my hand against the dark wood panel embossed with thorny vines and flowers, the sound echoing off the walls.

"This one," I said, my voice resolute. "I want access to this room."

Ty stiffened, his face growing tight as he looked at the door and then back at me. He hesitated, as though searching for the right words.

"No," he said at last, his voice strained. "That's…"

He trailed off, refusing to meet my eyes, his jaw clenched tightly.

I narrowed my gaze, crossing my arms.

"Then give me Ciaran's room," I demanded, my voice tinged with defiance.

He stood there in silence, his face shadowed and unreadable. I felt the tension tighten between us like a string ready to snap.

"You promised," I reminded him, my voice soft but relentless. "You can't keep me locked out of every room."

Ty's shoulders slumped, the fight draining from him. He let out a long, resigned sigh, his eyes meeting mine with a reluctant acceptance.

"Fine," he muttered, the word barely audible, like a reluctant admission.

I stepped aside so Ty could stand before the door. He

reached into his pocket and pulled out a slender, old-fashioned key. It must be a master key for the whole mansion.

I couldn't keep my eyes off it as he slipped it into the lock, turning it with a soft, metallic click. My pulse quickened at the sight of the key—the thought of it in my possession, the idea of all the other doors it could unlock.

But he was fast.

Before I could react, Ty slid the key back into his pocket, out of my reach, and stepped aside, pushing the door open with a somber look.

"Go on," he said, his tone unreadable.

I swallowed, my heart pounding as I crossed the threshold.

Inside, the room seemed almost untouched by time, as though it had been sealed off from the rest of Blackthorn Hall, preserved in amber.

A muted dusky-lavender canopy hung over the four-poster bed, its fabric faded but once rich, shrouding the room in a quiet, melancholic grace. The faint, powdery scent of faded rose perfume lingered in the air, mixing with the scent of aged wood and dust.

I moved farther in, my gaze catching on the vanity by the wall, its mirror clouded, reflecting only shadow.

Bottles of perfume sat undisturbed, dusted like forgotten relics of a life that once was.

An armchair by the fireplace slouched slightly, its cushions bearing the soft indentations of the owner's presence.

"This was my mother's room," Ty murmured. "I haven't been in here since she—"

He didn't look at me but stared off into the shadows, his face carved from stone.

Mona Donahue.

Her name floated through my memory, a whisper I'd heard among the Blackthorn staff years ago, yet never attached to a face.

There were no portraits, no photographs.

Ty and Ciaran's mother was a ghost erased by those she'd left behind, as if acknowledging her was a wound they couldn't bear to reopen.

A wave of guilt twisted through me for pushing him here, forcing him to peel back layers he'd buried so deeply.

"You never spoke about her," I said softly. "None of you did."

He remained silent, his lips pressed into a thin line.

The weight of the room settled over me like a shroud as I stepped farther in, my heart catching at every object that hinted at the woman who'd once lived here.

A woman's blush-colored coat hung on the closet door, delicate and elegant, and a sun hat rested on the back of the chair.

My gaze fell on a book lying open on the bedside table, a book left mid-sentence, as though Mona Donahue had only put it down for a moment, as though she had just left, intending to return in mere moments.

But the years had only added to the stillness, encasing the room in an untouched silent tomb.

Ty's voice broke the silence, low and hollow, echoing in the stillness. "Our mother was much younger than the professor. By nearly two decades. She was barely sixteen when they married."

A knot tightened in my stomach.

Sixteen—just a few years younger than I was now. The

thought of being married off at that age, bound to someone so much older, felt incomprehensible, wrong in a way that gnawed at me.

He let out a humorless laugh, brittle and sharp.

"Scandalous, isn't it? But back then, no one batted an eye. Women married young." He paused, his gaze darkening. "And... I doubt it was exactly her choice."

A chill prickled down my spine, the weight of his words settling in, filling the room with a suffocating heaviness. I swallowed, my throat tight.

"How did she...?" But I couldn't bring myself to finish the question.

Ty's jaw tensed, his hands curling into fists at his sides.

"She killed herself," he said, his voice barely more than a whisper. "She stole plants out of father's greenhouse and brewed herself a tea out of oleander."

*That's why the greenhouse was forbidden to us.*

He sat down heavily on the edge of the bed, the mattress creaking under his weight. He looked down, his fingers curling around the edge of the bedspread as if he needed something to hold on to.

My chest tightened as I watched Ty, his face etched with shadows I hadn't seen before, shadows that ran deeper than anything I'd imagined.

Without thinking, I sat down beside him. My hand found his, and though the logical part of me screamed to pull away, I didn't.

For reasons I couldn't explain, I wanted to comfort him, to ease some of the weight he carried—even though he was my captor.

I didn't understand it; maybe I didn't want to.

"Ciaran refused to talk about her," he continued, his gaze distant. "He wouldn't even say her name again. He rebelled, became... well, you know Ci."

He let out a faint, bitter laugh, and I could hear the complicated mix of resentment and admiration beneath it.

"And you?" I asked softly.

"I..." Ty hesitated, his eyes clouding with something deeper. "I threw myself into school, into debate club, chess club, *anything* that would keep me busy."

A wave of sorrow swept through me, mingling with a new kind of grief—not just for him, but for Ciaran too. The pain they must have endured when she abandoned them, no way to understand why she'd left.

"At the time, I didn't understand why she would leave me. Leave us." His voice was quiet, strained with a pain that had clearly been buried for years. "I thought... maybe if I had just been perfect... if I could have been everything she wanted... then maybe she would have loved me enough to stay."

The ache in his words hit me, raw and unguarded. It was the kind of confession that left no room for masks or games.

For the first time, I saw him—not as the man who'd trapped me here, but as a broken boy who'd blamed himself for not saving her.

I understood his fierce determination to save *me*—no matter how much it broke me.

Ty stood up suddenly. "Close the door on your way out when you're done."

He walked out abruptly, as if he couldn't stand to be in

her room any longer, his anger and pain trailing behind him like a shadow.

I watched him leave, his shoulders stiff with an unspoken weight. Ty's words echoed in my mind, leaving me torn.

Part of me wanted to follow him, to try to ease that torment, but another part held me back—a dark, gnawing curiosity pulling me deeper into his mother's room.

The room felt frozen in time, shrouded in sacred stillness. But the longer I lingered, the more unsettling the details became, small clues casting shadows over any sense of peace.

My gaze caught on a small wastebasket near the bed. Inside, a crumpled towel was stained with dried blood, faded yet unmistakable.

I took a step back, my stomach twisting as the room's darkness seemed to swell around me.

My heel struck something small and glass—a vial. It rolled across the floor, its sound hollow and haunting in the silence.

I swallowed back bile, my gaze falling on the bedposts, and a chill crept up my spine as I noticed the faint grooves in the wood, marks worn down from repeated use. The marks were on all four posts, like something heavy had been tied around them.

*Chains*, my mind whispered, horrified.

My heart pounded as I pieced it together. Mona had been drugged, bound, forced to endure some unimaginable suffering. Perhaps… she had been the *first* girl?

And I had been her twisted replacement.

A shiver ran down my spine as I tried to breathe past the wave of nausea.

His mother—Mona—had suffered here, trapped in her own bedroom, and for the first time, I felt a grim understanding of the woman whose ghost seemed to linger. Trapped, controlled, like I was now.

The mansion had always felt cursed, but now I felt the weight of its secrets bearing down on me.

My eyes fell on a delicate, ornate jewelry box on the dresser, its carvings intricate and aged. So similar to the jewelry box that Ty had left for me.

Without thinking, I ran my fingers over the floral design, feeling a small bloom beneath my thumb.

There was a soft click, and to my surprise, a hidden drawer sprang open.

I reached in, my hands trembling as I pulled out a bundle of letters, each one neatly folded and tied with a faded lavender ribbon. My breath caught as I carefully unfolded one, the parchment thin and fragile between my fingers.

The first words gripped me with a sick, hollow feeling.

The letters were Mona's.

They were prayers, or perhaps pleas, written to someone unnamed—maybe to God, or maybe just to the silence.

There was a desperation in her words, a kind of terror that seemed to reach out from the ink, echoing through the years.

And then—a dark truth. A terrible secret.

I staggered back, clutching the letters to my chest.

My gaze drifted toward the door, toward where Ty had vanished moments ago.

Should I show him? Should I lay this truth in front of

him? But as I looked down at the trembling letters in my hands, fear and doubt held me back.

Would he survive knowing the depth of her suffering? Or would it only destroy him more? Would it only push him further into darkness?

# THE SHADOW

I slapped Liath's abuser awake with the flat of my knife, the metal landing against his cheek with a dull smack.

I'd tied him up in the basement of my mansion, in a stress position restraint or as I liked to call it, a hog-tied hangman.

His wrists and ankles were tied behind his back but with a rope extending to a loop around his neck. The more he struggled, the tighter the noose got.

It was brutal and effective.

"Wake up," I muttered, every word laced with cold rage.

It had been laughably easy to catch him off guard. Men like him—entitled, bloated with privilege and self-assurance—never entertained the notion that they could be anyone's target.

They moved through life shielded by wealth, cushioned by arrogance, unaware of the raw, open wound their existence inflicted on those they considered beneath them.

Even after his involvement in Liath's disappearance, he

had gone about his daily routine like a man cloaked in invisibility, safe in the certainty that no one would ever dare approach him.

But he'd been wrong. He hadn't seen me coming.

And at the moment I struck, I saw the dawning horror on his face—the realization that, for the first time, *he* had become prey.

The irony of drugging and kidnapping him didn't escape me. Using his own weapons against him—binding, silencing, trapping him—brought a grim satisfaction I couldn't deny.

The difference, of course, was purpose.

His cruelty was born of pure domination, a sick exercise in control.

But mine was a means to an end—a desperation fueled by each day that passed without a trace of her. I could almost taste the urgency, sharp and unrelenting, gnawing away at me.

I needed information, needed answers on Ava's whereabouts *now*.

And this bastard was going to give it to me—or I would cut it out of him piece by piece.

Fachnan Byrne—Liath's father—woke up with a gasp, his head jerking to the side. For a heartbeat, his weathered face remained slack, disoriented, before terror flooded his features as he took in the dark, damp basement walls.

He began to struggle, but the ropes around his wrists and ankles tugged, pulling taut against his neck. Panic seized his eyes as he felt the pressure clamp around his throat, cutting his breath short, and he jerked again—only for the noose to tighten further.

"I wouldn't do that if I were you," I said, stepping forward out of the shadows and watching the realization wash over him, the terror in his eyes shifting to something deeper, more primal.

"Struggle and you'll cut off your own oxygen. And we wouldn't want that, would we? Not yet." I let the corner of my mouth tug up in a smile, watching as he froze, breathing shallowly.

"Help! Somebody—help!" His voice, a desperate croak, echoed around the basement walls.

I let out a sigh. Why did they always scream?

I held up my sharpened cleaver—one I named Babe—the large flat metal side gleaming in the dim light.

I'd learned from my torture session with Dr. Vale. Knives were not ergonomic when it came to dismembering fingers. And I expected that I'd have to take a few to get what I wanted out of him.

Couldn't risk getting RDI... Repetitive dismembering injury.

"Save your breath, Byrne." I waved the cleaver at him, catching his wide, terrified eyes with my own steady gaze.

"This place?" I scraped the edge of Babe against the thick stone walls. "Soundproof."

A flicker of hopelessness crossed his face as he realized he was completely trapped.

Byrne's bloodshot eyes found mine and he began stammering, groveling, begging for mercy I had no intention of giving him.

"Please," he gasped. "Please, I don't know what you want—"

"Where is Ava?" I gripped Babe's handle tighter, my own voice a low growl. "Where did the Sochai take her?"

His face twisted, panicked, his wrinkled chin wobbling. "I-I don't know who—"

I grabbed his ear and cleaved it off.

Byrne let out a howl as blood began to run from the side of his head.

"Let's not do this whole, 'I don't know who the Sochai are' shite," I said, waving Babe around, flicking blood back onto his face. "Because you only have one ear left."

"I s-swear, they don't have her," he stammered, his voice cracking. "Please, I don't know anything about it."

"Liar," I spat, pressing the cleaver edge under his chin, just enough to make him feel the bite of it, just enough to draw blood. "Try again."

"Please, I swear, I'm telling the truth! The Sochai—" He coughed as the ropes binding him cut into his throat as he tried to inch back away from me. "They didn't take her."

"Just like they didn't take Liath?"

His eyes widened in genuine fear. "I s-swear, I didn't want to hurt Liath."

"Stop *lying*," I yelled, cutting him off, my patience hanging by a thread.

Desperation clawed at me. Every lead I'd followed to find Ava had turned up empty, every path leading nowhere. Byrne was my last hope, my final shot at getting any answers.

I grabbed his hair in my fist and yanked his head back, holding the cleaver like I was about to scalp him. "Where is she?"

Byrne began to cry, loud pathetic sobs. "P-please, I don't know. I swear."

My grip on Babe slipped slightly, my hands trembling as the words caught in my throat. "Tell me where Ava is."

"I don't know."

"*Where* is she?"

"I don't know!" he screamed, his voice cracking as he fought against the restraints. "I swear to you—"

"Where. Is. Ava?" I shook him by his hair.

Byrne howled as hair popped from his scalp. "Please, stop. Have m-mercy…"

"WHERE THE FUCK IS SHE?"

Before I knew it, my anger had taken control. Red bled across my vision and in a blind, unthinking moment, my cleaver swept across his neck, severing his head from his shoulders.

His eyes went blank, his mouth opening as blood spurted out of his raw exposed neck.

His body slumped to the concrete floor, or at least as slumped as it could still being hog-tied.

I was left with his head in my hand, dangling like a dead fish from the roots, blood dripping from the stump.

The reality of what I'd done sinking in, a mix of satisfaction and dread tangled inside me.

Damn it. He was supposed to talk. He was supposed to lead me to Ava.

But I knew, somewhere in the hollow ache of my gut, that he wasn't lying about not knowing where Ava was. He truly didn't have a clue.

Yet his denial of the Society's involvement? That was bullshit. These secret societies moved in layers, cloaking their dirtiest secrets at the highest levels, where only a select few were in the know.

Someone in that inner circle had her. Someone powerful enough to keep her hidden from their underlings, men like Byrne.

The Society had Ava; that much I knew with a bitter certainty. It was just a matter of *who*—and *where*.

I forced myself to take a breath, to shake the red haze from my vision.

I stood and dropped Byrne's head. It bounced before rolling aside and staring off to the wall.

I glanced down at my trusty cleaver, Babe, dripping blood onto the floor.

"That'll do, pig," I whispered. "That'll do."

It was done now. Nothing would bring Byrne back.

At least Liath got justice; her abuser had paid with his life. And the whole world would know the truth—that she hadn't just run away.

On the TV screen installed on the wall, the news story ran of how Michael Byrne, a prominent politician and the Minister for Foreign Affairs, was implicated in the abuse of his adopted daughter, Liath Byrne. The news reporter called for another investigation into Liath Byrne's disappearance.

I'd sent the 'insurance' tape to every single news outlet in Ireland myself, even the smaller local ones, making sure it would get out. I even sent it to some foreign news outlets, especially the ones that the former Foreign Affairs Minister was heavily involved with like the UK and Germany.

I made sure that the evidence was disseminated so widely that the Society couldn't bury everything.

Liath's story would finally be heard.

And Byrne? He wouldn't be missed.

Not even by the Society. No doubt *they* would have made him disappear to avoid the scandal from leaking on to them. Really, it was a mercy that I had killed him instead.

When I snatched him, I'd made sure to take a few pieces from his bedroom—a suitcase, several pairs of clothes, and cash from his safe. Ironic, huh?

I'd also left a letter in Byrne's study, a 'goodbye' note scrawled in his own shaky handwriting that he was leaving Ireland, begging his wife to forgive him, to take his fortune as penance, to leave his memory in the past and move on.

It wouldn't take much convincing for her to accept that he'd fled the country in the wake of his sins coming to light.

Mrs. Byrne would get over it. She'd be fine.

But me? My fists clenched as I looked down at his lifeless body. If I lost Ava, there'd be no getting over this for me.

I changed the channel on the TV to a recording.

I stood over Byrne's lifeless body, his blood leaking around my boots as a recording of Ava showed on the screen of her sleeping in just a thin t-shirt and panties.

My fingers ached to brush her dark hair back from her face, to trace her parted lips, the hollow of her neck. I could almost feel the ghost of her warmth in my hands. Almost.

These images were all I had left of her now.

No, I couldn't think like that. I had to keep the faith that she was still alive. I'd know if she were dead. I'd *feel* it. I was tied to her, in life and in death.

On-screen my hand reached out and tugged on her t-shirt, giving her nipples some friction. They hardened deliciously and Ava let out a soft moan in her sleep, a sound that haunted me.

*Fuck.* I missed her.

My throat tightened, a well of grief rising that I couldn't control even as my dick began to swell at the sight of her curvy body laid out for me.

Memories flashed through my head—of her straining against my ropes even as her pussy wept for me, of the first time I thrust my cock inside her sweet cunt as I pinned her against the library shelves, and of the last time I saw her, glancing back at me over her shoulder, her dark hair curtaining half her face in the doorway of Dr. Vale's office.

If only I hadn't let her leave on her own.

I dropped the cleaver and freed my cock from my pants, the blood on my hand making everything slippery as I stroked myself.

The metallic scent of Byrne's blood mingled with the musty air of the dimly lit room as I stared at Ava's sleeping form on the screen, her chest rising and falling gently.

My hand moved faster, rougher, as the camera focused on that spot between her legs. To those maddening white panties with a little silk bow in the small of her back.

To the damp cotton cupping her pussy, the pussy I ached to be inside right now.

I let out a groan as pleasure swam through my body, mixing with hopelessness.

I shouldn't be doing this. Not here, not now.

I should be out there, kicking down the doors of Mr. Byrne's friends and interrogating them, leaving behind a bloody mess in my wake, as I followed the trail right to Ava.

But the sight of her soft skin, even if it was just on the

screen, the curve of her hip barely covered by thin cotton, ignited a primal need I couldn't ignore.

My dark queen liked it when I got a little bloody. When I got a little psycho.

When I was torturing Dr. Vale, I could see the way her nipples poked through her shirt and how she pressed her thighs together and squirmed in her seat.

If she were here…

My breath came in ragged gasps, echoing off the stone walls, as I imagined her dropping to her knees, sticky with Byrne's blood, her hot, wet mouth around my cock.

Tears streaming down her cheeks as I fisted her hair and made her gag, her eyes filling with hatred for me, but also her hand rubbing frantically between her legs because she loved to hate me.

Release came and I choked on a sob as hot strands of cum shot out from my cock and sprayed over Byrne's decapitated body.

I stumbled against the wall, sagging against it, trying to catch my breath, the TV screen where my sleeping Ava lay casting an eerie blue glow over Byrne's pale dismembered face, his unseeing eyes accusing me even in death.

I knew I should feel remorse, horror at what I'd done. Instead, all I felt was an aching emptiness that only Ava could fill.

Ava was gone.

And I wasn't sure I would ever get her back.

# AVA

Perhaps I was a coward. But I couldn't tell Ty.

Mona's letters lay hidden back where I'd found them, tucked into the secret drawer of the jewelry box.

I couldn't bear to show him what I'd found. Couldn't risk how it might unhinge him further. Couldn't stomach the look that revelation might carve into his face.

Perhaps that made me selfish. Or perhaps it was self-preservation.

As the days blurred together, the guilt became easier to ignore until it sank under the surface.

Just like this house, I let Mona Donahue fade into the shadows, her pain sinking into the walls, her suffering becoming another ghost, because all I felt—all I could bear to feel—was my own.

Ty's routines became my prison. He put me through daily workouts that left my muscles trembling, every inch of me aching and sore, reminding me I was alive only by the intensity of the pain.

And then there were the therapy sessions—those were worse, digging under my skin, peeling back layers I'd buried long ago. They shattered me, mind and soul, stripping me bare and leaving me raw.

Each day blurred into the next, a steady rhythm of agony, physical and emotional, until all I knew was pain.

Pain in every breath, every movement, and every memory I dared to unearth.

Yet somehow, the ache settled in, coiling around me until it was almost... normal. Predictable. Almost safe.

The irony wasn't lost on me—that even in the hands of my captor, routine could become a lifeline. There was something about the predictability of it, the steady beat of exertion and exhaustion, that felt like a twisted kind of comfort.

I hated admitting it, but the rhythm grounded me, each day as familiar as the last.

A prisoner's schedule, maybe, but it was something I could count on, a strange, bitter solace that held me steady in the storm.

And perhaps we might have kept going like that all summer, locked in that dark and painful familiarity, if it hadn't been for what I remembered.

Training got harder as I got fitter.

Ty made me run with him side by side on the treadmills, him managing my speed and incline without input from me.

Whenever I put my hands on the armrests to jump off the racing belt, Ty would shove them away. His simple "No" was all it took for me to pound my feet faster even as the garden outside the barred windows of the ballroom flashed with bright-white lights.

Ty would spot me, his intense stare focused, as I lifted the weights he'd selected, always heavier than I thought I could lift. And I was always surprised that I could.

He pushed me until my muscles trembled—one more rep, just one more rep—until I could barely walk. Until I could barely lift my arms.

Then he'd be there, pulling me into his arms and lowering me into yet another warm Epsom salt bath after he'd stripped me of my sweaty clothes.

In the boxing ring, Ty would circle me wearing only his gray sweatpants and a set of boxing wraps as black as the ink that branded him, my heart thudding hard and not just from exertion.

Sweat poured from our bodies and when we grappled together, it took clawing with nails to hold on.

He'd force me into a corner and push against me till I couldn't breathe, yanking on my braid till I was forced to turn my head and sink my teeth into his wrist.

He encouraged savagery and I liked pleasing him so I became savage.

Slowly, my body began to change. The soft lines becoming defined, muscles I didn't know I had emerging.

My mind shifted, too, but more painfully.

At first, after each therapy session, I'd shatter into a million pieces, denying the memories that surfaced—denying the pain, the truth—and he'd have to scoop all my jagged pieces up and hold me in a broken pile until I could put myself back together again.

Then I stopped shattering and became *angry*.

Ty would hold up his palms, bracing for impact, and let

me pummel them—pummel *him*—screaming until my raw knuckles split open and my throat burned.

His chest would bloom with bruises, black and blue, but he never flinched. He never stopped me. He never complained. He just stood there, took the rage I threw at him, swallowed it, and let me pour it all out until I was empty. Until he became the only safe place I had left.

Finally, my anger fizzled out from a wildfire to burning embers.

I tried to negotiate a way out—with myself, with him.

Maybe if I just went through the motions, if I let the memories stay buried where they belonged and just *pretended* to remember, I could still escape this nightmare.

But this never worked. My past was insidious, like a nightmare that never ended. Like a ghost that wouldn't stay buried.

I pleaded with Ty. "Can't I stop now? Isn't it enough that I remember most of it now?"

I promised to be good, to follow the rules, if only I didn't have to relive the past anymore.

I tried to convince him, and myself, that I didn't need to remember. "You can help me in other ways," I whispered, desperate to make it end without facing the whole truth.

But he would always say the same thing: "There's no way out until you face it all."

So I'd nod, defeated, and take the glass vial from him, hoping that maybe, just maybe, this time would be the last.

As promised, Ty opened more of the house to me. More and more rooms were opened up, unlocked for me.

A library which used to be my favorite room in the house, with soaring ceilings and heavy oak shelves skirted by sliding ladders that housed every kind of book under the sun.

A sunroom, bathed in natural light, where I'd sit at the window boxes and stare out at the wind rushing through the leaves or where I'd take my books to read with the sun dappled across my legs, warming them.

A game room, where Ty would challenge me to games of chess after dinner. Games I always seemed to win, despite my being a complete beginner.

But my favorite was the piano room, centered around a stark white grand piano that gleamed beneath the soft glow of the iron chandelier. The room was circular, with a high-domed ceiling that turned even the softest notes into rich, resonant sounds.

I gasped when I saw the piano, and memories flooded back—of a younger Ty, playing while I lingered in the doorway.

Back then, he played the classics—Mozart, Beethoven, Debussy—pieces I could easily recognize, even if I wasn't a musician.

But now, as he sat at the piano with me beside him at his insistence, his black sleeves rolled up over muscled forearms, he played melodies I'd never heard before.

Each note ached with haunting beauty, striking deep in my chest, stirring something raw inside me. Unshed tears burned at the backs of my eyes.

"It's beautiful," I said, after he'd finished yet another piece I didn't know.

His long fingers traced over the polished keys. "I called that one *Hummingbird's Hymn.*"

I blinked, his nickname for me pulling at my heartstrings. "Wait... *You* wrote them?"

He nodded, casually playing a few minor chords. "In prison, there wasn't much to do."

I frowned. "They had a piano in prison?"

He let out a short, humorless laugh. "No."

I stared at his profile, watching the way his hair fell into his face, the way he looked so focused, yet distant. "You wrote those songs in your *head*?"

He shrugged as if it were nothing.

"This one," he said, letting his fingers glide over the keys again, "I call *Ava's Lullaby*."

The music began to flow, softer now, intimate.

His forearm brushed mine as he played, and every touch sent shivers up my spine.

I closed my eyes, letting the melody wash over me, but my mind couldn't help drifting. I pictured him alone in his cell, composing these songs, thinking of me while I was out there—free.

Free... and having forgotten him.

Guilt surged through me, sharp and biting. He had been rotting in prison, while I had pushed all my memories of him so deep, I'd nearly erased him from my life.

And now, he was here, playing lullabies for the girl who had moved on, while he had been trapped in a world that no longer remembered him and didn't care.

My heart broke for him, and this time I let my tears fall freely, rolling down my cheeks, even after the last lingering note of the song had faded into silence.

I gasped when I felt his lips on my cheek, his warm breath, the softness of his tongue as he gently wiped away my tears. His tenderness caught me off guard, sending another wave of emotion through me.

"Don't cry for me, hummingbird," he murmured, his voice soft yet steady, a strange mixture of command and comfort.

I kept my eyes shut, unable to look at him. "But it's so... *sad*."

"Sadness... pain... they shape you," he said, his voice deeper now, thoughtful.

I opened my eyes, but he wasn't looking at me. His gaze was distant, as if he was seeing something beyond the walls of this room, beyond the mansion.

"Like how the wind shapes the cliffs over time, wearing them down but also revealing their strength. Trauma can do that to you—carve you into something better, something unbreakable."

His gaze flicked to mine, catching me in his stare. "The parts that hurt... they can become the most beautiful, if you let them."

Pain could break you, yes. But it could also transform you. And maybe, just maybe, it was transforming us *both* in ways we couldn't yet understand.

∼

Sunday, I came to realize, was therapy day. I came to hate Sundays. No matter how many times it rolled around, I dreaded it, the feeling settling like a stone in my gut.

The paralysis drug usually crept in slowly, a dark cloud of foreboding that started at the base of my spine and crawled its way upward.

But tonight it wasn't slow. It crawled up my back like a spider, skittering beneath my skin, fast and erratic.

Maybe, deep down, I already knew what was coming. I could feel the weight of it—darker than any memory I'd yet faced.

Heavier than last week's revelation.

*My stomach didn't feel good.*

*I tried to take another sip of my hot chocolate, because the professor said good little girls show that they're grateful by always finishing their sweet treats, but I gagged and spit it right back into the steaming mug.*

*There seemed to be too much saliva in my mouth and a strange heat churned in my belly.*

*Hot chocolate spilled over the wobbling edge of the mug when I set it down on the side table next to the red velvet couch.*

*I ran into the professor's bathroom with my hand over my mouth. But I did not make it to toilet.*

*I threw up on the cold, gray marble floor. I coughed and heaved till the muscles in my stomach burned.*

*Tears fell straight from my eyes into my mess, the acrid smell of it nearly making me sick again.*

*"What's going on in here? Ava?"*

The professor's voice cut through the air behind me, and I froze, a chill rushing down my spine as a wave of nausea twisted in my gut.

His tone was almost too calm, calculated—but there was something sharp beneath it.

I turned my head slowly, my stomach lurching as I faced him, trying to mask the dread clawing at me.

His eyes narrowed, his expression shifting as he registered my discomfort and the vomit on the tiles.

*A flicker of alarm broke through his usual controlled demeanor.*

"Ava," he pressed, his voice lower now, "how long have you been feeling sick?"

On the red couch, it felt like dozens of unseen hands were pressing me down, clammy fingers digging into my burning flesh, suffocating me.

I gasped for air, tried to scream *no!* but my lungs wouldn't expand, my limbs frozen against the velvet. Panic clawed at my chest.

For a moment, I saw Ty leaning over me, his eyes wide with fear, his lips moving to say something.

But then his face blurred and shifted, morphing into the professor's cold, calculating stare.

"Ava... when was the last time you had your period?"

The paralytic felt like it flooded my veins, faster and stronger than ever before, a merciless tide I couldn't hold back.

Panic jolted through me, fierce and helpless, as the drug latched on to my senses, drowning them in shadows.

No. I didn't want to know what waited in that darkness. I wasn't ready to know what came next, to watch the truth unspooling in vivid, brutal detail.

But I couldn't scream, couldn't claw my way out. I could only sink deeper, spiraling into the pitch-black depths that clawed back at me, closing in with a suffocating, inescapable grip.

*The light above me was so white and so blinding that even when I squeezed my eyes shut, I could feel it stabbing like a knife straight into my burning brain.*

*But when I tried to shield myself with my forearms, I discov-*

ered that my wrists were bound to the cold metal table I'd been laid out on. Panic surged like a shot of adrenaline through my veins. It only got worse when I realized it wasn't just my wrists, but my ankles, thighs, and chest.

I wasn't on the couch this time. The pad underneath me was firm, cool against my skin.

*Where was I?*

I struggled to lift my head to see where I was, but it was so heavy I could barely move it. Spots appeared like cigarette burns in my already hazy vision.

All I'd managed to see was a sea of shapes moving slowly in the dark.

*I must be in a hospital.*

I'd tried to hide my sickness from the professor. But even the smell of food made me want to vomit and I couldn't hide it.

He'd been so angry when he found out. So angry. And... afraid.

The clatter of medical tools on a metal tray beside me made me want to whimper and cry out, but I could no longer feel my lips. Somewhere, a door slammed, sounding very far away.

"How the fuck did this happen?" a gruffy older man's voice said. "I thought she was given the implant."

*That voice. It was... familiar. But I couldn't place it.*

"I'm sorry, a Thiarna Ard." High Lord. "I did not want to mar her lovely skin."

I recognized this second voice as...the professor.

He continued, "I used a contraceptive mixture that I—"

"You and your little concoctions," the first voice spat with disdain.

More harsh clattering of metal and cold hands propped my

*bare feet up in strange braces, causing my nightgown to slip down my legs.*

*I wanted to cover myself up, but I couldn't move. I couldn't even cry out.*

*"You make sure she never remembers this, do you hear me?"*

*A doctor wearing a surgical mask loomed over me and waved a light in my eyes, turning their features into a silhouette.*

*I tried to beg them to help me. But my voice box wouldn't work. I just screamed inside and pleaded with my eyes.*

*But for a moment, they froze.*

*But then they were gone, taking my hope with them.*

*I could hear whispers, then voices rising.*

*A loud crash made me jolt, like someone had thrown something across the room.*

*"You* dare *second-guess me?" the first voice yelled. "You are my fucking Heir. You will do as I say. Now... take care of it."*

Tears streamed from the sides of my paralyzed eyes as grief tore through me, sharp and sudden, like a knife slicing through my chest.

The memory rising up from the darkest corner of my mind, its edges blurred and fragmented, but unmistakable.

I had been pregnant.

Then they forced an abortion on me.

My body had once carried life, and now, there was nothing. The weight of that realization crushed me.

How had I not known? How could I have forgotten something like that?

Ty must have sensed things hadn't gone as usual. Because he hadn't even stripped me this time.

We weren't on the couch. We were in my bed as he held me to his body.

I dug my fingers into Ty's chest, needing to ground myself against the overwhelming tide of emotions threatening to sweep me under, the ache inside me spreading like poison, making my limbs feel heavy, my stomach sick.

My body had been violated in more ways than one, manipulated and used without my consent, and now, this—this hollow grief for a life I never had a chance to know.

"Ava, what did you see?" Ty's arms tightened around me, his steady heartbeat against my own, but it did little to soothe the turmoil inside.

The loss wasn't just physical. It was deeper than that. It was the loss of control over my own body, my own life. The violation of something so intimate, so personal.

I felt robbed, stripped bare of something precious I hadn't even known I possessed.

My body trembled, but it wasn't from the cold. It was from the raw, aching pain that seemed to consume every part of me.

And in Ty's arms, I was also grieving for myself—for the girl I had been, and for the woman who was now shattered beyond recognition.

"What did you remember?" he asked in a whisper.

"Leave me alone," I choked out, feeling the weight of those words settle over me like a crushing burden.

I gripped my stomach tightly, the knowledge of what had been done to me stabbing me like a knife.

Ty's fingers slid down my arm to rest over mine. They trembled slightly before slipping between mine to press against my belly.

*He knew. He fucking knew and he forced me to remember, anyway.*

I shoved his hands away, rage boiling up inside me, the grief I couldn't process turning to something hotter, fiercer.

"I hate you!" I screamed, pounding my fists against his chest.

Each hit was weak, fueled by the overwhelming emotions clawing inside me, but Ty just sat there, taking it.

His arms closed around me, pulling me against him, crushing me in his grip like he was afraid to let go.

I kept hitting him, harder, but he didn't flinch. Didn't react.

His silence only made the rage in me burn brighter, made the sobs twist deeper in my throat.

Slowly the strength ebbed from me, my fists falling limply against him as I collapsed, the anger bleeding out into deep, ugly howls.

I buried my face in his chest, crying until my throat felt raw, until the pain I couldn't name consumed me.

And through the sounds of my broken sobs, I heard him murmur, his voice like a cracked whisper in the darkness.

"I hate me, too."

# THE WARDEN

I entered Ava's bedroom, the tray of her usual breakfast in my hands as if nothing had changed, but everything had. I could feel it in the air, thick and suffocating.

My eyes darted from the untouched bed to where she sat, knees drawn up to her chest, crumpled on the floor. Her eyes were puffy, red from hours of crying, and the sight of her like that—broken—stabbed through me.

I hesitated for a second, the heaviness in my chest almost unbearable. Then I went to the bed, sitting on the edge and setting the tray down like I had a thousand times before.

"Come. Eat," I said, cutting into the omelet, trying to maintain the pretense of normalcy, though there was nothing normal about this anymore.

"I'm done." Her voice was hoarse, barely above a whisper. The defiance in her words was thin, like she was hanging on by a thread.

My jaw clenched. It always did when I felt something too deep to control.

I took a breath, trying not to let it show, but I saw her flinch.

God, she was afraid of me. I hated it. But if I had to make her afraid to make her do what needed to be done, then I'd become her monster.

She swallowed hard, her voice shaky with the weight of everything she'd been carrying. "I can't do it anymore, Ty."

The storm inside me churned, and I dropped my head, breathing through the whirlwind of emotions clawing their way to the surface. The tension in the room grew suffocating.

I could hear her small, shallow breaths, could feel the fear radiating off her. It cut me to the core.

"You can," I muttered through gritted teeth. "And you will."

I didn't raise my voice. I didn't need to. The weight of the words landed between us, and I saw her stiffen.

I wasn't making a threat. But she knew I would never stop.

I would never let her go.

"You can't make me," she said, her hands trembling as she bunched her nightgown tighter in her fists. "Even if you keep me locked in here forever. Shut me off from everything. Let me rot."

"You're so close," I said, my voice barely a breath. "You're so close to acceptance."

Her brow furrowed, confusion clouding her tear-streaked face. "What the hell are you talking about?"

"The five stages of grief," I replied. "You've gone through every single one—denial, anger, bargaining, depression—and now, you're almost there. So close."

*You're so close, Ty.*

Those words, spoken to me by my own warden, echoed in my mind.

I had hated him, too.

But he had not veered off the path. And neither would I.

"Fuck you," she hissed, her words filled with venom. "I'm not some fucking experiment."

"No." I shook my head, the intensity of it all rising in my chest, threatening to break free. "You're not an experiment. You're *everything* to me. I would take all your pain, all of it, if I could."

"Then spare me," she pleaded, her voice breaking as she begged. "If you love me, let me go."

"It's because I love you that I'm *never* letting you go," I said, the words leaving my mouth like a vow I couldn't break, even if I wanted to.

Her wrist was in my hand before I even knew what I was doing. My lips hovered over her skin, her pulse thrumming against the tip of my tongue. The feel of it, the warmth of her... I didn't just want her. I needed her.

But she yanked her arm away, her eyes blazing with fury. "I'm not *yours*."

"You *are* mine," I growled, the possessiveness burning in my chest. "Saying you're not won't make it so."

"I'm Ciaran's!" she screamed, and her words hit me harder than any blow ever could.

It was her turn to advance on me. I found myself backing up.

"When you touch me, I pretend it's his hands. When you fuck me, I'm imagining his cock. I'll always be his. Only his."

The ground vanished beneath me, my breath stolen, her confession hitting like a blow I hadn't seen coming.

My knees buckled, and I grabbed the bedpost to steady myself, my heart collapsing under the weight of her words.

"Ava—" The words died in my throat, the pain too great to bear.

She reached out, but I recoiled, a chasm opening between us that I couldn't cross. Not after that. Not after she'd said *that*.

I backed away, stumbling, forcing myself to the doorway, each step feeling like I was tearing myself apart. I barely registered the cold air of the hallway as I fell back, slamming the door shut and locking it behind me.

My body shook, and I slid down the door, pressing my back against it as if it could keep out her words, her presence—anything to numb the jagged, gaping wound she'd left.

Her words, thrown so carelessly at me, like poisoned knives made to hurt, were my worst nightmare.

I would suffer a thousand years in prison rather than hear them again. Rather than have them be true.

Her voice, her sobs echoed through the metal and wood, pleading, desperate.

"Ty, no, don't leave me alone!" she cried, pounding on the door. "Please. I didn't mean it."

But it didn't matter.

It was too late. Her words had already carved their place, cutting deep, slicing through the last part of me that had dared to hope.

That night I couldn't sleep. The weight of the day, and the years before it, pressed too heavily on my chest.

Drawn to the giant white beast in the piano room, I surrendered to the only outlet I had left. The keys. Music was my refuge when words failed me—when swallowing my emotions became second nature. Too many years spent silencing myself, chewing back my thoughts, had made speaking about the things that haunted me near impossible.

And it seemed my little hummingbird couldn't sleep either, drawn out of her bedroom via the secret panel, I guessed.

I felt her standing at the doorway of the piano room, long before she cleared her voice and spoke.

"That was beautiful. What did you name that one?"

I hesitated, my fingers still hovering over the keys.

"*Requiem for... Taibhse.*" The Irish word for *ghost*, sounding like tie-sha, caught in my throat. The nickname bringing back too many memories.

Her steps were light, hesitant as she moved closer.

"W-who are you mourning?" she asked, and her voice cracked at the edges like she wasn't sure she wanted to know the answer.

I couldn't answer her. Not in words.

My shame, my grief, my past—there was too much to explain, too much I hadn't admitted even to myself.

Yet how could I expect her to face her darkness, when there were parts of mine I still hadn't faced?

Perhaps, to save her, to pull her from the darkness, I would have to reveal the things that kept me in mine.

I'd have to confess the things that haunted *me*.

# THE WARDEN

⁂

I readied to confess my darkness to her. But the memories threatened to swallow me whole. My throat closed up, choked by all the things I couldn't say.

So instead, I closed my eyes, letting my fingers fall back to the keys.

I played *Requiem for Taibhse* again—the mourning for the boy I once was, the man I could have been. The ghost of me.

I hoped Ava might hear it too. That she might feel the pain, the regret, the longing I had buried for so long.

I felt her slip into the seat next to me, and as always, her nearness twisted something deep inside my chest.

I wore no shirt, just a pair of loose-fitting black cotton drawstring pants, and the warmth of her skin brushed against mine as she shifted beside me.

The whisper of her forearm against mine as I played sent a shiver through me, the simplest touch filling me with a longing I had no right to feel.

Every inch of me wanted to reach out, to pull her

closer, to hold her the way I'd dreamed of in the dark nights when all I had was her ghost to cling to, the memory of her, the only thing keeping me from going mad in that cell.

The last notes of *Requiem for Taibhse* faded and Ava's hand slid onto mine.

*Time to be brave, Taibhse*, I could almost hear Eamon saying to me.

Words lodged in my throat like stones, heavy and jagged. But sitting here now, beside Ava, I knew I had to let her in. To tell her the things I never thought I'd be able to say aloud.

"I was too soft when I went into prison." The words grated out of me, like they were scraped raw from the inside. "Seventeen. A boy trapped in a cage with men. With *monsters*."

My breath shuddered past my teeth, the memory tasting sour in my mouth. I forced it down, but it still clung to me like a bad dream.

I closed my eyes for a moment, seeing Skellig Mór prison rising up like a rotten tooth from the craggy remote island off the misty west coast of Ireland.

"Those men—they can smell weakness," I continued. "And they smelled it on me."

I paused, gripping the edge of the piano, my fingers digging into the smooth wood, trying to anchor myself, but the memories threatened to slip loose anyway.

I felt the cell walls closing in on me, feeling the damp concrete under my knees. The sound of their footsteps. The taunts. The pain. The violation.

"*Such a pretty boy.*" One of their voices slithered up from the past, making me nauseous. *"Open that pretty little mouth..."*

My gut clenched, and I shoved the memory down as hard as I could as I fought back the bile in my throat, fighting to keep my voice steady.

I found my fingers touching the scar on my lip and I snatched it away like it had burned me.

I couldn't look at Ava, couldn't bear the thought of her seeing the truth on my face, that shameful part of me.

"I suffered," I admitted. "For weeks. It never stopped. And, of course, the guards didn't step in. The only time I had peace was when they locked me in my cell at night."

Ava gasped beside me, and I felt her eyes on me, burning my skin, making my cheeks flush.

I waited for it—waited for the disgust, for her judgment to crush me all over again.

But it didn't come.

Instead, her fingers found mine on the keys. Soft. Gentle. Her warmth wrapping around my hand like a lifeline.

I glanced at her, bracing myself for what I'd see, but there was no judgment in her eyes. Just a quiet acceptance, a grief that mirrored my own.

Her hand tightened around mine, grounding me in a way nothing else had. Not even my own memories of her had ever felt this real.

For a moment, I was just a man who had survived hell—and she was the only reason I was still standing.

"And then there was you." My voice cracked, raw. "Dreams of you. Your ghost. Your memory. It kept me going."

Ava squeezed my hand in hers, so much knowing in it,

her understanding cutting deeper than anything else ever had.

Ava had to know the rest. She had to know *me*.

I continued, knowing that if I stopped talking, I might not get the nerve to start again. "Every day I thought, today is the day they kill me."

"But they didn't," she finished for me.

I shook my head. "One day I got a new cellmate. *Eamon.*"

I almost choked on the name I hadn't spoken in months, the name carrying so much weight, so many tangled emotions.

I shoved away the memory of him, of his broad shoulders and quiet strength, the lines that crinkled around his dark eyes from a rare smile, and the way his deep voice seemed to tickle something inside my ear.

I continued. "At the time, I hated him. He was tougher than the men who hurt me. Unpredictable and... vicious. They left me alone after that. But Eamon was... tough on me."

Ava's eyes widened. "He *hurt* you, too?"

"Not like that," I said quickly, shaking my head. "He taught me how to survive in there. How to hide my emotions. How to fight."

Eamon had been a lifeline in prison. A source of warmth and strength.

"I owe him." A small smile tugged at the corner of my lips as I allowed memories of him to surface—ones that ached with bittersweetness.

The way he'd stick the tip of his tongue out in concentration as I taught him to play chess.

The wolf howl he released along with that stupid

twerking dance he did every time I broke a personal best on the bench press.

The way he'd lay with his muscled arm hanging down over the edge of the top bunk so he could sleep with his pinkie pressed to mine so I wouldn't have to feel alone.

*"Good night, Taibhse."*

"Where is Eamon now?" Ava asked softly, cutting through my memories.

I shook my head, shrugging his ghosts off me. "He's...gone."

The sorrow clenched around my throat like a vise, making it hard to speak. There were no words for the weight of that loss.

Eamon had shaped me, hardened me in ways that were brutal but necessary. And now, he was lost to me, the silence where his presence once was, still gnawed at the edges of my mind.

"What happened to him?" she asked, her voice soft but probing.

I didn't answer.

Eamon—the truth about him, about *us*, the sacrifice he made for me—was a story for another day. A story I wasn't ready to tell, not yet. Maybe never.

"Do you have a tattoo for him?" Ava asked, her fingers brushing lightly over the ink on my arm.

I nodded and pointed to the tattoo on the inside of my right bicep, the one covering a knife scar about the size of a large coin.

"I hope you don't mind," I said, my voice low, almost hesitant.

"Why would I mind?" She frowned, confusion flickering across her face.

I met her eyes, feeling the strange tightness in my chest.

"Because the rest," I paused, my heart racing at the vulnerability I was about to expose, "the rest are for *you*."

Ava's breath hitched as she looked up at me, her eyes wide with a mix of shock and something else—something deeper.

For a moment, she didn't say anything, just stared at the tattoos that mapped my skin, the black ink that told a story of my devotion that she was only just beginning to understand.

With trembling hands, she began tracing the outline of my tattoo for Eamon, her fingertips featherlight as they followed the inked lines etched into my bicep—a Celtic cross turned into a key that fit into a broken lock—a small memorial and a way to cover the last scar he gave me.

She tilted her head as her fingers went over the raised scar, but she didn't ask about it.

My muscles twitched under her touch, a mixture of tension and something far more potent.

All this time, I'd been touching her. This was the first time in five long years that she had touched *me*.

When she finished with that tattoo, her fingers moved on to the next.

And the next.

Her soft fingers mapped out each piece of me, tracing the ink that honored her. Ava as my dream, my fantasies, my nightmares. Ava as my maiden, my whore, my savior, my downfall. My redemption.

No one, not in all these years, had ever touched me with such tenderness, with such heat and meaning.

Only her.

Always only her.

Perhaps it was pathetic how much I reacted under her simple touch. How much my head spun and my skin burned. How much need and pleasure coursed through my body, the tension rising until my breath grew ragged and shallow, my body trembling from restraint, and I fisted my hands against my thighs.

I wanted to cry, scream, purge every emotion locked inside me. But all that escaped was a deep, guttural moan, torn from my chest.

Her hands were salvation and damnation all the same.

Finally, her fingers traveled up my neck toward my lip. For a moment they hesitated, unsure, her eyes searching mine as if for permission.

I grabbed her hand roughly, making her gasp, and pushed her fingers to the scar on my top lip.

It was so sensitive that I flinched—as sensitive as the day those monsters split it open—split *me* open.

I let go of her hand, leaving her there, touching my raw wound. Giving her access to the most vulnerable part of me. Laying my broken soul out for her.

Showing her every terrible thing. And begging her to love it—love *me*—anyway.

She brushed the scar so gently, her voice broken and cracked as she whispered, "They gave you this, didn't they?"

For a moment all I could feel was a hand on the back of my head, shoving my face into the shower tiles, the copper flooding my mouth, and how I'd choked on it as they—

"It's *me*, Ty."

Ava's words were so soft, so achingly tender, they slammed me back into my body with a gasp.

"It's only ever me," she promised, using my own words against me as she leaned in, "*mo mhaor.*"

*Moh muh-waar.*

*My warden.*

Ava's plump lips were so warm against my scar as she kissed it, it felt like her mouth on my most private of parts.

I let out a groan and shuddered, blood surging through my veins.

Her hot breath on my cheeks felt like heaven and my lashes fluttered closed, my breath hitching as I waited—prayed, hoped, *begged*—for more.

She explored my lip with the tip of her tongue, feeling every bump and crease of my scar.

My cock ached because it felt like she was tasting *me*. Taking *me* into her mouth.

Need overwhelmed me. Every single cell in my fractured body demanded to throw her onto this piano, spread her and fuck her.

I rocked my hips against the seat, against air, as I held myself back. Barely. I gripped my pants, my short fingernails threatening to tear through the thin fabric.

I tasted salt as a tear, then another rolled from her lashes and caught between our mouths, cleansing me. Baptizing me anew. Reborn.

Then she pulled my top lip between hers and *sucked*.

It was too much.

I clutched at her shoulders as I came, as release flooded

through me, something physical but also, something that moved through my soul.

I was left breathless, unable to be embarrassed, leaning my head against hers as the room spun, the front of my pants wet.

Ava gaped. "Did you just…?"

I almost laughed. Yes, I'd just come off a kiss.

Before I knew what I was saying, I blurted out something I hadn't meant to. Something I hadn't planned for.

But wasn't that just Ava? She always pulled things out of me I didn't expect.

I blamed the moment, the closeness, the fact that all I wanted right then was to make her happy, to see her smile.

Once it was out, I couldn't take it back.

"Ava." The words tumbled out in a rush. "Do you want to go outside?"

# AVA

I tied back my hair with a silky white ribbon, watching myself in the mirror, heart hammering in my chest. I was too excited. Too nervous. A, because I was finally going outside and B, because I was going to escape.

I almost couldn't believe it when Ty promised to take me out into the garden.

I knew that this could be my best chance of escape, but I also knew the stakes. If I messed up, if Ty caught me, I wouldn't get another.

I took a breath, trying to calm the rush of adrenaline coursing through me. I couldn't afford to get sloppy.

The knock at the door sounded light, almost tentative, and a silly thought entered my head like if this were some other time, some other life, he would be knocking at my door to pick me up for a date.

I rushed to the door, my excitement momentarily stealing my breath as I opened it.

Ty stood there, his dark hair freshly washed, still a bit fluffy in the way it only got after a shower. His black sleeves were rolled up, exposing his forearms, and for a second, the color of his eyes—so shockingly blue—made me forget what I was supposed to be doing.

There was a faint pink blush dusting his cheeks, and something about the way he blinked at me, his gaze taking me in from head to toe, seemed almost... nervous. Almost shy.

I twirled, my lacy white dress flaring out around me, teasing him lightly. "Aren't you going to tell me how pretty I look?"

He swallowed hard, his gaze serious as it lingered on me.

"Pretty doesn't even begin to describe you," he said quietly, the sincerity in his voice catching me off guard. "If the flowers in the garden saw you, they'd wither out of jealousy and bow their heads in shame."

A blush spread across my cheeks, unbidden. Damn it. I shouldn't be reacting like this. I chastised myself, fighting the warmth rising in me. This wasn't some fairy-tale date. I was supposed to be figuring out my escape plan, not flirting with my kidnapper.

But God, the way he looked at me...

"Shall we?" I forced a smile and stepped past him, already trying to map out my route, but my heart still thudded in my chest, torn between excitement for the garden—and something else I refused to acknowledge.

My heart thudded harder as Ty led me down the long hallway downstairs, his footsteps barely making a sound on the polished floor.

He stopped in front of what looked like a simple wood panel, flush with the rest of the wall.

I'd passed it dozens of times without giving it a second

thought. But this time, he pressed his thumb to a small panel at waist height.

Huh, he must have this entire place rigged to open at his thumbprint.

So if I wanted to leave, he'd have to open the door.

Or, I thought with a wince, I'd have to cut off his thumb.

A quiet click echoed in the hallway, and the door fell ajar.

The anticipation coiled inside me like a spring.

It had been so long since I'd seen the sun, so long since I'd felt it on my skin. Weeks? Months? I couldn't even tell anymore.

I stepped forward but Ty stepped in front of me, blocking the door.

"Rules," he said, his voice steady but with a warning edge that made my heart tighten.

"Okay," I replied slowly, trying to keep my voice even, even as guilt gnawed at me. I was already betraying him by thinking about escape.

"No wandering off. No tricks. No trying to escape."

I nodded, feeling my pulse race.

"And…" I teased, "if I *don't* play by your rules?"

He had me pinned up against the wall with his hand around my throat so fast that I didn't have time to scream.

His breath seared my face as he leaned in close, eyes intense and unyielding. "Don't test me, Ava. You won't like me when I'm angry."

The intensity in his gaze pinned me in place, a heat rolling through me that I couldn't control.

My body betrayed me, trembling under his firm grip, and the worst part was all I wanted to do was melt into him.

Just as the tension thickened between us, he snatched his hand back as he straightened, leaving an aching emptiness where his touch had been.

He glared at me with a look that made my skin prickle. "Will you follow the rules, or do we turn back now?"

"No!" The word came out too fast. "No, please—I'll play by your rules. I promise."

The lie slipped from my lips as smoothly as a practiced line.

He studied me for a moment, and I forced a smile, hoping it would be enough to mask the chaos inside.

He finally stepped aside, letting me pass through the door, but the weight of his warning hung over me like a storm cloud.

I could feel his gaze on my back, sharp and knowing, and as I stepped out into the sun, I prayed that my plan, my escape, would be flawless. It had to be.

I had to shield my eyes from the sun; it was blinding after all the time spent in dim, windowless rooms.

When my eyes adjusted, my surroundings came into view. A beautiful, manicured garden sprawled before me, gravel paths weaving in and out of endless rows of rosebushes and meticulously trimmed hedges.

Memories crashed into me like a tidal wave—me picking out daises to weave into a crown, me lying on my stomach on a rug under that large oak tree and reading, Ty and Ciaran chasing me through this very garden when we were younger.

I gasped, stepping off the narrow side path that ran around the mansion and onto the soft grass, feeling the earth beneath my feet, solid and grounding.

My toes sank into the cool soil, and a groan of relief slipped from my lips as I tilted my head back, closing my eyes and letting the warmth bathe me.

I didn't know how long I stood there, wriggling my toes in the dirt, letting the sun soak into every part of me.

But when I opened my eyes, Ty was watching me, an unreadable expression on his face—a look that made my stupid heart flip in my chest.

"What?" I sassed, crossing my arms and trying not to feel self-conscious. "Haven't you ever seen someone enjoy the sun before?"

He nodded, his gaze intense, as though he was seeing something deeper in me. "It's how I felt when I escaped prison."

His words struck me, sympathy flooding my chest. Yesterday, he'd told me about his time in prison—about the hell he went through—and it confused me. I wasn't supposed to relate to him, wasn't supposed to feel sorry for my captor, to *feel* anything at all for him.

I shook the thoughts away, buried them deep down.

"So how did you escape?" I asked, hoping I could learn something from his story—something useful for my own freedom. "You never told me."

A shadow passed over Ty's face, darkening his features before he buried it beneath that practiced, cool mask. "With great sacrifice."

Before I could push any further, he held out his elbow, his voice a low command. "Walk with me."

As we walked through the dark hellebores, black tulips, and the crimson falling wisteria it became clear that the garden wasn't just familiar, it was *exactly* as it was five years ago.

I paused on the path to lean into the dark-red, almost-black petals of a black pearl lily, its rich sweet fragrance filling my nose, grounding me in memories of a past I'd thought I'd lost.

"Ty," I said, my voice betraying my disbelief, "I can't believe you kept the garden this way."

He stood close by, his hands in his pockets, just watching me. "It was a mess when I first arrived. It took a few months but…"

He shuffled his feet, his black boots sinking into the soft grass. "I thought you'd like it this way. That having it the same would make you feel… more at home."

I frowned, studying his expression, which was as guarded as ever. "You put this garden back this way for me?"

He didn't answer, only looked out over the garden.

"But," I said, my breath coming out in a rush, "if you never intended to let me outside…"

A shrug. "You could still see it from the house."

Ty was so confusing. Cold, stoic, and unreadable one moment, yet thoughtful in ways that pierced right through my defenses.

He was holding me captive, forcing me to relive memories I'd tried so hard to bury, yet somehow, at times, he seemed to care. Really care. Like I mattered to him *too* much.

Clearing my throat, I kept walking, pretending his words hadn't shaken me.

"You can't possibly maintain this all yourself?" I said.

"I don't," he replied as he walked beside me.

"So who does?"

Ty pursed his lips, hesitating like he was weighing something. "I have… gardeners come once a month."

My heart stuttered. That's why he bricked up my window. So when the gardeners came, they couldn't see me screaming for help at my window.

*Once a month.*

If I could figure out when they came, maybe I could get a message to one of them. Maybe I could sneak out of my bedroom using the secret passageway and catch their attention through another window or I could leave them a message, an SOS, tucked into a rosebush or in the stone fountain.

Perhaps there *was* a way out of here—a chance.

Ty paused, his boots crunching the gravel as he came to a halt. He stared at something in the distance, a moment of quiet tension settling over him, before he turned back toward the house. "We should go back."

My gaze drifted to where he'd been looking, and there it was—a fence, half-hidden by thick ivy at the edge of the garden. Beyond it, the world. Freedom.

My chest tightened with a sudden, almost desperate longing. Something inside me rebelled.

No. I couldn't wait for once a month. I couldn't stand another fucking week, another fucking day here.

All my plans for a well-thought-out escape disappeared. All I could see was that fence. My freedom, so close.

Before I could rethink my rash actions, I shoved him as hard as I could.

Perhaps Ty was caught unawares, because he actually fell

forward, sprawling in the gravel like I had that day Ciaran had pushed me over.

For a moment I hesitated, caught between wanting to help him up and wanting to run.

He looked up, shock flaring in his eyes, and I felt a brief flicker of guilt—until I heard the feral growl tearing from his lips.

This wasn't my best friend anymore. He was my fucking kidnapper. My enemy.

And this was my one chance.

Without another thought, I turned and sprinted toward the fence, my pulse thundering as I tore through the garden, my only focus on the ivy-covered boundary, the promise of freedom beyond.

"Ava!"

Ty's voice thundered behind me, furious and unyielding, his footsteps pounding through the garden as he closed the distance.

I pushed myself harder, my bare feet searing with each step over sharp twigs and rocks. Pain flared up my legs, but I didn't dare slow down. I wouldn't stop.

My breath tore ragged from my lungs, my heartbeat a relentless drumbeat in my ears, but his footsteps grew louder, closer.

I felt him gaining ground, his presence like fire licking at my back. A sharp tug at my hair—his fingers catching in the ribbon, pulling it loose.

He was right behind me.

No, I wouldn't let him catch me. I couldn't.

I swerved left, darting down a narrower path, ducking under a canopy of dark-crimson wisteria. The hanging blooms brushed my face, cool and silken, but I didn't have time to admire them.

I plunged forward, desperate, weaving through the maze of greenery.

Ty's footsteps didn't falter, echoing behind me, relentless as a predator on the hunt.

Up ahead I spotted the familiar greenhouse at the edge of the garden.

Even though a part of me screamed not to go in there, another part figured that this was my only chance at escape.

Out here in the gardens I was too exposed, too out in the open.

In the greenhouse I'd have a chance to hide, to slip past him.

I sprinted for it, my footsteps in time with those from my memories.

*I slammed against the glass door, the entire lower level of the greenhouse covered as always with a dark curtain, and I grabbed for the handle.*

*Behind me, Ty's voice shifted, panic creeping into his usually steady tone.*

*"No, Ava! Don't go in there!"*

I shoved open the creaky ivy-covered door, thanking God it was unlocked, and tumbled inside.

*"Ava, stop!"*

*But I didn't stop. His words only fueled the curiosity that had been bubbling inside me for months.*

*So I stepped farther in, my eyes adjusting to the dim light, taking in the strange shapes around me as the door shut behind me.*

Inside, the air wrapped me in a thick, almost claustrophobic warmth, thick with the scent of something sweet yet sickly veiling the tang of damp earth.

Dense tendrils of climbing ivy crawled up the wrought-iron frames, casting faint shadows that danced in the dim light.

Rows upon rows of plants lined the room, each one arranged with unsettling precision—dark leaves, twisting vines, and flowers that bloomed in shades of deep violet, bloodred, and warning yellow. They seemed alive in a way that made my skin crawl, like they were watching, waiting.

Footsteps echoed from outside.

My heart dropped. Ty was coming.

Panic surged, propelling me down the nearest row as I darted left and right, searching frantically for another exit.

But all I saw was endless glass, closing me in. No other doors. Just the one I'd entered through—the one that was now swinging open.

I crouched low, ducking under thick green leaves. The quiet click of the door shutting made my blood run cold.

I was trapped in here *with* Ty. An angry Ty. *"You don't want to make me angry."*

I snatched a small dibbler sitting on the edge of a workbench, a gardening tool to make holes in the dirt for bulbs, its wooden shaft tapering down to a smooth metal tip, almost daggerlike.

It was barely a weapon. But it was all I had.

With it clutched in my hand, I crawled beneath a table crowded with potted plants.

From my hiding place I spotted across the row the unmistakable pink bloom of the Belladonna Lily.

*"Belladonna Lilies. Aren't they pretty, Ava? Just like you."*

*They were. So pretty. The prettiest pink in the world. Would they smell pretty?*

*I reached out to tug a flower closer so I could push my nose into it.*

*The professor's strong hand grabbed my fingers, crushing them, making me cry out.*

*"Don't touch."* His voice turned cruel and hard. *"Never touch."*

*I sobbed as I clutched my hand to my chest.*

*It wasn't just the pain. His fury shocked me. Scared me as he towered over me, the gray light filtering into the greenhouse silhouetting his face.*

*"It's poisonous."*

I sucked in a gasp. This was the greenhouse from my memory. The professor had been the one who had taught me that Belladonna Lilies were poisonous.

The lilies that Scáth—Ciaran—used to leave me by my bedside.

A wave of sadness went through me. My Scáth. God, I missed him. I wonder whether he was still looking for me or whether he'd given me up for dead.

"Little hummingbird?" Ty's voice called out, deceptively soft, almost singsong, only a few rows away.

I clasped my free hand over my mouth, willing myself to be still.

If I waited long enough, maybe he'd go deeper into the greenhouse, and I could slip out behind him.

But with every second, my breathing grew harder to control, and my heart pounded loud enough, it seemed, for him to hear from across the room.

There was a faint crunch as he stepped forward, leaves

crumpling beneath his steady pace, each footfall shattering the thick, suffocating quiet.

Then… silence.

Time lost all meaning, slipping through my fingers like sand. Seconds stretched into minutes, maybe hours.

I crouched there, ears straining, every nerve on edge. Where the hell had he gone?

Even though I couldn't see him, the hairs on the back of my neck stood on end. He was watching me. I could swear it.

My pulse thundered in my veins, each beat filling me with unbearable tension. I couldn't stay here, hidden like prey. I needed to go. Now.

Crawling forward, I peered out from behind the heavy leaves into the silent greenhouse aisle.

Where had he—

A hand clamped around my ankle, yanking me back.

## AVA

A scream tore from my throat as Ty dragged me out from under the table. I thrashed, kicking out, trying to break free. But his grip was relentless, unyielding.

Gravel scraped against my stomach as my dress bunched around my legs.

"You broke the rules, Ava. And now there's a price."

A surge of instinct took over.

I twisted in his grip, clutching the dibber like a weapon, its tip gleaming in the pale light.

Without thinking, I drove it toward him, burying the metal tip into his upper arm. Blood welled up, flowing hot and dark around the shaft.

He cursed, his grip around my ankle loosening just enough.

I wrenched myself free and scrambled to my feet, bolting down the row, every step a heartbeat closer to the door—to freedom.

But his presence loomed right behind me, closing in, his breath hot on my neck. Despite the terror, something dark and electric sizzled down my spine. I could feel him there, just inches away.

Ty lunged, his arm snaking around my waist, pulling me to the ground. His body was a cage, solid and immovable.

"Bad Ava," he hissed, his voice a rough murmur that sent a thrill of fear through me, a promise of retribution.

His hand pressed my cheek into the dirty concrete floor and I winced, but my nipples were hard and my pussy was wet.

What was wrong with me?

I fought back, trying to buck him off, but all I succeeded in doing was rubbing my ass over his cock which was hardening in his pants.

"You fucking stabbed me." He waved the dibbler, red with his blood, in my face.

"You deserve to be stabbed." I spat back. Even though as he had me pinned down, his weight over me, I was in no position to sass.

There was just something about *this* Ty that made me want to fight him.

Ty chuckled and it was cold and cruel. "So do you."

Fear tightened around me, icy and unrelenting. *No*—Ty wouldn't actually hurt me... would he?

But he didn't hesitate. His hand wrapped firmly around my hips, pulling me back until my body was forced into a position of pure vulnerability. He twisted my arm up behind me, pinning me to the ground, my upper body pressed against the cool gravel.

Every instinct screamed at me to fight, but the way he held me—secure, unyielding—left me helpless, exposed.

A soft whimper escaped my lips. I was at his mercy, and he knew it.

He pushed my hem up over my ass, my dress bunching around my waist, then tore off my panties so my pussy was exposed. Cold air rushed against my wet folds, sending tingles across my skin.

I panted, even as I squirmed, trying to get away. But all I did was hurt my shoulder as he twisted my arm harder against my back.

"Ow!" My sharp exhale blew dust and dried leaves across the concrete floor. "Please stop. I'll be good."

"No, Ava," he growled. "You knew the rules. I warned you not to make me mad. You did it anyway."

I gasped as I felt something cold and metal at my pussy entrance.

"You must be punished."

I had just enough time to realize it was the dibbler I'd stabbed into his arm before he thrust it into me.

The metal spread apart my pussy, my walls clenching around the foreign object, even as a wave of pleasure shot through me.

I cried out, a mixture of shock and unwanted pleasure, the cold metal warming inside me, my body betraying me as it responded to the intrusion.

Ty's breath was hot on my neck as he leaned over me, his chest pressed against my back.

"That's it," he murmured, his voice a dark caress. "Take your punishment like a good girl."

He began to thrust the dibbler in and out with agonizing

roughness as he ground against me, his hard cock against my thigh.

Each thrust, on the verge of pleasure and pain, sent sparks of sensation through my core. I bit my lip, trying to stifle the moans that threatened to escape.

The greenhouse filled with the obscene sounds of my wetness as Ty worked the tool inside me.

"Fuck, Ava, you're so fucking wet."

The scent of my arousal mingled with the metallic tang of blood from his arm.

My fingers of my free hand clawed at the floor, seeking purchase against the onslaught of sensations.

Then he pulled it out and I slumped to the concrete in relief and, strangely, disappointment. My punishment was over.

But I had the thought too soon. He rubbed the wet dibbler against my puckered back hole. I flinched against it. No. No one had ever.

And yet a part of me ached to be violated in that way.

A whimper escaped my lips as Ty pressed the blunt tip of the dibbler against my virgin hole.

My body trembled, torn between fear and a perverse curiosity.

"Please," I whispered, though I wasn't sure if I was begging him to stop or continue.

Ty's grip on my arm loosened slightly, his thumb caressing my skin in an oddly tender gesture.

"Relax," he murmured. "It'll hurt less if you don't fight it."

I felt the pressure increase as he slowly pushed the tool inside. The stretch burned, my body resisting the invasion.

Tears pricked my eyes, but I forced myself to breathe deeply, willing my muscles to relax.

Inch by torturous inch, the dibbler slid deeper. The pain mingled with an unexpected pleasure, sending shock waves through my body.

Then I heard his belt clinking as he undid it, heard his zipper lower.

And I felt the head of his cock at my pussy entrance.

My breath caught in my throat as I felt the hot, velvety tip of Ty's cock press against my slick folds. A shudder ran through me—fear, anticipation, and shameful desire all tangled together.

"You're mine, Ava," Ty growled, his voice low and dangerous. "Every. Inch. Of. You."

With each word, he pushed into me, stretching me wider than the dibbler had. The dual sensations of fullness—his cock in my pussy and the metal tool in my ass—were overwhelming.

I cried out, my body trembling as it struggled to accommodate him.

Ty's hand snaked around to seize my throat, muffling my cries.

"Go on," he whispered, his lips brushing my ear. "Scream. No one can hear you."

Ty began to fuck me, his thrusts hard and punishing. Each one pushed the dibbler deeper into my ass, sending jolts of pain and pleasure through my body.

I whimpered against the violation, tears streaming down my face.

The greenhouse seemed to close in around us, the air thick with the scent of earth and arousal. The plants that surrounded us were silent witnesses to my punishment, their leaves rustling softly as if in sympathy.

"That's it," he murmured, his voice a dark caress. "Take it all. Maybe next time you'll think twice before defying me."

My body betrayed me, responding to his touch despite my mind's protests. Heat pooled in my lower belly, a familiar tension building.

I hated myself for it, but I couldn't deny the pleasure that mingled with the pain.

Ty hissed. "Fuck. So tight. Not going to last long."

Neither was I, my own orgasm barreling toward me no matter how much I didn't want it. *Shouldn't* want it.

This was a betrayal to my shadow.

But my warden was determined to ruin me.

Ty snaked his hand around my waist, his fingers finding my clit. He rubbed it in tight, furious circles.

"Come for me."

"No," I choked out.

This was wrong. I couldn't let myself come. I couldn't betray Ciaran like that.

Finding release during Ty's twisted therapy was one thing. But this?

I was thinking clearly, no drugs in my system, or at least, my mind was thinking. My body had already given in.

*"Yes."*

Ty slapped my clit and a sharp burst of pain cut through my protests.

That was all it took. All it took to break the dam.

I couldn't help it. *I'm sorry, Ciaran.*

My body exploded with sensation, every nerve ending firing at once. The orgasm ripped through me with brutal intensity, my walls clenching around Ty's cock and the metal dibbler in my ass as waves of pleasure crashed over me.

I screamed but it came out a mere croak against his hand squeezing around my throat, my vision going white as my back arched.

Ty growled, his rhythm faltering as my pussy milked him. With a final, punishing thrust, he pulled out, his hot cum lashing across my back, marking me as his.

For a long moment, the greenhouse was silent save for our ragged breaths and soft rain beginning to patter on the glass roof. The scent of sex hung heavy in the air, mingling with the earthy smell of soil and green things.

Slowly, Ty pulled the dibbler from my ass and I whimpered, hearing it clatter to the ground as he tossed it aside.

He unbuttoned his black shirt, wincing as he shrugged it off his injured arm, then folded the fabric and, with surprising gentleness, used it to clean me up between my legs.

The tenderness in his touch stunned me, a jarring contrast to the ruthless punisher he'd been just seconds ago, almost as if he was... sorry for what he'd done. Almost.

I shoved his hand away, reminding myself that I was supposed to be angry at him.

Ty sat back on his heels, watching me, his sex and blood-soaked shirt crumpled in his lap, the flow from the puncture wound in his arm gradually slowing.

For a long moment, we just stared at each other, tension thickening the air between us.

Finally, I cleared my throat. "You're bleeding."

He glanced down at the wound, a faint smirk tugging at the corners of his mouth. "Ay, ay, a scratch, a scratch."

I fought back a reluctant smile, only Ty would quote Shakespeare in a moment like this.

My gaze drifted over the rows of plants in the greenhouse, each one steeped in a strange, ominous beauty.

I recognized the dark-green winding tendrils of the South American vine known to produce curare, the poison Seamus had once told me was used in the drug I found in Liath's bedroom.

Farther down, I spotted the delicate white hemlock flowers, untouched by the breeze that managed to sneak in through the open greenhouse door.

Then I noticed foxgloves with their tall spikes of tubular blooms, a vibrant shade of violet, and deadly nightshade, its purple-black berries nestled among drooping deep-green leaves.

A sudden realization hit me like a punch to the gut.

Every single plant in this greenhouse... was *poisonous*.

Then I spotted it—the oleander.

Its clusters of pale-pink and white flowers deceptively beautiful, with thick, waxy leaves glistening in the low light.

This was the plant that had ended her life.

My chest tightened as I remembered the letters I'd found in Mona's room, her desperate words, her pleas in those fading ink stains.

A chill ran through me, an unshakeable feeling of dread and grief, mixed with the burden of knowing.

The memory of Ty's face, his anguish and his intensity, flashed through my mind. Ty spent years haunted by his mother's death.

No matter how much I wanted to keep the truth hidden, no matter how much it would hurt him, I knew I couldn't.

He needed to know the truth.

I took a shaky breath, feeling the weight of the decision settle on my shoulders.

"Ty, I have something to show you."

# THE WARDEN

My mother's bed creaked softly as I sat on the edge of it, the faint scent of rose perfume wrapping around me, filling the room like she'd just left moments ago.

I hated being in here, hated the way her ghost clung to everything—the soft pinks and blues she used to wear, the lavender canopy of the bed I used to crawl into when I had nightmares, the dust settled over her silent tomb.

It made my skin crawl, made my chest tight with memories that had no business resurfacing.

I watched Ava as she crossed the room, every step deliberate, a strange seriousness shadowing her face.

My stomach twisted with the urge to stop her, to say I didn't want to know whatever it was she was about to show me.

I wasn't ready for this—I doubted I ever would be.

But the words caught in my throat, and I just sat there, waiting, feeling like a child awaiting punishment.

She paused by my mother's jewelry box, her fingers tracing its edges, then clicked open a hidden drawer with a quiet, practiced motion.

I blinked, realizing I'd never known about that drawer.

A feeling like I barely knew my mother at all crept up my spine in a shiver.

Ava turned around, and in her hand, she held a small stack of letters, tied with a faded lavender ribbon. Her ribbon. I remember seeing it nestled in her dark hair like a bird caught in a net.

I felt something crack inside me just looking at it, like the faintest sign of her was enough to shake the walls I'd carefully constructed.

Ava walked back to me, her face soft with something I couldn't read. She set the letters in my lap, then sank down beside me, wrapping her arms around my waist, her touch grounding me.

It felt as though she knew—maybe even better than I did—that whatever was inside those letters was about to tear me apart.

Her hands tightened, holding me close, keeping me from slipping off the edge.

I stared at the letters, my fingers numb as I undid the ribbon.

The knot slipped loose, and the ribbon fell away, trailing across my lap like a whisper of the past.

My hands trembled as I unfolded the first letter, and there it was—her handwriting, familiar and painfully delicate, like she'd written each word with a quiet desperation I hadn't known to look for.

The words began to blur as my eyes traced each letter, each curve of ink pulling me deeper into the memories, each line scraping at wounds that had barely begun to heal.

And with every sentence, I felt myself unraveling, piece by piece.

*My dearest boys,*

*I write this with a heart weighed down by things I can barely bring myself to say.*

*The man I once thought I could endure has become someone I cannot live beside any longer.*

*His experiments—oh, they have twisted into something terrible, something dark and unspeakable that seeps into every corner of my soul.*

*I am afraid it will soon destroy what's left of me.*

*There are nights I wish for peace, for an end to this, but that would mean leaving you both behind and I can't bear the thought of leaving you behind in this world with* him.

*My precious boys, you are all that's kept me here, breathing, hoping for a way out of this darkness.*

*But I am lost, not knowing where to turn or how to escape without abandoning you to that monster.*

*Please know that I love you, more than life itself. If there is any strength left in me, I will find a way to protect you, no matter the cost.*

*With all my heart,*

*Momama.*

My finger traced over her signature at the bottom of the page. A faint laugh caught in my throat, and I choked it back, feeling the bittersweet sting of the memory.

*Momama*—Ciaran had come up with it, smashing her name, *Mona,* and *Mama* together in that way only a toddler could, and somehow it had stuck.

She'd loved it, letting the name settle around her like a second skin, wearing it with the kind of joy she so rarely found in this house.

Something slipped from between the pages, fluttering into my lap.

I picked it up—a photo, worn and faded, its edges softened by time, deeps folds etched into it. She must have opened and closed it a hundred times, the lines deepened by years of careful fingers.

It was of her sitting in the garden under her favorite rosebush: the black baccara rose, with a dark, almost black-red hued velvety petals that deepen in color depending on the light.

And of us, her boys, both of us pressing sloppy, eager kisses against her cheeks as she laughed, her eyes sparkling alight with a happiness I'd almost forgotten.

It had been a rare moment, a sunny winter day when the cold couldn't touch us, when her laughter seemed to chase away every shadow.

I felt Ava's hand on my shoulder.

"You have to keep reading, Ty." Ava's voice was barely a whisper, cracked and swollen with the pain she was feeling on my behalf.

I didn't have to look at her to know that whatever was in these letters, this wasn't the worst of it.

She'd already read them. She already knew.

My heart felt as if it might split open, but I turned to the next letter.

The words blurred for a moment, then sharpened as I began to read, bracing myself for the truth waiting within those faded lines.

*My dearest boys,*

*My hands are still trembling as I write this. I can hardly think of the fury in his eyes, how close he came to taking that anger out on you both.*

*I feel like I'm holding my breath, waiting, knowing he'll strike back for my betrayal.*

*And Mrs. Buckley... God, I fear for her. I don't know what he'll do to her for helping us, and it's tearing me apart.*

*Last night, I thought we'd finally done it. I thought we'd escaped with her help. But Adam... he was waiting. I don't know how he knew, but he did.*

*If anything were to happen to you because of my mistakes, I don't think I could bear it.*

*I'll keep trying, my loves. I'll keep searching for a way out.*

*Know that I loved you more than anything in this world, more than my own life.*

*But if I can't... if I fail again... please, forgive me.*

*Momama.*

Horror seized my throat, choking off my breath. Had she... had she been a prisoner all along?

I struggled to comprehend it, but then, when had I ever seen my mother beyond the walls of Blackthorn Hall?

Ciaran and I left every morning for school, free to walk out into the world, but her?

I didn't recall her being anywhere but *here*.

The walls of Blackthorn Hall had kept her in, and she'd kept that from us.

The word *escape* reverberated in my mind. She had tried to escape. My mother had tried to flee this place—and failed. When had that even happened?

Fragments of memories surfaced, as sharp and painful as broken glass.

I could almost hear her voice, hushed and trembling as she'd woken me in the middle of the night, her panic barely hidden beneath forced calm.

Then, a darker memory, one I hadn't let myself recall in years: our father, his shadow looming in the faint light, his fury like a storm barely contained, blocking the small servants' gate.

I'd been too young to understand the danger, too small to fight it, too naïve to recognize that she'd needed more from me than I could ever give. To her, I'd been nothing more than a helpless weight, something to protect.

A shudder ran through me as the truth settled in, tearing me apart. Tears blurred my vision, and I couldn't hold back the surge of emotions rising up, each wave stronger than the last.

She'd been trapped, desperate, and she'd carried that weight alone, hiding her suffering to shield us.

And I'd never even known.

"I'm sorry, Ty. But there's… one more." Ava's voice broke through the haze of my grief, soft and tentative, like she knew the weight this last letter might carry.

I forced myself to look down, turning to the final page. Tears blurred my vision, smudging the words into faint, unreadable lines.

I had to close my eyes, take a breath, and try to pull myself back together. I wasn't ready, but something told me that whatever lay here would be the final blow—the one that cut deepest.

A sense of dread coiled in my stomach, a raw ache that felt like it might tear me apart.

With hands that shook, I opened my eyes and began to read.

*Boys,*

*I don't know how much time I have left.*

*Adam... he is so angry with me. I'm so afraid of what he might do.*

*I wanted so much to protect you both, to keep you from following into his madness, but I may not have that chance.*

*If anything happens to me—if I'm not here to watch over you—I need you to know that I never stopped loving y*

The letter cut off, the last words hanging unfinished, as though her life had been snatched away mid-thought, mid-sentence.

"*She* didn't leave you, Ty," Ava said, her voice a reverent hush. "She loved you."

She hadn't killed herself.

My father murdered her and faked her suicide.

That *monster* had taken everything from her, from us.

From *me*.

The letters fell from my hands.

I felt a surge of anger—raw, vicious—burning through the hollow ache in my chest.

All the anger I'd buried, forced down for years, erupted, spilling out in a tidal wave that I couldn't hold back.

Rage against my father, whose cruelty had shaped every dark corner of my life.

Rage against the system that locked me away, caging me like an animal.

Rage against the faceless monsters who had hurt me, who left me broken and haunted.

And beneath it all, a deep, bitter fury at Ciaran—for taking the *one* person who'd ever made me feel whole, for stealing the love that should have been mine.

Suddenly, I was on my feet, lashing out, *destroying*.

My hands gripped the back of my mother's favorite armchair, hoisting it up and slamming it against the floor, against the wall, against her favorite Monet painting of the garden in Paris that she'd never visit.

The wood splintered, the delicate fabric tearing as I struck it again and again, each hit releasing a sliver of the fury and helplessness clawing inside me.

Her antique mirror smashed, fracturing my reflection.

Bottles of her perfume, preserved and untouched for years, shattered across the floor, glass scattering like tiny prisms.

The jewelry box followed, clattering to the ground, spilling its contents in a mess of splintered wood and broken memories.

Everything she'd left behind, every trace of her presence, lay in ruins around me.

As the shards settled, regret pierced through me, sharper than any piece of glass on the floor.

I dropped to my knees, breath heaving, the cuts on my hands and arms stinging as I pressed my palms to the cold floor, the broken remains of her things all around me.

But I couldn't bring myself to care about the pain. I couldn't feel anything beyond the hollow ache of knowing that her life was cut short, her last words left unfinished.

But most of all, her story—the truth—had been left buried, rotting and unhonored.

Ava dropped beside me, her hands gentle as she pushed her way into my lap.

She didn't say anything; she just sank against me, straddling me, her arms wrapping around my neck, holding me close.

I buried my face in her shoulder, the smell of her jasmine washing away the stench of rotten roses, the warmth of her body grounding me, her embrace soothing the raw edges of my grief.

Her fingers combed softly through my hair, her steady breath against my ear, a reminder that I wasn't alone. She was here, a silent, steady presence, comforting me the same way I'd held her when she'd faced her own nightmares.

And in that moment, I clung to her, letting the fury and anguish bleed away, until all that remained was the hollow ache and the weight of her arms around me, holding me together.

Finally, she pulled back, her gaze steady and intense.

"It all started here, Ty. Your father and his... drugs." Her voice was barely more than a whisper, thick with the weight of what she'd uncovered.

A sick feeling churned in my gut. I'd known my father's vile paralytic had reached beyond Ava, but I'd never imagined he'd perfected his sick concoction on my own mother. The realization hit like a punch to the chest, each beat of my heart tightening with fury and disgust.

"But it's bigger than him now," she continued, her voice trembling. "Liath's abuser used that same paralytic on her. And the other missing girls. And Dr. Vale..."

Her voice faded, her lips pressing together as though holding back a truth too dark to speak. "I don't know exactly how they're connected, but they are."

My father's journal, the one he'd kept of *Ava*—the one I'd found tucked beside his bed—flickered in my mind, each page brimming with notes, instructions, and his disgusting secrets.

Did he have a journal for my mother, too? What other twisted truths had he hidden, even from me?

Ava's voice broke through my thoughts. "Ty, we have to go back to Darkmoor. They could be doing this to more girls. We can't let them get away with it."

"We will," I assured her.

"No, Ty, we have to go now!" Her voice grew desperate, each word laced with urgency. "If we can expose them, if we take this evidence—"

"No," I cut her off, firmer this time.

She stared at me, her eyes wide, the fight still blazing within them. I didn't think it possible but I fell even more in love with her—my fiery warrior, my fierce hummingbird.

But I couldn't let her rush into this—not yet.

"We'll go back to Darkmoor," I promised. "But not until you're strong enough."

"But—"

"No." I held her gaze, unflinching.

There were pieces of her past still hidden in the shadows, truths she hadn't yet remembered, each one scrawled in my father's handwriting.

I couldn't risk her unraveling in the midst of this battle —not when she was so close to reclaiming what he'd stolen from her.

"First," I said, softer but unwavering, "you need to finish your therapy."

## AVA

When I agreed to return to therapy, I expected more pain, more choking darkness. I expected to remember more violations on the red couch. But what I didn't expect was this.

Perhaps it was because I'd finally remembered the greenhouse that it had unlocked this part of my memories. Who the fuck knows.

*I crouched low under the worn workbench in the greenhouse, tangled in a mess of trembling limbs and shattered breaths, the concrete biting into my knees.*

*The air felt thick, heavy—cloying with the sweetness of oleanders, sickly and suffocating, clawing its way down my throat, rooting itself in the pit of my stomach as my panic pressed in on me.*

*My pulse pounded a frantic beat in my ears, drowning out every other thought, leaving me with only that question spiraling through my mind.*

*What had I just done?*

*Maybe it was reversible. Maybe it wasn't too late to stop it.*

*But I knew that was a lie.*

*Shadows pooled in the corners of the greenhouse, creeping toward me with every second, like hands reaching out, ready to pull me into their grasp.*

*And yet nothing moved. Nothing dared disturb the silence but the faint rustle of leaves against the glass and the maddening, relentless beat of my own heart.*

*Each time I let my eyes flicker up to the door, dread twisted tighter in my chest. I couldn't hear anything beyond the glass, no footsteps, no voices—but I knew they were searching for me.*

*I'd fled so quickly when I realized what I'd done.*

*Someone would find me, hiding where my unforgivable sin began.*

*And when they did...*

*No. I pressed a hand over my mouth, swallowing a panicked gasp.*

*I had to flee this place—flee Blackthorn Hall. Now.*

*But where would I go? I had no one else. And soon, I wouldn't even have this place. They'd never forgive me.*

*Never.*

*Something deeper rooted me in place—fear, guilt, shame, maybe all of it.*

*"Oh God," I whispered, staring at my guilty dirt-streaked fingers as the realization sank in, heavier than the humid air.*

*"What have I done?"*

I blinked, and the heavy fog around me began to dissipate. The rough concrete floor softened beneath me, turning to the plush velvet of the red couch, warm against my back.

The damp scent of soil twisted into the lingering smell

of tobacco and old wood that filled this room, creeping into my lungs and making my pulse stutter.

The overhanging leaves turned into the softness of Ty's face as he sat by me.

I blinked, disoriented, my breath catching as I realized I was back—back in the professor's old bedroom.

My fingers twitched against Ty's slacks as he pulled me into his lap as he always did, the paralytic ebbing from my system.

I could lift my head now, the weight of it lessening, my vision sharpening.

Ty's face was inches away now, his expression unreadable, like a mask cracked in places but not enough to reveal the man behind it.

I knew he was waiting for me to speak about what I remembered.

"I... I did something," I murmured, my voice thin and foreign. Shame curled at the edges of my words. "Something... bad."

His eyes darkened, and I could feel his gaze burrow deeper, peeling back layers of memory I wasn't yet ready to touch.

"So," he said quietly, each syllable carved from stone, "you remember what you did?"

A hollow, twisting feeling coiled in my stomach. I couldn't say why, but something in his voice, in his carefully measured words, told me that whatever I'd done was worse than I'd ever imagined.

It wasn't just a mistake or a regret; it was something that had set off a chain of events, a domino effect leading to... here.

"No… not exactly," I whispered, desperation clawing its way up my throat. "Please, tell me. What did I do?"

"No." His tone held finality, a wall between us. "You have to remember it yourself."

"What?" My voice trembled, the fear morphing into anger as I sat up straighter in his lap, gripping his corded forearms for support. "Why can't you just tell me?"

His face shifted, going from guarded to stone-cold in an instant. "That's not how therapy works."

"*Fuck* therapy." My voice rose, raw and strained as I shifted on his lap. "Fuck you and fuck—"

"Ava." His voice cut through mine, low and sharp, his gaze hardening as he clamped his hands down on my hips. "Stop. Moving."

Then I felt it. His cock getting hard.

Anger surged through me, fierce and uncontainable. I was losing my damn mind not knowing, torn between fury and desperation, pleading with him and he was sitting here getting *off*?

I was going to punch him in his fucking face. No, I was going to punch him in his arm where I stabbed him.

I pulled back my fist, curling my fingers under the way he had taught me.

But I had no leverage pinned down in his lap.

And he was too used to reading my movements. Besides my anger, my glare at the bulge under his shirt where he'd wrapped a bandage around his wound, telegraphed my intentions too much.

He caught my wrist before I could do any more damage to him.

For a moment I fought against him, pushing my arm

against his immovable grip, torn between letting my anger get the better of me or pleading again.

But I knew—pleading was useless.

Ty was ice. Unmovable, unbreakable, no matter how much I screamed or begged.

Still, another idea began to unfurl in my mind, a thrill of possibility twisting in my stomach as my gaze flickered to his lips—to that scar.

Guilt shot through me as I remembered how he'd gotten it, the pain he'd endured, the suffering.

I shouldn't use his feelings against him. I was Ciaran's, and when this was over, I'd go back to him. Leading Ty on was cruel.

But before I could tear my gaze away, memories rushed in—of pressing my mouth to his scar, tracing the rough edge of it with my tongue, feeling his pulse beneath my touch.

My logic faded. I leaned closer, drawn toward him as though that scar held a magnetic pull.

His lips parted on an intake of breath.

"Please," I whispered. "Tell me."

I closed the gap between us, drawn in by the heat of him, my mind short-circuiting, forgetting what I was doing in the first place.

I just needed to feel his lips on mine.

Before my lips crashed onto his, he moved, his hands grasping me by the waist and causing me to gasp.

With a firm, almost careless strength, he lifted me, setting me back on the couch like I was nothing more than a restless child.

"Therapy's over," he said, his voice flat, eyes cold and distant.

Without another glance, he stood and left, leaving me stranded in the silence, every nerve aching with embarrassment and longing.

For a moment, I just sat there, breathless, rage curling in my fists.

Something glinted on the floor near the edge of the couch—the empty vial.

The moment flashed back to the start of therapy: my fingers loosening as I dropped it, the glass rolling into shadow, Ty overlooking it.

And he still hadn't noticed.

I could feel my heart thudding as I reached down, fingers closing around the smooth glass. It was small enough to tuck into my palm. I glanced at the empty doorway, my thoughts racing.

And an idea for escape flared, dangerous and alive, lighting up every nerve in my body.

∼

I didn't bring it up again. Not during training the next day or dinner or when we leaned over the chessboard afterward.

I let Ty think I had given in, that I had accepted that I'd just have to remember my guilty shame during more fucking therapy. That I'd have to wait yet another week for answers. Answers that might not come.

But I was planning my next move.

I didn't know where Ty hid his cameras in the bedroom,

but I was sure they were there. I knew him well enough to know that he wouldn't leave an inch of the bedroom unmonitored.

So at night, with my eyes closed and pretending to sleep, and the down duvet pulled up to my nose, I practiced hiding it in my palm. I practiced rolling the empty vial along my fingers, swapping it for a small empty perfume bottle in my palm.

It was the only time Ty had slipped up, forgetting the vial the session before when it fell from my fingers and rolled beneath the couch.

I intended to make him pay for his mistake, because I didn't trust that I'd ever get another chance.

Day after day, I pretended everything was fine, wearing a mask as carefully constructed as Ty's. He'd taught me well.

Night after night, I practiced my treachery, rehearsing every move, even though each step made me feel like I was unraveling.

It felt like months had dragged by, but it was only seven days before therapy came around again—a week of waiting, scheming, and keeping my plan hidden beneath layers of forced calm.

I slipped the empty vial into the pocket of my silk robe, which I tied over my clean and washed body like a shield.

By the time Ty's footsteps sounded in the hallway, my palms were so sweaty that I feared the reverberations would make the vial slip as I held it hidden in my palm with my pinkie.

I trembled as I sat on my bed when Ty entered my bedroom, but I hoped that he attributed it to my fear of the drug and my memories. The jasmine of my shampoo was suddenly overwhelming and I fought against the feeling of lightheadedness.

My stomach lurched when Ty's long, pale fingers shifted into view of my lowered gaze. He held out a full vial, the clear liquid refracting the candlelight.

I took a steadying breath and with the empty vial tucked against my palm, I reached out.

I bowed my head even farther, hiding my hands with my hair and with Ty's black boots filling my vision, I switched the vials.

I "drank" the empty vial before offering it to him and he smiled down at me as always.

"Good girl."

Adrenaline was throbbing in my veins, but I knew I couldn't rush my performance. I let my hands fall first, pretending that the paralytic was taking over, hiding the full vial under my pillow as I "fell."

Ty kneeled to wrap his arms around me and I forced my limbs into a dead weight as he lifted me into his arms.

I closed my eyes, afraid that he'd see through my charade, afraid that my heart was beating so hard against his that he'd know I was faking.

If I couldn't fool him now, there was no chance I'd fool him when the therapy started.

He carried me down the narrow passageway to the library and I steadied myself, trying to calm my racing mind.

This was my last chance to prepare myself for what I knew was to come.

I couldn't bear to think what his punishment might be if he found out I was faking it.

# AVA

Ty arranged me like always on the couch. If my chest rose and fell more dramatically than it should have, he didn't seem to notice as he untied my robe strings and pushed it off my body.

My heavy breath through my loosely parted lips sounded so loud to me that I was sure Ty would find me out.

My whole body tensed in anticipation of Ty's tongue as he leaned over my naked body. It was only with the greatest exertion that I did not flinch when he flicked it over my nipple, then sucked, hard.

I held back a deep groan.

God. It was going to only get harder not to move, not to groan or rock my hips, begging for more.

Ty always made me come, even if it took hours.

Ty licked my skin with a savageness that had me dripping between my legs.

I wanted to tremble for him, shudder onto his tongue,

beg him with my hips grinding into his face for more, but it would all be over if I even flinched.

He'd know I'd swapped out the drug.

Ty was so attuned with my body that he'd notice anything other than perfect stillness.

"I'm going to cleanse you of him until there's only me."

I'd always assumed that he'd been talking about the professor when he said those things, but now that I had all my senses, a thought entered my head.

Maybe he was talking about Ciaran.

He lowered his face between my legs and sweat broke out all up and down my naked flesh from the strain of holding back as he lapped at my pussy, his fingers burying deep into the meat of my hips.

Inside my head I was screaming.

It was unbearable pain and it was unimaginable pleasure, the two clashing in my body like opposing waves.

I was sure I couldn't survive to the end. I was sure my body would betray me.

Ty was normally so quiet, diligent and focused. Always in control. But the noises that filled the soaring heights of the professor's bedroom were primal, vicious, blood hungry.

If he'd been silent, my traitorous gasps as he sucked frantically at my clit surely would have been heard.

"Mine. Mine. *Mine*," he chanted, his voice oscillating from hungry to painfully desperate.

So much so that my heart tugged in my chest and I had to force down the bitter guilt.

No. *He* betrayed me by forcing me to stay here. I wasn't doing anything wrong.

I was merely doing what I had to do to get back to Ciaran, to Dublin, and to uncover the bastards who were hurting Darkmoor girls.

My mind was thick with a hot haze as the wave inside of me rose higher and higher from Ty's ceaseless tongue.

My self-control was slipping. I felt fucking high. Fucking drunk.

I wanted nothing more than to give in, to claw at Ty's back, to wrap my thighs around his ears, to damn the consequences.

But I had to stay still. I had to keep it all inside.

No, I couldn't hold it back. I would scream his name when I went crashing over the edge and I wouldn't be able to stop it.

But my gaze landed on the secret panel on the opposite side of the library.

I thought I saw the secret panel shift, the memory of Ciaran's burning eyes flashing in the dark and the sharp line of his jaw just visible enough for me to see it tighten.

I held on to his furious gaze even as Ty slid two of his fingers into my pussy and curled them around. Pleasure slammed through me so hard that I thought I might pass out.

I came, with Ty's fingers inside me and his tongue on my clit, and my gaze locked on the phantom of Ciaran.

It was the ghost of his memory that kept me from screaming and revealing my treachery to Ty. His strength was mine.

My promise to return to him steeled inside me.

The full vial of paralytic burned in my mind like a

forbidden promise, a tangible glimmer of freedom tucked discreetly under my pillow.

Escape.

All I had to do was find the right moment, slip it into Ty's drink, and watch as the same paralysis that had bound me countless times finally took him down.

The very idea sparked a thrill of hope—of returning to Darkmoor, to Ciaran. Of freeing myself from this twisted cycle of "therapy" that was as torturous as it was healing.

But even as I held on to this plan, the thrill dulled with a creeping guilt.

If I used it, if I left Ty behind, I'd be leaving more than *him* behind. I'd be severing myself from everything he'd tried to unearth in me, every piece of my fractured past he had forced me to confront.

Wasn't that the whole purpose of therapy? Had I gone down this long dark road, suffered every raw and painful step, just to quit now?

And somehow, hadn't he—Ty, with all his dark, complicated intensity—started to mean something more to me?

Not in the way that Ciaran did, but in a way I couldn't easily dismiss, no matter how hard I tried.

Ciaran.

I could almost see his face staring out at me through the secret panel, the flash of his smirk, could almost feel the brush of his protective arms around me.

My heart tugged in his direction, as if it belonged with him, waiting for me to come back.

But had he felt this pull—this ache—when I was gone? Or had he managed to let me go, to start over without me?

It had been almost three months, the whole summer, of me "missing."

The thought struck hard, as if my escape might mean stepping back into a world where he'd moved on, where he'd left Ireland without me as we'd planned, leaving me with only the haunting memory of what we'd once shared.

And then there was Ty.

How many times had I pleaded with him to stop, to let me go, only to find him holding me through every memory, coaxing the truth from me like it was our shared burden?

He'd suffered, too, in ways I couldn't begin to understand, yet I'd seen his control crack, his humanity bleed through the armor he wore.

If I drugged him, if I escaped, would I be betraying that side of him—the one who'd stayed by my side, even as I fought and screamed and clawed against the memories? I'd be betraying my best friend who suffered through prison and fought his way out so he could come back to me.

And yet... every time Ty touched me, I felt Ciaran's ghost between us, a wall of loyalty and guilt that I couldn't seem to break down.

Could I keep enduring Ty's version of "therapy," knowing it chipped away at that bond, knowing that with every session I was betraying the man I loved?

Or would breaking free of Ty be my only way to hold on to Ciaran, to make sure that when I returned, I could look him in the eyes without shame?

As usual, Ty pulled me into his arms. I laid my head on his shoulder as I "recovered" from the paralytic, keeping my movements slow and heavy as if the drug was only just wearing off.

Ciaran's shadow watched me from the secret panel, his tortured eyes pleading with me to choose *him*.

As Ty pressed tender kisses along my spent, limp body, every argument clashed, pulling me in opposite directions.

The vial could mean escape or betrayal, a step toward freedom or a descent back into the dark memories that haunted me.

It was my decision, my responsibility, and the weight of it pressed down on me until I felt like I might break under it.

What would I lose if I left? And what would be left of me if I stayed?

# AVA

All day, the small vial of paralytic burned a hole in my mind.

The idea of drugging Ty and escaping hung over me like a storm cloud, constantly shifting between hope and dread.

I could slip it into his drink, watch him go limp, and finally get out of Blackthorn Hall.

I'd be free.

But there was no denying the risks—the thought of his furious gaze, the potential consequences if he caught me, sent chills down my spine.

I went back and forth in my mind, wavering, one second resolute, the next hesitant.

The vial felt heavier by the hour, the guilt gnawing at me as much as the desperation for freedom did.

Ty wasn't just my captor; he was complicated—sometimes kind, sometimes cruel, always unreadable. And there was this unsettling truth that, despite everything, some part of me didn't want to betray him like that.

But wasn't he the one betraying me by keeping me here?

A sudden sound of the door panel sliding aside pulled me from my thoughts. I glanced at the door to find a small silver tray with a bowl being pushed inside the panel door.

The scent of the strawberries washed over me as I brought them to my spot on the couch, a scent that pulled me back—way back. A memory surfaced, unbidden, so vivid it might as well have been happening before my eyes.

*Ciaran set me roughly on the bench in the kitchen. "What the fuck were you thinking, Ava?"*

*I listed to the side, a hiccup falling from my mouth as my head lolled.*

*"Jesus—" he muttered as he caught me and set me right again, the roughness of his hands stirring something in me that scared me more than his fury.*

*I pushed his hands away and forced myself to sit upright. "I'm f-fine."*

*"You're drunk." Ciaran shot me a judgmental glare before he walked stiffly to the sink.*

*Moonlight drifted in from the window and cast strange shadows from the fragrant mint, lavender, and wild thyme the professor had hung to dry.*

*The muscles along Ciaran's strong back tensed and flexed as he poured water into a glass and despite the alcohol warming my insides, I shivered.*

*I'd called the wrong twin to come rescue me from the underage high school party.*

*Ty never would treat me with such contempt.*

*If it had been Ty who picked me up off the floor of that spinning bathroom, he would have taken me to his bed here at Black-*

thorn Hall and applied cold compresses to my pounding forehead while whispering that I was safe in his arms.

Why did I instinctively call the boy who despised me instead?

Ciaran gripped the edge of the farm sink with knuckles which shined white in the moonlight and dropped his head to breathe sharp, ragged breaths.

I considered making a run for it.

How quickly could Ty come to me if I called his name down the long dark hallway? What would Ciaran do if he caught me first?

My uncertainty paralyzed me and soon it was too late as Ciaran turned to me in the dark.

I could feel his shadowed eyes on me and adrenaline battled the alcohol in my veins.

He crossed to the fridge and I tracked his every step, fearful of what he would do next. The glare of bluish-white light made me wince and when I shielded my stinging eyes, I lost my balance again. I would have fallen had Ciaran not wrenched angrily at my shoulder to right me.

His fingers hurt me, surely digging in deep enough to bruise later. With tears pricking at my eyes, I twisted out of his grip.

"I said I was fine," I slurred.

Ciaran remained dangerously silent as he struck a match in the dark. He lit a candle, thick with drips of wax, and set it on the table behind me.

I felt the heat of his eyes, which seemed almost black against the flame.

He pressed the cool glass against my lips.

"Drink," Ciaran commanded, his voice strained and tight.

Parting my dry lips and tipping up my chin, I closed my eyes to drink. I'd never tasted water so fresh and delicious.

*I drank till Ciaran pulled the glass away, whispering, "Easy."*

*I opened my eyes to see that Ciaran's hands were shaking as he placed the glass back on the table. Did I disgust him so much? Was I that unbearable to be near?*

*With heavy, irritable breathing, Ciaran forced my knees apart, wedging his legs between mine.*

*I felt vulnerable in that position, pinned between his hard body and the cupboard behind my head, my chest heaving in fear, the breeze from the window stealing under my miniskirt.*

*Ciaran did nothing to make me feel more comfortable. If anything, his anger seemed to grow as he stared down at me, unmoving, unspeaking.*

*His stillness terrified me even as his proximity inflamed my skin from head to toe.*

*When Ciaran reached for something beside me, I flinched.*

*He held up a strawberry which he'd plucked from the bowl beside me.*

*I was so anxious and still really drunk. The words tumbled out before I could stop them.*

*"One day... in my future house... I want a strawberry patch."*

*I searched Ciaran's face for any reaction at all. But his gaze was icy beneath his dark brows and his beautiful lips did not even twitch.*

*"Eat."*

*I opened my mouth for him. His gaze followed the strawberry as I gently bit down on it.*

*I felt the heat of his fury and almost couldn't swallow.*

*I chewed slowly, taking more and more tiny bites until I'd reached the stem, my eyes only on him.*

*He plucked another strawberry from the bowl and held it up.*

*This time when I opened my mouth, Ciaran traced it around*

my lips. I could feel the juice smearing onto my skin; I longed to lick it, but he plunged it deep into my mouth.

I bit the whole strawberry off, stickiness gathering around my mouth, his eyes fixed on my lips, pupils flashing black in the candlelight.

"What else do you want?" Ciaran asked, surprising me.

I didn't think he heard me. Or if he did, he didn't care.

I tried to tell myself to keep quiet. I didn't want to share what I held so precious inside my heart. I feared in his cruelty that he would crush it, my fragile dreams.

But I was drunk and nervous around Ciaran. And I'd secretly longed for someone to share myself with, just like all lonely orphans always do.

"I want a big library with a view of the sea," I said before I could stop myself. "It will be filled with light. The shelves will be the color of driftwood and the couches the color of sea glass. And the books will be faded from the sun with pages bent and yellowed from long days on the beach."

My knees trembled against Ciaran's legs and my heart pounded painfully in my chest. I felt like I was getting more drunk instead of less.

I continued. "Each room will be light and airy and have blue drapes the color of..." Your eyes. "...of cornflowers. And our—my —bedroom will have a peaked ceiling and overlook the sea. There'll be an antique writing desk beside a sunny window. And a large comfortable bed piled high with the softest pillows."

I watched, sure that I'd said something wrong, as Ciaran bit into a strawberry, the red juice as bright as blood in the flickering flame. The corners of his wet lips curled up and my veins went cold with fear.

If he laughed at me, I would die.

*I was frozen in place, expectant of the worst, as he leaned forward and motioned for me to take a bite myself.*

*I kept my eyes fixed on his, searching for a hint about how he would hurt me. Because Ciaran always found a way to hurt me.*

*He caught a drop of juice from my lower lip. "Would you have a porch... where we could drink tea?"*

*His hair brushed along my cheek as he reached past me to grab another strawberry. He'd left me staring, wide-eyed and wary.*

*I didn't trust the sincerity in his voice, but when he touched the strawberry gently to my lips, I saw in his eyes that he was still waiting for an answer.*

*"Yes, a large wraparound porch," I whispered before I bit the fruit he offered, letting the sweet taste melt on my tongue.*

*I didn't tell him that there had always been a boy on my porch, too. Always in the shadows. Always just a silhouette. I hadn't let myself paint him in. Yet.*

*Ciaran's face moved dangerously close to mine.*

*I gripped the bench more tightly.*

*"What about a forest nearby so I could chase you through it?" he asked.*

*Goosebumps erupted along my arms.*

*Pine drifted in through my nostrils, even through the thick fragrance of the drying herbs. Pine and salt water. Rich earth and his musk.*

*"Yes," I said, hypnotized by his eyes. "Pines, I think."*

*"Pines," he echoed.*

*The candlelight seemed to enclose us in a world of our own. I had only meant to show Ciaran my dream house, not open the doors to it.*

*But whether it was the alcohol or the steadying pressure of his legs against mine, I suddenly found him there wherever I looked.*

"The house shouldn't be too big," I said, breathing a little too quickly, "so that we can always find each other without having to yell."

"Unless I'm up on the small rooftop terrace with the telescope," he replied, encouraging another bite of strawberry.

Though it was fleeting and hesitant, Ciaran smiled, and for a moment, it transformed him. It softened the hard edges of his face, a rare warmth breaking through his usual cruel mask.

His lips curved slightly, almost uncertain, but the effect was undeniable—it was beautiful, a glimpse of something hidden beneath the layers of darkness he carried.

I clung to the rare sight of it like a shooting star. But just like the shooting stars, it was gone too soon.

Ciaran ran his thumb along my cheek. I shivered from his touch.

"But we should always go together to count the stars," I said.

"Yes," he whispered. "I promise to never look at the stars without you."

Ciaran seemed distant as he took another strawberry from the plate. I saw in his eyes that he wasn't there with me in the glow of the candle in the kitchen of Blackthorn Hall.

He was already at the house, *our* house.

My heart leaped with a cold panic. He had to take me with him. I wouldn't let him go there without me.

When Ciaran absentmindedly brought the strawberry to his lips, I snatched it from his fingers and replaced it at his lips with my own. A deep warmth spread through me as I kissed him. He kissed me back, if only for a moment.

He stood abruptly and I fell back against the edge of the table behind me, my legs still spread between his. The next time the *breeze came in through the window, carrying with it a soft hint of lavender, it chilled a small wet spot on my panties.*

*Ciaran was breathing heavily, just like me.*

My feelings for my bully made sense.

That's when I fell in love with Ciaran.

It should have been Ty. The kind brother.

But for the stupidest reason, I'd fallen in love with my bully *first* all those years ago.

It sealed my choice.

I promised my shadow that I would do what I had to do to come back to him. I would make the sacrifices. Suffer the penalties. Carry the weight of the consequences.

Nothing mattered more than him.

I would find my way back to him. No matter what.

I would drug Ty.

And I would escape.

## AVA

In the library after dinner, the damp of my freshly washed hair chilled me more than usual despite the warm summer breeze that blew through the crack in the barred bay windows.

The Blackthorn library was one of my favorite rooms, the only place it seemed I could mentally escape my prison.

The towering bookshelves stretched up to the vaulted ceiling, their dark wood softened by the low golden light of the iron chandeliers. Dust floated lazily in the beams filtering through the tall arched windows, casting the entire room in a soft, mysterious haze.

The spiral staircase wound its way up to the mezzanine level and sliding ladders rose up to the higher shelves, inviting me to lose myself in the stories waiting in the shadows.

My fingertips shook as I turned a page of a book that I hadn't read a single word of. My cheeks burned feverishly because I was sure Ty knew that I planned to betray him.

He sat on the other end of the large cushioned window box with my bare feet in his lap.

I didn't dare glance over to check, but I was sure that he was watching me over the top of his book.

He'd caught me biting nervously at my lip. He'd noticed the quickness of my breath stirring the delicate lace of my slip. He'd guessed at the reason for my marble-cold skin.

He knew.

"Did I tell you you're in Croatia now?" Ty spoke casually, softly, innocently, but still I flinched.

For a second I was confused until I remembered that he was faking my "summer sailing vacation."

I gripped my book tighter.

The silence between us was stretching too thin and I feared what would happen when it snapped.

With tension aching in every little muscle of my jaw, I said, "I must be enjoying the sunshine."

I fixed my gaze on the page, even as the words blurred in front of me. My heart pounded as I waited for Ty's reply.

My pulse throbbed against the full vial, which was tucked between my palm and the leather-bound cover of the book.

I nearly screamed when Ty's hand wrapped around my foot.

"You seem... tense." His thumb massaged small circles into the balls of my feet.

The tender gesture made another flood of guilt wash through me.

But I shook it off. No. I'd made up my mind. I'd chosen my path. My path led me back to Ciaran. I would not be swayed by guilt.

No matter how kind Ty was being, he was still my kidnapper, my captor, my tormenter.

And I would escape him.

I shrugged. "No more than usual."

Ty let out a small hum but I forced my focus back to the book in my lap.

The hidden vial felt like it was searing a hole into my skin. Every word on the page blurred together, unreadable through the tension winding tight in my stomach.

"Interesting book?" he asked, his tone unreadable.

"Riveting," I muttered through clenched teeth, my fingers clinging to the book as if it could shield me from his attention.

"It's upside down."

I startled, fumbling with the book, almost dropping both it and the vial hidden within its pages. My heart lurched.

I glanced down, but the words were right side up—he was trying to trick me. Trying to goad me into giving away my plan to betray him.

I shot my gaze back up, prepared to fire a glare his way, but he was already watching me, a small crooked smile tugging at his lips, a hint of mischief in his gaze. That smile—just the faintest quirk—sent my pulse into chaos.

Damn him. Even now, even with everything, his smile was breathtaking.

For a second, I felt something unsteady under my anger, some dangerous part of me that wanted to smile back.

And then it hit me—he was *joking*.

Tynan Roderick Donahue, the cold, unflinching warden who held me captive, was making a joke.

It was like a crack in his otherwise impenetrable armor, and for a moment, it made him seem almost... human.

It left me speechless.

"More wine?" he said, nodding at the empty wineglass sitting on the small table at my elbow. I'd gulped the whole glass down earlier to try to calm my nerves.

I cleared my throat. "You... you never let me have a second glass."

He stood, slipping out from beneath my feet, and walked toward me.

I snapped the book closed around the vial and pulled it into my chest. If he took the book from me, the vial would fall out. I'd be caught. I'd be so fucked.

I remembered the way he'd "punished" me on the floor of the greenhouse for trying to escape the last time and repressed a shiver.

For a moment he just stood there, staring down at me, my heart in my throat.

Then he reached out and grabbed my glass, shrugging. "Maybe you've been a good girl lately. Maybe you deserve a second glass."

Guilt clenched around my chest, sharp and suffocating, while a bitter wave of disappointment surged through me. I wanted to be good. I didn't want to let him down, didn't want to see that flash of disappointment shadow his beautiful face when he realized I'd betrayed him.

*But you won't see it, Ava*, I reminded myself fiercely. *You'll be gone by then, far away from this prison, free from your cruel warden.*

Ty turned on his heel, his footsteps echoing all the way

up around the beautiful, towering ceiling as he walked over to the small ornate silver bar cart, his back to me.

The flood of adrenaline and relief in my blood made me want to throw up.

I clutched the book and vial to my stomach as torment tugged violently at my chest. I believed Ty was onto me, but if I wanted to take my chance, this was it. I had to move.

I leaned forward toward Ty's own glass, still half-full of rich burgundy wine, perched on the small ledge wedged between the window box cushions and the window, the vial of paralytic gripped in my palm feeling like a burning coal.

From where Ty stood with his back to me, the stopper on the red wine popped and glass clinked as he refilled my glass, making a soft melodic murmuring sound—was that Ty *humming?*—under his breath.

When I realized he was humming *Ava's Lullaby*, a song he wrote for me while he'd been in prison, it momentarily broke my heart.

No. I couldn't go through with it.

I shook this crack in my armor off. No, I *had* to do it.

*Fuck Ty. Fuck his therapy and fuck this Stockholm Syndrome shite.*

I had to return to Darkmoor. To Ciaran. To the missing girls and the vile society that preyed on them. I was the only one who could help them. The only one who would fight for them.

I had to betray Ty. Even if… even if a part of me didn't want to. Even if a part of me craved Ty and his darkness like a captive craves his captor.

I poured the contents of the vial into Ty's glass of wine.

# AVA

For a second I stared at the swirling wine laced with paralytic in Ty's glass. Shit. I couldn't believe I'd just done it.

I'd drugged his drink.

The pop of a cork going back into a wine stopper snapped me back into action.

As Ty turned, my glass in his hands, I leaned back, shoved the empty vial between the couch cushions, and opened up my book in my lap again, feigning innocence.

My heart jolted with terror, sure it was all over, at the sound of his footsteps returning.

But Ty placed the glass at my elbow and rearranged himself back where he'd been sitting, once again placing my feet back onto his lap.

"Well?" he asked.

My head was so muddled with terror and guilt that it took a second for me to realize he was talking about the wine he'd brought me.

"Oh. Yes. The wine. Thank you."

I managed a smile even as I felt the moisture along my cupid's bow.

When he reached for his glass of wine, I hardly dared to let out a breath. I was positive he would have been able to smell the drug I'd poured in there, the faint scent of strawberries.

Ty raised the glass to his lips and I almost cried out for him to stop.

I hated that I was still conflicted over taking my chance at escape. I was being disloyal to Ty, but my heart was being disloyal to me.

In the end it was Ciaran's face in my mind that caused me to bite my lip, swallowing back the protests.

As Ty sipped his wine, I watched his throat bob as he swallowed, sure I could see the paralytic descending.

Did his eyebrows twitch toward each other, a slight frown drawing down the corners of his beautiful lips? Did he taste my treachery? The hint of strawberries in his wine?

Meeting Ty's eyes, I searched for signs of anger and betrayal. But finding none was no consolation. I knew the godly level of self-control Ty exerted over himself.

I took a sip of my own wine, actually tasting it this time. It was lush and fruity. Please God, make it fruity enough to cover up the taste of strawberries.

Ty set aside his wine and returned to my feet, rubbing his thumbs on the pads and making me want to sink back into the cushions and groan.

And for a moment that's what I did.

I peered at Ty over the edge of my book, watching his gaze drift to my feet as he worked his way up my arches.

Dammit. As heavenly as his focus felt, he was barely touching his wine. Just the occasional leisurely sip, like he had all the time in the world.

A flaw in my plan.

If he kept going at this pace, he could take all night to finish the glass. I needed him to drink more—and fast. But how?

My eyes dropped to my own untouched glass, a flicker of an idea sparking to life.

If he wouldn't drink of his own accord, I'd just have to give him a reason.

"How about a game?" I said as I set aside my book, keeping my voice light.

Ty's brow rose, curiosity glinting in his eyes. "A game?"

"Two Truths and a Lie," I said, conjuring up the memories of playing this scandalous yet always hilarious drinking game at college parties, always with Lisa and Aisling and… Liath.

Her name hit me in the chest and my resolve hardened. I *had* to make Ty play, had to make him drink his damn wine. Had to get back to Darkmoor.

Ty tilted his head and hummed. "Not a game they taught us in prison. Explain the rules."

I leaned forward, playing with the rim of my wine. "You say three statements, two true and one false. I have to guess the lie, and if I'm wrong, I drink. Then it's my turn. And we keep going until one of us… can't anymore."

I raised my glass in a faux toast, trying not to look like I had ulterior motives.

Ty's expression shifted thoughtfully, all cool detachment, his fingers paused on my feet. "This is hardly a frat party, Ava."

I shrugged, pretending like I didn't care if he didn't play. "Okay. If you're not game... *Ciaran* was always up for a bit of fun."

I saw Ty flinch, caught the slight scowl before he straightened.

"All right," he said, voice low, a competitive smirk playing at his lips. "Let's play."

My heart skipped. *Yes*, I fist-pumped internally. Nothing like pitting two brothers against each other.

Ty picked up his glass and tilted it toward me. "Ladies first."

I hadn't really thought through my own turn. I couldn't let him make me drink too much. I couldn't exactly escape properly if I was falling down drunk.

I'd always been a lightweight, but all these months as a captive with barely any alcohol had made me a two-drink drunk.

I needed to choose something I could reveal without giving away too much. I had to choose carefully so that *he* drank but I didn't.

I swallowed and took a breath.

"Okay." I ticked them off on my fingers. "I've climbed the roof of Darkmoor chapel. I got kicked out of a college club for pranking the dean. And... I love lilies."

Ty's smile was barely there, his eyes piercing me with that relentless intensity. The silence stretched between us.

"You didn't get kicked out of any club," he said finally. "The only one you ever joined was the *Darkmoor Diaries*."

I blinked, feeling a spark of irritation as he nailed it without flinching. How did he *know* that?

I frowned. Was Ciaran feeding him information in prison all those years? Or did he have someone else on the outside keeping tabs on me?

"Right. That's... correct." I took a drink, the sharpness of the wine sliding down my throat.

Not exactly according to plan, but it was fine. That would be the last sip he'd make me take.

I gestured for him to take his turn, hiding my nerves behind the glass.

He was quiet for a moment, considering, then spoke in that too-casual tone. "I can speak six languages. I hate heights. And I've killed a man with a teaspoon."

I blinked, caught off guard, then squinted at him. "You don't hate heights."

His mouth quirked up in a low chuckle, the sound sending a strange shiver through me. "Actually, I do. I just don't ever let it show."

"Well, I know you don't speak six lang—" I cut off, my mind catching on his last statement. "How the hell do you kill a man with a teaspoon?"

Ty smirked. "Maybe if you're a good girl, I'll show you."

My face heated as I took a bigger sip this time, fighting the embarrassment creeping up.

"Okay," I said, glancing at my glass, feeling the tipsy warmth spreading through me, loosening my tongue. "I've never stolen anything. I once stayed in the library overnight after hours... and I miss Ebony."

Ty's gaze softened, something deep and raw flashing in his eyes. "You never stayed in the library overnight."

My chest tightened, my mouth going dry. I blinked. He was right, though I'd thought I was careful.

I obeyed, the sharp edge of the wine a poor cover for the bitterness I felt.

The game went on, each turn loosening something in me. I wasn't sure if it was the wine or the game or the way he kept looking at me, his gaze softening every time I got something right—or terribly wrong.

His stare was unrelenting, like he could reach into me, drag out every secret. And in a rush, I realized I was drifting closer to him, feeling the pull of his warmth, the presence that unnerved me.

I was slipping, forgetting the plan.

And somehow, we found ourselves seated cross-legged in front of each other, my leg burning where our knees were touching.

Ty's breath was warm as he leaned close, his voice low and intimate, like he wanted every word to reach me. "I spent every night in prison dreaming about you. I planned your therapy for a year. And... I never wanted to hurt you."

The words hung in the air between us, heavy with meaning that I didn't dare unpack.

"The lie," I whispered, "is that you never wanted to hurt me."

He didn't answer right away, just held my gaze, his hand lingering on his glass.

"Drink," he said finally, his voice dropping to a command.

"But—"

"I spent *more* than a year planning your therapy."

His casual confession of his utter obsession with me sent a shiver through me.

I was right to try and escape.

Ty would *never* let me go.

I lifted the glass to my lips and paused, realizing there was only one mouthful left. I let out a soft huff and tossed it back, warmth spreading through me as my head spun.

Well, that didn't go as planned.

At least Ty had also almost finished his wine. Almost.

Jeez, when did it get so hot in here?

"I guess you win," I said, setting the glass aside and crossing my arms.

"Have I?" he whispered.

His tone was so heavy with meaning, so achingly hopeful, it made my heart clench. He wasn't just talking about a simple game.

He leaned in, his gaze trailing down to my mouth, growing hungry as if he wanted to kiss me.

I found myself leaning forward, drawn into him, my own gaze locking on his parted lips.

I wanted to kiss him.

No, that was stupid. I didn't want to *kiss* my kidnapper. I was drunk. That was all.

He murmured, "Ava…"

His hand lifted toward me, fingers trembling as they reached for my face. But halfway there, his arm faltered and fell back to his lap, a flicker of confusion crossing his features.

I stilled, caught between exhilaration and dread as I watched him sway, the drug clearly taking hold.

His brows knit together, realization dawning as he

struggled to lift his hand again, his expression hardening into something dark and accusing.

His voice was a low, dangerous growl, his tone sending chills down my spine.

"What have you done?"

Ty lunged for me and I screamed.

# THE WARDEN

I should have known something was wrong.

There was a look in Ava's eyes—intense, unguarded, like she was studying every line of my face, her gaze drifting over me with a strange, hungry focus. The kind of look that held an edge I couldn't quite place.

But then she smiled at me and I forgot everything but the warmth of her knee pressed to mine, the way a stray lock of her hair had slipped loose, framing her face in soft, dark waves, her lips parted slightly as she sipped her own wine, her gaze never leaving mine.

I let myself sink into that moment, into her nearness, leaning into her as she leaned into me.

"Ava…"

My hand lifted toward her, fingers trembling as I reached for her face. But halfway there, my arm faltered, heavy and unresponsive, before falling back into my lap.

I blinked, trying to shake it off, but the warmth that had filled me moments ago felt heavier now, a thick, weighted warmth spreading through my arms, my legs. A faint numbness began settling in my fingers, turning the empty glass heavy in my hand.

She froze, her wide eyes fixed on me, a mix of something electric and fearful flashing across her face.

I struggled to lift my hand again. But my muscles refused to obey, weighed down by something insidious.

A chill prickled down my spine as realization dawned.

She had done this.

*The wine.*

My mind raced, piecing it together—she must have saved a vial, pretended to be drugged all along. She'd hidden it, reserved it just for me.

*She'd planned this.* She had planned her escape.

*Just like my mother.*

A stab of horror sliced through me, freezing me in place.

This was my worst nightmare—Ava, scheming, waiting for the moment she could break free, leaving me like my mother had tried to leave my father.

Had I fought my whole life to be anyone else, but inadvertently become *him*?

"What have you done?" I growled, the words sharp, edged with disbelief. The betrayal cut deeper than any blade, a fierce heat roaring through me as I grabbed her wrist.

She twisted against my hold, yanking back with a move called a wrist release—*ironic*, given that I'd taught her that trick myself.

Passed down from Eamon to me, from me to her.

Now, the student had become the master. The captor had become the captive.

Even without the paralytic, Ava had gotten under my skin. Dug into me, invading my mind, my senses. Making me helpless against her, my willpower crumbling at every turn when it came to her.

She'd studied me, learned me, and now... she was using everything I'd taught her to break free.

I'd applaud my perfect student if I wasn't so desperate to stop her.

With one final, frantic twist, she wrenched out of my grasp, scrambling back from the window box.

I lunged forward, my hand reaching for her, my fingers brushing the fabric of her dress before she slipped out of reach.

"Ava!" I snarled, my voice thick and heavy.

She didn't stop.

She pushed herself to her feet and ran through the library, her footsteps echoing in the vast, quiet space.

My body protested as I forced myself forward, each step a battle against the creeping numbness overtaking me. The drug fought to pull me down, but I pushed through the fog, feeling her betrayal like acid in my veins.

This wasn't the first time she'd chosen Ciaran over me.

I remembered watching from across the crowded school cafeteria on Ava's first day at our school, the way Ciaran's charm had lit up Ava's face, her laughter ringing out in response to something he'd said.

My gut had twisted with jealousy, an aching fear that she already belonged to him.

Ciaran had always been the charismatic one, the reckless one, the bad boy, and I'd feared that was what she wanted.

But then something shifted. I didn't understand it at the time, but overnight his behavior toward her changed.

Ciaran became distant, even dismissive.

He'd scowl at her, his gaze dark and unreadable as she tried to talk to him. He brushed her off with a cruel edge. It was as if he wanted to push her away, to drive her back.

And every time he did, she turned to me, her eyes uncertain, her voice soft, looking for something Ciaran refused to give.

I was there for her.

Every small moment in between his mood swings and his games, I was the one who listened.

When Ciaran shoved her over, hurting her, I'd carried her to the nurse's office. I'd sat with her, bandaging her knees, feeling her trust in me, feeling… seen.

And I thought she saw me.

Finally chosen me.

From then on, it was always Ty and Ava—whispered conversations, inside jokes, shared glances that I held on to, desperately trying to convince myself they meant something.

All the while, Ciaran pulled away, treating Ava with such cruelty that she stayed away from him, could barely say his name.

But then it happened. That awful shift I hadn't seen coming.

Ava started looking at him again, with that same softness in her gaze, that same light. It was a look I wanted, needed, to be directed at me, not him.

A memory crashed into me with a bitter clarity, as vivid as if it were happening all over again.

*Gravel crunched under my shoes as I crossed the shadowed path winding through the small cemetery. Ivy twisted around ancient headstones, the moss-covered statues leaning as if whispering secrets to each other. A chill hung in the late afternoon air, thick with the damp smell of earth and old stone, a place no one ventured unless they wanted to be left alone.*

*Perfect for the bad boy of Blackthorn.*

*Ciaran leaned against a crumbling angel statue, one foot pressed against the base, his blazer unbuttoned, shirt rumpled, collar askew. He flicked the ash from his cigarette, letting the thin smoke curl up into the thick branches of an overhanging yew tree.*

*Shadows played across his face, sharpening his already angular features, his eyes dark and unreadable as he saw me approach.*

*He didn't move, only raised an eyebrow, that infuriating smirk tugging at his mouth, like he'd been expecting me.*

"Hello, brother, did you miss me?" *he drawled, taking another drag, his tone as dismissive as ever.*

"Did you kiss her?" *The words came out rougher than I intended, my voice cutting through the stillness.*

*Ciaran's expression barely shifted, only his eyebrow arched, a glint of mischief sparking in his eyes.*

"Who?" *he asked, voice dripping with feigned innocence.* "I kiss so many girls, Ty. You'll have to be more specific."

*I felt my jaw clench, my fists tightening by my sides.*

*He knew exactly who I was talking about.*

"Don't play games with me, Ciaran," *I growled, the anger boiling over.* "You know damn well who I mean."

*He laughed, a quiet, taunting chuckle, his gaze never wavering.*

"You mean... Ava?" *He flicked ash from his cigarette, that insufferable smirk tugging at his lips as he watched my reaction, like a cat playing with a wounded bird. "Our sweet, little* sister?"

*I flinched, the word hitting me like a slap.*

*Sister.*

*He said it with a smirk, as though he'd seen right through me, knew exactly what lay under my skin.*

*The word was wrong—too wrong.*

*Ava wasn't my sister, not in any way that mattered to me. But even hearing it out loud made something sink, heavy and sickening, in my gut.*

*I knew what I felt wasn't allowed, wasn't supposed to be spoken.*

*But it didn't change the way my heart stammered whenever I saw her. The way I'd felt since that first moment we'd met, since her eyes had met mine.*

"What did you do to Ava?" *I demanded.* "One second she was mine— And now she... she won't stop looking for you, talking about you, asking about you."

*I scowled at my brother, cursing him, jealousy burning hot over the effortless way he made girls love him.*

*While I tried so fucking hard to be perfect and nobody loved* me.

*Ciaran shrugged, exhaling smoke that drifted lazily around us, dissipating into the cool, damp air.* "Can't help if your girlfriend would rather fuck me."

*The casual, almost mocking indifference in his tone ignited a raw fury in my chest.*

*He knew what she meant to me, how much I cared about her, and yet he couldn't resist stirring the knife.*

*Without thinking, I shoved him, hard enough to make him stumble.*

*"She's mine,"* I snarled, my fists clenched, barely keeping the rage in check.

*He scowled as he straightened his jacket, the smoke casting shadows over his face.*

*"You can fucking have her,"* he spat out. *"But careful, Ty. She's not who you think she is."*

The memory faded, swallowed up by the present as I stumbled through the library, chasing after Ava once more, feeling the effects of the paralytic clawing at my limbs.

No, Ava wasn't who I thought she was. She was sharper, more cunning, more relentless than I'd ever realized.

She hadn't given up on escape; she'd lulled me into a false sense of security, a carefully crafted illusion of unity, only to strike when I least expected it.

*That's my girl.*

A twisted surge of pride flared in me, fierce and undeniable, even as the sting of betrayal burned through it. She'd played me perfectly.

My muscles were sluggish, each step harder than the last, but I refused to let it overpower me. I was determined to push through.

I tumbled out of the library and there she was, down the hallway, her wide eyes betraying her shock. She'd clearly expected me to have been taken down by now, paralyzed and helpless.

"Ava," I rasped, my voice rougher than I'd intended, my vision blurring just slightly.

Her gaze flitted over me, assessing, calculating, and then she spun, bolting down the hallway once again.

I staggered forward, forcing one foot in front of the

other, gritting my teeth against the tremors that threatened to betray me.

She thought she could escape, but I wasn't going to let her go that easily.

*Ready or not...*

# AVA

Ty's movements were uncoordinated but fueled by sheer desperation as he chased me down the hallway, the echo of his uneven footsteps following me.

"Ava!" he shouted, the sound raw and cracked.

I didn't want to look back, didn't want to see the hurt I knew was there.

But pain and betrayal laced through his voice. It sliced through me, twisting like a knife as I pushed onward.

The hallways of Blackthorn loomed, shadowed and sprawling, each familiar corner seemingly foreign in the low light.

My mind spun, tipsy from the wine and adrenaline, and my steps wavered, but I tried to focus, tried to sort through my fragmented memories of this place. I had to find a way out.

The front door! If I could just find my way to the main foyer, I could get out through the front door.

My bare feet slapped against the stone floors as I ran, the cold seeping into my skin, sharp and grounding.

Behind me, I could hear Ty stumbling after me, banging off the walls like a pinball, his footsteps heavy and unsteady.

He should have been paralyzed by now, but he was still moving, still following me.

Realization dawned cold and sickening—the dose I'd given him wasn't nearly enough.

Ty was precise. He would calculate and measure out the exact amount of paralytic required for me. The amount in the vial was designed for someone of *my* height and weight. He was ten inches taller and almost twice my weight of muscle.

Shit. The contents of the vial weren't enough to fully take Ty down.

He was fighting through it, sheer willpower and fury propelling him forward.

"Don't... do this," he called out, voice thick with betrayal. "Ava..."

Each word seared into me, the weight of his voice making my knees weak, but I shoved the feeling down. I couldn't let his words stop me.

My breath came in ragged gasps as I skidded around another corner, feeling the walls close in with every step.

I stumbled into the main foyer, the grand staircase looming above me, its sweeping curves casting shadows over the marble floor.

Desperation clawed at me as I sprinted to the front door, only to find it sealed tight—paneled in cold metal just like my bedroom door with no handle in sight. In its place, a sleek panel gleamed where the handle should have been, Ty's fingerprint was the only key.

A shadow fell across the doorway to the foyer, and Ty's voice, now a low, chilling murmur, drifted to me. "It doesn't matter where you run, Ava. I will hunt you down."

My mind spun, desperate and wild, as I tore up the stairs toward the second floor. Each step echoed up the spiral, a drumbeat of fear pulsing through me.

Shit. I was being forced farther into the house.

Ty's heavy footsteps drifted up from below, steady and persistent, the sound digging deep under my skin.

An idea struck me—the secret passageway, the one Ciaran's shadowed face had peered out from in the professor's bedroom.

Maybe that passageway might lead out?

I had no idea if it would. Or if I could even discover the way to open it, but I had to try.

I tumbled onto the second floor, Ty's sluggish footfalls following my panicked steps.

My bare feet slapped against the wooden floor, each step jarring as I tried to focus, to keep my balance. The hallways seemed to close in, the shadows deepening, as if the very walls were conspiring to trap me.

My fingers brushed against the rough damask wallpaper as I stumbled around a corner, the textured patterns catching at my skin, grounding me for one frantic second.

There was the professor's room at the very end, its dark wooden door mocking me, taunting me with ghosts.

I pushed forward, lungs burning, my skin prickling with the chill of fear, my mind racing to keep going, to find a way to escape before he was upon me.

I burst into my foster father's bedroom, into the vortex of my haunting, fighting the panic that threatened to claw up my throat.

This place would *not* break me.

I ignored the glaring red couch and ran to the far wall where I remembered seeing Ciaran's face peering out from. I scanned the wall for a way to unlock the panel, heart pounding so hard it seemed to echo off every surface. Where was it? Where was the opening?

My hands scrambled along the wall, pressing at anything that might give, searching for some latch, some hidden lever.

Footsteps sounded in the hallway, a heavy tread full of hurt and determination, growing closer with each second. Ty's long shadow stretched across the threshold, his silhouette blocking out the hallway light.

Panic clawed its way up my throat.

I swiped my hands along the wooden panel, along the ornate moldings, willing them to yield under my touch, willing them to be the sanctuary I needed.

I felt a faint click under my fingertips.

*Yes!*

The panel swung inward, revealing a narrow, twisting iron staircase spiraling down into a black void, a thick, musty odor of trapped air rising up, mingling with the scent of damp stone.

Every instinct told me not to go down there. The shadows seemed to shift, whispering of terrible things hidden in the dark below.

But I didn't have a choice—if I hesitated, Ty would catch me.

"Ava..."

He loomed in the doorway, his eyes finding me even in the dim glow. Fury and something far worse—a raw betrayal—darkened his expression, making my stomach clench. His gaze was relentless, burning into me as if he could pin me to the spot with just a look.

"Stop!" His voice was hoarse, urgent, his hand reaching toward me just as I slipped through the gap, slamming the panel closed and plunging myself into the darkness below.

The darkness in the narrow twisting staircase enveloped me, cool and close, the musty scent of damp stone and dust thick in the air. The only light came from a faint skylight far above my head, revealing the fading dusk.

Ty's muffled voice echoed faintly from the other side of the panel, calling my name, laced with an anger that rattled me to my core.

He couldn't see me now. He couldn't reach me here. But it would be moments before he figured out how to open the panel. Then he'd be on my heels again.

I hurried down the twisting staircase. The only sounds were my shallow breaths and the faint pounding on the other side of the hidden door.

At the bottom of the stairs, another secret panel opened into an unfamiliar room.

I stumbled forward, the automatic sconces casting a faint yellow glow as they flickered to life, illuminating a gothic laboratory steeped in shadows. The air was thick with the sharp, metallic tang of chemicals, mingling with an all-too-familiar herbal musk—the same sickly-sweet scent from the drug I'd found in Liath's room.

My stomach twisted as I took it in.

Everywhere, there were rows of workbenches cluttered with glass beakers and vials, some filled with strange, glinting substances, others empty but stained with dark, dried remnants of experiments long past.

I could almost hear the hollow clink of glass as I brushed against one of the benches.

Shelves lined the stone walls, each crammed with dark bottles labeled in Latin, some with peeling labels that revealed the sinister symbols and names of toxic plants.

As I passed the heavy mahogany desk at the far end, I saw it held a chaotic sprawl of journals and notebooks, each bearing a familiar emblem.

This... this was the emblem I'd seen on Dr. Vale's signet ring.

I froze, my pulse racing as I flipped open a page on the nearest journal.

My eyes darted across the notes in the professor's unmistakable handwriting.

Evidence was here, I could feel it.

This place—it held answers.

My hand trembled, torn between the urge to stay and uncover everything, to piece together what the professor and the Society had done, and the need to keep moving, to escape.

Ty's voice echoed down the passageway behind me, angry and desperate, the sound slurring, but still close. He'd found the secret panel.

A knot of fear twisted in my chest. I had to go.

Leaving the journals scattered as they were, I turned and sprinted for the other door, bursting through it, and to my surprise, the cool glass and greenery of the greenhouse swallowed me in a rush.

I staggered forward, nearly tripping over a loose stone on the greenhouse floor, my hands pinwheeling for balance.

I tore through the rows of purple nightshade berries, drooping dark hellebores and tangled vines, my bare feet slipping on the mossy stones as I sprinted for the greenhouse exit.

My heart pounded with each desperate step, Ty's footsteps echoing behind me.

I shoved past the last towering plant and burst out the door into the clean open air.

The garden stretched out around me, vast and eerily quiet under the night sky, and there—in the distance—was the fence. Half-hidden in ivy, its metal edges glinting faintly in the shadows, it felt as unreal as a mirage.

But it was real. A path to freedom, a promise of escape, so close I could almost touch it.

My breath came in gasps as I stared, the garden stretching between me and the fence like some kind of twisted maze.

My pulse raced, and yet a paralyzing fear clawed at me. What if he caught me before I made it? What if the fence wasn't climbable, wasn't strong enough to hold my weight?

I glanced back, knowing Ty was just steps behind, his footsteps growing louder, steadier. I couldn't wait. I couldn't pause to dwell on my fears. I had to *act*.

Gritting my teeth, I pushed forward, my legs carrying me across the soft grass toward the distant glint of metal.

I was so close to the edge of this property, this prison.

But I was nowhere near freedom. Not by a long shot.

I crashed into the fence, the iron bars cold and unyielding as my chest collided against them, knocking the air from my lungs. My breath left me in a sharp gasp, and for a moment, I could barely think, could barely breathe.

I clutched the bars, fingers trembling as I looked up, my heart sinking.

The fence stretched high above me, each iron bar slick with rain and rust, topped with cruel, twisted spikes that glinted in the dim light.

My chest tightened, the chill of hopelessness seeping in as the reality of the barrier loomed over me.

There was no way I could climb it; a fall from the top would mean a broken ankle, maybe worse.

And then I'd be right back in his hands.

I swallowed, fighting down the frustration clawing up my throat.

There had to be a gate.

I closed my eyes, digging deep into my memories of this place, trying to summon anything that might help. A faint recollection flickered to life.

The front gate.

West. I had a memory of a gate somewhere west.

It felt hazy, like something half-forgotten, but it was all I had.

I turned and hurried along the fence, my fingers grazing the metal and then the thick ivy that covered half of it like it was trying to swallow up the boundary of this cursed place.

I moved as fast as I could without losing my footing in the dusk.

Time stretched endlessly, each step fueled by hope that was beginning to fray around the edges.

After what felt like hours of racing along the fence line, I stumbled upon it—the main gates of Blackthorn Hall, looming tall and imposing, crafted from wrought iron twisted into intricate, gothic patterns of thorned vines and dark roses.

Rusted over time, the iron had taken on a deep, weathered patina, sharp spikes crowning each bar like silent, menacing guards, flanked by heavy stone pillars.

Relief washed over me, but when I reached out and tugged, it refused to budge.

I shook the gates, yanked at the thick central lock, desperation overcoming me, the bars rattling in their place. But still they remained locked to me.

I stared up at the soaring gates, just as tall as the fence, if not taller, and just as unscalable, with spikes like a thorny crown.

My chest tightened, a surge of despair gripping me, the air cold and thick as I tried to think, to breathe, to not let the hopelessness set in.

I had thought I'd escaped Blackthorn Hall, but this cursed place had claws that reached far beyond its mansion walls, pulling me back when I least expected it.

My mind flickered to Mona—how she, too, had tried to flee, only to be thwarted at the gates.

A pang of empathy twisted in my chest for the woman I'd never met, separated from me by years, yet tied to me by a dark painful secret.

I could not quit. I could not fail. I could not let him recapture me.

I kept running down the fence line, wishing, hoping, *praying* for another way out.

Up ahead, a faint shape loomed into the sky, silhouetted in the fading sunlight filtering through the trees.

I squinted, and my heart lurched.

The treehouse.

Hidden among the dense branches, its faded boards and dark silhouette whispered of memories and broken promises, and a memory slammed into me.

*I sat cross-legged on the wooden floor of the treehouse, doodling in my journal as I waited for Ty.*

*But as the hatch creaked open, it wasn't Ty's warm face that peeked through.*

*It was Ciaran's.*

*He climbed up, barely sparing me a glance as he swung himself onto the platform. His expression shifted into a scowl when he noticed me sitting there, but he said nothing, just stepped over me, the slight smell of smoke trailing him as he moved toward the window.*

*I watched, confused, as he leaned out and threw one leg over the sill, perching on the ledge with a reckless kind of ease that made my heart stop.*

*"What are you doing?" I asked, leaping to my feet and grabbing his arm instinctively. "You'll fall!"*

*He shook me off, his eyes glinting with defiance. "I'm a big boy, Ava. I know what I'm doing."*

*I lost my grip on his arm, feeling the sting of rejection that came with his dismissal. My fingers fell away, and I looked down, heat prickling my cheeks.*

*He threw his other leg over the ledge, steadying himself with one hand on the frame as he turned to face in.*

*We were suddenly face-to-face, close enough that I could see the glint of determination in his eyes.*

*For a moment he just stared back at me, his usual hatred falling away, revealing something softer.*

*My gaze dropped to his lips, my heart fluttering as I imagined, just for a second, what it might feel like if he leaned forward.*

*His gaze dropped to my mouth.*

*Oh God. Was he going to...*

"Ever ridden a motorbike?" *His voice broke through my thoughts.*

*Surprised, I shook my head.*

"Want to come for a ride?" *he asked, a daring smirk on his face that sent a thrill through me.*

*I hesitated, a part of me painfully aware that Ty would be here any minute.*

"I'm waiting for Ty," *I said, my voice soft and uncertain, feeling torn.*

*Ciaran's smirk shifted into a scoff, his tone dismissive.* "Suit yourself."

*He started to climb down, disappearing halfway out the window.*

*I leaned out the window of the treehouse, watching him climb down the other side of the fence using the overgrown ivy.*

*Below him a black motorbike stood waiting, half-hidden by the ivy.*

*This must be his escape route, the way he snuck out of the stuffy mansion to the world outside of Blackthorn.*

"Wait!" *I heard myself yelling.*

*He paused, glancing up at me, eyebrows raised, waiting. There was a challenge in his eyes, and I knew he wouldn't wait forever.*

*I chewed my lip, torn. If I left with him, I'd be letting Ty down.*

*But if I stayed, I might lose my one chance to do something wild, something reckless with Ciaran.*

*"I'll come," I said, the words barely louder than a whisper, but he heard me.*

*To my surprise, his face softened into a rare, genuine smile as he held out his hand.*

*And before I could talk myself out of it, I reached forward and took it, feeling a strange sense of excitement and freedom course through me as his fingers closed around mine.*

The treehouse had been my escape route then.

It would be my escape route now.

I sprinted across the grass, my bare feet stinging as they struck sharp stones and the rough edges of the pathway.

But I didn't slow down.

The treehouse loomed in the distance, tucked near the high fence, just like in my memories. My heart hammered with a strange blend of hope and desperation—my way out was finally clear.

I just had to hope Ty wouldn't realize that I'd found a way out.

## AVA

I climbed down the fence, my legs scraping against the cold metal as I landed with a heavy thud on the other side.

Just like I had all those years ago with Ciaran.

But this time there was no villainous prince in a black leather jacket waiting to speed me away on his mechanical chariot.

A dirt road stretched out before me, trailing off in either direction, east and west, both paths looking identical in their dusty desolation.

I didn't have time to wait for a passing car—if any ever came this way. I had to move, now, before Ty found me.

But which direction?

I cast one last look at the looming shadows of Blackthorn Hall behind me, feeling a wave of dread press down on my shoulders.

Then I turned east, trusting the pull in my gut and praying it wouldn't lead me back into some twisted circle, right back into the jaws of hell.

The dry earth kicked up clouds as I broke into a jog, every strained breath filling my lungs with the taste of dust.

The dirt road felt like sandpaper against my bare feet, every step sending fresh stabs of pain up my legs. The sharp rocks and grit embedded in the earth pressed into my soles, scraping raw patches that burned with each stride.

I bit my lip, refusing to slow down.

I had no choice—every step away from Blackthorn was a step closer to freedom, even if it tore my feet apart, a silent chant of "keep going" echoing in my head.

The irony of it wasn't lost on me—Ty's grueling fitness regime had strengthened my muscles, given me endurance. It was that same training that was allowing me to push forward now, miles passing beneath me.

Even at the end of summer, the night air in the west of Ireland was cool, prickling my skin as I moved along the desolate road. The chill bit through the thin fabric of my slip, seeping into my bones, a constant reminder of just how exposed I was.

At least the jogging kept me warm enough to ignore it, my pounding heartbeat pushing heat through me.

But I couldn't keep running forever. When I finally had to stop, when exhaustion won, I'd have to lie down somewhere.

The thought sent a shiver through me; lying exposed on the hard ground, no walls or roof to shield me, didn't promise a restful night.

It would be cold, miserable even, and if I didn't find shelter, I'd be at the mercy of the elements as much as anything—or anyone else—lurking out here.

The road wound through the remote Irish countryside,

bordered in sections by thick, scraggly hedges of gorse that bloomed with yellow flowers, their faint scent of coconut drifting in the air.

Here and there, low stone walls took the gorse's place, the gray rocks stacked with ancient precision and overgrown with moss and lichen, marking the boundaries of quiet farmland.

The road ambled up and down gently rolling hills, each descent revealing a new stretch of quiet fields under the purple sky.

But no sign of other humans. Nowhere to settle for the night. Nowhere to hide.

In the middle of many fields stood solitary trees—fairy trees, left untouched for generations. Their twisted, haunting silhouettes rose defiantly against the night sky, sacred in their own right, protected by local superstition.

No matter how expansive the field or modern the farmer, these trees were left undisturbed, a mark of respect for the old ways, reminders of the land's secrets and the quiet power it held over its people.

If I got desperate, I'd hike into one of those fields and sleep under the fairy tree. I would tie the ribbon in my hair onto a branch—an offering to the fairy that called the tree home—and make a wish.

*Please, let me get back to Scáth. Let me see him again.*

Every so often, the cool, damp air carried a distant rustle, the faint hum of something unseen moving in the hedgerows, and a shiver ran up my spine. I kept my eyes on the narrow, winding road ahead, feeling like I was traveling deeper into the endless maw of an unfriendly beast.

Just when I thought my legs couldn't carry me any

farther, a shape appeared on the horizon, cutting into the violent hues of the dusk sky.

It was a farmhouse, distant but unmistakable. The closest neighbor to Blackthorn Hall.

My pulse quickened with something I hadn't felt in days: hope. I stumbled to a stop, staring at the silhouette, feeling a flicker of recognition pulse somewhere deep inside me.

*Did I know this place?*

I fixed my eyes on the farmhouse ahead, a dark shape on the horizon, and pushed forward.

Finally, I stumbled onto the wooden porch, each step bringing a dull, stinging pain up from my bare feet.

The single porch light flickered above, casting a harsh glow over me. Out here, surrounded by endless dark fields and the deep, inky sky, it felt like I was under a spotlight.

The farmhouse itself, with the wide wraparound porch and peeling blue door, seemed almost spectral in its familiarity, like a hazy memory brushing against the edge of my mind.

I knew this place, or something about it, but the details were blurred, slipping away every time I tried to grasp them. I couldn't be sure if the people who lived here were friend or foe.

But the night had fully settled in, the air growing colder with each passing second. My throat ached with thirst, and I could barely feel my feet anymore.

It was too late, too cold, and I was too desperate to hesitate any longer. I knocked, the sound almost hollow in the night.

A shuffle of movement sounded from inside, and then

the door creaked open to reveal a figure—a man, older now than the memory I'd held of him.

My voice was barely a whisper. "I'm sorry to barge in on you like this—"

"I know you…"

The door creaked open a bit wider, and he stepped forward, into the faint light spilling in from the hallway. He wore a thick sweater layered over his shirt, and in his hands, he held a hunting rifle. His face, rugged and lined with age, softened as he took me in, recognition dawning.

"Ava?" His voice was low, laced with both surprise and concern. "Is that you, girl?"

The memory clicked, sharp and clear—Mr. Buckley, the Blackthorns' neighbor.

Memories of him surfaced. He'd patiently fixed my flat bike tire when I'd popped it in front of his house. He'd given me sweet tea to drink and invited me to pick blackberries from the patch behind his farmhouse.

"Yes." It came out in a rush.

He held me in his gaze, a stunned awe settling over him. "Jesus… it's been, what? Five years? I thought they sent you away after…"

After Ty killed his father.

But there was no time for a long-winded explanation, not here, not now.

"Please, Mr. Buckley… I need help," I managed.

Without another word, he stepped aside and gestured me in.

Inside, the warmth hit me first, cozy and faintly scented with peat smoke. The living room was lit by a single lamp, casting a warm glow over the worn, homely furniture.

Mr. Buckley poured me a glass of water and returned, handing it to me, his watchful eyes never leaving me as I gulped it down.

"Lord save us—what's put ya in this state, girl?" he asked, his brow furrowing with concern as he scanned my disheveled state.

I could see him piecing together the gaps as he took in my bare bleeding feet, the scratches on my arms, the exhaustion in my face.

When I didn't respond, his eyes narrowed, and his voice dropped to a murmur. "Did you... come from Blackthorn?"

I couldn't bring myself to confirm it. Something inside me flinched, still too tangled up with conflicting emotions to speak Ty's name, even after everything.

But I didn't have to answer.

Mr. Buckley shook his head, a dark look settling in his eyes. "That place has been cursed with death for as long as I can remember. Even before that boy murdered your foster father," he muttered, more to himself than to me.

A weight seemed to settle over his words, like he knew more about Blackthorn Hall than he was saying.

For a moment, I felt like pressing him—asking about the shadowed history of that place and the tragedies lurking within its walls, perhaps something about Ty and Ciaran's mother, too.

But not now. Not yet. Right now, I needed to get as far from Blackthorn as I could, even if every step away tore something inside of me.

"I can't go back there," I choked out, my voice trembling as panic crept into every word. "You can't let him take me."

Mr. Buckley's gaze hardened, his weathered hands tightening around the rifle, pulling it close as if to reassure both of us. "I promise ye, girl. No one's takin' ya. Over my dead body."

He moved purposefully toward the side table, reaching for the old rotary phone. My stomach dropped.

"Please," I blurted out, placing my hand over his. "No police."

He paused, eyes searching mine for a reason. I could see his frown deepening, but he hesitated. "Girl, you're shakin' like a leaf and look like the devil himself chased ya here. The garda could put an end to this."

My mind raced, scrambling for an explanation. I couldn't just blurt out the truth—it sounded insane, like something out of a nightmare.

As much as I resented Ty, as much as I wanted to hate him, I didn't want him to get in trouble. Locked up again, trapped behind bars... I couldn't do *that* to him.

The thought of it twisted inside me, leaving me caught between fear and a loyalty I could barely admit to myself.

I took a deep, steadying breath, my heart pounding in my chest. "Mr. Buckley, I can't... I can't explain everything, not now. But please—just believe me when I say that the police can't help."

He studied me for a long, silent moment, his jaw clenched. Then he gave a sharp nod. "That place has had evil in it since long before yer time. But alright, girl, no police. We'll keep this quiet as the grave if that's what ya need."

He gave my hand a gentle pat, then took a step back, watching me for a moment as if ensuring I was real, alive, and not a phantom from the haunted halls of Blackthorn.

There was something dark and knowing in his eyes,

something that made my skin prickle with curiosity and dread.

I swallowed, my heart pounding painfully against my ribs. "Please, Mr. Buckley... could I use your phone?"

He nodded, gesturing toward the rotary phone on the side table. "Course ya can, lass. I'll make sure every door and window's bolted proper. We'll have none sneakin' up on us tonight."

As he moved to the door, rifle tucked against his side, I reached for the phone, the cool metal of the receiver grounding me.

If I knew Scáth's number by heart, I'd call him. But I didn't.

There was only one number I knew—she made me memorize it years ago just in case I ever found myself stranded and in need of help.

Back then, I'd rolled my eyes, brushing off her worries as overbearing. But now, with desperation tightening my chest, I silently thanked her.

I took a shaky breath and dialed, each turn of the rotary feeling like an eternity.

Behind me, Mr. Buckley's voice echoed softly through the hall as he muttered to himself, his footsteps creaking through the old farmhouse while he checked the locks.

When the line finally connected, I steadied myself, forcing calm into my voice. "Ebony? It's me. Ava."

"Ava?" Her familiar voice was warm but laced with surprise. It sank into my bones and I almost started crying right there. "Is that really you?"

I forced a small laugh, hoping it sounded natural, as I

brushed aside a tear that threatened to spill over. "Hey! Yeah, it's me."

"Oh, my darling girl. It's been so long. I thought you were in Croatia for the rest of the holidays?"

For a moment my brain short-circuited on Croatia, before I remembered that Ty had been updating everyone on my socials about my "Mediterranean summer."

"Oh, yeah. Right. I thought I'd surprise everyone, caught an early flight home. Only, uh, my flight to Dublin got redirected... I'm stuck near Shannon Airport."

I glanced over my shoulder, wondering if Mr. Buckley was nearby and if he could hear me. I didn't want to have to explain why I was lying to my own mother.

Lowering my voice, I added, "I'm staying at the Sheraton hotel by the airport for the night. Could you send someone to pick me up tomorrow morning? Around ten?"

"Of course, Ava," she replied, her tone softening. There was a pause, and in that silence, I felt her worry, her relief. "I've... I've missed you."

I closed my eyes as a wave of emotion washed over me, tightening my throat. "I've missed you too, Ebony."

For the first time in weeks, I felt like I was close to home, close to the life that had seemed so distant, almost unreachable. So close to Ciaran.

*Just one more night, Scáth. I'm coming home.*

I hung up and turned around, nearly stumbling as I realized Mr. Buckley was standing right behind me, his gaze steady and far too knowing.

My mouth went dry, and I scrambled for words to explain the lie I'd just spun on the phone. "I, uh—"

He silenced me with a small, understanding smile and

placed a gentle hand over mine, calloused and warm, grounding me in a way that nearly unraveled everything I'd been trying to hold together.

"You look tired, lass," he murmured, his voice soft. "Let's get you to bed. I'll fix up a proper breakfast before I drive you to the Sheraton tomorrow morning. Do you like pancakes?"

For a moment, the simple kindness hit me like a tidal wave, overwhelming the fear and tension that had knotted in my chest.

I nodded, words escaping me, a swell of gratitude filling the emptiness.

He pointed to the nearest door. "That's me, just in case you need anything during the night."

Then he led me down the narrow hall, showing me a bathroom where I could wash up, and then to a cozy guest room, its low, beamed ceiling adding to the sense of warmth.

The double bed was already made up with soft, clean sheets, and on the edge of the bed lay a clean towel and small stack of folded clothes. At the base of the bed were worn but clean ladies' work boots.

"My late wife's," he said, his voice dropping to a reverent hush. "She... she was about your size before she passed. Figured they'd fit you. The shoes might be a touch big, though."

A flicker of sadness traced his features, and I sensed an unspoken story in his words, something he wasn't ready to share.

I realized that Mrs. Buckley—his wife—had been the one to help Mona try and escape with her boys all those years ago. Had... had the professor *done* something to her to punish her for helping Mona?

I didn't press him, but the weight of his loss brushed against me, resonating with my own hollow spaces. I touched the soft fabric of the clothes, my fingers trembling.

"Thank you," I whispered, the words feeling woefully inadequate.

He offered a nod, his hand lingering on the doorknob as if making sure I'd be safe here.

I made a mental note to send something to him once I was back in Dublin. Maybe I'd buy him a large expensive armchair or... I chuckled to myself, a new phone, like something from this *decade*.

With the warmth of the room wrapping around me, the clean clothes waiting, and a bed that looked softer than any I'd seen in what felt like years, I felt something I hadn't allowed myself to feel in so long—hope.

After a hot shower, I slipped into Mrs. Buckley's old nightgown, soft and worn. I crawled into the bed, sinking into layers that felt like clouds around me.

The farmhouse was quiet, each creak and distant murmur of wind outside somehow comforting in its simplicity, and for the first time in months, I felt something close to peace.

I closed my eyes, and Ciaran's face filled the dark—his familiar intensity, the way his eyes softened when he looked at me, his touch that I longed to feel again.

My heart sped up, love and anxious hope filling every beat. I couldn't wait to see him. I *needed* to see him. But... what would he think? How would he look at me when he learned the truth?

Fear chilled the warmth from my skin. His brother. His own brother lied to him, made him believe he was dead. Would he even believe me?

And how could I tell him about Ty... about the way he'd kept me, made me relive my past under the guise of therapy? How could I explain the things that happened? Could things between us ever be the same?

I squeezed my eyes tighter, the worry churning in my stomach. I wanted nothing more than for Ciaran to take me in his arms, to tell me we'd leave this place together like we always planned.

But... could he even forgive me? Would he still want me if he knew that I couldn't walk away?

The Society was there, woven into everything I'd been through, everything that had twisted my life and the lives of so many others. I had to stay, to dismantle them piece by piece.

And I needed Ciaran's help. Even if he hated me a little for choosing to stay, for dragging him deeper into this fight.

And then Ty drifted into my mind, unbidden.

My stomach twisted, and I pushed the thought away, but it crept back, trailing guilt and confusion. I'd drugged him, betrayed him, left him behind.

But he'd forced my hand; he'd given me no choice.

Still, I couldn't shake the fear of what he'd do when he found out I'd returned to Ciaran. The two of them—their rivalry, their dark history—I could feel the collision building like a storm on the horizon, inevitable and unstoppable.

They were brothers, yes, but could they really let it go, even for each other?

I swallowed hard, telling myself that they loved each other. Deep down, somewhere. No matter how much they fought or how much pain lay between them, they wouldn't hurt each other. Right?

And yet a strange ache pricked at me, unwanted, almost shameful.

I missed Ty. Missed his warmth, the steady way he wrapped himself around my back every night. I'd grown used to it, to him, and the hollow space left behind felt like a betrayal.

I closed my eyes, skimming my hands under my clothes, trying to picture Ciaran, trying to focus on the way his arms would feel around me, his breath against my skin, his hands on my body, his mouth and tongue on my breasts, his cock inside me.

But Ty's face, Ty's touch haunted me, mingling with Ciaran's until I couldn't tell them apart.

In my mind, Ciaran's clean, classic tattoos—simple lines and beautiful symbols—morphed into the haunting ink scrawled across Ty's skin, twisted designs that spoke of pain, anguish, endurance, of ravens with broken wings and dark broken dolls.

I could see Ty's scars, puckered and raw, slipping into the places where Ciaran's skin was smooth, each mark a painful story etched into his body.

And the memory of Ciaran's scent in my nose, his leather and spice, blended with Ty's, heavier, darker—sandalwood laced with something primal, something that filled the air between us with an unspoken intensity.

The lines blurred, and for a single, frightening moment, I didn't know who I longed for more—whose touch I missed, whose presence I wanted to feel beside me in this dark, quiet room.

With a frustrated sigh, I rolled over, burying my face in the pillow and letting exhaustion carry me into sleep.

But it wasn't long until a noise woke me up. I lay there in bed, gasping, mind whirling, momentarily disoriented from the unfamiliar bedroom.

There it was again, the sound of metal scraping on metal.

Someone was breaking into the farmhouse.

Oh God. Ty had found me.

# AVA

My heart lurched with a sickening twist of fear at the thought that Ty had found me.

No, I couldn't go back. I wouldn't survive that. I couldn't.

I took a deep breath, trying to calm the panic clawing up my throat. Don't panic. It could be nothing. It had to be nothing. I had to check first.

Sliding out of bed, my bare feet touched the rough wooden floor, grounding me in the present.

I tiptoed to the bedroom door and pressed my ear against it, straining to pick up any sounds in the farmhouse.

A soft creak from the front of the house sent a jolt of adrenaline through me.

My breath hitched, but I forced myself to open the door a crack, just enough to peer out.

In the dim moonlight filtering through the windows, I saw a man entering through the front door.

He wore a mask that obscured most of his face, but even from this distance, I could tell it *wasn't* Ty. He wasn't tall enough, nor did he move like Ty. This man wasn't as quiet, his steps heavier, more lumbering.

But that only made it worse. It had to be someone from the Society.

My mind spun. How had they found me? I hadn't even told Ebony where I was, had only mentioned the Sheraton.

And then it struck me like a punch to the gut.

I could hear Ciaran's voice in my head, sharp and cutting. *"...If I were them, looking for you? The first thing I'd do is bug Ebony's phone in case you called her."*

Of course. They'd traced the call here. Stupid, stupid Ava.

A hollow pit of dread formed in my stomach, and I squeezed my fists tight, fighting back the wave of nausea.

Ciaran was right; it was too dangerous. I wasn't just risking myself. I was risking anyone who tried to help me.

Just then, Mr. Buckley's voice cut through the silence, low and firm. "Who are you?"

He appeared from the doorway of the main bedroom, closest to the masked man, determination in his stance, the hard line of his mouth set in defiance.

He didn't wait for an answer; he raised the rifle, aiming straight at the intruder.

The masked man lunged forward, tackling Mr. Buckley as the rifle went off, the bullet hitting something in the living room with a smash.

I screamed and flinched.

My heart thundered in my chest as the two men grappled, the rifle twisting between them.

Mr. Buckley's grip wavered as they struggled over the weapon.

"Run, Ava!" Mr. Buckley's voice tore through the air, desperate and panicked.

But I didn't run. No, I couldn't leave him, couldn't keep running forever. I was sick of hiding, sick of being hunted down. He was fighting for me, and I had to help him. I couldn't just run.

I scanned the darkened bedroom frantically, my eyes catching on the bedside lamp. I yanked it from the wall, the cord snapping loose, and I sprinted for the living room where the struggle was happening.

Every step thundered in my ears, fear flooding my veins, but I forced it down, focusing on one thing only: stopping this man.

The masked figure was grappling with Mr. Buckley, wrestling for control of the rifle. The old man's hands trembled as the barrel turned to point at him.

Without thinking, I raised the lamp high and brought it down on the intruder's head. The impact sent a dull crack through the room, and for a brief second, he faltered, his grip on the rifle loosening.

But he didn't let go.

Dread clawed up my spine. I needed something else—something stronger. Deadlier.

I raced for the kitchen, the adrenaline pulsing faster than my fear. I snatched a large knife from the block, its cold weight a strange comfort in my hand, a tiny fragment of power in the chaos.

But just as I whirled around, ready to strike, a loud crack exploded through the air. The rifle had fired again.

"No!" The scream ripped from my throat as I watched

Mr. Buckley's body jerk, his face draining of color as he staggered and collapsed to the floor.

My stomach lurched with a violent, nauseating grief. My heart hammered painfully against my chest, my pulse roaring in my ears as I took in the masked man, now turning his gaze—and the rifle—on me.

His eyes narrowed, his movements calm, methodical.

"Stop or I'll shoot." His voice was cold, unfamiliar, and unmoved by the life he'd just taken.

A raw instinct flooded my mind, silencing every rational thought. There was no way in hell I was going to let him take me. Not alive.

Without hesitating, I pivoted and sprinted toward the side door, my feet pounding on the wooden floor as I flung myself against it. The knob was cold under my hand, and I twisted it frantically. Locked.

Dammit, no, no, no! I was trapped.

Behind me, I heard the sharp click of the rifle as he pulled the trigger. But there was no bang.

I froze for half a second, processing it. Out of bullets. Thank Christ.

I turned to face the masked man as he tossed the useless rifle aside, tightening my grip on the knife.

The tiles were cool under my bare feet, and I spread my stance, trying to remember everything Ty had drilled into me.

*Keep your weight balanced. Stay light on your feet. Watch his eyes, not the weapon.* It all came rushing back in fragments, adrenaline pushing it to the surface.

The man chuckled, low and dark as he raised his hands

to me. "Give me the knife before you hurt yourself, princess."

I swallowed the tremor of fear and steadied my breath. I lunged toward him, feigning to the left before shifting my weight and stabbing forward with all my strength.

The blade sliced through his shirt and bit into his side.

He lurched back, clutching his wound with a curse, his cocky smile twisting into a grimace.

"Bitch," he spat, his voice laced with anger. "You'll pay for that."

He lunged forward, but I sidestepped, ducking under his reach and circling back to his exposed side. The world narrowed to this single, brutal moment.

I didn't think—I acted, gripping the knife tightly and driving it into his abdomen. I felt the blade sink in, deeper than I'd meant, and a hot, sticky warmth coated my hand.

His eyes widened as the color drained from his face, and he staggered back, clutching at the wound with both hands, a strangled curse escaping his lips.

His knees buckled, and he dropped heavily to the floor, gasping as his blood began to pool around him.

My heart thundered as I stared at him, the harsh reality of what I'd done sinking in, but I shoved it down. I didn't have time to think about it.

*Mr. Buckley!*

I spun around, racing across the room to my kind old neighbor, who lay motionless, the pool of blood around him darkening the floorboards.

My knees hit the ground, pain flaring which I ignored, my knife clattering to the tiles as I slid beside him, my hands trembling as I searched for a sign, any sign, that he was still alive.

His shirt was dark and sticky, the blood seeping from the wound in his chest.

But then I saw it—a faint rise and fall. He was breathing, just barely.

"Oh God, Mr. Buckley?" I whispered, panic clawing at my voice.

His eyes fluttered open, glazed with pain, and he coughed, a thin line of blood bubbling on his lips. "Ava…"

"I'm going to get help," I said, forcing a calmness I didn't feel.

I had to move quickly, had to get someone here before it was too late. Even if it meant I was risking my own life.

I scrambled to my feet, heart pounding as I reached for the old rotary phone.

My fingers fumbled over the receiver, but as I pressed it to my ear, dread pooled in my stomach.

Silence. No dial tone.

I tried again, slamming the phone down and picking it back up, but it was dead.

They must have cut the phone line.

*No!*

My mind raced, every thought colliding in panic as I stared at Mr. Buckley, his chest barely lifting with each ragged breath. He wasn't going to last long.

I cursed under my breath, my hands pressing down harder on the wound, feeling the warm, sticky blood seeping through the tea towel.

"Hang on, Mr. Buckley," I whispered, my voice trembling

as I tried to steady my hands. I needed to do something. Anything.

*Ty.* Ty was the only one who could help him now.

I had to fetch him, to beg for his help. I'd promise to return to my prison, return to therapy, *anything*, but I'd do it to save Mr. Buckley.

I had no choice. There was no one else.

I grabbed his hand, pressing it firmly on the tea towel over his wound, feeling him flinch beneath my touch.

"Keep this here," I said, my voice low but urgent. "The phone's dead. I need to run and get help, but you hold on, okay? Just hold on."

His eyes were glassy, but he nodded weakly, his hand clenching over the towel with whatever strength he had left.

I stood, a surge of desperation pushing me forward as I sprinted for the door, my heart pounding with a mix of fear and hope.

But just as I reached for the handle, the door swung open.

A second masked man stood there, blocking my escape. The sight of him made my blood run cold.

He towered over me, his figure shadowed by the dim moonlight spilling in from behind him.

No. This couldn't be happening. My pulse hammered in my throat, and I took a shaky step back, panic clawing at my insides.

"No... no, no, no," I whispered, dread pooling in my stomach.

The masked man's gaze swept over the scene, and he shook his head, his eyes narrowing on me. The casual way he looked at his friend's blood-streaked body on the floor made bile rise in my throat.

"You've made the Sochai very angry with your little games, Ava." His unfamiliar voice was low and mocking. His eyes met mine, glinting with a dark, twisted amusement. "But no more. You're coming with me."

The realization hit me hard—I'd slipped through Ty's grasp, only to fall into something far darker, something I might not survive.

# AVA

I had escaped one prison just to be dragged back into another by this masked man.

No, I was not going to let him take me.

As he advanced, I backed away, pressing myself against the wall, my mind racing as I searched for any way out.

But there was none. I was cornered, caged. Every escape route was blocked.

The man lunged toward me, his hand outstretched, fingers closing in.

Before he could touch me, a dark shape loomed up behind him, swift and silent as a shadow, and I caught the glint of a wire garrote wrapping around his neck.

The newcomer's face appeared beside the masked man's from behind, a streak of moonlight falling across his strong features.

Ty.

Relief flooded through me, a warmth so deep it nearly buckled my knees.

Ty's arms tightened, his muscles taut with controlled

fury as he leaned close to the man's ear and hissed, his voice low and dangerous, "Your threats to her will be your last words."

The man thrashed, clawing at the garrote, but Ty was relentless, holding him steady, unfazed by the desperate struggle.

Ty's blazing blue eyes were fixed on me, holding my gaze with an intensity that felt like a physical weight pressing down on my chest, as though nothing else existed.

My stomach twisted with something dark and hot.

The man's choked gasps faded, his face turning ashen as his strength ebbed.

Still, Ty held him, inches from death, his focus never wavering from me.

"Pick up the knife, Ava." Ty's voice, calm and cold, sliced through the air. "And finish it."

I froze, my breath hitching.

The bloody knife lay near Mr. Buckley, gleaming under the light. Finish it?

My heart hammered against my ribs as the realization hit me—Ty was giving me the power to end this, to take control in a way I'd never imagined.

My hand trembled as I reached for the knife, my fingers wrapping around the handle.

As I stood before him, the masked man's gasps turned to weak, desperate pleas, his eyes wide and terrified as he tried to mouth words that never came, his weak fingers clawing to get under the wire that was cutting into his neck, blood already seeping out.

I looked at Ty, searching his face for any sign of hesitation, any trace of softness.

But his gaze was unflinching, steady, as though this act—this offering—was something *intimate*.

My nipples hardened to points under my bed shirt and I tried to tell myself it was just because I was cold. But I couldn't deny the dark thrill racing in my veins like a drug, making my breath catch in my throat.

"Good girl," Ty murmured, guiding me with a slight nod. "Aim for the heart."

I kept my eyes locked on his, grounding myself in his dark, knowing gaze as I lifted the knife.

On an exhale, I stepped forward and drove the blade between the masked man's ribs, my hand steady, my focus unwavering.

The man's struggling ceased, his body slackening as silence fell.

I let go of the knife slowly, unable to look away from Ty, the strange, intimate understanding that passed between us wrapping around my heart, leaving a mark deeper than any scar.

Ty let the man drop to the floor, his expression cold and unfeeling as he stepped over the crumpled body to get to me.

His hands were warm as they slid around my cheeks, his thumbs brushing away the tears I hadn't realized had fallen.

"Did he hurt you?" His voice was a mixture of fury and concern.

Before I could answer, I heard a low groan.

My heart plummeted. "Mr. Buckley!"

I wrenched away from Ty and ran to Mr. Buckley's side, dropping to my knees.

I pulled his head gently onto my lap. "Ty, help him. *Please.*"

Mr. Buckley's breathing was shallow, each rise and fall more labored than the last.

Ty kneeled beside us, inspecting the wound with his experienced, calculating gaze, and when he looked up, I saw it—the grim finality.

"I'm sorry," he whispered.

*No... no, no, no.*

Panic surged through me, crushed under an avalanche of guilt.

"There must be something we can do," I begged, my voice breaking as I searched his face for any glimmer of hope. "Oh God. This is my fault. All my fault."

The helplessness gripped me with an intensity that felt like it might tear me apart.

Mr. Buckley's trembling hand moved over mine.

"Couldn't... save her..." he murmured, his words trailing off as his gaze grew distant, his breaths slowing. "But glad... I saved..."

His voice stopped, his hand falling limp, his kind eyes empty.

The grief tore through me, breaking me open in a way I'd never felt before.

I collapsed over him, my body racked with shudders over the man who had taken me in tonight, had given me shelter when I'd had nowhere else to turn.

And who, in the end, gave his life for me.

Ty's arms closed around me, his embrace firm yet gentle as he pulled me away. "We have to go."

"No," I moaned, but I couldn't stop him, couldn't resist as he gathered me into his arms and carried me out to his car.

He gently lowered me into the passenger seat, the weight of his arm brushing against my breasts as he fastened the seat belt.

Despite everything, a shiver ran through me at his touch, my nipples hardening, the warmth of his hand lingering where he'd clipped me in.

I hated the way my body reacted, the way my pulse fluttered under his hands even now, when every piece of me felt shattered.

Ty shut the door, but he didn't go to the driver's side.

Instead, he turned and walked back into the house.

I sat, numb and hollow, my eyes fixed on the farmhouse, the darkness pressing in around me.

A few moments passed before Ty emerged, his face shadowed.

He slid into the driver's seat, turned on the ignition, and without a word, steered the car down the gravel drive.

In the rearview mirror, I saw the first flickers of orange, small licks of fire climbing up the side of the wooden porch, curling around the walls, the dark smoke twisting into the night sky like some ghostly omen.

Ty was taking me back to Blackthorn. I knew it.

But in that moment, with the weight of grief pressing down on me, I was too broken to care.

# AVA

Ty carried me up the winding main staircase of Blackthorn Hall, the scent of polished wood and dried roses thick in the air, pulling at old memories.

I felt the familiar apprehension creep up my spine, but beneath it, there was something almost... comforting. A part of me felt like I'd come home.

I expected him to take me to my bedroom, but Ty continued past it, his grip firm as he strode farther down the hall.

I lifted my head as he nudged open the door to another room with a gentle kick.

The room was dark, masculine, almost intimidating. It took me a second to realize where he'd taken me.

*His* bedroom.

He carried me over to a polished mahogany side table and seated me there carefully, his hands lingering a moment on my shoulders before he turned on a side lamp and stepped back.

"Stay," he commanded, his voice low and firm.

For the moment, I had no desire to fight him. No energy to disobey.

He disappeared into the en suite, and I heard the sounds of drawers sliding open and the rustle of items being gathered.

Through the open door where a warm light spilled out from, I could see a black claw-foot tub lined with thick stubbed candles and a large black and gold marble vanity.

Despite how wretched I felt, curiosity bloomed inside me, and before I could stop myself, my gaze wandered over his sacred space, his inner sanctum.

You can learn a lot about someone by their bedroom. Even though Ty had been my childhood best friend, there was so much about him now—about him as a *man*—I didn't know.

Dark-navy walls framed the space, punctuated with rich black velvet drapes hanging heavily over the unbarred window, which filtered in the faintest trace of moonlight. Ornate gold accents glinted on the edges of the furniture, catching the glow from the single lamp.

A massive four-poster bed loomed in the center, draped in a midnight-blue canopy that flowed like shadows around the bedposts. The carved wood details and heavy gothic shapes whispered of power and solitude. Everything about it felt intensely private.

A large black fireplace dominated one wall and on the mantle, my gaze fell on a small framed photo—an image of us, me and Ty, younger, smiling at the camera, a moment I barely remembered.

Surrounding it were other photographs, each one of... *me*.

A pang of surprise and unease flickered through me as I took them in, each capturing me in different moments from long ago.

There was one of me lying on my belly in the treehouse, hair falling over my face as I scribbled in my journal, completely absorbed.

Another captured me laughing, chasing a butterfly through the garden, my expression alight with wonder.

And one where I stood on the steps of our private school on my first day, clutching my books, glancing up at the gothic buildings with wide, hesitant eyes.

I hadn't known he'd taken these. In each one, I was so unaware, so... watched.

I trembled with an odd blend of nostalgia and dark heat.

Ty returned to the room, his face shadowed, tension vibrating off him in waves as he placed a first aid kit beside me.

He stepped between my legs, pressing my knees apart with his hips. In that close proximity, I could feel the heat radiating from him, the silent fury and relief tangled together in his posture.

The silence thickened as he pulled out wipes and took my hands gently, though his fingers trembled as he wiped away the dried blood.

The intimacy of his touch made my skin prickle. His thumb brushed over my knuckles, rough yet careful, as he inspected the cuts there.

My breath caught in my throat, but he said nothing, just

shifted his attention to my thighs, pushing the hem of my borrowed nightgown up to reveal the grazes on my knees.

His jaw clenched, his brows knitting together as he eyed the red, raw skin.

He swiped an alcohol wipe across the wound, and the sting shot up my leg, making me jerk.

"Ow!" I gasped, trying instinctively to pull away, but he caught both my wrists in one hand, holding me still.

He scrubbed the alcohol wipe against my knee again, harder this time, the sting like fire searing my skin.

"That hurts, Ty." I yanked at his hand like an iron band around my wrists, but he didn't yield.

His movements were no longer careful but sharp, precise, almost punishing.

"*That* hurts? God*dammit*, Ava."

His voice was low, rough and seething. There was more than anger in it—a dark edge, a desperation.

"You're mad at me," I murmured as I winced, a statement rather than a question.

He snorted, though the sound was laced with bitterness. "For drugging me, for stabbing me, for running away. Take your pick."

He snatched another wipe and moved to my other knee, his touch rougher this time, almost as though he couldn't hold back his frustration.

All I could do was whimper in pain.

"You could have…" He shook his head, his voice tapering off on a growl, and he tossed the wipe aside, letting go of my wrists abruptly, his hands curling into fists against his eyes.

"I almost lost you," he whispered, his voice breaking on

the words, his chest heaving, his arms shaking as if holding back something vast and terrible. "If I had been even thirty seconds later…"

The pain in his voice cut through me, a raw vulnerability I wasn't used to seeing from him.

Before I could think, I reached forward, pulling him into my arms.

His body tensed, caught off guard, but slowly he softened, his arms wrapping tightly around me as if he were afraid I'd vanish. He pressed his face into the curve of my neck, his breath warm against my skin, and he inhaled deeply, like he was trying to hold on to me with every sense he had.

"You got there in time," I whispered, running my hand gently over his back, feeling the taut muscles beneath his shirt, trying to calm him. "I'm right here, *mhaor.*"

*Warden.*

His arms tightened around me, his fingers pressing into my skin with a desperate need. The weight of his hold, the solid, unyielding way he clung to me—it felt as if he were grounding himself in the fact that I was alive, that he hadn't lost me.

He'd shown up right when he did, his timing like some kind of cursed magic—how had he known exactly where to find me?

I frowned, feeling a shiver of unease in my chest, a sense that I wouldn't like the answer. "How did you find me so quickly?"

Ty's grip around me tightened, his fingers pressing into my back. He didn't answer immediately.

"I told you," he finally murmured against my shoulder. "I'd always find you."

I pulled back. There was something evasive in his tone, a flicker in his eyes that sent a pulse of suspicion through me.

I swallowed hard, searching his face. "What do you mean by that?"

"Ava, it's late. We've had a rough night. Let's talk in the morning when things are—"

"No," I interrupted, my voice steely as I pushed back against him. "Now, Ty. Tell me."

I slipped out of his hold, my heartbeat thrumming in my chest as I faced him, crossing my arms tightly.

He let out a long sigh, dragging a hand over his face, but when he looked back at me, his expression was unreadable—almost unapologetic.

"I put a tracking device in you," he said finally, his voice low but unyielding. "In the back of your neck."

The words struck me like a blow.

Memories flashed across my mind: waking up on that first day, confused, trapped, a sore spot on the back of my neck burning when I'd moved.

I'd thought... I'd thought it was a cut or a bruise, a remnant of my abduction. But it was Ty's doing all along.

"You did... what?" I whispered, barely able to breathe, my voice thick with a mixture of anger and disbelief.

I reached back to the spot and felt around with my fingers, still unable to believe what he'd done to me—this *violation* worse than anything he'd done before.

But there it was, just under my skin, a hard bump like a small pebble when I moved my fingers over it.

The room spun, and my head filled with a sickening buzz of disbelief.

"Take it out," I demanded, my voice low and trembling as I lowered my fists to my sides.

He didn't move, he just looked at me with that icy stare that I wanted to rip off his fucking face.

"No."

A dizzying sense of betrayal washed over me, and I couldn't breathe, couldn't think past the furious pounding in my chest.

His hand reached for me, but I slapped it away, every inch of me recoiling.

"Take it the fuck out," I repeated, my voice breaking, "or I'll rip it out myself."

I pressed my nails into my neck, dragging them over my skin as if I could claw the fucking thing out. My skin felt like bugs were running underneath it.

"That's enough," he snapped, his face flashing with something dark, unyielding.

Ty lunged forward, catching my wrists in an iron grip and slamming them against the wall above my head. His face was inches from mine, the intensity of his stare fierce and raw.

I spat in his face as I fought against him, my voice raw with fury. "Get it out. Get it out now!"

He didn't even flinch as my spit ran down his cheek. He even stuck out his tongue to lick it as it ran past his mouth.

I hated that as I writhed in his grasp, his cock thickened against my upper thighs, causing wet heat to gather between my legs.

Fuck him for getting turned on right now.

Fuck my stupid body for joining in.

With a quick wrench of my wrist, I broke free from his grip, recalling one of his own techniques he'd taught me.

My fist connected with his jaw, a burst of satisfaction surging through me as he let out a curse.

But it was short-lived; his hand closed around the wrist, my knuckles throbbing, before pinning it back against the wall with unrelenting strength.

"I can't lose you again," he roared, his voice echoing off the walls, each word jagged and desperate.

His chest heaved, his arms trembling as he held me there, his face so close I could see every pained line, every shadow of grief and need.

Tears burned behind my eyes, stinging, the rage blurring into something softer, more vulnerable as I noticed the tremor in his hands, the way his breaths came unsteady, erratic.

His forehead rested against mine as he shut his eyes, his jaw tight as if battling against his own emotions.

He was terrified. The realization shocked me.

He was frightened, desperate. His love for me—a twisted, fevered need—had fueled everything he'd done, every action, no matter how wrong.

Something broke inside me. I didn't want to think about the betrayal, the grief, the rage boiling in my chest. I just wanted to feel something else, anything else.

Before I knew what I was doing, I surged forward, capturing his mouth with mine.

## AVA

My kiss was raw, demanding, fueled by the anger and despair clawing inside me.

Ty's reaction was instant, his hands tightening around my wrists as he returned the kiss with an intensity that bordered on violence, his lips rough, desperate, as though he was trying to erase the last few hours.

He released my wrists and tangled his fingers in my hair, tugging it and making my scalp sting, a reminder of the anger still running under his skin.

Part of me wanted to resist, to shove him away, to scream—but I kissed him back with a hunger that surprised even me.

I dug my nails into his shoulders, dragging against his skin with a vengeance, as if somehow this might make up for the tracker in my neck, for Mr. Buckley's death, for *everything*.

He just pulled me in closer, his cock flush against my wet pussy, his grip bruising, his lips harsh against mine, but I didn't care.

I kissed him harder, feeling the desperation pouring out of both of us, the anger, the fear, all twisted together in a way that made it impossible to stop.

And in that moment, I didn't want to.

I wanted *more*.

I reached for his shirt, his belt, for his zipper. He only broke away long enough to help me tug off his shirt and kick off his pants.

His cock sprung free, thick and hard, the veins almost angry.

He grabbed my bloody gown by the neckline and ripped it clean off me.

He positioned his cock at my entrance. "Beg for it."

"W-what?" I gasped.

"Beg."

"Please, fuck m—"

He thrust into me, swift and brutal.

I cried out, my nails raking down his back, leaving angry red trails in their wake. He hissed, his teeth grazing my neck, biting down hard enough to bruise.

God, he was so thick it felt like he was splitting me open. In a way, he was, carving my heart in two. Two men, same face, two sides of my heart.

He began to fuck me and I fucked him back, wrapping my legs around his waist. Two hot bodies. Feeling. Needing. Aching.

"Fuck," he groaned. "I love you more."

"I hate you," I replied, as we moved together in a frenzied rhythm, our bodies colliding with a force that bordered on punishment, the side table slamming against the wall.

Each thrust was an outlet for our rage, our fear, our helplessness. The sound of skin slapping against skin echoed in the room, punctuated by our ragged breaths and guttural moans.

"That's not the truth," he said, and his thumb found my clit as he added, "Or at least not all of it."

I betrayed myself with a desperate moan and before I realized it, the truth was flowing from my lips. "I hate that I don't hate you."

Pleasure mixed with desperation and fury inside me, the pressure building until I couldn't take it anymore.

He wrapped his hand around my throat, trapping the breath from my lungs, but I didn't care. I wanted the pain, craved it even. It was real, tangible, unlike the emotional turmoil threatening to consume me.

I came hard.

My body shuddered violently, clenching around him as waves of pleasure crashed over me. I gasped for air as his grip on my throat loosened, my vision swimming with black spots.

Ty didn't slow down. If anything, my orgasm spurred him on, his thrusts becoming even more frantic, more punishing. His fingers dug into my hips, sure to leave bruises, as he relentlessly pounded into me.

I could feel another climax building, impossibly soon after the first. Every nerve ending in my body was on fire, raw and overstimulated.

It was too much, and yet not enough.

"Fuck," Ty growled, his voice rough and strained. "I can feel you getting close again."

He lifted up my thigh so he could get deeper, shifting his

angle slightly, hitting that spot deep inside me that made me see stars.

I cried out, my back arching as my body flooded with pleasure again. I writhed as I was trapped in his arms, feeling like the orgasm was wringing me out.

Ty soon followed, thrusting into me one last time, a guttural groan falling from his mouth as he came inside me. He placed his sweaty forehead on mine, his breaths uneven and ragged.

His bedroom smelled of sex and copper, a heady mix that made my head spin.

For a moment, we just stayed there, our hearts pounding against each other, the reality of what we'd done slowly seeping in.

"Shit," I said. "We didn't use a condom."

"You're not going to fall pregnant."

Men. Maybe if *they* were the ones burdened with growing the new humans, they'd care more about using protection.

"Unless your swimmers are defunct," I snipped, "you can't know that."

Ty froze, a shadow flickering in his eyes, his shoulders tensing with something unspoken.

I pulled back, narrowing my gaze. "What is it?"

He tried to shrug it off, his tone casual, almost dismissive. "It's nothing. Don't worry about it."

I blinked, frustration building as I sensed he was hiding something. "No, tell me. *Now.*"

He shifted slightly, as if to distance himself, pulling back just enough to make my grip tighten on his arm.

I held him in place with my legs around his waist, my voice firm, leaving no room for evasion. "Ty?"

A heavy sigh escaped him, his gaze dropping, the hint of vulnerability flashing through the usual hardened exterior.

"As a precaution, I implanted a contraceptive rod in..." his voice trailed off.

A wave of guilt surged through me, twisting into something darker, something raw—disgust at the liberties he'd taken, the choices he'd made without me. Violations, each one carving deeper.

Without thinking, I shoved him back, putting space between us, his hot cum trickling out of me.

"What?" he said as he stumbled back. "I mean, you don't want a baby right now, right? Surely?"

"No, of course not." I shook my head, frustration making me want to *hurt* him. "That's not the point."

"I mean, maybe one day..." he said, his voice growing wistful.

I hopped down from the side table and swung at him, this time landing my fist square on his mouth. His lip split open, blood glistening against his teeth.

"Ow," I hissed, clutching my throbbing hand, bruised twice now on his maddeningly gorgeous face.

For a fleeting second, I almost felt guilty for reopening that scar. Almost.

I braced myself, half expecting Ty to lose it, to unleash his anger after I'd hit him yet again.

Instead, he touched his fingers to his mouth, glancing at the blood smeared across his fingertips with a blank expression.

He pursed his lips as he looked back up at me. "Your

stance was off. You'd have hit me with more force if you'd followed through with your hip."

A sound of pure frustration slipped out of me, somewhere between a growl and a groan. Nothing fazed him. Nothing.

I stomped off toward the bathroom and turned on the water, letting it fill the claw-foot tub. I needed to clean myself up—and clear my head.

I gripped the edge of the tub, staring into my reflection in the mirror as the enormity of what I'd done hit me like a sledgehammer.

I'd fucked Ty.

Worse than that—I'd wanted to.

I had *begged*.

Begged him to fuck me.

I couldn't hide behind the excuse of therapy or punishment, no rationale to shield me from the truth. I'd been the one to lean in, to instigate the kiss and *more*.

My heart hammered with shame and a sickening sense of guilt. What had I done?

I pressed my fingers to my swollen lips, as though I could erase the memory, the taste of him still lingering.

But I couldn't shake the feeling of Ty's mouth on mine, the way his cock had buried deep inside me, stirring something deep and volatile within my soul. Something I couldn't deny, something I'd tried so hard to bury.

And now, I'd betrayed Ciaran in the worst possible way. The person whom I loved, who loved me, and I'd betrayed him.

With Ty.

With his twin brother.

God. I wanted to scream.

I'd allowed myself to indulge in the twisted intimacy Ty offered, the warmth that felt dangerously like comfort, like belonging. I'd let go of the boundaries I'd sworn I'd hold, given in to something dark and selfish that I couldn't take back.

I'd let Ty *in*, if I was being painfully honest with myself.

What would Ciaran think if he knew? If he saw me now, with Ty's finger marks bruising my skin, his cum inside me, his stain on my soul?

I'd torn a hole through everything Ciaran and I had once shared, breaking trust that he didn't even know I'd betrayed. I tried to swallow the rising panic, the sickening realization that I might have destroyed everything.

I felt Ty's presence behind me, the warmth radiating from him brushing my back, an unbidden shiver tracing up my spine.

He walked so fucking quietly.

I forced myself to ignore him, clamping down on the confusing whirlwind inside me. Anger. Guilt. Confusion. All of it boiling beneath my skin, almost too much to contain. How had I let it come to this?

His voice, firm and determined, vibrated behind me. "If you want babies, I'll take that implant out now and keep you in bed until your belly is round. If you want to leave and never step foot in Blackthorn again, I'll burn it down behind us. And..."

"And?"

"And if you want to return to Darkmoor and destroy the Society—"

"Let me guess," I said with a snort, "you'd burn them down for me."

"No. I'd stand by your side and hand you the match."

I didn't say anything.

Because I feared he was lying. That this was all just some trick.

"Ava, I'll go back to Darkmoor with you."

I whirled around, barely able to believe it. I must have misheard him over the rush of water from the tub faucet.

For a moment we just stood there, both of us still so very, *very* naked. The only noise was the rushing of water. The only movement was the steam curling around us.

"W-what are you saying?" I asked.

"We'll take down the Society. Together."

I felt a flicker of disbelief, something twisting in my chest that I didn't dare call hope. This had to be a trick, a ploy, some twisted attempt to manipulate me back to his side.

I braced myself, waiting for him to reveal whatever strings were attached.

But he just looked at me, his face steady and unreadable, like this was an offer without conditions.

"You're ready," he added.

The words lingered, an unexpected note of finality in his tone that stopped my breath.

Yes. I was leaving this cursed place. Going home. Back to Dublin. Back to Ebony and Lisa and Darkmoor and…

*Scáth.*

The relief was short-lived, dread settling in like a heavy stone.

How would Ciaran react, seeing me arrive with his

brother—the brother he thought dead, the brother he believed was just a ghost of a memory? How could he ever look at me the same, knowing whom I'd chosen to bring along with me?

Ty cleared his throat. "But first…"

I almost snorted. Right. There was the other fucking shoe.

"There's one last… session." His tone darkened, a quiet insistence settling into each word. "One more memory left for you to unlock. One final thing you need to remember."

A fresh chill slipped down my spine, colder this time, and I fought against the desire to cover up my nakedness from him. "One more… memory?"

The question hung between us, and though I fought it, curiosity and a trace of dread filled me.

Ty nodded, his face as solemn as I'd ever seen it.

"You need to remember what you did."

# THE SHADOW

"I can't... I can't find her." My voice wavered, then broke. "Ava... she's just *gone*."

My hands clawed at the ground, nails scratching into the dirt, every word scraped out of my raw throat, as I barely held it together. "Every lead, every damn lead, *dead*. Cold."

I had nothing.

Nothing.

Nothing.

*Nothing*.

Ava was out there somewhere, I knew it, I could feel it, but every step was wrong, every door slammed shut, and the walls—they were closing, *closing*, CLOSING in, tighter and tighter.

"Tell me what to do," I whispered, my voice a thin, desperate thread. "Tell me. You... you always knew, didn't you? Always knew the answer, had the plan."

I stared at the grave marker, cold and unmoving, the

stone angel above it frozen mid-sorrow, her face twisted in eternal grief, eyes hollow and unseeing.

*Tynan Roderick Donahue.*

The name looked strange carved in stone, formal and stiff, like a stranger's. Nobody ever called him Tynan—except our father.

He was Ty.

Ty, the kind brother whom everyone liked.

Ty, the smart, dedicated brother who would go places, be someone, do something great with his life.

Ty, the *favorite* brother.

A hollow laugh tore out of me, sharp and splintered.

And now *Ty*, the perfect brother, was taunting me from beyond the grave. Keeping his secrets to himself.

Was Ava there with him in the afterlife? Had she found her way back to him after all? Had she left this earth?

Left *me*?

Had Ty won after all?

I could almost hear him mocking me. *"Serve you right for losing Ava. She never belonged to you in the first fucking place, did she?"*

"Shut up, you *bastard*," I screamed, my voice echoing through the old cemetery.

My fist hit the marker, pain flaring in my knuckles, grounding me for a heartbeat. One heartbeat before it all fell apart again.

"I'm sorry." I brushed the gravestone, smearing the blood I'd left from my knuckles like I was wiping away his tears. "S-sorry. I didn't mean it."

I could feel the panic clawing up, scraping at the edges of my sanity, curling around my throat like hands squeezing, choking. The sky spun, or maybe it was just me, dizzy, unsteady, grasping at air, at nothing.

"You have to tell me, Ty." I grasped the sides of the stone as if I were shaking Ty's shoulders. "Tell me where she is. Just... one sign. Give me something, give me *anything*."

"P-please... let me go." The voice trembled, weak, barely a whisper above the ghostly wind.

I snapped my gaze toward Dr. Edward Hickey—the father of one of the other missing girls.

He was sprawled across the neighboring grave, bound and helpless, his head awkwardly propped against a bouquet of dried roses someone had left behind.

"Don't you know it's rude to interrupt?" I snapped, glaring down at him. "I was having a conversation here."

His eyes widened, a glint of something bordering on disbelief flickering across his face as he stared between me and Ty's gravestone.

He should've been trembling. Should've been pleading.

Instead, he looked at me like I was *insane*, which was ballsy, considering his position.

Hmm. Maybe I was.

"You have a brother, right?" I asked as I crouched down in front of him, close enough to see the confusion swirling in his gaze. "Ever fall for the same girl?"

"What?" he managed, his voice barely a squeak.

"Say there was someone you both wanted," I continued, undeterred by his blank stare. "Someone you both... loved. And let's say... let's say, in a moment of guilt, you promised your brother that he could have her but... say he just fucking up and died, the bastard."

My fingers tapped against the headstone beside Dr.

Hickey, a rhythm that echoed the beat of my heart, too loud in the quiet of Glasnevin Cemetery.

Celtic crosses and elaborate Victorian headstones rose from the earth, each one worn and weathered, its inscriptions softened by time, some markers tilted slightly, leaning under the weight of decades.

Towering yew and cypress trees lined the winding gravel paths, their branches twisting overhead to form dark, natural arches that cast shadows even on the brightest days.

It was a perfect place for my lost twin to haunt for all eternity.

"So?" I asked Dr. Hickey, my voice betraying my impatience. "What would you do?"

Dr. Hickey's eyes flickered, and I could almost hear his thoughts racing, trying to piece together whatever fractured logic I was laying out for him.

But I was already leaning closer, a conspiratorial smile tugging at my lips.

"I mean, do those kinds of promises extend to death?" I asked, my voice a thread of something dark and bitter. "Am I really betraying him if... if he's gone? No, right? So why, Doctor, do I feel so fucking *guilty*?"

I watched him, waiting, as if he actually had an answer.

He blinked, mouth opening and closing, a look of utter bewilderment spreading across his face.

"I... I don't understand," he stammered, his voice thick with confusion, panic edging in as he glanced between me and the headstone.

"Seeing as you're *so* full of great advice," I said, my gaze narrowing on Dr. Hickey's face, watching the flicker of fear in his eyes as he realized he wasn't done here, "if you were me, how would you take the Sochai down?"

He swallowed hard, his gaze darting around like a trapped animal. "I-I'm not part of the Society. I don't know what you're talking about."

I shook my head, a mocking smile tugging at my lips. "Liar."

I leaned closer, my voice dropping to a dangerous whisper. "I know all about how the Society works. How they take adopted girls, place them with members, drug them... abuse them. Thought you'd keep that hidden, did you?"

He tried to protest, but I cut him off, reaching into my pocket and pulling out a drug vial along with a needle.

"Look what I found in your safe," I said, my tone casual, like we were discussing the weather.

His eyes widened as I held them up, a silent threat hanging in the air between us.

"T-that's..."

"Yes, from your personal stash of vile paralytics. I know what you did to Sarah, you sick bastard."

I twisted the cap off the vial, drawing the clear liquid into the syringe, moving slowly, deliberately, letting each second stretch out until I could practically hear his heartbeat.

His face paled.

I moved closer, pressing the needle against the side of his neck, just enough for him to feel the prick of metal on his skin. "You're going to tell me everything, or you'll get a taste of your own medicine."

"Okay, okay!" His voice wobbled, thick with fear as he struggled uselessly. "Please, don't... don't hurt me."

"Start talking," I murmured, my voice cold and calm, "or I plunge."

"Okay, yes—you're right," Hickey stammered, his eyes darting away from mine. "The Society uses girls. It rewards its members with... *daughters*."

The word twisted in my mind, sharp and sickening.

I felt bile rising, disgust seeping into every corner of my thoughts.

*Daughters.*

They were giving away girls, handing them over like prizes to monsters.

My throat tightened as the realization hit, cold and brutal.

Ava had been a *daughter*.

"We're given... drugs. Safeguards. The... the rules are... don't ever let them remember." Hickey's voice shook, his eyes pleading, but I wasn't feeling merciful.

"Then why make them disappear?" I demanded, my tone harder, angrier. "Why pretend they're runaways?"

He swallowed, his face paling. "I don't know. I swear. But... the order came down. One by one, we were told to get rid of our *daughters*. Make it seem like they ran away. So no one would bother investigating."

The rage simmered in my blood, nearly blinding me.

"Ava too," I ground out.

"N-no," he stammered, shaking his head as much as he could without moving away from the needle. "Specifically *not* Ava. At least not at first."

My brow furrowed, the tension pulling tight across my shoulders.

"Why not Ava?" The question burned on my tongue.

"I don't know," he whispered, almost to himself. "The High Lord gave specific orders that she wasn't to be touched. It caused... discontent. Dissension among the members."

My grip on the syringe tightened. "This High Lord. Who is he?"

"I don't know. No one does. He's too careful... hides his identity from everyone." Hickey's gaze darted around, desperation flickering in his eyes, his voice dropping to a fearful whisper. "But he's *always* watching."

I felt my pulse pound, the fury rising again, but I forced myself to keep focused and calm.

"But then Ava started investigating," Hickey said, his voice barely a whisper. "Uncovering too much. Remembering too much. She was getting too close. It became too dangerous to leave her alive."

I felt a chill crawl down my spine. "So the Society *did* take her."

He didn't answer, his silence hanging thick in the air, the confirmation I didn't want to hear.

My voice dropped, dangerous and low. "What would they do with her?"

Hickey swallowed, his face ashen.

"If she's... lucky," he murmured, his voice barely audible, "they'd kill her. Quickly."

Red bled into my vision. No, Ava could *not* be dead.

Suddenly the needle had been tossed aside and my hands were wrapped around Hickey's throat.

I watched myself, as if I were a floating above my body, choke the life out of him. I saw the life draining from his eyes but there was nothing I could do about it.

I only slammed back into my body the moment that his life snuffed out and he became a wraith.

Horror flooded through me as I stumbled back, my hands trembling. Dr. Hickey lay motionless, his glassy eyes staring blankly up at the sky, mouth frozen in a final, silent scream.

I'd killed him.

I hadn't meant to, hadn't planned for it to end this way. But the anger, the desperation—it took over. I'd lost control. Again.

A cold emptiness spread in my chest as I stared down at him, his lifeless form a brutal reminder of my failure.

He was my last lead.

The only thread I had left to finding Ava... and now he was gone, just like that.

I scrambled back to Ty's gravestone, my knees hitting the ground hard as I kneeled before it, my heart pounding against my ribs.

"I'm sorry, Ty," I whispered as I clutched the cold stone, my voice breaking. "I watched over her all those years, just like I promised you I would. But I didn't mean to betray you."

Ty remained silent and I felt the hollowness yawning beneath me, swallowing my words.

"I had always wanted her," I confessed. "You know I did. But watching her all those years, I saw in her what you had always seen."

The memories flooded in, each one sharper than the last, her laughter, her fire, the way she moved through the world like she didn't realize how special she was.

"I fell in love with her, too."

My voice dropped to a whisper, rough with desperation. "If you could come back—if you'd just bring her back with you—then I swear, I'd let her go. She'd be yours, like she was always meant to be. I'd step aside, watch you both live the life you deserved. I'd disappear. I'd do whatever it took... just to have her alive. Both of you. Alive."

A cold wind blew and the cemetery seemed to shiver around me.

I closed my eyes, swallowing hard, trying to steady myself as memories and regrets surged up like a flood I couldn't contain.

"Do you know that in Japan, they have a way to... to regain honor? Even after one has done something... unforgiveable."

*Like I had.*

I had stolen my brother's girl.

Then I'd let her die.

I sank back to the heels of my feet and wiped my face with my hands, my voice growing softer, almost reverent.

"It's about taking responsibility for failure, showing that... that you meant something, that there was honor in what you tried to do, even if you lost everything along the way."

My hand slipped to my pocket, pulling out the knife, its handle cold and steady in my grip.

"Seppuku," I explained to Ty's grave. "Ritual suicide."

I pressed the tip of the blade against my stomach, the weight of it grounding me in a way that nothing else had in months.

This knife, I'd named *Ty*.

It was fitting that my brother would end up killing me.

"Forgive me, Ty," I whispered to him one last time, the blade trembling in my hand. "If she's gone, then… I don't want to live."

~

Continue reading the Lovely Broken Doll trilogy in the final book, Claiming Pretty.
*Out 7 March*

## AUTHOR'S NOTE

If you or someone you know has been impacted by suicide, please know you are not alone. Scenes like Ciaran's can bring those emotions and experiences to the surface, and it's important to honor those feelings.

If you are grieving a loss or struggling with thoughts of suicide, please reach out to someone who can help. You are valued, and your voice matters.

US and Canada: 988

Ireland: +4408457909090

International: https://blog.opencounseling.com/suicide-hotlines/

## BOOKS BY SIENNA BLAKE

### LOVELY BROKEN DOLL

Hunting Pretty

Catching Pretty

Claiming Pretty ~ *out March 2025*

### DUBLIN INK

Dublin Ink

Dirty Ink

Dark Ink

Devilish Ink

### IRISH KISS

Irish Kiss

Professor's Kiss

Fighter's Kiss

The Irish Lottery

My Brother's Girl

Player's Kiss

My Secret Irish Baby

## ALL HER MEN

Three Irish Brothers
My Irish Kings
Royally Screwed
Cassidy Brothers

## DARK ROMEO UNIVERSE

Dark Romeo (standalone)
Bound by Lies (#1)
Bound Forever (#2)

## A GOOD WIFE

Beautiful Revenge
Mr. Blackwell's Bride

## BILLIONAIRES DOWN UNDER

*(with Sarah Willows)*
To Have & To Hoax
The Paw-fect Mix-up
Riding His Longboard
Maid For You
I Do (Hate You)
Man Toy (Newsletter Exclusive)

Paper Dolls (standalone)

# ABOUT SIENNA

New York Times bestseller Sienna Blake writes angsty and dark romance reads. When she's not busy writing about morally grey villains and the strong women who bring them to their knees, she spends her time reading or binge-watching mafia shows, hanging off aerial silks, or adding to her personal reverse harem of Irish men.

Made in the USA
Middletown, DE
18 February 2025